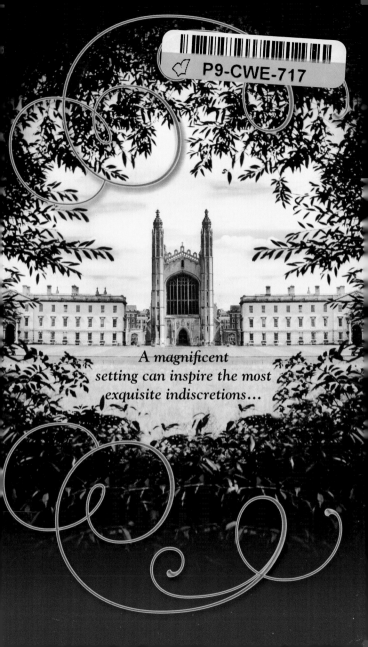

*A magnificent
setting can inspire the most
exquisite indiscretions…*

A SHOCKING KISS

"You may be the most intelligent woman I have ever met but unfortunately, you're the most stubborn as well." He threw the document in his hand back on the pile then circled the table toward her. "And at times, you haven't a brain in your head."

"That's exactly what I want to hear right now, thank you very much. I am well aware of any number of stupid mistakes I have made in the past." She glared and brushed a persistent strand of hair away from her face. "And there's absolutely no reason why you should be quite so annoyed with me. All I was—"

He grabbed her, pulled her hard into his arms, and gazed into her eyes. "And you don't *see* anything."

She stared up at him and her breath caught. "What do you mean?"

"Good God, if I have to explain it to you . . ."

Without another word he pulled her tighter against him and pressed his lips to hers in a kiss demanding and possessive and utterly wonderful . . .

Books by Victoria Alexander

THE PERFECT MISTRESS

HIS MISTRESS BY CHRISTMAS

MY WICKED LITTLE LIES

WHAT HAPPENS AT CHRISTMAS

THE IMPORTANCE OF BEING WICKED

THE SCANDALOUS ADVENTURES
OF THE SISTER OF THE BRIDE

THE SHOCKING SECRET
OF A GUEST AT THE WEDDING

Published by Kensington Publishing Corporation

The Shocking Secret of a Guest at the Wedding

VICTORIA ALEXANDER

ZEBRA BOOKS
KENSINGTON PUBLISHING CORP.
http://www.kensingtonbooks.com

ZEBRA BOOKS are published by

Kensington Publishing Corp.
119 West 40th Street
New York, NY 10018

All Kensington titles, imprints and distributed lines are available at special quantity discounts for bulk purchases for sales promotion, premiums, fund-raising, educational or institutional use.

Special book excerpts or customized printings can also be created to fit specific needs. For details, write or phone the office of the Kensington Special Sales Manager. Attn.: Special Sales Department. Kensington Publishing Corp., 119 West 40th Street, New York, NY 10018. Phone: 1-800-221-2647.

Zebra and the Z logo Reg. U.S. Pat. & TM Off.

First Printing: November 2014
ISBN-13: 978-1-4201-3226-7
ISBN-10: 1-4201-3226-1

First Electronic Edition: November 2014
eISBN-13: 978-1-4201-3227-4
eISBN-10: 1-4201-3227-X

10 9 8 7 6 5 4 3 2 1

Printed in the United States of America

*As this book took shape,
a thread developed about the relationship
between mothers and their adult children.*

*A relationship that can be as adversarial
as it is loving, as combative as it is affectionate,
as annoying as it is funny.*

*So it seems only right that I dedicate this book
with a great deal of love and gratitude
to the mothers in my life—
to my stepmother Mary and
my mother-in-law Anna and
to the memory of my mother,
Rosemarie.*

They taught me well.

My children should be grateful, too.

Chapter One

September 1887,
The Fifth Avenue home of Jackson Quincy Graham,
President and Chairman of the board of Graham,
Merryweather and Lockwood Banking and Trust,
his daughter, Mrs. Elizabeth Channing, and
her son, Jackson Quincy Graham Channing.
New York City . . .

Jackson Quincy Graham Channing isn't the man he thought he was.

A scant five minutes ago, the youngest vice-president in the storied history of Graham, Merryweather and Lockwood Banking and Trust, was not merely accepting of his lot in life but considered himself quite content. Oh certainly, when he was six years of age he had wanted to become Jack the intrepid pirate king and live a life of adventure on the high seas. A notion that vanished when he was seven and decided the adventurous life of Jack the heroic scout in the vast uncivilized recesses of the West would be much more exciting. When he turned eight, he had realized Jack the hunter of lost treasures and seeker of adventures in the jungles of the

Amazon or the desert of Egypt, a hero of epic proportions, was much more to his liking. But by the time he was nine, Jackson Quincy Graham Channing understood the duty, the responsibility, and the destiny of the great-grandson of one of the founders of Graham, Merryweather and Lockwood Banking and Trust was to follow in the not quite as adventurous footsteps of his grandfather and his great-grandfather before him. And so he did, exactly as planned.

In five years, Jackson Quincy Graham would turn over the presidency of Graham, Merryweather and Lockwood to his grandson who would soon be officially engaged to Lucinda Merryweather, also an offspring of one of the bank's founders. They would marry in the spring, shortly after her twenty-fourth birthday, just as both families had planned from the day Lucy was born. They would have an appropriate number of children including at least one boy who would grow up to take his place as the head of Graham, Merryweather and Lockwood Banking and Trust.

Life was unfolding exactly as expected, precisely according to plan, with no unseemly excitement, little opportunity for adventure, save that to be found in the world of banking and finance, and few surprises.

That Jackson Quincy Graham Channing now found himself taken completely by surprise was most unsettling. He couldn't recall ever having been at a loss for words before. Obviously his shock now was due directly to the fact that the importance of the moment was rivaled only by its absurdity. No doubt why he said the first thing that popped into his head.

"But you're dead."

His mother winced. The tall, distinguished, older British gentleman standing beside her in his grandfather's wood-paneled library in their grand house on Fifth Avenue, the man who was apparently his father, *his dead father,* smiled in a wry manner. "Actually, I'm very much alive."

"So it would seem." Jack studied the older man closely.

Colonel Basil Channing looked decidedly familiar although they had never met. But his eyes, his nose, everything about him was as familiar to Jack as . . . his stomach twisted. *As if he was looking in a mirror.* Granted that mirror was considerably older but there wasn't a doubt in Jack's mind that this man was who his mother said he was. Until a minute ago Jack was under the impression his father had died in an Indian uprising before Jack was born. It was a tragic story that his mother never wished to talk about. For more reasons than one, obviously.

"Forgive me for being blunt but surely you understand why I am more than a little taken aback." Jack's gaze slid to his mother. "And extremely confused."

"Yes, well, you might have a question or two," his mother said under her breath, refusing to meet his eyes.

"I might?" His tone rang harder than expected but it seemed ire went hand in hand with shock. "Only one or two you think?"

"Or more." His father's eyes narrowed. "God knows I do."

"Do you?" Jack's brow rose. "How very interesting as most of my questions are for you. First and foremost where have you been for the last thirty years, *Father?*"

"You would do best to watch yourself, my boy." The colonel's casual tone belied the hard look in his eye. "Until you know all the facts. Wouldn't you agree, Elizabeth?"

"One should always have all the facts before passing judgment." Elizabeth Channing calmly crossed the library to where a decanter of brandy sat, as always, on a corner of his grandfather's desk.

The ever-present decanter marked this room as a gentleman's domain every bit as much as did the commanding, century-old mahogany desk, the floor-to-ceiling shelves filled with precisely arranged, finely bound volumes, the well-worn costly leather sofa, and the imposing portrait of Jack's great-grandfather over the fireplace. This was his grandfather's sanctuary and would one day be Jack's. Exactly as it should be.

"You would be wise to remember that as well, Basil." Mother poured herself a glass and only a slight tremble in her hand indicated she was anything other than completely composed. Interesting as Jack had never seen his mother anything less than completely composed.

His father was right, of course. Besides, Jack never allowed emotion to overcome logic and logic dictated he wait to have the facts of the matter before reaching any conclusions. It was the sensible, rational way to proceed even if there was nothing sensible and rational about any of this.

"Yes, of course." Jack drew a deep breath. "Then perhaps you would be so good as to explain."

"Quite honestly, there's little I can explain. As I said, I have as many questions as you. Until a week ago, I had no idea I had a son." The older man's gaze shifted to Jack's mother. "Nor was I aware that I still had a wife."

Jack's gaze turned to his mother who was doing her best to look anywhere but at him. Or his father.

"Well?" both men said in unison, then exchanged startled glances.

"We're waiting, Mother," Jack said.

"Out with it, Elizabeth," his father said at the same time.

"I have no intention of being interrogated like a common criminal," his mother said in a lofty manner and tossed back a good portion of her brandy. That too was interesting. She did not normally indulge in quite so reckless a manner.

"Why didn't I know that I had a father?" Jack said.

"Everyone has a father, dear," Mother said coolly. "It's rather odd that you thought you didn't."

"You're right. My apologies. Allow me to restate my question." Jack's voice hardened. "Why didn't I know my father was alive?"

"I have no idea." She raised a shoulder in an offhand manner. "I never told you he was dead."

"Not in so many words, I suppose. But you led me to believe he was dead. That he was killed in an Indian uprising before I was born."

"That might have been your grandfather's doing," Mother said under her breath.

"I was in India in '57," his father said. "Sepoy Rebellion."

Jack stared. "Not that kind of Indian."

"Nonetheless, as you can see, I was not killed." He turned toward his wife. "You let him think I was dead."

"How was I to know you weren't? You could have been." She sniffed. "It's not as if you kept in contact with me."

"I wrote to you. At least in the beginning." Indignation sounded in the older man's voice. "Admittedly, it took me a week or so to realize your admonition that it would be best if we did not contact one another was ridiculous. I wrote you once a month for the next, oh, eight months if I recall."

"Yes, well, the ninth month was when I might well have responded," she snapped.

"At that point it seemed hopeless." His father's tone matched his mother's. "As far as I knew, you had returned to America to have our marriage annulled and never wanted to see me again."

"That was the original plan." Mother's eyes narrowed. "However an annulment is difficult when one is going to have a child."

"The two of you were actually married then?" Jack interrupted.

"Of course we were married." She huffed. "I certainly would never have had a child if I had been unmarried. I can't believe you would ask such a question."

"Do forgive me, Mother."

"Sarcasm is not the way to handle an awkward situation, Jackson."

Jack's jaw clenched. "Again, my apologies."

"It's been thirty years, Elizabeth." The colonel's gaze met his wife's. "I would think that at some point during that time, you would have seen your way clear to inform me of the birth of my son."

"You needn't look at me that way. I didn't deliberately not tell you. Indeed, I can't count the number of times I put pen to paper to write to you. Why, I probably wrote a good two dozen letters or more through the years."

"And yet I never received even one."

"Yes, well, I didn't say I actually mailed them." She shrugged. "I really didn't know where to send them. I didn't know if you were still in the army or wandering the world. Regardless, I had no idea where to find you." She studied her husband. "You were an adventurous sort, remember? Always talking about what you wished to see and do, the places you wanted to go."

"If I recall, you wished to see those places with me."

She sipped her brandy. "I was very young and extremely foolish."

The colonel's eyes narrowed. "Weren't we all."

"And therein lies the problem," she snapped.

"One of many," he said sharply, then drew a deep breath. "You could have sent your letters to Millworth Manor. I would have received them eventually."

"I suppose I could have but I didn't." She waved off his comment. "It's really a moot point now. You know everything and—"

"I don't know anything at all." His father's brow furrowed. "Aside from the basic facts that I have a wife and a son, I don't—"

"Oh, come now, Basil, you needn't be so indignant." She rolled her gaze toward the ceiling. "I'll have you know it's remarkably difficult to inform a man he's a father who is not even aware he's still married. And while admittedly I should have, oh, made a greater effort perhaps, this is really not my fault."

"Not your fault?" father and son said in unison.

Mother's annoyed gaze slid from one man to the other.

"We're never going to get anywhere if the two of you keep doing that. I find it most disconcerting."

"We certainly wouldn't want you to feel ill at ease, Mother," Jack said.

"Thank you, Jackson," she said in a lofty manner.

The men traded glances. Jack drew a deep breath.

"Nonetheless, I must agree with . . ." He looked at his father. What was he supposed to call this man he had just met? "*Him*. We both have questions and an explanation as to your actions for the past thirty years is certainly in order and long overdue."

"Possibly, I suppose. But it really is a long story and we do have guests." She glanced at her husband. "Only Mr. Lockwood, my father of course, and the Merryweathers and their daughter Lucinda. Jackson and Lucinda will more than likely marry within the year."

The older man glanced at his son. "My heartiest congratulations."

"Nothing is settled yet," Jack said without thinking, ignoring the voice in the back of his head that wondered why it was that nothing was settled. And why it didn't seem to bother him. Or Lucy.

"You've come in the middle of a small dinner party, Basil. Nothing elaborate but as you were neither expected nor invited, it was most inconsiderate of you."

"Do forgive me," the colonel said wryly. "I would hate to be an inconvenience."

"Furthermore, I have said all I intend to say at the moment." Mother started toward the door. "We can clear up all this confusion later."

Jack stepped to block her way. "Absolutely not."

"This is far too important a matter to blithely put off." His father glared.

"Nonsense." She scoffed. "Admittedly, it might seem urgent to the two of you but it's not. This, oh, revelation for want of a better word, is thirty years in the making. It can certainly wait until after dinner."

Jack stared at her. "I'm not the least bit hungry."

"I could use a bite, myself," his father murmured.

"You were not invited," Mother said firmly.

"And yet here I am." His father grinned. It was a surprisingly infectious grin and Jack found himself biting back a smile of his own. "Surely you can see your way clear to allow me to join you for dinner, Betty."

Her jaw tightened. "Don't call me Betty. Betty is not my name nor has it ever been my name."

Amusement shone in the colonel's eyes. "As I remember you used to like it when I called you Betty."

"There are any number of things that I liked in my youth." Her eyes narrowed. "That I have grown out of."

"Have you now?" The colonel moved closer to her, plucked the half-filled glass of brandy from her hand, and took a sip. "Does that include me?"

She ignored the question and cast a pointed glance at her glass. "I'd be happy to get you a brandy of your own."

"I'm fine with this, thank you." His father chuckled. "And you didn't answer my question."

She heaved a resigned sigh. "Goodness, Basil, we were married for less than a week—"

"Plus thirty years," Jack murmured.

"There was no need to grow out of you. I simply had to come to my senses."

"And did you?" The older man swirled the brandy in the glass.

"Of course I did," she said sharply.

"Then tell me this, Elizabeth." He leaned closer, his gaze boring into hers. "Why did you never seek to obtain a divorce?"

She lifted her chin. "No one has ever had a divorce in this family and I have no intention of being the first."

"I see." The colonel nodded thoughtfully. "And I thought

it might be because then you would have to confess all. That we were still married. And that I had a son."

She paused. "Well, I suppose that might have been a factor—"

"And that you still harbored some affection for me."

"Don't be absurd." She crossed her arms over her chest. "I certainly haven't been pining away for you if that's what you think."

"I don't know what to think. This has all been something of a shock."

"For all of us," Jack added.

"It's not been particularly easy for me either," his mother said under her breath.

"Good God, Elizabeth." His father glared. "For all you knew, I could have remarried."

"Nonsense." She sniffed. "You were not the marrying type."

"I married you, didn't I?"

"That scarcely counts." She glared back at him. "Besides, you agreed that it was a mistake."

"Only because I couldn't fight your parents who were determined that our marriage be annulled. And you were completely under their thumbs."

"I was not!" She hesitated. "Well, perhaps I was but I was a mere girl of eighteen and it did seem that we had been impulsive and—"

"And as much as I hate to interrupt and suggest that the two of you work out your marital *entanglements* another time there are other issues to settle at the moment." Jack turned his gaze to his mother. "While I can probably make allowances for your failure to tell him he had a son, I don't understand why you never told me I had a father. A *living* father."

"I intended to. It just never seemed quite the right time, that's all." She shrugged as if it didn't matter but the evasive look in her eyes and the set of her shoulders said more than words that she knew how very much it did. "First you were too young to understand. And even as you grew older it was difficult to find the right words. And then you were, well, an adult with your own life and it didn't really seem to be of significance one way or the other. After a while, I suppose you could say that it simply slipped my mind."

"It slipped your mind?" Jack stared at her. "Didn't I have a right to know?"

"Didn't *I* have a right to know?" his father added.

"And what about me?" She fisted her hands on her hips. "I am your mother and your"—she closed her eyes as if praying for strength—"*wife*. Don't I have any rights?"

"Mother, don't be absurd. You're a woman." The words were out of his mouth an instant before he realized what a mistake they were.

His father choked.

Mother's glare shifted from one man to the other. "Well, you certainly are his son. I'm surprised I haven't noticed it before. Now then, I am going to return to the dining room." She directed an annoyed look at her husband. "Basil, do honor us with your presence for dinner."

His father's eyes twinkled with triumph. "I would be delighted."

"On one condition," she said firmly. "There is to be no mention, from either of you, that he is my husband."

"You think they won't notice the similarities in name?" Jack said.

"I could be the cousin of your late husband," Father said in a helpful manner that should have earned him credit but elicited a scathing look from Mother nonetheless.

"I am not trying to orchestrate a theatrical production." She heaved a resigned sigh. "But yes, I think that might work, however—"

A knock sounded at the door and it opened almost at once.

"I do beg your pardon but is anything wrong?" Lucinda

Merryweather stepped into the room and glanced around. "You've been gone so long we were wondering if there was a problem." Lucy smiled her familiar, bright smile.

Jack had known Lucy for all of her life. She was unfailingly cheerful, possessed a fine mind, and was really quite lovely with her fair hair and slightly turned-up nose. Marrying Lucy would not be a hardship. Their families had planned their marriage since the day she was born and they were well suited to one another. In very many ways she had long been his dearest friend. And he did love her of course. Who wouldn't?

They had never kept anything from each other and Jack saw no reason why he should start keeping anything from her now. Especially a matter of this magnitude. She was to be his wife one day after all.

"Come in, Lucy, and please close the door behind you." Jack cast an affectionate smile at the young woman he was almost, nearly, practically engaged to.

"Do you think that's wise?" Annoyance sounded in his mother's voice.

"Lucy and I have no secrets, Mother," Jack said firmly. "She deserves to know what is going on."

"Secrets?" Lucy's blue eyes widened with delight. "Oh, I simply adore a good secret." She turned her attention to the colonel. "And I suspect that has to do with you, doesn't it?"

His father chuckled. "I'm afraid so."

Mother sighed and moved back toward the brandy decanter.

Lucy stepped toward the older man and extended her hand. "We haven't met but you are obviously related to Jackson."

Jack's father took her hand, a pleased note in his voice. "Do you think so?"

"Oh my, yes. The resemblance is unmistakable. You share the same coloring and in spite of the gray, it's obvious your hair was once as dark as his. And the blue of your eyes is very nearly the exact same shade as his." Lucy directed her words to Jack even as her gaze stayed on his father's face. "Goodness, Jackson, do you realize this is exactly how you will look in twenty or thirty years?" A flirtatious twinkle shone in Lucy's eye. "I must say, I am going to like it."

"Lucy." Jack drew a deep breath. "This is my—"

"Oh, I know who he is," she said, studying his father curiously. "This is Colonel Basil Channing. I read an article about him." She glanced at Jack. "The similarity in name, you know, caught my eye although I must say his photographs don't do him justice. I didn't notice any sort of resemblance at all until now." She nodded. "He's quite famous."

"I wouldn't say famous," his father said in a modest manner. "Well known perhaps, in certain circles."

"He's an, oh, what's the word? Adventurer I suppose." She shivered with delight. "How very exciting."

"What on earth have you been reading?" Mother said under her breath and poured a new glass of brandy.

"And better yet, you're part of the family." Lucy beamed. "Just how are the two of you related?"

"He's Jackson's father's brother," Mother said quickly. "Or his cousin, something like that. Now, we should return to the others."

"No, he's not." Jack braced himself. "He's my father."

"Really?" Lucy's eyes widened. "How delightful. And that does explain the resemblance." She leaned toward the colonel in a confidential manner. "But aren't you supposed to be dead?"

"Rumor." His father shrugged. "Nothing more than that."

Lucy nodded solemnly. "Rumors can be dreadfully hard to stop once they take hold. And in your case, one might say they were positively . . ." Her eyes twinkled with laughter. "Fatal?"

The colonel chuckled. "One could say that." His father glanced at Jack. "I like her."

"Everyone likes Lucinda, Basil." Mother took a fast swig of her drink.

"Of course they do," Lucy said. "I am unfailingly pleasant, cordial to a fault, and I am rather more intelligent than is seemly in a woman but I am clever enough to keep that to myself." She smiled in an overly sweet manner. "For example, right this very moment, I am well aware that there is more to this meeting than any of you have revealed thus far. Admittedly, it doesn't take a great deal of intelligence to ascertain that. After all, it isn't every day that a man's dead father and a woman's late husband appears just in time for dinner. Add to that the fact that Mrs. Channing is drinking brandy before dinner, which I have never seen her do before, and Jackson has the oddest sort of stunned look in his eyes, well, as I said there is more to this story." She settled on the sofa and looked at the gathering expectedly. "A story I would very much like to hear."

"Yes, well, it's not a story I wish to tell at the moment." Mother inched toward the door. "And there is dinner—"

"Dinner can wait, as I would like to hear this story as well." Jack glanced at Lucy. "She's been remarkably reticent to reveal anything at all thus far."

"Imagine my surprise," Lucy murmured.

"Go on, Mother," Jack said in his best banking and trust vice-presidential voice. "Tell us your story."

"I really don't think now . . ." Mother glanced around the room then sighed. "Oh, very well." She downed the rest of her brandy and drew a deep breath. "Thirty years ago, my father served as a financial advisor to an American company that had interests in India. The position required him to travel to that part of the world. Mother and I accompanied him as neither of us had traveled extensively. It was quite exciting as I recall." She glanced at her son. "Travel is extremely broadening, you know."

"I am well aware of that, Mother." Jack had always thought he would have a grand tour when he finished his studies. But he had started at the bank and one thing had led to another and he had never quite had the time a grand tour would require. He had responsibilities after all.

"I have always wanted to travel," Lucy said under her breath.

"Continue, Mother."

"While in India, I met a young, dashing, handsome British officer. He was quite, well, irresistible."

Father tried and failed to hide a satisfied grin.

"We knew each other for only a few weeks but I fancied myself madly in love, the way only someone young and inexperienced can be. It was all terribly romantic." She shrugged. "In a moment of mad, starry-eyed impulse we eloped."

"Scarcely a moment," his father said. "As I recall it took quite a bit of secrecy and several days of machinations to arrange. It was not at all easy." He smiled at his wife. "But well worth it."

"Don't try to be flirtatious with me, Basil." Mother huffed. "I am long past the time when that sort of thing will work on me. Especially coming from you."

"My apologies, Elizabeth." His father struggled to keep a smile off his face. "You can't blame me for trying."

"I most certainly can." Mother paused. "Now where was I? Oh yes, we were married. My parents were not at all pleased. In fact, Father was livid. He thought I had surely lost my mind. I had never been an impulsive sort. They pointed out Basil and I had nothing in common. He was English after all and I was American."

"That doesn't seem like a great deal to overcome," Jack said.

"That wasn't all. They said we were being reckless and irresponsible. That marriage was forever and we hadn't given it due consideration. They said our marrying was nothing more than the foolish actions of youth. There was more, of course, but I don't remember all of it now. Suffice it to say, they convinced me"—she looked at her husband—"or rather they convinced *us* we had made a dreadful mistake." She shook her head. "You must understand I did not have nearly the strength of character than that I do now."

"The biggest mistake I made was allowing them to convince me," his father said.

"Stop it, Basil." Mother glared at him and continued. "My parents said the best way to resolve the situation was to return to America and have the marriage annulled. And so your father and I parted. By the time I returned home I realized I was, well, you were going to arrive, which made an annulment impossible." She raised a shoulder in a casual shrug. "And that's all there is to it really."

Jack stared at his mother. "Although I believe you have left out the part where you never mentioned to my father that he had a son. Or the part where you failed to tell me I had a father who was very much alive."

She waved off Jack's comments. "You already know that part. I didn't think it necessary to repeat it. So." She cast them her brightest smile. "Shall we go in to dinner?"

"No." Jack shook his head. "You really have given no good reason as to why you didn't tell me about my father. What you've said thus far is not a satisfactory explanation. I think I—I think *we*—deserve better."

"Nonetheless that's all I have." Mother's jaw tightened. "Would you prefer that I say I was afraid? Afraid that your father would snatch you away from me? Afraid that you would hate me if you learned what I'd kept from you? Is that what you want to hear?"

"Only if it's the truth," Jack said slowly.

"Very well, then I suppose that was part of it." She shook her head. "I had no desire to lose my only child."

"Did you really think I would do that?" his father said quietly.

"How did I know what you would do? I barely knew you after all." She paused and her voice softened. "I truly did try to write to you, Basil, but I couldn't find the words. And the longer I put it off, the harder it was. Surely you understand?"

Lucy nodded. "It's like running into someone you've met over and over again, but you can't remember their name. And the longer that you go on without asking what their name is the harder it is to ask." She shook her head. "That can be most embarrassing."

"Exactly." Mother thought for a moment. "Well not exactly but you do understand my dilemma." Her gaze shifted from Lucy to Jack to her husband. "Do you? Understand, that is?"

"Not really," Jack muttered. "Especially since this is far more important than not being able to remember someone's name."

"But surely you can forgive me?" A hopeful note sounded in Mother's voice. "It is all water under the bridge now, isn't it?"

"There's really no need to hold a grudge." His father studied his mother carefully. "It's not as if we can go back thirty years and undo what was done."

Mother stared at him. "You're much more forgiving than I expected."

"And probably more than you deserve," Lucy said helpfully.

"I for one am not sure I'm ready to forgive you." Jack blew a long breath. "However, my . . . *father* is right. What's done is done. It can't be changed. No sense in looking backward."

"Good." Mother breathed a sigh of relief. "That's that then. Perhaps now we can go to dinner."

"I don't think we're quite done yet, Elizabeth." His father chose his words with care. "There's a great deal yet to discuss and a great many more questions that still remain."

"I really can't imagine what those might be." Mother set her glass on the desk and moved toward the door. "And we do have guests waiting. So perhaps—"

"Perhaps we need to discuss the future and what happens now." His father absently tapped his finger against his glass and studied her for a moment. "You were right about one thing though."

Mother's brow arched upward. "Oh?"

He smiled slowly. "I do intend to take your son."

Chapter Two

Mother sucked in a sharp breath and her eyes narrowed. "Over my dead body!"

"That seems appropriate," the colonel said in a hard tone. "As you've essentially had him all these years over my dead body."

"One wonders how they managed to stay married for a full week," Lucy said under her breath to Jack.

"Might I point out to both of you, I am not a child to be squabbled over." Jack glared at his parents. "Nor am I a possession to be divided between the two of you."

"Of course not, dear." A conciliatory note sounded in his mother's voice. "You're an intelligent adult with a position of responsibility and authority. You make important decisions every day and you are more than capable of making decisions about your own life. For your father to make such a threat in the first place is utterly absurd."

"It's not a threat," his father said coolly. "Although perhaps I misstated my intention."

Mother huffed. "I should think so."

"My apologies, Elizabeth."

Mother snorted in disdain.

"As I said, it was not a threat. It was simply a statement

of fact." He turned to Jack. "Forgive me if I am not saying this as well as I might but you must understand, until last week, I had no idea of your existence. Most men have months to come to terms with the possibility of having a son. I've had only a week and most of that was spent onboard a ship although admittedly it did give me plenty of time to consider the ramifications of your existence. Not that I'm not pleased," he added quickly. "I had quite frankly resigned myself years ago to the idea that I would never have children of my own."

Jack smiled. "Well, I never expected to have a father either."

"How lovely," Lucy said. "You have something else in common."

"Delightful," Mother said through clenched teeth.

"There is however more at stake here, Jackson." He considered his offspring for a moment. "Did your mother tell you anything about me? Anything at all?"

"No." Jack shot an annoyed look at his mother. "From as far back as I can remember, the very mention of your name upset her. I learned as a young boy that you were a part of her life she did not want to be reminded of. I always thought it was lingering grief."

"A love so tragic she could not bear to have it brought to mind. The kind you read about in novels." Lucy sighed. "So very romantic."

Mother stared at her. "We must look at your reading material, dear."

"I grew up believing my father had died fighting Indians in a Western territory, Nebraska or somewhere."

"I never told you that," his mother said quickly.

"No, that was Grandfather's doing." Jack thought for a moment. "Although you never saw fit to correct the impression he gave me either. Admittedly, it was all rather vague. More implication than anything else. Grandfather never wanted to speak of my father either."

"Imagine that," Lucy murmured.

"Then we are starting from scratch as it were?" Father asked.

"I'm afraid so." Jack drew a deep breath. "But I do feel some sort of apology is in order. I should have made further inquiries about you. At least as I grew older. Even though you did seem a topic to be avoided, that's no excuse. I should have made an effort to learn more about you. I was curious but . . . Perhaps if I had asked—"

"Rubbish, my boy." His father scoffed. "No apology is necessary. At least not from you. Indeed, you were being a thoughtful and considerate son not to bring up a topic that distressed your mother. You are not to blame for any of this." He cast a pointed look at his wife.

"Oh, for goodness' sake." Mother threw up her arms in surrender. "Very well then. I'll accept the blame. I did what I thought was best, what I thought was right—"

"For whom?" both men said in unison.

"That doesn't scare me, you know," Mother said sharply. "The way the two of you have been spouting the same words at the same time. Why, it's probably to be expected. Runs in the blood and all. I'm not frightened of either of you."

"Perhaps you should be," Lucy said helpfully. "After all, you did keep father and son apart for thirty years. One might even say that you stole something from them. Part of their lives, really. It seems to me that some kind of, oh, I don't know, retribution or punishment is in order. Yes, that's it—punishment. You should pay for your crime. It seems only fair."

"And we do want to be fair." Mother fairly spit the words.

One wouldn't have thought the evening could get any stranger and yet there was Mother glaring at the young woman she'd always thought of as a daughter. And there was Lucy challenging her at every turn. This was not the ordinary kind of evening Jack had expected when he'd heard Uncle Daniel, Lucy, and her parents were to join him,

Grandfather, and Mother for dinner to mark his thirtieth birthday a few days ago. And he had expected it to be extremely ordinary, as such a gathering, even to observe a birthday, usually was. Now, he preferred not to speculate as to what might happen next.

"It's pointless to look behind us. We must move forward," Father said firmly.

"And what exactly does moving forward mean?" Caution edged Mother's voice.

"Perhaps you should sit down," Father said.

"I don't want—fine," Mother snapped and sat on the sofa, as far away from Lucy as possible.

"First, you should know about your family, Jackson," Father began.

"He does know about his family," Mother said under her breath.

Father ignored her and continued. "There are Channings all over England, mostly distant relations and you needn't be overly concerned with them."

"Although it is nice to know they exist," Lucy said.

"Exactly." Father nodded. "And I daresay you'll meet them all eventually."

"I really don't see—" Mother began.

"Quiet, Mother." Jack nodded at his father. "Go on."

"For the most part, they're not especially important although admittedly some of them are most amusing. Eccentric is probably the kindest description." The colonel lowered his voice in a confidential manner. "There is Cousin Wilfred on my father's side. He was quite convinced he could fly. He couldn't, of course. Pity, as it turned out." Father shook his head in a regretful manner. "But as I was saying, you needn't bother concerning yourself with anyone aside from the immediate family. At least for now."

"The immediate family?" Jack said.

"You, my boy, have an uncle, my twin brother, Nigel, and an aunt, his wife, Bernadette. They have three daughters, charming girls, all of them. They've grown up quite nicely, all things considered. Oddly enough, I am not the only brother whose wife preferred to let his offspring believe he was dead."

Lucy stared.

"Although in Nigel's case, he did rather deserve it. But that's neither here nor there at the moment." Father's brow furrowed thoughtfully. "Let me think. The eldest girls are older than you and are twins. One is married, the other a widow and about to be married again. The youngest, Delilah, is also a widow. So you can see how the revelation that I have a son changes, well, everything. Especially the future. The family's and yours."

"Basil." A warning sounded in Mother's voice. "This is not how I wanted—"

"It no longer matters what you want, Elizabeth. You've had what you wanted for far too long." Father cast her a hard look.

"I'm not certain I understand," Jack said slowly. "I know I am as shocked by your existence as you are by mine. And this does change a lot, for any number of reasons. But while it certainly is significant, in a personal sense, I fail to see what effect my having a living father, and you having a son has on your future or mine. Not that I don't like the idea, mind you," he added quickly. "It would be different if we were having this, oh, *reunion* I suppose is the only word for it, when I was ten years old or even twenty. But I am an adult. I have a position of responsibility at the bank and a sound, solid career ahead of me there. My future is well planned out."

"Exactly," Mother said under her breath.

"It might well have been planned out yesterday or this morning or even a few hours ago but now . . ." His father's gaze met his. "Now, your future is entirely different."

Jack drew his brows together. "I still don't see—"

"My brother is the Earl of Briston." Father paused to allow the others to grasp the significance of his pronouncement.

"Jackson, your uncle is an earl," Lucy said with delight. "How very interesting."

"It's more than merely interesting, my dear girl," Father said. "I know it's not the same in your country—"

"We don't have earls for one thing." Mother sniffed.

"But in my country"—he met Jack's gaze—"your country as well, titles and property are often tied together in what is called an entailment. Are you familiar with it?"

"Vaguely." Jack nodded. "We deal on occasion with English financial institutions and I've seen reference to it in correspondence. It has to do with inheritance, doesn't it?"

"Exactly." His father studied him closely. "A title is tied to a family's property, they are passed on together. In our case, Millworth Manor, the estate that has been in our family for generations, as well as some other properties, are tied to the title. The title can only be inherited by the closest male relative. If my brother died, I would be next in line to be the Earl of Briston. If I died . . ."

Lucy gasped.

Mother sighed.

Jack stared. "Are you saying that I would be the next earl?"

"That's exactly what I'm saying." Father nodded. "And thank God, too. We were all afraid Millworth and the title would eventually go to Wilfred's son." He shuddered. "And believe me no one wanted that."

For the second time tonight, Jack was at a loss for words. The idea of being an English earl was interesting but not something that had ever before crossed his mind. Why would it? He was, after all, an American. He wasn't sure he'd like being an earl, not that he had any idea what that might involve. Regardless that his surname was Channing, what he knew was how to be a Graham and follow in his grandfather Graham's footsteps and the footsteps of the Grahams before him. It was part and parcel of his responsibility to his family. It was who he was. Banking was in his blood.

Although it did now appear banking was not all that was in his blood.

"Jackson," his mother began. "You don't—"

"Did you know about this?" He met his mother's gaze directly. "Is this something else that slipped your mind?"

"I really haven't given it much thought. I'm sure it will come as a surprise to both you and your father but I have not spent the last thirty years plotting as to how to keep the two of you apart. The entire question rarely crossed my mind." She heaved a long-suffering sigh. "But yes, I will admit that I was aware that your father's brother had a title and that he had no male heirs."

"Ah-ha!" Triumph rang in Father's voice. "Then you did know that I was alive and where to find me."

Mother sighed in surrender. "Of course I knew you were alive. I hadn't heard that you were dead and it did seem, well, prudent, to make inquiries on occasion to see if you had remarried. I would have felt compelled to contact you if that had happened."

"Ha!" Father's eyes narrowed. "To have me jailed for bigamy no doubt."

"I hadn't thought of that." Mother smiled in a decidedly wicked manner. "But it's a pleasant idea."

"You're admitting that you knew how to contact me."

"I'm admitting no such thing." Mother's gaze locked with her husband's. "Yes, I knew you continued to draw breath. No, I did not know where you were at any given time. You are—as Lucinda so enthusiastically put it—an adventurer. You have never stayed long in one place, Basil. You simply roam from country to country, from one *adventure* to the next. One would think you were running away from something. Or trying to hide."

"I had nothing to hide from nor did I have anything or anyone to run from." Father narrowed his eyes. "However both running away and hiding can certainly be done without taking so much as a single step."

"There are any number of things that I am guilty of but hiding from you is not one of them." She glared at her husband. "You knew exactly where I was these past thirty years."

The colonel stared at his wife. "So to punish me for not seeking you out, you kept my son from me?"

"Don't be absurd. That never occurred to me." She paused. "But you certainly could have made some sort of overture through the years, aside from a handful of letters in the beginning, that is."

"Of course I could have but you, and your parents, made it clear that such a gesture on my part would be both foolish and futile." Father drew a calming breath. "Regardless, this is not the time to debate who should have done what, who was more at fault—"

"Not a doubt in my mind," Lucy murmured.

"As I said, that's in the past. Jackson." He turned to his son. "Unfortunately, this is to be the briefest of trips. I took the first ship here as soon as I learned about you, thanks to a chance conversation with a new acquaintance in London. It seemed to me we had lost enough time and I didn't want to lose any more."

Jack nodded.

"I only arrived today but I have to return to England at once. My niece, your cousin, is to be wed next week. She would never forgive me if I failed to appear." Father paused. "A wedding is an excellent way to meet a large number of members of a family. I have booked passage on a ship leaving tomorrow." His gaze met his son's. "Actually, I have booked two passages."

"You're asking me to go with you?" Jack said slowly.

"Don't be absurd." Mother scoffed. "He can't simply leave without a moment's notice. He is a vice-president of the bank. It's an extremely responsible position. Vice-presidents simply don't go off to foreign countries without so much as a by your leave."

She was right. The very idea was absurd.

"I'm not asking you to stay forever, to take up permanent residence. Nor am I asking you for a decision as to your future. Not at the moment. You might not even like England after all." His father's tone was matter-of-fact, as if he didn't care if Jack decided to accompany him or not. But the look in his eyes told an entirely different story. "However, it does seem that this is the perfect opportunity to meet my—*your*—family."

"Perhaps another time." Mother stood, her posture as always straight and perfect, and clasped her hands in front of her.

Jack wasn't the type of man to act on impulse. A trip to England would involve planning and a great deal of due consideration. Arrangements would have to be made.

"I would have to take a leave of absence," Jack said thoughtfully.

"It would also give us the chance to get to know one another. The voyage is nearly a week," his father added in an offhand manner.

Still, now that he had discovered he had a father, it wouldn't be at all ill-advised to spend time with him. One might say it would be impolite to do otherwise.

"A week there and a week back," Mother began. "Why you'd be gone at least a month. And doesn't that place poor Lucinda in an awkward position."

"Oh, don't bother yourselves about me." Lucy rose to her feet, excitement glittering in her eyes. "I think it's a splendid idea, simply splendid."

Mother's eyes narrowed. "But weren't you planning on announcing your engagement soon?"

"Don't be silly, that can wait." Lucy waved off the objection. "It's not as if we haven't put off our engagement before and for far less important reasons than this."

"You're not getting any younger, dear," Mother said pointedly.

Jack raised a brow. "You wouldn't mind postponing it again?"

"Not at all," Lucy said staunchly. "I think you should go. I think it would be a mistake for you not to go. One you might well regret."

"Do you really?"

"Without question." She nodded. "Goodness, Jackson, it isn't often that a man discovers his father has come back from the grave." She leaned toward him in a confidential manner and lowered her voice. "Although I do think you should ask how it happened that your father and his brother were both believed to be dead by their children. It's a rather startling coincidence, don't you think?"

Jack glanced at his mother. "Not if my aunt is anything like my mother."

"There is that." Lucy stepped closer and rested her hand on his arm. "Don't forget, Jackson, I know you as well as I know myself. You already feel a certain amount of foolish guilt because you accepted everything your mother and grandfather said, or didn't say, about your father." She met his gaze firmly. "Besides, it would be terribly selfish of me to think only of myself. This is the perfect opportunity to meet your family and find out exactly, oh I don't know, who you are, I suppose. To find the answers to all those questions you've had all these years and I think you should take it."

Certainly the bank could get along without him.

"One thing I should warn you about." Father chose his words with care. "No one knows of your existence. I should have taken the time to inform my brother but it did seem to me that time was of the essence." He shrugged. "I was eager to get here, you see. For all I knew, you had no interest in meeting me. But I had to find out."

Jack smiled. "I'm glad you did."

"As am I." The older man chuckled. "This is going to be quite a surprise for the rest of the family. I suspect Nigel will be quite pleased but I have no idea what the girls will think. The women in our family can be most headstrong and stubborn."

"Then Jackson will feel right at home," Lucy said under her breath.

"I can't believe you're even considering this." Shock sounded in Mother's voice. "At some point perhaps but now, well, it's ridiculous and I absolutely forbid it."

Lucy winced.

Jack stared at his mother. He couldn't recall ever having been at odds with her before. They were usually in agreement over important matters, of one mind as it were.

In that moment, his entire life, all thirty years, came into focus with crystal clarity. Without warning it struck him that he had spent his life trying to make up for the fact that his father wasn't around, trying to make his mother's life better, out of some sort of misplaced sense of guilt. As if it was his responsibility. As if his father's absence was somehow his fault. It was silly of course, as he had believed his father was dead.

The anger that had simmered within him from the moment he realized his mother had lied to him his entire life, indeed that much of his life was little more than a lie, blazed into flames.

"Do you?" Jack said coolly.

"Forbid might be the wrong word," Mother said quickly. "But you haven't thought this through."

"Didn't you say that I was more than capable of making my own decisions about my life?"

"Yes, of course, but this particular decision is . . . well . . ." Mother squared her shoulders. "It's ill-advised, Jackson. That's what it is. I have never known you to make poor decisions before. Obviously, it's his influence." She aimed a furious look at her husband who grinned back at her.

"Perhaps then I should stay here." Jack's gaze narrowed and he considered his mother. "As you and I have a great deal to sort out."

"Well, yes," she said weakly.

"You should know, Mother, that I have never been as furious with anyone as I am with you. Never imagined I could be." His gaze bored into his mother's. "Lucy was right. You have stolen something from me and from my father as well. The idea of putting an ocean between us has a great deal of appeal especially since, at the moment, I don't know that I can forgive you."

"Regardless." She pulled a deep breath. "I don't think you should go."

Lucy raised her chin in a defiant manner. "And I think you should."

"As do I." His grandfather stepped into the library and closed the doors behind him.

"Do you?" Jack's tone was harsher than he had intended but he didn't care. "And what part did you play in all this, Grandfather?"

"Channing." Grandfather nodded at the colonel. "I never thought I'd see you again."

"No doubt," Lucy said under her breath.

Mother shot her a sharp look.

"Life is full of surprises, Mr. Graham," his father said in a clipped tone. "But you haven't answered my son's question."

"It's not an easy question to answer. Odd, as it used to be." Grandfather turned toward Jack. "I did what I thought was best at the time."

"Are you talking about separating my parents or the decision not to tell me my father was very much alive?" Jack asked.

"Both." He glanced at his daughter. "Your mother had made what I had considered to be the sort of mistake that could ruin a life. She was entirely too young and rather foolish."

Mother's jaw tightened. "Thank you, Father."

"You've grown out of it," Grandfather said coolly and turned to Jack. "As for not telling you, I wouldn't say that was a deliberate decision. More of an, oh . . ." Grandfather's brow furrowed in thought. "An evolution, if you will. As the years went on, it really didn't seem necessary. You were perfectly content without a father." Grandfather paused. "It might not have been right in the strictly moral sense of the word but I think it turned out quite well. Given the same circumstances I would probably do it again. And I have no intention of defending decisions made decades ago."

Jack stared. "You have no regrets about denying me the chance to know my father all these years? About allowing me to believe he was dead?"

"Regrets are pointless, Jackson. One never knows how the end result of one's actions will play out. One does what one believes to be the proper course of action at the time and then moves on. Do I now think that it might have been a mistake?" Grandfather shrugged. "Possibly. But, as I said, I would probably do it again."

Jack struggled to keep his temper in check. He could not remember having to do so before, at least not with his family. Indeed, he considered himself every bit as even-tempered as he was rational. But then there was nothing the least bit rational about this evening.

"At least you are willing to admit that you were wrong." Anger sharpened Jack's voice.

"I admitted no such thing," Grandfather said. "I simply allowed for the possibility that I might have made an error in judgment. One's decisions are always easier to evaluate in hindsight. However, one's perspective on life does change as one grows older." He paused for a moment, then drew a deep breath. "I suspect I would be most irate to discover after thirty years that I had a son, or a father for that matter."

Jack stared at the elderly man. "Did you ever intend to tell me?"

Grandfather met his gaze firmly. "I don't know."

Again a knock sounded at the door and it opened without pause. Uncle Daniel popped his head in the door. "I hate to interrupt whatever is going on here but the rest of us are wondering if we've been abandoned. If there was some sort of crisis or worse."

"Definitely worse," Lucy murmured.

Daniel stepped into the library and surveyed the gathering. "From the looks on your faces, I'd say a crisis was fairly accurate."

Daniel Lockwood's father had become a partner in the banking and trust some forty years ago. Jack had called him Uncle Daniel for as long as he could remember and he was as much a part of the family as if he was a blood relation. In many ways, Daniel had taken the place of Jack's father for both Jack and his mother. He had long been Elizabeth's escort for various social functions and it was obvious to everyone, except perhaps Elizabeth herself, that Daniel was in love with her. Jack had always wondered why they hadn't married although the answer to that was now clear.

Daniel nodded at Lucy. "You might want to join your parents. They're getting restless."

"Yes, of course," Lucy said, but made no move to leave.

Daniel's questioning gaze settled on Jack's father. "Isn't anyone going to introduce us?"

"No," Mother snapped, then sighed. "Yes, well I suppose someone should."

Jack drew a deep breath. "Uncle Daniel, this is Colonel Basil Channing."

"Channing?" Daniel's brow arched upward. "Are you related to Elizabeth's late husband?"

His father nodded. "One could say that."

"Oh, my," Lucy said under her breath, her gaze shifting between Jack's mother and Daniel. "The plot does thicken now."

Mother slanted her a scathing look.

"Elizabeth?" Daniel said. "Wasn't your late husband's name Basil?"

"Yes, well . . ." Mother wrung her hands together and

straightened her shoulders. "He's not quite as late as one had hoped."

"Thank you, Elizabeth," Father said and took a sip of his brandy.

"Daniel." Jack met the older man's gaze. "This is my father."

"Your father?" Shock followed by realization washed across Daniel's face. "And your *husband?*"

Mother winced. "I'm afraid so."

Daniel studied the Englishman. "Not dead then?"

Father chuckled. "Not yet."

"I see." Daniel nodded slowly. "That explains quite a lot."

"Brandy, Mr. Lockwood?" Lucy headed for the brandy decanter without waiting for a response. Grandfather joined her, poured two glasses, and handed them to Lucy. She promptly crossed the room and gave one to Daniel.

"Thank you," Daniel said absently and tossed back half the glass.

"The poor man's had quite a shock, you know," Lucy said quietly for Jack's ears alone, handing him the second brandy on her way back to her seat. Brandy did seem like an excellent idea although good Scottish whisky might be better.

"Haven't we all," Jack murmured and gratefully sipped the liquor. Lucy would make an excellent hostess one day.

"Daniel." A placating note sounded in his mother's voice and she stepped toward the other man. "I'm sure you have a great many questions."

Daniel stared at her. "I most certainly do."

Mother nodded. "Yes, I did think that you—"

"At the top of that list . . ." Daniel's brow furrowed in anger and he directed his words toward Jack's father. "What kind of man abandons his wife and child?"

Mother winced. Lucy choked. Grandfather poured a brandy of his own.

"I'm afraid you're jumping to conclusions, old man." Father swirled the brandy in his glass.

"It's not what you think," Jack said quickly. "You have it all wrong."

"It's seems pretty obvious to me. In fact, it clears up a lot of discrepancies I've noticed through the years." Righteous indignation sounded in Daniel's voice. "Answer my question, Channing."

"I'm afraid I can't." Father shrugged in an offhand manner. "I don't know the answer to that particular question."

"Oh, come now. What kind of a fool—"

"He didn't know," Mother blurted, then heaved a resigned sigh. "Basil had no idea he was a father. Nor did he know that our marriage was not annulled."

"Annulled?" Daniel shook his head in confusion. "I thought he was dead."

"Not yet," Father said again and raised his glass in a toast.

"I don't understand this." Daniel rubbed his forehead. "Any of this." He paused and stared at Mother. "You're not a widow?"

"Not in the strictest definition of the word," Mother said. "But I do feel—"

"All these years and you were still married?" Shock shone in Daniel's eyes, betrayal sounded in his voice. "All that nonsense about waiting until Jackson was settled and married before you and I—"

"Really, Daniel." Mother huffed. "That's quite enough. I'll explain everything later and we can discuss all of it. At the moment we have more important issues to deal with."

"More important?" Disbelief rang in Daniel's voice. Grandfather appeared beside him and refilled his glass. "What could possibly be more important than a dead husband coming back from the grave?"

"Not really coming back," Father said pleasantly, "as I was never actually in the grave."

"Basil wants to take Jackson back with him to England. To meet the rest of his family," Mother said.

"Jackson's family," his father said firmly.

Mother ignored him. "Basil's brother is an earl and Jackson will one day inherit the title."

Daniel stared at her. "And?"

"And . . ." Mother chose her words with care. "If he leaves he might never come home." A pleading note rang in her voice and she moved closer to Daniel. "Don't you see, we could lose him entirely."

Daniel studied her for a moment, then turned his attention to Jack. "What are you going to do, Jack?"

Jack stared at the other man. Daniel hadn't called him Jack since he was a little boy. His heart twisted for the man who had been just as badly treated by his mother as he and his father.

Jack shook his head. "I haven't decided yet."

"It's a big decision." Daniel nodded thoughtfully. "If you want my advice, I think you should go."

Mother gasped. "Daniel!"

"You've always wanted to travel, this is your chance." Daniel favored him with a half-hearted smile. "And you've always wanted a father. This is your chance for that, too."

"I think it would be a mistake for you not to go, Jackson." Lucy met his gaze directly. "You've always done exactly what was expected of you. This would be, oh, an adventure I think and you should seize it. Go against everything you've always done. Why, you don't have an impulsive bone in your body. You're steadfast and reliable and not at all the type of man prone to adventure."

"Thank you?" Jack said.

She waved off his words. "You know what I mean. You're responsible and sensible. You don't take risks. You don't head off into the unknown—"

"Good Lord, Lucinda, it's only England," Grandfather said. "He's not going off to explore deepest, darkest Africa. England is quite civilized. And I am sorry, Elizabeth, but this is his decision. The bank will be here when he returns." He met his grandson's gaze. "No regrets, Jackson, but I do apologize, for whatever it's worth."

Jack nodded. "Thank you."

"Well?" Mother's eyes held a mixture of fear and hope. "Are you going with him or not?"

Jack stared at his mother for a long moment. No matter what she had done, no matter how many poor choices she had made, she was still his mother. He didn't doubt that she wanted what was best for him. He had never gone against her wishes before.

If someone had asked Jack last week or yesterday or even an hour ago if he had so much as a single rebellious bone in his body, he would have laughed in a wry manner and said no. His gaze shifted from one expectant face to the next. He had known all but one of them for most of his life. In that moment Jackson Quincy Graham Channing realized while he had no particular desire to be an English lord, he wasn't sure he really wanted to be a New York banker either. At that moment he realized what he really truly wanted in life . . .

Was to escape.

Chapter Three

Eight days later, October 1887,
Millworth Manor,
the country estate of the
Earl and Countess of Briston . . .

Jack resisted the ridiculous urge to hide behind one of the potted palms clustered decoratively around the perimeter of the grand Millworth Manor ballroom.

That he was ill at ease in a social setting was a new experience. He wasn't used to feeling both somewhat invisible and altogether conspicuous. But then what hadn't been a new experience in the last week?

His gaze drifted over the wedding guests now enjoying the wedding ball and lingered on a lovely, tall, red-haired woman who seemed to be in charge. A friend of the family no doubt. One he would probably meet at some point. If his father ever returned.

He sipped his champagne and considered the odd twist his life had taken since the moment he had stepped into his grandfather's library and met his father. *His father.* He was still trying to get used to the idea although nearly a week on-board ship together helped. He had learned a great deal about Colonel Basil Channing, about his family and his years spent in the army and the adventurous life he had lived since. Jack suspected there were few spots on the globe his father hadn't visited. He had been on safari in Africa, traveled down the Amazon, seen for himself China's Great Wall and the ancient temples of Angkor. He had hunted for treasure in the West Indies and the deserts of Egypt and narrowly escaped headhunters on the islands of Polynesia.

They had forged a rapport during their voyage that was part friendship, part father and son. With each day in his father's company, Jack liked him more and more. Trusted him more and more. Onboard ship, his father had delighted in introducing Jack as his son and always with a note of pride in his voice. As odd as it was to now be someone's son, there was something about publicly acknowledging their relationship that struck Jack as right, as it should be. As it always should have been. And if, when the conversation turned to family and home, there was a touch of wistfulness in the older man's voice, Jack diplomatically ignored it. But that too served to strengthen the growing bond between them.

And his father called him Jack, which was as natural, *as right,* as everything else.

Once they arrived in England, his father was as apprehensive as his son. They agreed the colonel should find just the right moment to present his newfound offspring to the rest of the family. Jack had stayed at an inn in a nearby village last night while his father went on to Millworth Manor.

He had joined his father at the family's ancestral home a few minutes before the late afternoon wedding. Father had decided, given the chaos at Millworth upon his arrival, to wait until after the wedding to reveal Jack's existence to the family. While the colonel assured Jack of his welcome, it was obvious he didn't entirely believe his own words. Jack was more than willing to take a seat in the back of the manor's chapel for the ceremony while the colonel joined the rest of the family in the front.

Perhaps she was a member of the family? Jack's gaze again settled on the red-haired beauty, drawn back as if of its own accord. Not that it mattered what her connection to his family was. He had Lucy to consider after all even if she had essentially broken things off with him before he left New York.

Lucy had said, as they were not officially engaged and he might well be starting a new life, and, as there would be an ocean between them, he shouldn't for a moment consider himself under any obligation to her while he was away. She said he should regard himself as completely unencumbered. Besides, she had pointed out, this was the opportunity for both of them to discover if they were really meant to be more than good friends or if they had just assumed they were meant for each other to please their families. Why, when one thought about it, wasn't it significant that they had both put off announcing their engagement over and over again? And really, wouldn't it be dreadful if they married and then later discovered it was a mistake? He had objected, of course, but she had been adamant and, in the end, he had reluctantly agreed with her. He had discussed the matter during the voyage with his father who agreed that women, as a rule, were incomprehensible. His father had also noted that it was his experience that women who gave a man his freedom often did so because they wanted freedom themselves. Jack had scoffed at the time, this was Lucy they were talking about after all, but a few days later he found himself wondering why it was so easy for them to part. Why neither of them had declared their love for the other. And why that now bothered him even though there was also a distinct sense of relief. Which bothered him as well.

He took another sip of his wine and watched the redhead move from one group of guests to the next. There were a surprising number of Americans present. His father had explained that the groom, Grayson Elliott, had spent nearly a decade in America. Jack didn't realize until he saw the man at the altar that they'd met but were no more than acquaintances. There were other Americans here too that Jack had met in the course of business although no one he knew more than casually. He thought it best to avoid them for now given that he wasn't at all sure how to explain his presence.

He and his father had avoided the other guests after the ceremony as well. Instead of joining family and friends for an early supper in advance of the wedding ball, the colonel had escorted his son on a tour of Millworth's extensive and impressive grounds. His father took him to the pond where he and his brother had skated in the winter and learned to swim in the summer, in spite of governesses who had forbidden them to go near the water. Father showed him the Grecian-style folly that was built by a long-ago owner of Millworth for his wife and told him the story of the star-crossed lovers that were said to haunt not only this folly but one exactly like it on the grounds of a nearby estate. It was foolish, of course, no sensible man believed in spirits. But it was also poignant and romantic and touching, even if one was a sensible man who did not believe in such nonsense.

And everywhere they went, everything they saw, brought to mind a memory for his father. He told Jack stories about his brother and his brother's children, the girls who had grown up here. He talked about those long-gone generations of Channings who had made Millworth their home and spoke of heritage and history. But with everything his father told him, everything they talked about, the one thing his father didn't say was the one thing that hung unspoken in the air between them: *One day all this will be yours.*

Jack still wasn't sure how he felt about that. If he wanted to be the next earl, wanted everything that went along with it, or not. And even if by virtue of blood he was half English, in mind and spirit he was firmly American. Still, there was no need to make a decision about his future yet. His father had recommended he take one step at a time and Jack had to meet his new family first. His father was even now breaking the news of his existence to them.

The red-haired woman laughed at something said to her and even at a distance it sounded delightful and genuine.

Onboard ship his father had said there was nothing that made a man feel more optimistic about life than a dance and a flirtation with a beautiful woman. Jack could use a bit of optimism at the moment. He hadn't felt this ill at ease in a social setting since his first ball more than a decade ago. Even now he remembered the discomfort of the stiff, starched collar of his formal attire. The collar he wore now was every bit as annoying as the first but he no longer noticed. Odd how one grew accustomed to even the most uncomfortable things with time and age and experience. Although he suspected he would never grow used to feeling out of place.

Well, enough of that nonsense. It was only nerves. He had no real reason to feel anything other than completely confident. Jack studied the redhead and adjusted the onyx studs at his cuffs. He was, after all, a successful banker with an exceptional heritage on both sides of his family. Granted, his family connections were far more complicated than they had been a month ago but the circumstances of one's life changed and one needed to be able to change with them.

He started toward the woman who had caught his eye. Besides, he was an excellent dancer.

Lady Theodosia Winslow resisted the urge to allow the pride and elation that comes from the satisfaction of a job expertly accomplished to show on her face. It wouldn't be at all proper to smirk.

Teddy stood off to one side of the ballroom and surveyed the ball, the final festivity of the day. Oh certainly, the wedding of Camille, Lady Lydingham, and Grayson Elliott was not entirely perfect but then what wedding was not without its moments of disorder and impending disaster? All of which had been skillfully averted, avoided, or circumvented by Teddy's capable hands. Not that it was particularly easy as Camille had alternated between fits of temper, overwhelming apprehension, and the firm belief that her wedding would be nothing short of a catastrophe.

It wasn't of course. And those moments of *imperfection* that did occur were vanquished as if by magic the moment Camille walked down the aisle on the arm of her father to marry the love of her life.

At this point, the hardest part was over. Teddy studied the gathering with a practiced eye. The ceremony was completed, dinner had been served without incident, and now Camille and Grayson's family and friends could simply celebrate with the happy couple although admittedly she wasn't quite sure exactly where the happy couple was at the moment. Not that it really mattered.

Guests were now enjoying the twelve-piece chamber orchestra Teddy had first employed last year for the Christmas Eve ball given by the Duchess of Roxborough. Yet another successful event coordinated and planned by Lady Theodosia and her mother, the Countess of Sallwick.

A good portion of those present tonight were on the dance floor just as Teddy had intended. There would be no wallflowers at this ball if she could help it. She had pointedly mentioned to several of the unmarried gentlemen in attendance that it never hurt to exert their charm toward those young ladies who had not been asked to dance. After all, one never knew if a less than extraordinary face hid a fine mind and a wicked sense of the absurd. She also subtly reminded them that heiresses did not wear signs indicating them as such. Not that nearly everyone here, with the exception of the Americans, didn't know, or know of, everyone here. Still, family circumstances changed with an unexpected and alarming frequency. Teddy's own life was a prime example.

She had also had a private word with the mothers of several of the young, unmarried ladies present and suggested their daughters might wish to extend the hand of English friendship to those American friends—those very *wealthy* American friends—of the groom who had traveled such a long way to attend his wedding. Even though Grayson had grown up at Fairborough, a nearby estate, he had spent more than a decade making his fortune in America and he had apparently invited everyone he had ever met there to celebrate his nuptials. It did seem that for every two of Her Majesty's subjects there was at least one American visitor. Even those mothers determined to snare their daughters a lofty title were practical enough to see the benefits of a liaison with a rich American. Eligible men with respectable titles and decent fortunes were in short supply these days.

Teddy's gaze constantly shifted between the guests and the hired waiters. Millworth Manor simply did not have the staff necessary for a gathering of this size. Part and parcel of her job was doing all in her power to make certain every guest had as good a time as possible. It would not do for a dissatisfied guest to gossip about what a dreadful time he or she'd had. She stopped a passing waiter and directed him to a group of gentlemen discussing whatever it was gentlemen were compelled to discuss when they clustered together at social events. But the gentlemen's glasses were empty and that would never do.

Those not dancing milled and mingled, renewing old acquaintances, sharing the latest bit of gossip and, without question, dissecting every detail of Camille and Grayson's wedding. Teddy allowed herself a small, satisfied smile. Such dissection would only serve to greater solidify Teddy and her mother's position as one of the preeminent planners of society events in England. When they had started planning parties and weddings, they had been engaged primarily because there was nothing society hostesses liked better than having the socially prominent Countess of Sallwick and her daughter organize their events. Then too, not everyone could afford their exorbitant rates, which only served to add to the social prestige of the hostess hiring them. Rates her mother explained to prospective clients with a blithe wave of her hand as she charmingly pointed out there was a high price to be paid for the very best.

Of course, charm was Mother's greatest contribution to their efforts, a reality of their new life Teddy had realized almost from the beginning. Teddy knew as well that the functions they planned had best be rousing successes if their business was to succeed. She might not have been born to the world of business but she understood that even a prestigious name would not make up for shoddy service. Teddy could name quite a few ladies who still suffered the taint of unsuccessful soirees held years ago. But social successes were not as easy as they looked. Teddy never imagined the organization of parties, fetes, soirees, and weddings would be quite as all-consuming as it was. She had never worked like this in her life. Still, it was worth it. They'd come a long way in a few short years.

Teddy gazed out over the crowd and wondered what these people would say if they knew this wasn't just the eccentric hobby of the countess and her daughter. If they knew her father's death four years ago had left them very nearly penniless and with debts still to be paid off. Only her closest and oldest friend, the bride's sister Delilah, Lady Hargate, knew the truth. But Dee would take Teddy's secret to the grave if necessary. There were any number of sins the upper ten thousand would forgive. Poverty was not one of them.

"You do realize that you've missed someone," an American voice said behind her.

She turned and adopted her most pleasant smile. "I beg your pardon."

"You missed someone," he said again.

She was tall but he was taller and she had to raise her chin to meet his gaze. His eyes were a rich blue that complemented the dark shade of his hair. His jaw was square, his shoulders broad, and while not shockingly handsome, he was certainly an attractive-looking man. There was the vaguest air of familiarity about him although she was sure they had never met. He was obviously one of Grayson's American friends.

"Did I?"

"I've been watching you and I couldn't help but notice that you seem to be making sure everyone is dancing or otherwise engaged."

"You've been watching me?" She raised a brow. "I'm not certain if I should be flattered or alarmed."

He smiled, a charming, infectious sort of smile. "I assure you, my intentions are strictly honorable."

"Then tell me." She glanced around the room. "Who have I missed?"

"Me of course." He paused. "And you."

"I see." She considered him for a moment.

It was not uncommon for Teddy to join in the festivities at an event. Indeed, one of the benefits of hiring Teddy was having Lady Theodosia present at a social event. She was from a prominent family, the daughter of an earl, and was once one of the most sought after marriageable ladies in the country. Of course, that was several years ago. She was twenty-six now and while her mirror told her she had never looked better, age was as much of a stigma in her world as poverty. Not that she didn't wish to marry, the right man had simply never happened her way. And the one she had thought was right had turned out to be very, very wrong.

"One dance, that's all," he said quickly. "Save me from the dire fate of having only myself for company."

"That does sound dreadful."

"You have no idea." His brow furrowed. "I don't seem

to be doing this well." The American leaned closer in a confidential manner. "May I be perfectly honest with you?"

She smiled. "I much prefer honesty to dishonesty."

"Good." A decidedly uncomfortable look crossed his face.

"I accompanied my father here but he seems to have disappeared. And aside from him, I don't know anyone else here to speak of. I feel both invisible and conspicuous, if that's at all possible. I'm not used to feeling out of place and it's, well, disconcerting."

"And dancing will help?"

"I am considered a good dancer and I promise I won't step on your feet."

"Well, I—"

"The point I am trying to make is that I feel like a fish stranded out of water at the moment. A large American fish. Just flapping around in the sand."

She bit back a smile.

"So please take pity on a fish and do me the very great honor of joining me for a dance." He cast her a hopeful smile. "I would be forever in your debt."

"Well," she said slowly, "I have always been fond of fish. Although I usually prefer it with a dilled cream sauce."

"Then you've obviously never had baked flounder stuffed with crab." Amusement glimmered in his eyes. "Nothing is better than crab-stuffed baked flounder."

"Unless perhaps it is a native American fish stranded on the beach?"

He stared at her for a moment, then laughed and held out his hand. "Shall we?"

She hesitated, then placed her hand on his. "You should know I don't make it a habit to dance with men I have not been properly introduced to."

"Understandable." He nodded and led her onto the floor. "Then this will be a new experience for you. For both of us really. We should think of it as an adventure."

"As adventures go, I'm afraid this one is rather minor."

Although there was something to be said for dancing with a handsome stranger. "Surely you can think of something better?"

"I wish I could." He took her in his arms and they moved to the strains of a sedate waltz. "But one has to start somewhere. With adventures, that is. One step at a time, you know."

"I suspect you're right." She shook her head. "I've always rather fancied adventure although I've never been an especially adventurous sort myself."

"You don't need to be."

She drew her brows together in confusion. "I don't?"

"Of course not." He skillfully led her through a turn. He was right—he was good. "You're a beautiful woman with hair the color of fine mahogany, flashing emerald eyes, and an air of confidence and assurance about you. You *are* an adventure."

"Oh." She had no idea what to say. It was perhaps the nicest compliment she had ever received. And it had been some time since she'd had such a compliment. She wasn't used to being at a loss for words and promptly changed the subject. "Forgive me but I am a bit confused. You said you didn't know anyone here but your father. There are a great many American friends of the groom's in attendance. I assumed you were one of them."

"I'm afraid not." He shook his head. "I have met him, the groom that is, but I didn't realize that until I arrived."

"Now I am even more confused."

"As are we all." He smiled. "My story is long and convoluted. One I promise not to bore you with."

"But I do so enjoy a long and convoluted tale." She tilted her head and studied him. "Is it a good one?"

"That remains to be seen."

"Well then, does it end well?"

"The ending too is yet to be determined."

"How very interesting," she murmured. What an enigmatic

sort this American was. "Will you be staying in England long?"

"I'm not sure."

"My goodness." She stared up at him. "Are you being deliberately vague?"

He laughed. "Not really. My life is something of a, oh, a question mark at the moment, I would say. I can't answer your questions because I don't have the answers."

"I see. Well, do you have a name?"

"I do." He smiled. "But, in the interest of elevating our dance from a minor adventure to something more interesting, maybe we should postpone introductions for now." A firm note sounded in his voice. Whatever his story was, whoever he was, it was obvious he did not wish to discuss it further. How very intriguing. "And at the moment, I would much prefer to talk about you. You seem to be running things here. Are you a friend of the family?"

She nodded. "The bride's younger sister, Dee, or rather Delilah, Lady Hargate that is, is my oldest and dearest friend. My mother and I organize social events including weddings although my mother is not here today. I planned this one."

"It looks as though you've done an excellent job."

"It has turned out nicely." She couldn't keep a note of pride from her voice.

"So this is, well, a business enterprise for you?" Doubt sounded in his voice.

"When my father died, my mother and I found ourselves at loose ends." The well-rehearsed story flowed easily from her lips. "Mother was well known for the elaborate parties she gave and she trained me well. It began, and indeed it remains, more of a hobby than anything else. Something to fill our idle hours. Although we do charge for our services. There is nothing that says prosperity in society more than paying outrageous sums for something you could probably do yourself."

He nodded. "Yes, of course."

For a few moments they danced in silence but he was obviously pondering her comments. "It must be difficult work though."

"Not at all. It's quite enjoyable." She shrugged as best she could in his arms. "Mother and I both enjoy entertaining but there are only so many parties one can give. Planning social events for others provides us with a great deal of variety and an extra bit of pin money."

"I see." There was a slight hint of disapproval in his tone.

"You think we should do this for nothing?"

"No, but it's, well . . ."

"It's what?"

"Somewhat unseemly, isn't it?"

She narrowed her eyes. "What makes it unseemly?"

"You're charging for your services which takes it out of the realm of an innocent pastime and into the definition of business."

"Yes, I suppose one could look at it that way." His attitude was nothing she hadn't encountered before. Still, it was most annoying. She smiled and gazed into his eyes. "I prefer to see it as providing assistance to those ladies who can barely manage a household let alone a ball for two hundred people or an evening of music and cards for ninety or a grand, extravagant wedding."

"Perhaps but—"

"And if we did not charge for our services, which as you said makes it perilously close to a business endeavor—"

He nodded.

"They would not be the least bit valuable. As much as I hate to admit it, especially to a foreigner, but the upper echelon of society here is frightfully shallow about things like this." She cast him her brightest smile and changed the subject. "And are you in business as Mr. Elliott is? Another American entrepreneur? A captain of industry perhaps?"

"Not exactly." He shook his head. "I'm engaged in banking, in the banking and trust founded by my great-grandfather."

"I don't believe I have ever danced with a banker before."

"Yet another factor that makes it more of an adventure for you," he said firmly. "Although bankers by their very nature are not adventurous men."

"And yet you strike me as a man well suited to adventure."

"Do I?" He executed another complicated turn. "Why do you think so?"

She considered him coolly. "For one thing, there is an air of assurance about you. You have the look of a man certain of himself and his world."

"And yet, only moments ago, I confessed to feeling completely out of place."

"Ah, but you hide it nicely. If you hadn't said it, I would never have known you were anything other than completely at ease. I suspect you conceal your other secrets equally as well. Which are probably most shocking."

"Oh, without question."

She smiled. "Which makes you a man of mystery and intrigue."

He laughed. "I've never been described as either mysterious or secretive and certainly not intriguing."

"And I've never had gentlemen describe me as an adventure," she said without thinking.

"Then they were unobservant fools." He held her a tiny bit closer than was proper. "And are you a woman of mystery and secrets as well?"

"No, of course not." She scoffed, then gazed up into his endless blue eyes. Her breath caught. "Perhaps."

He smiled a slow, irresistible smile. A smile fraught with unspoken meaning or promise or something else completely absurd. Something absolutely improper. Something that held the vaguest, tempting hint of true adventure. The music ended and they drew to a stop yet his gaze still locked with hers. "Then I was right. You are an adventure."

For a long moment she stared at him, lost in his smile and his eyes, ignoring a voice in the back of her head telling her enough of this nonsense was enough. Noting she had things to attend to. Chastising her for allowing this stranger to hold her spellbound. And yet there was something about him, something in his eyes, something unknown, something perhaps quite wonderful she was loath to abandon.

A throat cleared behind her. "Might I have a word, my lady."

The voice yanked her back to the here and now and she turned. "Yes?"

Clement, Millworth's butler, inclined his head toward her in a discreet manner and lowered his voice for her ears alone. "I do hate to interrupt, but you're needed in the kitchen."

"I'll be right there." She nodded at the butler, then turned back to her stranger. "Forgive me, but I do have duties to attend to."

"Understandable." He took her hand and drew it to his lips. "Thank you for coming to the rescue of a poor flounder." He flashed a quick grin. "And for a most enjoyable adventure."

She smiled, nodded, and hurried off, ignoring the heat that flushed her face and a distinct sense of disappointment. Absurd, of course. It was no more than a single dance with an unidentified gentleman. There was no need for her to think even for an instant that it was more than it was. Besides, she had other concerns at the moment.

Still, once she had resolved the problem—a simple matter of locating misplaced cases of champagne—and returned to the ballroom she couldn't help casually looking for her handsome American. He seemed to have vanished, exactly what one would expect from a mysterious stranger. Blast it all, she never did get the man's name and now he was nowhere to be found. How could she inquire about him if she didn't have his name? Although, it was probably for the best. The last thing she wanted, now or ever, was another man in her life with secrets.

Her gaze wandered over the crowd of celebrants and the thought occurred to her, as it always did when she organized a wedding, that this was very much the sort of wedding she had always planned on for herself. The wedding she expected to have when she married the man she was expected to marry. A man with a lofty title and a sizable fortune. It was what the daughter of the Earl of Sallwick was born and bred for.

Perhaps it was something the American had said or maybe it was simply inevitable, but for the first time it struck her that what she had expected of her life was not how it was ever going to be. Wasn't it time to stop thinking of what she and her mother did to support themselves as a temporary measure? As nothing more than a passing solution and that one day their lives would be back on the course they were always expected to take.

The American was right. She was a woman of business and bloody well good at it too. Maybe it was time to accept who and what she was. To accept that she would never have the kind of wedding she had expected to have. Or that she would never marry the kind of man she had expected to marry. In fact, now that she thought about it, marriage was no longer what she wanted at all.

As a young girl she had longed for independence. And why not? The new century was fast approaching and with it progress and new ideas. Why, weren't women already working for suffrage? And while being an independent woman of business was not something she would proclaim to society—it would ruin them after all—it was time, past time, really, to embrace it within herself and stop looking back at what her life was supposed to be. But rather look at what it was. And what it could be.

Without thinking she raised her chin as if facing the future head-on. No, Lady Theodosia Winslow was not born and bred to be an independent woman of business but it was exactly what she was.

Teddy smiled at the thought. And that, my dear mysterious American, might well be the grandest adventure of all.

Chapter Four

Colonel Basil Channing considered himself a man of action and courage. Why, among his many adventures, hadn't he once faced a charging rhinoceros on the African plains? Hadn't he escaped the clutches of bloodthirsty natives in the South Seas? Hadn't he been presented at court to Her Majesty? Still, none of those, with the possible exception of his introduction to the queen, had proved as daunting as the task before him now.

He surveyed the expectant expressions on the faces of his family in the large, gracious Millworth dining room, the scene of any number of announcements, proclamations, and revelations through the years. Indeed, it seemed whenever there was a critical issue affecting the family it was revealed and discussed here. It had become something of a tradition. It was assumed when a request was made to meet in the dining room it would be a family matter of some importance.

"I am sorry to interrupt," he said with an apologetic smile although everyone was in excellent spirits. Exactly why this had struck him as the perfect moment to say what had to be said. One should always seize an opportunity when it presented itself. "I didn't think this could wait any longer. In truth, I shouldn't have waited this long. But it's rare that the entire family is together in one place. I didn't want to take the chance that some of you would scatter in the morning so I thought it best to do this now." This was an announcement he did not want to repeat.

Basil nodded at the newlyweds. "But I do apologize for taking you away from the festivities."

"Nonsense, Uncle Basil," Camille said with the sort of smile that could only come from someone truly happy. "The ball is well under way and no one will miss us for a few minutes."

Basil had asked his brother and sister-in-law, their twin daughters, Beryl and Camille, along with Beryl's husband, Lionel, Lord Dunwell, and Grayson, as well as the youngest Channing daughter, Delilah, to join him. Delilah was accompanied by an American, a Mr. Russell. From what Basil had heard last night, there was a question as to whether Mr. Russell would be here at all but judging by the way he and Delilah looked at one another, they had resolved whatever problems they'd had.

"I must confess, you have us all dying of curiosity," Beryl said. Beryl always did come straight to the point.

"And a certain amount of apprehension." Nigel studied his brother closely. "It's not like you to be preoccupied and on edge but you have been since you arrived at Millworth."

"I will try to keep this as succinct as possible." Even though Basil had rehearsed any number of times since he had learned of Jack's existence, the right words evaded him now. He braced himself and met his twin's gaze directly. "I know you have been concerned about the fate of Millworth as you have no sons. And upon our respective deaths, your title, the estate, and everything associated with it will be inherited by some distant relative we scarcely even know."

"It's the way of the world." Nigel shrugged as if it didn't matter but both brothers knew it did. "I've made my peace with it."

"As have we all," Delilah said. "Admittedly, it will be rather sad to see Millworth pass into unfamiliar hands but it's not as if any of us will be left penniless."

"Thanks to appropriate first marriages," Bernadette said smugly.

Bernadette had done an excellent job of raising the girls on her own after Nigel had gone off to wander the world. She had made it her mission in life to make certain her daughters would not face financial insecurity should their husbands decide to seek adventure rather than live up to their responsibilities. The first marriages for all three girls were to older gentlemen with substantial fortunes. No matter what happened in the future, their financial security was assured.

"That is one less thing to be concerned with," Basil said under his breath.

It was only in widowhood that Beryl and Camille, and now apparently Delilah, had found what looked to be genuine love. Exactly as their mother had planned. Something Bernadette had admitted to Basil but would never admit to her daughters. It was one of many confidences she and her brother-in-law had shared through the twenty years of Nigel's absence from his family. Not that Nigel hadn't realized his mistake very nearly from the start. But Bernadette had thought it better to let her daughters think their father was dead rather than know he had abandoned them.

Basil had been his twin's champion through the years and had argued repeatedly with Bernadette about allowing Nigel to return home. Nigel had pled his own case in frequent letters but Bernadette was unyielding. While to some she might have seemed overly stubborn, Basil knew his brother's actions had hurt her deeply. So Basil had become his sister-in-law's confidant and close friend and had fulfilled the role of father for the girls when he was in England. But his restless nature had kept him seeking travel and adventure and he was gone more than he was present. Basil never would have admitted it even to Bernadette but it was often difficult to see the life and family his brother had freely forsaken, the life Basil would never have. The life he could have had if only . . . Basil firmly thrust the thought aside. It was pointless to dwell on the past and what might have been. His brother had been a fool but then, in many ways, so had Basil.

It was only this past Christmas that Nigel had at last found the courage to come home in spite of his wife's objections. As it happened, she was waiting for him to do so. After twenty years apart they had found one another again. Bernadette had, if not completely forgiven her husband, at least been willing to overlook his transgressions and move forward. After all, twenty years was a long time. Not as long as thirty . . .

"I do wish you would tell us what this is all about." Annoyance sounded in Bernadette's voice. "We do have a ball to return to, you know."

"Of course, I know," Basil snapped, then drew a calming breath. "This isn't easy, Bernadette. I'm trying to think of the right way to say this."

"Just say it." His sister-in-law glared. Patience had never been one of Bernadette's virtues. "The more you dissemble, the more the rest of us think this is something truly dreadful."

"It's not dreadful," Basil said staunchly. "In many ways it's something of a miracle."

"Go on then." Nigel's brow furrowed with concern and he studied his brother. "Out with it, Basil."

"Very well." Basil paused to pull his words together. This was every bit as difficult as he had thought it would be. "It's a long story but I shall try to make it short."

"Too late," Beryl murmured.

Basil braced himself. "A very long time ago, I met a lovely young woman, the daughter of an American banker." He chose his words with care. "We fancied ourselves in love and did what young people in love often do . . ."

Bernadette's jaw clenched with impatience. "Do get on with it, Basil."

He ignored her. "We eloped."

A collective gasp washed around the room.

"Her parents were appalled and convinced the marriage was a terrible mistake. They convinced us of that as well."

Nigel stared, shock and disbelief in his eyes. "You never told me any of this."

"It was not something I was particularly proud of." Basil's voice was sharper than he intended. He had always regretted letting Elizabeth go. Now it seemed it was the biggest mistake of his life. "At any rate, she returned to America and was to have the marriage annulled. Her father would see to that."

Beryl studied her uncle closely. "*Was* to have the marriage annulled?"

"Yes, well, that's apparently difficult to do if the bride is with child." Basil shook his head. "I only recently learned about this."

Camille's eyes widened. "Then you're still married?"

"And you have a child?" Shock rang in Delilah's voice.

"Basil," Nigel said in a hard tone and met his brother's gaze. "What exactly are you trying to tell us?"

"I'm trying to tell you I have a son." Basil drew a deep breath. "I'm trying to tell you there is a new heir to Millworth Manor. And he's American."

Shock hung in the air. For a long moment no one said a word. Then the dam broke.

"Good Lord, Uncle Basil." Beryl stared at him. "How could you have been so careless as to misplace a son?"

"And in America no less." Delilah scoffed in a derisive manner earning her a raised brow from Mr. Russell. "Not that it's not a fine enough place to lose a son," she added quickly.

"Although where you lost him is really beside the point, isn't it?" Camille said.

Bernadette shook her head in amazement. "How could you, Basil?"

"First of all, I'll have you know, all of you, that I knew nothing about this." Basil blew a long breath. "Elizabeth, his mother, *my wife,* did not see fit to tell me that we were still married nor did she inform me as to the birth of my son who has, by the way, recently marked his thirtieth birthday. So you see, my dear niece"—he pinned Beryl with a firm look—"I did not misplace him as I was unaware of his existence." His gaze shifted to Delilah. "New York is the home of his mother's family and again I did not lose him as I didn't know he existed." He directed his gaze to Camille. "And yes, where he was is entirely beside the point although I daresay had he been born and raised in England I might well have stumbled onto him before now." He narrowed his gaze at Bernadette. "And as to how could I, how could I what, Bernadette? Fall in love with a woman and then fail to fight for her? Admittedly, that was a mistake that I realized nearly from the beginning. And while I wrote to her, it seemed she wanted nothing more to do with me. Should I have pursued her in spite of that? In hindsight, of course I should have." His gaze pinned his sister-in-law's. "But we all make mistakes out of passion or pride or pain, mistakes that have unexpected repercussions. Don't we, Bernadette?"

"Well, yes, I suppose." Bernadette muttered and had the good grace to look chagrined.

"When did you find out about this?" Delilah asked.

"A few weeks ago. I took the first ship to New York. But of course, I couldn't stay." He glanced at Camille. "I couldn't miss your wedding."

"Thank you," Camille murmured with a weak smile.

Beryl shook her head. "You must be furious."

"My anger is greatly diminished by my, well, I suppose my joy is the only good word for it." He smiled wryly. "It isn't every day that one discovers one has a full-grown offspring, and a son at that."

"Still, I would be hard-pressed to forgive something of this magnitude," Beryl said firmly. "Why, I know I shall never be able to forgive this woman on your behalf."

"Thank you, my dear, for your loyalty." Basil smiled and shook his head. "I don't know that I have forgiven Elizabeth or that I ever will. Regardless, what's done is done and we need to move forward from here."

"Father." Camille turned to Nigel. "You haven't said a word."

"This is quite a lot to digest," Nigel said thoughtfully. "Not the least of which is my brother failing to tell me about his marriage."

"I apologize for that. I put it all behind me and went on with my life. It seemed pointless to bring it up. Now, of course, it's an entirely different matter that affects us all." Basil held his breath. "I know this is a shock but I would appreciate it if you would say something, Nigel, anything. I have no idea what you're thinking."

"I'm not entirely sure what to say. As you said, it's all a bit of a shock. Completely unexpected. And the consequences . . ." Nigel's gaze met his brother's. "Cousin Wilfred's dolt of a son will be most disappointed. I however . . ." A slow smile spread across his face. "I couldn't be more pleased."

Basil grinned at his brother. "It is something of a surprise."

"A surprise? Good God, man." Nigel crossed to his brother and embraced him. "You said it was a miracle and I'd say you're right. It's a bloody great miracle. Millworth and the title going to your son, my nephew. Nothing could make me happier."

"But Father." Delilah cast an apologetic look at Mr. Russell. "He's American. You can't have an American Earl of Briston."

"I don't see why not," Mr. Russell said in a casual manner

and glanced at Lionel. "Is there any legal reason why an American couldn't inherit an English title?"

Beryl's husband was a political sort, a member of Parliament, and if anyone knew the legal repercussions of any question, Lionel did. Or, as Basil had always suspected, he simply thought he did. "From what I gather thus far, Colonel Channing was, and still is apparently, legally married to this man's mother so legitimacy is not an issue. Regardless of where he resides or where he was born, he is the colonel's legal heir and, after the colonel, Lord Briston's closest male relative. As his father is English, he would be considered a subject of the Crown even though his American birth gives him citizenship in that country as well. The way I see it, and I very much doubt that I'm wrong on this, he is considered a citizen of both countries."

"Entirely more than we wanted to know, dear," Beryl said to her husband.

"Quite right." Lionel nodded. "Well, I don't see any impediment to his inheriting at all."

Perhaps Lionel was as clever as he thought himself after all. Beryl's smile of pride said she certainly thought so.

"But in every way that truly counts, he's an American." Horror sounded in Delilah's voice.

Grayson inclined his head toward Mr. Russell and lowered his voice. "I suspect that sort of thing is going to be most annoying in the future."

"Oh, I'm not worried. She'll come around. You'd be surprised at how willing she is to compromise." Mr. Russell grinned confidently, his gaze firmly on Delilah. "Besides, we have a contract."

Grayson frowned in confusion. "A what?"

"None of your concern." Delilah huffed and a blush washed up her face.

"So then . . ." Camille said slowly. "You've met him? The new son, that is?"

"Goodness, Camille." Beryl sighed. "Why do you think he went to New York?"

"I don't know," Camille snapped. "Why does anyone go to New York?"

"I went to meet my son, of course." Basil frowned at the twins. "And I brought him back with me."

Bernadette's eyes widened. "You what?"

"He's here?" Camille stared. "He came to my wedding?"

"I do hope he brought a nice gift," Beryl murmured.

"Yes," Basil said in the hard, quiet, commanding tone that had once made grown men shake. "I brought him to Millworth to make the acquaintance of his family. To his cousin's wedding."

"Excellent." Nigel beamed. "When can we meet him?"

"I sent a footman to fetch him."

An awkward silence fell over the group. For the first time in Basil's memory, none of the female members of his family had anything to say. Although their faces clearly gave away their thoughts.

"There is nothing that makes me more uncomfortable than when we're all thinking a myriad of different thoughts and yet none of us have the courage to speak them aloud." Beryl rose to her feet. "Well, I for one, think it's splendid, just splendid." She directed a brilliant smile at her uncle. "Congratulations, Uncle Basil, on the birth of your son."

"It's not quite that easy," Bernadette said thoughtfully. "There will be a great deal of talk, you know."

"Gossip." Delilah sighed. "Again."

"Oh, we have certainly weathered gossip before." Bernadette waved a dismissive hand. "And emerged none the worse for it really. Delilah is the only one who has ever been especially bothered by it. And Basil." She smiled at her brother-in-law. "You have my heartfelt congratulations as well. I too think it's splendid that you have found your son."

"Besides," Beryl continued. "This is exactly the sort of thing expected from our family."

"She's right." Camille ticked the points off on her fingers. "Why, we've had Father come back from the dead. Mother has always had various deposed noblemen in residence at Millworth at Christmas. And there's been all kinds of other assorted scandalous behavior through the years."

"Not from me," Delilah said under her breath.

Mr. Russell choked back a laugh.

"Why, for this family, a long lost son is scarcely worth mentioning at all." Beryl grinned.

"Even if he's American?" Basil pinned Delilah with a firm look.

Delilah glanced at Mr. Russell, then managed a weak smile. "I'm certain that will only make him more interesting."

"You'll accept him then? All of you?" Basil's gaze circled the room. "As a member of the family?"

"Of course we will," Nigel said staunchly.

"And with a great deal of enthusiasm." Bernadette nodded in a firm manner.

"I look forward to welcoming him into the family." Camille cast her uncle a bright smile.

"As do I." Delilah heaved a resigned sigh, then smiled. "He is half English after all."

"I told you," Mr. Russell said under his breath to Grayson.

"The real question, Uncle Basil, isn't whether we're willing to accept him," Beryl said thoughtfully. "But is he willing to accept us?"

Jack followed the footman out of the ballroom and down the stairs to the ground floor, through the gallery that opened up off the main doors, past several parlors to a closed door.

The footman glanced back at him. "I'll inform Colonel Channing that you've arrived, sir."

"If you must." It took Jack an instant to realize he had said that aloud. "Sorry, of course."

The footman cast him a curious look, obviously wondering

why the colonel and his family had left the festivities to gather in the dining room. And what part this American stranger played in it. Not that every servant in the house probably wouldn't know the answer by morning if not sooner. Jack suspected that servants here were no different than those in his grandfather's house. No one knew more about what went on in a residence than its servants.

The young man nodded, knocked sharply, then opened the door and stepped into the room. He cleared his throat and his voice drifted back to Jack. "I beg your pardon, Colonel Channing . . ."

This was absurd. Jack shouldn't be nervous about this. Absently, he adjusted his necktie. He was about to meet his family after all. Nothing terrifying about that. Aside from the fact that they were about to meet a relative they had no idea even existed. A stranger, a foreigner, who stood to inherit all they held dear. He groaned to himself. Oh, no, nothing to be anxious about at all.

The footman returned, gave Jack a slight encouraging smile, then took his leave. His father stepped into the corridor an instant later.

"I've broken the news to them." The colonel studied his son closely. "They took it quite well. There's no need to be the least bit apprehensive."

"Oh?" Jack's brow rose. "And you weren't apprehensive when you faced them?"

"I was bloody well terrified." His father chuckled. "But it's turned out quite well really, you'll see." His father's firm gaze met his. "Trust me on this, my boy."

"All right." Jack took a deep breath and followed his father into the dining room.

His immediate impression was of a very grand room, a table far too small for the room although he suspected it expanded, and eight faces turned toward him expectantly. He recognized nearly all of them from the wedding ceremony. The bride and groom of course, Camille and her new husband, Grayson. The attendant who looked exactly like the bride was Camille's twin sister, Beryl, which meant the other young woman in the room was the younger sister, Delilah. He couldn't fail to recognize Lord Briston, his uncle Nigel, even if he hadn't seen him at the ceremony as it was clear he was his father's twin. The older woman was obviously his wife, his aunt Bernadette. He had no idea who the unidentified man was but the other was an American, Samuel Russell, a successful entrepreneur and industrialist. A voice in the back of his head, that might have been his grandfather's, pointed out what a coup it would be to get this man's holdings, as well as Mr. Elliott's, firmly in the vaults of Graham, Merryweather and Lockwood. He dismissed the thought. Now was not the time for business. They moved closer to the table.

"Allow me to introduce Jackson Channing." Pride sounded in his father's voice and eased Jack's discomfort. "My son."

Unfortunately, no one had told his new family how impolite it was to stare in silence. Fortunately, it lasted less than a moment. Those sitting rose to their feet.

Lord Briston stepped forward and clasped his hand. "I can't tell you what an unexpected pleasure it is to meet you." His uncle smiled into Jack's eyes. "Welcome, Jackson, to Millworth Manor."

"Jack," Jack said without thinking, then realized he had never introduced himself as anything other than Jackson before. At least not since he was a very small boy. His father's influence no doubt.

"Jack it is then." His uncle's smile widened. "Allow me to introduce you to your aunt Bernadette."

"Good Lord, you look exactly like Basil and Nigel looked at your age." Astonishment shone on her face. "There certainly isn't any doubt as to whose son you are."

One of his cousins groaned. "Mother."

She cast an annoyed look at her daughters. "Come now,

we were all thinking it." She took Jack's hand, leaned forward, and kissed his cheek. "How very good it is to meet you, Jack."

"Thank you." He smiled, relieved to note his apprehension had, if not gone completely, then certainly lessened.

The next few minutes were filled with introductions. The man he didn't know turned out to be Lionel, Lord Dunwell, Beryl's husband and a member of Parliament no less.

"We've met, haven't we?" Mr. Elliott said, shaking Jack's hand.

"We have." Jack nodded. "But it wasn't until today at your wedding that I realized that. My father said his niece was getting married but I don't think he ever mentioned the groom by name."

"We had a great many other things to discuss," his father said quickly.

"I don't doubt it." Elliott studied Jack's face. "I'm rather disappointed that I didn't make the connection myself. The resemblance, you know, and of course the name. And I daresay you've met Mr. Russell."

"Once or twice." Jack shook the other American's hand.

"I've had business with your bank on occasion," Russell said with a smile.

"And were we helpful?"

Russell grinned. "Not always."

Jack laughed, marveling that he was at ease enough to do so.

"Really, Jack," Camille said, taking his hands in hers. "I can't tell you how very happy we are to meet you and we all want to get to know you better, but at the moment . . ." She glanced at her new husband. "We should return to our guests."

"Of course." Elliott nodded.

"Teddy will be furious if we don't return at once," Delilah said. "If she isn't already."

"Teddy?" Jack said without thinking. "Is that the beautiful red-haired woman?"

"Why, yes it is, Jack." Aunt Bernadette hooked her arm in his and steered him toward the door. "How perceptive of you to notice. Have you met? Oh, you should meet her. She's a lovely young woman. Why, I've known Teddy—"

"Goodness, Mother." Beryl rolled her gaze toward the ceiling. "The man has barely arrived in this country. He doesn't need you interfering in his personal life."

"Don't be absurd, Beryl." Aunt Bernadette cast him an innocent smile. "I never interfere in the lives of my children, Jack. You should know that about me. And I certainly wouldn't interfere in yours."

The look the three sisters traded said otherwise.

Beryl heaved a long-suffering sigh. "For all you know he could be married."

"He's not," his father said helpfully.

"Or engaged," his cousin added.

"No, I'm not married or engaged," Jack said perhaps a shade quicker than he should. His father threw him a considering look.

"You'll stay here of course," Aunt Bernadette continued.

"I have a room in the village."

"Nonsense," she said firmly "I—we—wouldn't dream of you staying anywhere but here. Regardless of the circumstances, this is your family home. This is where you belong." Aunt Bernadette released his arm and continued toward the door. "I'll have Clement send for your things at once."

"In the meantime, we should get back to the festivities." Uncle Nigel nodded, turned toward the door, then paused. "But it might be best if we all"—he shot a pointed look at Beryl—"refrained from mentioning Jack's connection to the family. At least for tonight."

Relief washed through Jack. It was awkward enough to

meet his new family tonight. He would prefer to do this as his father had suggested—one step at a time. Being acknowledged publicly as a newly discovered heir could wait.

"Why did you look at me when you said that?" Beryl's brow furrowed in indignation. "I can certainly keep a secret."

"Not so anyone would notice," her twin murmured.

"You are the undisputed queen of gossip," Delilah said.

"Thank you, dear." A smug smile curved Beryl's lips. "Might I point out that all of you are most appreciative of that when you want some sort of information. And might I remind you . . ." Her gaze shifted from one sister to the next. "That there are any number of secrets I have kept quite well. Why, I know all sorts of things about both of you which, if I was not good at keeping your confidences, I might be inclined to reveal. Take, just as an example, the time when Camille—"

"I don't think any of us need to hear that," Camille said quickly.

"Or," Beryl continued, "when Delilah went to—"

"My apologies, Beryl." Delilah glared at her sister. "I don't know what I was thinking. Obviously, you can keep a secret."

Jack stifled a smile.

"I agree, Nigel." His father nodded. "Now is not the best time to make Jack's existence known. We should probably write to Cousin Wilfred first. I would hate for him to learn his son will not be the next earl from anyone other than family."

Jack glanced at his father. They had agreed it would be best not to tell the family that Jack's future as to whether he would stay in England and eventually take up the duties of the earldom was still undetermined. Regardless of his decision though, his father had explained he would be the earl one day whether he decided to fully embrace all that went with the title or ignore it.

"I would like to settle in first," Jack added. "Get my bearings, that sort of thing." He glanced from one face to the next. "I know this has come as a surprise to all of you, a shock really, and for me as well. I'm still trying to accept it myself. I always thought my father was dead."

"That does seem to run in the family," Camille said under her breath.

"Besides." Jack smiled at Camille. "This is your day and your celebration. I would hate to intrude on it. The only reason I'm here now is because my father thought it was a good idea to meet everyone at once."

Uncle Nigel nodded. "Clever of you, Basil."

"I have my moments." His father chuckled and the brothers exchanged looks of affection.

"Now then." Uncle Nigel gestured toward the door. "Let us return to the festivities before our absence is noted and remarked upon."

"We wouldn't want that," Delilah muttered.

The family filed out the door, chatting about plans and the future and any number of other things judging from the snatches of conversation Jack caught.

Elliott hung back and paused beside Jack, lowering his voice. "I've known this family for much of my life. His lordship and the colonel are good men. As for the Channing women, well, they're lovely and charming and amusing and—"

"Difficult?" Russell joined them. "Stubborn? Opinionated? Demanding?"

Gray chuckled. "On their good days."

"Do you have sisters, Mr. Channing?" Russell said.

"No and Jack will do."

"Good. I'm Sam and this is Gray." Sam nodded. "Any female relatives at all? Cousins or something?"

"No." Jack shook his head. "Just my mother."

"Then you have no real experience. And they've never had anything approaching a brother." Sam and Gray traded glances. "What do you think?"

"Oh, he'll definitely need help," Gray said.

"Help?" Jack laughed. "For what?"

"Navigating, negotiating, simple survival really. They will, each and every one, try to take you in hand," Gray said. "And you're not married?"

"No."

"Pity you let that be known. Even worse, you expressed something that could be construed as interest in Teddy." Gray shook his head. "Lady Briston might well take that as a challenge."

"A challenge?" Jack stared. "What do you mean?"

"Probably nothing." Gray shrugged. "But marrying the next earl off to a nice Englishwoman from a good family, a woman she is exceptionally fond of, would certainly take any sort of sting out of the earl's being American. In fact, now that I think about it, marrying you off to any acceptable female subject of Her Majesty's would work quite nicely. Secure Millworth's future for at least another generation and that sort of thing. With any luck, this hasn't even occurred to Lady Briston yet but from the look in her eye, I doubt it."

"She said she didn't interfere." The barest hint of unease sounded in Jack's tone. It was one thing to engage in innocent flirtation during an equally innocent dance and quite another to be led down the aisle to marry a woman he hadn't even been introduced to. And then there was Lucy to consider, even if she did seem like a minor consideration given all she had said to him. And hadn't he just escaped from a mother trying to run his life?

Sam scoffed. "I suspect your mother would say the same. I know mine would."

"I suppose," Jack said slowly. And in his mother's case, it would definitely be a lie. His mother had interfered in his life since before he was born.

"I've only recently met the lady but if she's anything like her daughters . . ." Sam shook his head. "As one American who will soon join this family to another who has already become a part of it, just know I'm willing to lend my help if you need it."

Gray nodded. "As am I."

Jack looked from one man to the next. Surely they weren't serious about any of this. "I appreciate the offer but—"

"Are you gentlemen coming?" Camille called from the doorway.

"We're right behind you," Gray said, then turned back to Jack. "Welcome to the family, Jack." He started after his wife.

"I wouldn't worry about it." Sam shrugged. "We probably shouldn't have said anything."

"I'm not worried," Jack said with a confidence he didn't quite feel. "I thought this meeting with the family went well."

"So did I," Sam said thoughtfully.

"Too well?"

Sam hesitated, then scoffed. "Of course not. There's no such thing as too well." He grinned. "Come on, we should join the others."

"Yes, of course." Jack nodded and followed his fellow American toward the door.

It really didn't matter if his aunt was already plotting a match for him. In fact, it might keep her too busy to consider other matters. He shuddered to think what any of them would say if they knew there was so much as a question about whether he'd chosen life as an earl or return to the only life he had ever known in New York. His father was obviously hoping for the former but was wise enough not to press his newfound offspring.

It was clear that his uncle Nigel saw him as not only a miracle but a savior as well. Jack had no desire to be anyone's savior but he didn't know what he did want. His entire life had been turned upside down. He had a father he had never known and a heritage he had never expected. Still, there was no need to decide anything tonight.

For now, he would follow his father's advice and take this one step at a time. Even if he had no idea where those steps would lead.

Chapter Five

Teddy closed her bedroom door behind her and started down the long corridor to the main stairway, heading toward the dining room for a leisurely late morning breakfast. She had slept later than usual this morning but then she always did sleep soundly the night after a successful event. Besides, she had no desire to be engulfed by the chaos and bustle surrounding today's departing guests.

Millworth had been filled with assorted relatives and distant friends, some of whom had arrived at the manor as early as a few weeks ago. Most of them intended to leave today and with luck Teddy had missed those departures. Camille and Grayson did not intend to take any sort of wedding trip until the spring and Teddy planned to stay a few more days to assist Camille with cataloguing those gifts that had arrived in the past few days.

Then Teddy would return to London to resume her life. No, she amended that thought. To start her new life. Already she was going over a list in her head of upcoming events and a second list of how to increase and expand business. If she was going to be an independent woman of business she was going to be a brilliantly successful one.

The ball had wound down in the wee hours of the morning

with Teddy on hand to make certain the additional staff she had hired began the task of cleaning up. She hadn't stayed long. Clement had insisted she retire for the night and assured her he would oversee the work. As the butler's nose was more than a bit out of joint that Teddy had seen fit to hire outsiders in the first place, she graciously and gratefully accepted his assistance and turned this last task over to him. She did plan to surreptitiously check on the ballroom after breakfast to make sure all was in order although she had no intention of allowing the butler to know she did so.

Hopefully she would see Dee at breakfast. She'd only spoken to her in passing last night. Her friend had said she had a great deal to tell Teddy, most of it quite astonishing, but it was best to speak in private so they wouldn't be overheard. Teddy suspected it had to do with Sam. Yesterday morning, Dee wasn't certain he would even appear at the wedding given the discord between them, although he and Grayson were good friends. Obviously, he had come around and just as obviously, given her observation of her friend dancing in the arms of the American at the ball, he and Dee had resolved their differences. Teddy wasn't sure she'd term that *astonishing*. In truth, she would have been quite shocked if they hadn't worked things out between them as Dee was so clearly in love with the man. And he was so obviously in love with her.

Teddy didn't catch sight of her mysterious American again, which was something of a pity. He had been most intriguing and there had been something . . . It scarcely mattered really. She had no wish to be distracted by a man in her life right now. Even if he was handsome and charming with an endearing smile and compelling blue eyes. It was probably for the best that she didn't know his name and would more than likely never see him again. Her heart twisted slightly at the thought. She ignored it.

Teddy reached the foot of the stairs, avoided the large

gathering of departing guests at the front entry, and headed toward the dining room.

"There you are." Dee appeared from the front parlor. "I was wondering when you were finally going to make an appearance."

Teddy nodded toward the entry. "I was trying to avoid the crush of departing guests. Have they all gone now?"

"Most of the relatives have left, I believe. Frankly, we were glad to see them go. The last thing we need at the moment is distant relatives hanging about. And I think those American friends of Grayson's that were staying here have all headed toward London. Business and that sort of thing. One or two might be lingering though."

"Is there anyone still at breakfast?"

"I don't know, I'm just headed to the dining room myself. I do know Mother is making Father help her bid good-bye to the departing guests. He wasn't especially pleased about it but she said it was the least he could do. I suspect Father understood exactly what she meant by that. Lord knows, the rest of us did. I was just about to go and find you. You never sleep this late." Dee's assessing gaze swept over her friend. "But you do look tired."

"So good to know, thank you, Dee," Teddy said wryly. "But I usually sleep a little later on the morning after a successful event." She cast her friend a satisfied smile. "And it was successful, wasn't it?"

"Oh my, yes." Dee nodded. "It was everything Camille wanted. Why, it was practically perfect." She lowered her voice in a confidential manner. "In fact, I think it was even more perfect than Camille's first wedding although I would never say that in front of Mother. Believe me, Mother certainly made that a grand affair."

"More perfect because of the festivities?" Teddy smiled. "Or because of the groom?"

"Both." Dee grinned, then drew a deep breath. "You will plan mine as well, won't you?"

Teddy widened her eyes as if she had no idea what Dee was talking about. "Your what?"

"My wedding."

"To . . ."

"To Sam, of course."

"Mr. Russell?" Teddy adopted an innocent tone. "Why, the last I heard you were sending him home to America to live his life—"

"That was the day before the wedding." Dee smiled in a slow, wicked sort of way. "The day after the wedding is another matter entirely."

Teddy arched a brow. "Then you and he . . ."

"We have a contract."

"A what?"

"A contract, you know. The sort of thing where he agrees to certain terms and I agree to various conditions." Dee thought for a moment. "One might call it, oh, a compromise I suppose."

"A compromise?" Teddy stared. "You?"

"I know." Dee sighed. "I find it hard to believe myself." She grinned. "But quite, quite wonderful." She hooked her arm through her friend's and they started for the dining room.

"It is wonderful and I'm very happy for you," Teddy said. "Although I'm not sure I would call it astonishing. Quite honestly, I would be astonished if you and Sam had not reconciled."

"As would I. Both of us can be quite stubborn and—" She pulled up short and stared at her friend. "Oh, but this isn't what is so astonishing although I suppose one could say—"

Teddy laughed. "Goodness, Dee, what are you talking about now?"

"We agreed we wouldn't mention this, at least not yet, but you are practically a member of the family."

"Now, I am curious." Teddy studied the other woman. "Well?"

"Well . . ." Dee glanced from side to side as if to assure herself they would not be overheard. She leaned close and lowered her voice. "Uncle Basil is married."

"The colonel?" Teddy gasped. "Why, he's always struck me as a confirmed bachelor as well as an outrageous flirt." Teddy shook her head in disbelief although admittedly Colonel Channing was still a fine figure of a man. He and his brother had passed their fiftieth year and yet Lord Briston looked every bit his age whereas the colonel appeared somewhat younger. Apparently, abandoning your responsibilities for a life of freedom took a greater toll on a man than choosing a life of adventure with no encumbrances. She did hope the colonel hadn't married an extremely young woman. While Dee and her sisters had married older men, and indeed, it was not at all uncommon, Teddy had always thought it vaguely unseemly and rather a shame for the young woman. Although, in the colonel's case, Teddy could well understand the attraction for a woman of any age. "When did he marry and, I suppose more to the point, whom?"

"The answer to whom is an American woman although I daresay we'll never meet her." Dee wrinkled her nose. "Nor do any of us particularly care to, I suspect."

Teddy stared in confusion. "Why on earth wouldn't you want to meet her?"

"Because there's much, much more. Although Uncle Basil didn't say it outright, it's apparent she broke his heart. As to the when . . ." Dee paused in the manner of an expert storyteller.

"Don't stop now. When did he marry?"

"Thirty years ago." A smug note sounded in Dee's voice.

"Good Lord! And he's just now getting around to mentioning it to his family?" Teddy drew her brows together. "Rather inconsiderate of him I would think."

"Not at all. You see, he didn't know. He just recently discovered this."

"How could he not know he was married? That sort of thing is usually hard to miss."

"Don't be absurd." Dee scoffed. "He knew he had been married. What he didn't know is that he was still married. His wife never told him."

Teddy shook her head. "As usual with your family, this makes no sense at all."

"Uncle Basil thought his wife, Elizabeth, I think, had returned to America to have the marriage annulled a bare week after they were wed. Her parents were completely against the marriage. But she didn't."

"Didn't return to America? Or didn't have the marriage annulled?"

"Oh she returned to America but she didn't have the marriage annulled."

Obviously, Dee was enjoying telling her story far too much to get to the point.

"Why not?"

"This is where it becomes really interesting."

"I thought it was interesting enough already although I do wish I didn't have to drag every detail out of you." Teddy huffed an impatient sigh. "Go on."

"Well, she didn't pursue an annulment because . . ." Dee paused in an overly dramatic manner. She had obviously missed her calling, the woman could have gone on the stage. Still, it was most effective. And annoying.

"Out with it, Dee."

"Because she was going to have a child," Dee said with a flourish.

It was all Teddy could do to keep her mouth from dropping open. "Colonel Channing has a child?"

"Uncle Basil has a son." Dee smirked.

"And this was thirty years ago?"

Dee nodded.

"Then the son . . ."

"The son is just turned thirty . . ." Again Dee paused for effect. "And he is my father's heir. An American is the next Earl of Briston."

Teddy stared at her friend. "You're right, this is astonishing."

"Isn't it though? No one had any idea. Uncle Basil had never mentioned his marriage to anyone, not even my father. We're all quite shocked about it." She thought for a moment. "But pleased for the most part. Father is ecstatic. A nephew is the next best thing to having a son of his own. He had no desire to have his title go to a distant relative."

"I can certainly understand that." Teddy understood better than most.

It was the nature of the world they lived in and, as such, had to be expected despite the appalling unfairness of it all. Upon the death of Teddy's father, his title and their family's ancestral estate had gone to Simon Winslow, her father's second cousin's son. Fortunately, her mother had managed to retain ownership of a house in London she had inherited from a great-aunt so Teddy and her mother were not left completely homeless. Still, it was harder than she had expected to see her heritage go to someone she barely knew even if Simon was a decent enough sort. She studied her friend closely. "And you're not bothered by all this?"

"It has never seemed fair that we had to forfeit our home because we were born female but there was nothing anyone could do about it. I long ago accepted that, because Father had no sons, Millworth would end up in the hands of Cousin Wilfred's son. It would have been quite distressing and very sad but it's a fact of life." She paused. "I will admit the idea of an American being the next earl was disconcerting at first but Sam pointed out that, as his father is English, he really would be considered more English than American. I thought that was an excellent way to look at it."

Teddy raised a brow. "Another compromise?"

"So it would appear."

"What has happened to you?"

"Apparently I have been quite thoroughly corrupted by yet another American." Dee grinned, linked her arm with Teddy's, and once again they started for the dining room. "Uncle Basil gathered us all together during the ball to announce, well, the birth of his son. But, as we were in the middle of Camille's wedding celebration, we didn't have a chance to do little more than meet the man and welcome—"

Teddy stopped short outside the door to the dining room and stared at her friend. "He's here?"

"Oh my, yes." Dee's eyes widened. "Didn't I tell you that part?"

"No, you failed to mention that rather important point."

"Well, there were so many other important points." Dee shrugged. "But yes, he was one of the Americans at the wedding and at the ball afterward. Although I don't think he returned to the ballroom after Uncle Basil's announcement. He and Uncle Basil and, oh, and they invited Sam as well, escaped to the billiards room and Father joined them after the festivities ended. Father is very eager to know his new nephew better and they stayed well into the night." She sighed. "Entirely too long."

"And Sam discussed all this with you this morning?" Teddy asked with feigned innocence.

Dee grinned. "Yes, let's say that, shall we?" Dee shook her head. "It's amazing how quickly things change. Barely a day ago I was quite miserable and now . . ."

"Now, my dear friend." Teddy took the other woman's hands. "Now you have reconciled with the man you want to spend the rest of your life with."

"I know." Wonder shone in Dee's blue eyes. "And I'm

happy, Teddy. Truly, truly happy." She grinned. "I suppose it is astonishing at that."

"Not at all," Teddy said staunchly. "It's no more than you deserve."

"You're absolutely right. I do deserve it." Dee laughed and the women stepped into the dining room.

The room was nearly empty. Colonel Channing and Sam sat at the table finishing their breakfast and engaging in quite an animated discussion about something. Probably Sam's horseless carriage—or rather *motorwagon*—as that did seem to be the one thing that created such enthusiasm with nearly every gentleman who came near it. Although admittedly it was quite remarkable. As the colonel hadn't arrived at the manor until the day before the wedding, he hadn't seen the vehicle before Sam had had it transported to London.

One of the American guests greeted them in the doorway, then continued on his way. Another man stood with his back to the door, filling his plate at the sideboard still brimming with breakfast offerings. Obviously the cook wanted to make certain the departing guests had no reason to complain as to the manor's hospitality.

"Mrs. Dooley has outdone herself yet again." Dee's gaze shifted between the sideboard and her new fiancé as if she couldn't decide which to head for first. "I must say, I'm starving," she murmured but adopted a pleasant smile and moved to greet Sam.

Dee usually was hungry when she was happy. Teddy stifled a laugh and stepped to the sideboard.

The gentleman filling his plate glanced at her and his gaze met hers.

Her breath caught. "You!"

"Good day," he said with a smile. "I was hoping to see you again."

Teddy stared and at once realized the truth. She was shocked she hadn't noticed last night but then last night she never would have suspected the truth. The man looked vaguely familiar because he looked very much like the colonel—*his father.* He had the same boyish good looks and infectious grin and his eyes were very nearly the same shade of blue as Dee's and her sisters. He'd said he had come with his father and said as well his story was a convoluted one. That was certainly an understatement. Nothing the man said had been a lie, as far as she knew, yet the most unreasonable sense of having been deceived swept through her.

"Good morning, Jack," Dee said, returning to the sideboard and perusing the offerings, much like a general planning a campaign. "Have the two of you met?"

"No," Teddy snapped.

"Yes," he said at the same time.

Dee's eyes narrowed and her gaze shifted between Teddy and the American.

"Not really." Teddy shrugged.

"In a manner of speaking," he said, again at the same time.

"I see," Dee said slowly. Teddy refused to hazard a guess as to what exactly the other woman was thinking but whatever it was, Dee was wrong. "Well then, just to make certain as neither of you seem entirely sure, Teddy, may I present my cousin, Mr. Jackson Channing. Jack, this is my dearest friend in the world, Lady Theodosia Winslow."

Without thinking Teddy held out her hand. Mr. Channing looked for a place on the sideboard to put his plate. Good Lord, what was she doing? The man had her, well, flustered. She pulled back her hand but he passed his plate to Dee, then took Teddy's hand.

"A pleasure to meet you, Lady Theodosia." He frowned. "Or is it Lady Winslow?"

"Oh, you can call her Teddy. She's practically a member of the family," Dee said absently, her gaze fixed on Mr. Channing's plate. "This looks wonderful."

"You'd best reclaim your breakfast from Dee before she claims it for herself." Teddy pulled her hand free from his.

"Don't be ridiculous. I would never . . ." Dee handed him back his plate and grinned. "But I am famished." She stepped around Mr. Channing and took a plate of her own.

Mr. Channing leaned closer and lowered his voice. "Do you mind? My calling you by your first name, that is? Is it acceptable?" Doubt shown in his blue eyes. At once she recalled his comments about being a fish out of water.

"It's quite all right." Teddy smiled up at him. It probably wasn't fair for her to feel any indignation about their conversation last night. He hadn't misled her, indeed, he hadn't really said much of significance at all. Still, the feeling lingered. "Dee and I have been close since our school days together so I've known her family for a long time. And you are a member of the family after all."

"Good." He breathed a sigh of relief. "I don't mind telling you it's going to take some time to understand the rules of your titles. When it's Lady Firstname and when it's Lady Lastname."

Teddy nodded. "I imagine it is most confusing for someone new to it all."

"Maybe . . . "A casual note sounded in his voice. "You could give me some pointers, if you're willing, that is," he added quickly.

"Oh, I'm certain anyone in the family would be happy to help you with that."

"Of course." Disappointment flashed in his eyes.

She regretted her words the moment they were out of her mouth. He was a visitor to her country, even if it was now his country as well. "But please, Mr. Channing, do feel free to ask anything that might come to mind."

"Jack," he said firmly and smiled. Admittedly, it was a most charming smile. But then, so was his father's. "And I suspect I'm going to need all the help I can get."

"Probably." She cast him a dismissive smile and took a plate of her own.

She knew he was still looking at her but she ignored him and pretended to be completely engrossed in selecting a sausage. Absurd of course, no one spent that much time choosing a sausage. After a moment he joined the other gentlemen at the table. Good, she had no desire for aimless chat with an . . . an interloper. A man who was less than forthright even if he didn't, by definition, lie. Subtle deceit was far worse than outright dishonesty. She would not be led down that road again.

Dee stepped up beside her and sliced a piece of pheasant pie. "What was that all about?"

"What was what all about?"

Dee slid the pie onto her plate. "That nonsense with you saying you hadn't met him and him saying you had."

"Simply a bit of confusion, that's all." Teddy selected a coddled egg and added it to her plate. "We shared a dance together but we were not introduced."

"I see. Still, you were a bit curt with him."

"Was I?" Teddy shrugged. "I hadn't noticed."

"I did. It's not at all like you."

"Perhaps I simply don't like being played for a fool by men who appear to be one thing when they are something else entirely."

Dee stared in confusion. "What?"

"Oh, certainly he was charming enough with his mysterious manner and his unfinished story and his shocking secrets. But does he seem the least bit out of place to you?"

"Not if he doesn't open his mouth," Dee said slowly.

"No, he certainly does not. And his *you are an adventure* nonsense. Entirely too polished and well rehearsed. It takes a great deal of practice to sound that sincere." Teddy slapped a piece of bacon onto her plate. "Lord save me from men who claim they wish to be perfectly honest."

"What are you talking about?"

"I'm talking about . . ." Teddy stared at her friend. Dear Lord, what was wrong with her? The man really hadn't done anything to earn her annoyance except not confide his identity to her. What he had or hadn't said was of no consequence really even if last night there had been something, a spark, a recognition, just for a moment . . . a moment easily explained away now by his resemblance to his father. Of course she would be attracted to the man. The first crush she'd ever had was on his father. Regardless, that was no reason—indeed—there was no reason at all why she should be so irate with him.

And yet she was.

She drew a deep breath. "Forgive me, Dee. I must be more tired than I suspected. You're absolutely right. I was a bit curt." She glanced at the table where Jack had joined his father and Sam. "I should probably apologize."

"Although I suppose it makes sense if you don't like him."

Teddy started. "I never said I didn't like him."

"It would certainly be understandable."

Teddy drew her brows together. "Why?"

"On my behalf, that is."

"Again why?"

"Well, just like your cousin Simon, Jack has swept in here, where he has never belonged, and, through nothing more than a twist of hereditary fate, will be handed Millworth Manor and all that goes with it. My home and my heritage. As much as I might say that I have accepted it, it's still difficult. Don't you agree?"

Teddy nodded.

"That's it, isn't it? Why you were so sharp with him." Dee cast her friend an innocent smile.

Teddy stared. She knew this woman as well as she knew herself. And knew from the look in her eyes, Dee didn't believe what she was saying for one moment. But her dear friend was giving her a means of escape, a rational explanation for irrational behavior even Teddy herself couldn't explain. She breathed a sigh of relief and nodded. "Yes, of course, you're right."

"I knew it." Dee smiled. "You're a very good friend, Theodosia Winslow, and I am most grateful to have you. However . . ." Dee plopped an egg onto her plate. "You shall have to put aside your dislike. The man is now a part of this family. And I must confess, the more I think about it, the more I like it. And I cannot have my dearest friend at odds with my father's heir. It would be most distressing."

"And we wouldn't want to distress you."

"No, we would not," Dee said firmly.

"Then I shall just have to carry on." It shouldn't be at all difficult to be pleasant to the man. Once Teddy left Mill-worth, it might be months before she ran into him again. Surely by then this irrational annoyance he elicited would have eased.

"As do we all." Dee glanced at the men at the table. "You do have to admit, he is rather handsome."

Teddy shrugged. "I hadn't noticed."

"He looks very much like Uncle Basil and Father do in that portrait of them in the upstairs gallery. They were handsome devils."

"Your uncle still is."

"You've always thought so."

"I know." Teddy sighed. She'd been smitten with the dashing Colonel Channing since the first time she'd met him more than a decade ago. That he never saw her as anything other than a friend of his youngest niece was a source of great dismay in her youth. Fortunately, she had grown out of both the disappointment and the infatuation.

"His son seems pleasant enough." Dee studied her cousin for a moment. "If a tiny bit lost. He strikes me as rather quiet as well."

"It's never easy to get a word in with your family," Teddy murmured.

"Of course, it must be quite a shock to discover an entirely new family you never knew you had."

"One would think so."

"We should be as nice to him as possible." Dee slanted her friend a sharp look. "All of us."

"Why?" Teddy shrugged. "He's not my cousin. I have a cousin of my own who has already laid claim to my family's heritage. You should be grateful you have your own finances and your future is not dependent upon what happens to Millworth."

"Oh I am, most grateful." Dee had very nearly lost everything she had when a false claim was made against her late husband's estate. "I thank God every day for that. Every day that I remember to do so, that is." She nodded and crossed the room to the table.

Teddy wished she had waited a bit longer to come down for breakfast but there was nothing to be done about it now. Surely she could be nice to the man for the remainder of her stay. She adopted a pleasant smile and joined the others.

The gentlemen rose to their feet at once upon the ladies' arrival.

"Teddy, my dear." The colonel took her hand and raised it to his lips, in a manner romantically old-fashioned and completely enchanting. Just as he had the first time she'd met him when she'd been barely thirteen. The first man to ever do so. "You look lovely today."

"And you, Colonel, are as charming as ever." Teddy cast him a brilliant smile. "Fatherhood obviously agrees with you."

"And no one is more surprised by that than I." He chuckled and glanced at his son. "Jack, have you met Teddy?"

"I have had that pleasure." Jack smiled.

"She is as brilliant and efficient as she is beautiful." The colonel glanced at his son. "Beauty and brains is a rare combination, my boy."

"Dare I ask what the three of you were so immersed in discussing?" Dee said and took her place at the table.

"I was just telling your uncle about my motorwagon." Sam sat down as did the other gentlemen.

"That is a surprise." Dee nodded knowingly at Teddy. "So what are your thoughts about it, Uncle Basil?"

"I think it's most intriguing." the colonel said. "Sam has been explaining this German fellow's—"

"Mr. Karl Benz," Sam said.

"Yes, yes, Benz has made some remarkable advances regarding the—"

"No, no, Uncle Basil." Dee thrust her hand out to quiet him. "I don't want to know your assessment of the inner workings of the beast. I just want to know what you think about it." She leaned forward and met her uncle's gaze. "Sam thinks it's the way of the future and I must say I agree with him."

Teddy choked back a laugh. It wasn't so long ago that Dee had called Sam's horseless carriage a waste of time, money, effort, and energy. She certainly was embracing compromise wholeheartedly. Perhaps astonishing was the best word after all.

"I would take you for a ride in it, Colonel." Sam shrugged apologetically. "But we've already moved it to London."

"A ride shall have to wait then," the older man said. "At least for a few days. I was thinking we should go to London. What do you think, Jack?"

"I've never been to London aside from our arrival," Jack said slowly. "Besides, I'd like to see this horseless carriage myself."

"Well, that's that." Lady Briston swept into the room trailed by her husband. "Everyone is finally on their way."

"At last," Lord Briston said under his breath.

"Do stay seated, gentlemen." Lady Briston waved at the men at the table. "It's only family left now. No need to stand on formalities. Teddy, my dear." She cast the younger woman a brilliant smile and took a seat at the table. "You did a superb job, simply superb. Everyone said so."

"I'm so glad you're pleased." Teddy smiled at the older woman. She wanted each and every event she planned to be as perfect as possible, of course, but this one was a little more special. Lady Briston had always made Teddy feel like one of the family.

"And I do hope you'll agree to take on another event, even if it is on short notice."

"I'd be delighted," Teddy said cautiously.

"Excellent." Lady Briston beamed. "Because I have had a brilliant idea."

Chapter Six

Even to a newcomer, the faces around the table said it all. Delilah and Teddy shared a vague but distinct look of apprehension. His father and Uncle Nigel traded glances. Apparently, this was not Aunt Bernadette's first brilliant idea.

Delilah smiled weakly. "What kind of brilliant idea?"

"Oh, don't look at me like that." Aunt Bernadette cast her daughter a chiding look. "It's not the least bit odd, simply brilliant." She glanced at the door. "I had hoped to bring this up with Camille and Beryl here but who knows when we'll see the newlyweds. Lionel returned to London this morning and Beryl has always run on her own clock."

"So tell us, what is this latest brilliant idea?" his uncle said.

"I think we should have a grand ball here at Millworth to introduce Jack to, well, to the world." Aunt Bernadette beamed. "What do you think, Teddy?"

"It certainly is brilliant," Teddy said with somewhat less enthusiasm. Although Jack might have been the only one to notice as he was probably the only one watching her.

He thought he and Teddy had gotten along quite well last night. In fact, there had been a moment . . . But of course that was absurd.

"Mother." Delilah's tone was similar to what one might use for a small child. "We just had a grand ball."

"I know that, dear." Aunt Bernadette waved off the objection. "But that was to celebrate Camille's wedding. This is a different matter entirely."

"I must say, my dear." Uncle Nigel grinned at his wife. "I quite agree. That is brilliant."

Still, Jack had thought she at least liked him. He had certainly liked her.

"Not a bad idea," his father said slowly. "But I had planned to take Jack to London in a few days, and begin introductions there."

"There's no reason why we can't do both," his aunt said firmly. "But I would like it to be as soon as possible." She turned to Teddy. "How quickly can you arrange it?"

"I don't know." Teddy shook her head. "I have a number of engagements already scheduled in London. I shall have to look at my book. And we will need to discuss exactly what you have in mind."

Today, Jack had the distinct impression she didn't like him at all.

"I'm not thinking of anything outrageous, mind you."

"Simply, oh, grand?" Teddy said weakly.

"Exactly." The older woman nodded. "Although a masked ball might be nice."

How could she not like him? Granted, he wasn't as, well, exciting as some other men might be. He was a banker after all.

"And we could play a guessing game and have guests try to pick out which among them is the new heir?" An innocent note sounded in Delilah's voice.

Sam coughed, obviously to hide a laugh.

Aunt Bernadette narrowed her eyes at her daughter. "That was not amusing, dear."

But people generally liked him. Women in particular had always liked him. He was a very likable kind of man.

"And I thought it was." Delilah smiled sweetly and sipped her tea. "Whatever you do, it will have to be soon."

"My thoughts exactly." His aunt nodded. "I would hate for word of Jack's existence to become fodder for gossip although a certain amount can't be helped I suppose, unless we hid him under a rock or something of that nature."

"I'd prefer not to hide under a rock, if it's all the same to you, Aunt Bernadette," Jack said.

Really, how could the woman know if she liked him or didn't like him?

"And I'm not going to delay introducing my son around London until you have yet another social spectacle," his father said in a firm tone.

"Nor do I expect you to, Basil." Aunt Bernadette huffed. "This is simply on the order of, oh, a coming-out party one might say."

His father had described Teddy as brilliant and efficient. It didn't seem especially *brilliant* or *efficient* to dismiss someone on the basis of one brief conversation and a single dance.

"Still . . ." His father shook his head. "I'm not sure—"

"Let me put it to you this way, Basil." Aunt Bernadette pinned his father with an unyielding look. "Word of your son is not going to be secret for long—"

"Nor do I wish it to be," Father said staunchly. "I have no desire to hide him from the world."

"And certainly not under a rock," Delilah murmured.

"And," Aunt Bernadette continued, "as the circumstances of his joining this family are unusual to say the least, gossips will have a field day. Why, they will say all sorts of things. At the very least they'll question his legitimacy."

"Can't have that," Uncle Nigel muttered.

"Don't you think it's better if we, as a family, publicly and formally embrace him?" Aunt Bernadette tapped her finger on the table to emphasize her words. "Show the world that he is not some sort of American usurper but that he is an accepted and welcome part of the family? That we aren't the least bit upset at discovering this new heir but rather thrilled and delighted?" Challenge shone in his aunt's eyes. "Well, Basil, tell me I'm wrong. Go on."

"I would love to say exactly that," his father said sharply, then sighed. "But I can't. You may be right."

"I know I'm right." Satisfaction curved his aunt's lips.

At the very least it wasn't at all fair of Teddy.

"What about you, Jack?" His uncle studied him. "Are you ready to be introduced to the world as a future Earl of Briston."

Was he going to allow her to dismiss him out of hand?

"Jack?"

"Absolutely not," Jack said without thinking, then realized his mistake. His father threw him a sharp look. "What I mean is that this has all happened so fast." Jack shook his head. "A mere two weeks ago, there were absolutely no questions in my life. My father was dead and my future was laid out for me. I was—*I am*—a vice-president of Graham, Merryweather and Lockwood Banking and Trust."

"Youngest in the history of the bank," his father said in an aside to his brother.

"I would expect nothing less," Uncle Nigel said.

"I appreciate how warmly you've welcomed me." The last thing he wanted was a grand announcement at a grand ball. "But I don't know that I'm prepared to face the world, your world, as a member of this family yet. I can barely remember your names as it is. The last thing I want is to make some sort of embarrassing mistake. I can't imagine society here is any more forgiving of that kind of thing than it is in New York. I think I'd like to feel more a member of this family before I'm presented as one. There's a lot to consider here and well . . ." He wasn't sure what else to say without coming straight out and telling them all that he didn't know that this life they were expecting him to step right into was what he wanted. "I just don't think I'm ready for that."

"Of course not, dear. Perfectly understandable." Aunt Bernadette smiled brightly. "When do you think you will be ready?"

"It will be at least a month before I manage something like this," Teddy said quickly. "Possibly six weeks and then we're perilously close to Christmas and I have several events already scheduled and—"

"Why not welcome the New Year and introduce Jack at the same time?" Delilah looked at him. "That gives you a little more than two months to accustom yourself to, well, everything."

"That's not a bad idea, dear." Aunt Bernadette thought for a moment. "But as we have discarded the suggestion of hiding him under a rock, word will trickle out. It isn't everyday a family discovers a new member, you know. There will certainly be rumor, speculation, innuendo, and more than a little gossip."

"Goodness, Mother." Beryl sauntered into the room and gestured for the men to stay seated. "I should think you would know how to handle gossip by now. Lord knows we've been the subject of enough of it. But never fear." She leaned over and plucked a piece of toast from a rack on the table. "I shall take care of that part of it."

Delilah's eyes narrowed. "How?"

"The best way to handle gossip is to control it. And the best way to control it is to start it yourself." Beryl took a bite of her toast. "I'll come up with something."

Delilah stared in horror. "What?"

"I don't know yet." Beryl took another bite of toast and chewed thoughtfully. "Perhaps something along the lines of long-lost lovers, separated by fate and distance and misunderstanding. That sort of thing." She glanced at Jack. "I don't suppose you'd be willing to let people think your mother has been in an asylum for the past thirty years?"

"Most certainly not." Jack stared at his cousin. "My mother may be many things but she's not mad."

"Are you sure?" Aunt Bernadette asked hopefully.

"Yes," Jack said firmly, although mad was one of the kinder things he had thought about his mother's actions since he had learned the truth about his father.

"I don't like that either." His father's hard gaze pinned Beryl's. "Should I hear so much as a mention of madness—"

"Goodness, Uncle Basil, it was only the first thing that came to mind." Beryl huffed. "I shall certainly think of something better. The last thing we need is anyone suspecting actual lunacy runs in the family." She thought for a moment. "Amnesia is always nice though."

Jack drew his brows together. "Amnesia?"

"There is nothing like amnesia to make even the most absurd story sound legitimate." Delilah nodded. "The best part is that when anyone questions a detail the answer is always, "Oh, but she didn't remember, you see."

Aunt Bernadette nodded in agreement. Teddy seemed to be the only one among the women who didn't appreciate the idea of amnesia. Perhaps lunacy did run in the family after all.

"I'm not sure I like the idea of people thinking my mother has had a faulty memory for thirty years." Indignation sounded in Jack's voice. "And I don't like the idea of gossip at all."

"Come now, Jack." Beryl cast him a pitying look. "Unless you're prepared to let the entire world know your mother deceived your father about your very existence, which I must say casts her in an even worse light than if she were truly mad, we do need to come up with some sort of story."

"Perhaps something closer to the truth?" his father murmured.

"I shall think of something plausible." Beryl's gaze shifted to Jack. "I know all this is awkward for you, I heard your comments from the door. But I must say I was pleased to hear you finally speak out. You scarcely said more than a few words last night. I was beginning to think, in spite of your resemblance to Uncle Basil, that you weren't related after all. No one in this family ever hesitates to speak their mind."

"It was difficult to get a word in last night," Jack said wryly. "But I will try to do better."

Beryl smiled in a thoughtful manner. "Yes, I suspect you will."

"Teddy, dear, why don't you go look in that book of yours and see if a New Year's Eve ball is a possibility," Aunt Bernadette said. "It is silly to even consider if Teddy can't manage it. Of course, we could do it without her . . ."

"I'll check on the date," Teddy said quickly and stood. "It should only take a few minutes." She turned and took her leave.

"I know we are more than capable of arranging this ourselves, Mother," Delilah said in a quiet voice. "But Teddy is my dearest friend and an event like this will only strengthen her reputation and increase demand for her and—"

"I know, dear," Aunt Bernadette met her daughter's gaze. Delilah's eyes widened. "You do?"

"I know far more than you give me credit for." Aunt Bernadette reached over and put her hand on Delilah's. "I have always thought of Teddy as another daughter and I will do all that I can, whenever I can, to assist her."

Jack had no idea what they were talking about but then his father and uncle's puzzled expressions said neither did they. It struck him that it would be quite some time before he knew the histories and backgrounds of the various players in this new world. The secrets and mysteries that were common knowledge in this family.

Still, there was one mystery he could solve right now.

"If you will excuse me," he said and got to his feet. "I'll be right back." He turned and started after Teddy.

"Where on earth is he going?" his aunt's voice trailed after him.

"I suspect, Mother, the answer to . . ."

He caught up with Teddy at the main stairway. She was already halfway up the stairs. "May I speak with you for a minute?"

Her eyes widened. "I really don't have time right now. I do need to check my schedule if your aunt's brilliant idea has any chance of coming to fruition."

"I understand that but I promise, I'll be brief."

She paused, then sighed. "Very well then." She came back down the steps to his level. "What is it?"

"Why don't you like me?" he said, then cringed to himself. He hadn't meant to sound quite so, well, pathetic.

"I don't dislike you."

"But you don't like me either."

"Nonsense." She scoffed but her objection didn't ring true. Not to him anyway and, given the uncomfortable look in her eyes, not to her either.

"Have I done something to offend you?"

"No, of course not." She waved off his question.

"If so," he continued, "it was unintentional on my part and you have my sincere apologies."

She hesitated, then sighed again. "You really have nothing to apologize for."

"If my behavior in some way—"

"Not at all. You were quite . . . charming."

"I was?" She thought he was charming? And wasn't that unexpected.

"Yes." She nodded. "If that's all—"

"It's not." He studied her closely. "I thought that last night, well . . ."

"Last night?" Her brow arched upward. "Are you referring to our *minor* adventure?"

"Well, yes, to our dance and our talk."

"One and the same, aren't they?"

"I had a very nice time with you, Teddy. In fact, it was one of the best parts of the evening for me. You and I, well, it seemed, maybe just for a moment . . . I thought . . ." He drew a deep breath. "And I thought you enjoyed it as well."

"Goodness, Jack." She shrugged. "It was only a dance. We agreed, as adventures went, it was minor. Less than minor really as I danced with several gentlemen last night." She paused. "But yes, I did enjoy it."

"And yet, in spite of that, today you act like I am the last person you want to ever see again. I want to know why."

"Very well then." Her voice sharpened. "Last night, while knowing full well my connection to this family, and while claiming to prefer honesty to dishonesty, you proceeded to mislead me."

He frowned in confusion. "How did I mislead you?"

"All that nonsense about your story being long and convoluted—"

"It is."

"And that the end has yet to be decided."

"It hasn't."

"And refusing to give me your name."

"But we agreed that made it more of an adventure." His father was right, women were incomprehensible.

"Admittedly dancing with a handsome, dashing stranger might well be considered an adventure, a *minor* adventure, but when one discovers that stranger is hiding a fact of great importance that affects the lives of my dearest friend and her family, one can't help but feel, from the moment you asked me to rescue you to the moment you vanished, you had some sort of . . . of . . . of ulterior motive."

Obviously this lovely creature was as mad as the rest of them. He shook his head in confusion. "Ulterior motive?"

"Yes!"

"And what might that be?"

"I don't know," she said in a haughty manner.

He stared at her for a long moment. He hadn't lied to her, not once. He didn't think he had misled her either, not really.

Certainly he had been vague but for her to be so irate with him made absolutely no sense. Unless . . .

He smiled slowly. "You did like me."

"Honestly, men are all the same." She rolled her gaze toward the ceiling. "And you are as arrogant as the rest of them."

"Arrogant? Me?" He widened his eyes in surprise. "I've always thought I was one of the least arrogant men I know."

"Then your circle of acquaintances must be very small."

"I don't think you liked me last night out of any sense of arrogance." He leaned closer. "I know it because I liked you, too. And today, I still like you although for whatever reason, today you don't like me."

"Don't be absurd. I said I don't dislike you."

"You also said I was handsome and dashing."

"That was no more than a simple observation," she snapped. "After all, you look very much like your father. And even at his age, the colonel is still quite attractive and perhaps the most dashing man I have ever met."

He chuckled. "But you didn't say it about my father, you said it about me."

"Very well then." She heaved a frustrated sigh. "You are handsome and dashing just like your father. And, exactly like your father, you are an outrageous flirt as well."

He stared in disbelief. He had never considered himself the least bit flirtatious. "Am I?"

"You know full well you are." She scoffed. "You *are* an adventure. My God, how long did you practice that?"

"I've never said that before in my life." Indignation rang in his voice.

"Well, it certainly sounded like you had." In spite of her words, doubt flickered in her eyes.

"And yet." His gaze locked with hers. "You seemed to have been quite flustered by it."

"Rubbish." She shrugged. "I wasn't the least bit flustered. I simply had other matters on my mind, that's all."

"One of which being that you liked me." He grinned.

"I wish you would stop saying that." Her fists clenched at her side. "Will you let the matter drop if I allow that there is the most minuscule possibility, that for the briefest of moments last night, there was perhaps a chance that I might have liked you?"

"Absolutely not." He laughed, obviously a mistake.

She glared at him, turned, and started back up the stairs.

"Admit it," he called after her. "Last night you liked me."

"I will do no such thing!"

"My God, you're stubborn."

"Thank you!"

"And one more thing."

She stopped in midstep, turned, and stared down at him. "What?"

"I liked you last night and I like you today." He shook his head. "God only knows why."

Her eyes narrowed.

"But I think it's probably because, in spite of your obvious dislike, which I am fairly sure I didn't earn, I still think . . ." He met her gaze firmly. "You, Lady Theodosia Winslow, are definitely an adventure."

She stared at him for a long silent moment. At last, a slow smile spread across her lovely face. Her green eyes flashed. "I know."

She nodded and continued up the stairs, the bustle of her dress swaying with every step.

Jack watched until she disappeared from sight. In the span of less than a day this woman had called him mysterious, secretive, intriguing, handsome, dashing, flirtatious, charming, and arrogant. As far as he could recall, and he did think he would remember that kind of thing, no woman had ever used those words about him. He was usually described as . . . nice.

Jack considered himself a rational, logical, sensible man. A man who routinely dealt with facts and figures. He sank down on the stairs and considered the matter. The facts here made no sense whatsoever.

Fact number one: for whatever reason, he wanted Teddy to like him. It made no particular sense but there it was. Facts that made no sense could be discarded for the moment.

Fact number two: while he was confident she had liked him last night, when he was a stranger, today it was obvious she did not. Therefore one might think it was the revelation of his identity that had affected her view of him. Which in itself was odd as the Channing family appeared pleased at the discovery of his existence. So that made no sense either and again could be set aside.

Fact number three: she claimed he had misled her and further charged that he had an ulterior motive, which was absurd. He'd had no intentions of misleading her. It simply hadn't seemed wise to give his name at that particular moment. Besides, he was enjoying the, well, the romance of it all he supposed. She wasn't the only one dancing with an attractive stranger.

Now that he thought about it, when he had been introduced to her, and to everyone else from the day he met his father, he had introduced himself as Jack. His father called him Jack but he hadn't introduced himself as Jack since he was eight years old and had bid farewell to childish dreams of adventure. That he did so now was interesting. Until this moment, he wasn't sure he had even realized it himself.

Was it possible that something as simple as what name he chose to be known by could change his entire life? No, of course not. The very idea was absurd. Besides, there were any number of other factors that had recently changed his entire life.

He had come to England without any particular plan in mind, which in itself was unusual for him. He'd had no idea how long he would stay. Now, of course, he would have to remain at least until his aunt's ball. To leave before then would not only be rude but would adversely affect his relationship with his new family. Besides, Teddy would be arranging the ball and they'd have to spend a certain amount of time together. He'd write to his grandfather and let him know he would be staying longer than he had expected. He ignored a twinge of guilt at not wanting to write to his mother.

Ten days ago, he was Jackson Quincy Graham Channing, great-grandson of the founder of Graham, Merryweather and Lockwood Banking and Trust. A solid, sensible man not known for impulse or reckless behavior. Now he was Jack Channing, heir to the Earl of Briston and the son of a man of travel and adventure.

Of course he was still the same man. Wasn't he? And more to the point—did he want to be?

Jackson Quincy Graham Channing would never have been called mysterious or flirtatious or intriguing. And he was certainly not a man of adventure. Banking was in his blood.

Jack Channing was another story entirely. And wasn't his father's blood flowing just as strongly in his veins as his mother's?

Perhaps he'd accept the duties of the next earl or possibly he'd eventually return to the bank. He had no idea at the moment, nor did it seem to matter. He was the son of a man of adventure and it was past time he had an adventure or two of his own.

And he knew exactly what—or rather who—his first adventure would be.

Chapter Seven

Teddy made a few final notations in the book that was as much an appendage as her arms or her legs in the course of a social event. Tonight's Explorers Club Ball was no exception.

Teddy's mother had secured the commission for the ball but, as had become her custom, had begged off actually attending, and assisting, because of a conflicting engagement. An engagement Mother said was crucial for her to attend. After all, one did need to keep up with the comings and goings of society if one was to be of assistance to those in society who might need it. Mother was a great deal like a wolf cutting an innocent lamb from the flock.

Teddy stopped a waiter headed for the ballroom and suggested he fill the glasses on his tray more than halfway. At this point in the evening, supper, accompanied by endless speeches by each and every one of the club's ruling body, had concluded and dancing had begun. The ball would continue for another few hours but, for the most part, her work was done. She could, indeed, she was *expected* to make an appearance now that would be strictly social. While ordinarily she wouldn't have thought twice about it under other circumstances, tonight was different.

He was here.

Teddy had scarcely given Jack Channing a second thought in the three weeks since she'd left Millworth Manor. Or rather she'd tried not to give him a second thought although it was extraordinarily difficult to do so. For one thing, Lady Briston had come into London four times thus far to discuss the New Year's ball. Admittedly, Teddy had used the ball as an excuse to leave Millworth earlier than she had planned, within a few hours after Lady Briston had announced her brilliant idea. Given her abrupt departure, it was understandable that the older lady would wish to talk about the ball. Although she did tend to talk as much, if not more, about her newly discovered nephew.

Did Teddy know that Jack was the youngest vice-president in the history of Someone, Whosit and Whomever Banking and Trust? Teddy had heard that, yes. And was Teddy aware that Jack had distinguished himself in his studies at some prestigious university Lady Briston couldn't for the life of her remember but was most impressive nonetheless? Why no, Teddy was not aware of that. And that he was considered financially astute, even brilliant? No, Teddy was not aware of that either. Or that while this was Jack's first trip outside of America, he was quite interested in extended travel and hadn't Teddy long expressed an interest in travel as well? And wasn't that a coincidence? Teddy had smiled weakly, agreed it was a remarkable coincidence, and firmly steered the discussion back to the guest list.

Still, it was very nearly impossible to dissuade Lady Briston from a course she was determined to follow. As subtle as the older lady thought she was, there wasn't a doubt in Teddy's mind that her closest friend's mother was determined to bring Teddy into the family.

One did wonder if her nephew was amenable to that.

Even if Lady Briston hadn't been relentless in the singing of Jack's praises, Teddy still found him lingering in the back of her head. Like an annoying melody one keeps humming even if one doesn't care for it.

Or perhaps it was guilt that kept him firmly in her mind. She hadn't been at all fair to him. In hindsight, he hadn't really misled her or at least she was fairly certain it hadn't been deliberate on his part. The man was just being prudent and she could scarcely fault him for that. It wouldn't have been at all wise to confess everything to a woman he had just met. Certainly, if he had done so she would probably now be questioning his judgment or lack of it. But then she was rather sensitive to men who misled her, deliberately or not.

Teddy fully intended to apologize to the man on their next meeting. According to his aunt, Jack and his father had been in London for over a week now and, as he was here tonight, there was no time like the present. She wasn't used to apologizing, she rarely had anything to apologize for. She was usually even-tempered and unfailingly polite. Unfortunately, Jack Channing did seem to bring out her less admirable qualities.

She tucked her book into the large bag she carried when coordinating an event and removed the smock she always wore over her gown when in a serving area or kitchen—it would not do to appear in soiled clothing and one never knew what might happen behind the scenes. She ignored the thought that her gown was a few years out of fashion but that couldn't be helped. She tucked the smock in her bag and stowed it in the corner of what had once been the plate room of the mansion that was now the home of the Explorers Club and tonight served as a station for the waiters providing guests with a never-ending offering of champagne or fruit punch. Everything was well in hand and Teddy could take her leave without undue concern. She started toward the ballroom through the maze of private corridors that wound around the building.

The Explorers Club was housed in a grand mansion in Bloomsbury near the British Museum, presented to the club by a previous benefactor some fifty or so years ago. Another later patron had donated funds for an addition to the original house that provided lecture halls and a large meeting room that also served as a ballroom when called upon to do so. According to Teddy's mother, this was the first year the club had employed an outside agency to coordinate the ball as usually this was handled by a committee of wives of club members. This year, however, those dutiful spouses had apparently rebelled in support of the effort by a small group of stalwart and very vocal ladies who were insisting club membership be opened to women. While privately, Teddy's mother thought it was disgraceful, it was to their benefit and a few appropriately placed comments was all it took to secure the event. Teddy was not merely grateful to those ladies attempting to storm the male stronghold but rather proud of them as well. It was yet one more thing she and her mother disagreed about.

As annoying as it was, it was probably for the best that her mother wasn't here tonight. Since the death of Teddy's father, her mother had carried on a concerted campaign to convince her daughter to marry the relative who had inherited her husband's title. A campaign that, for reasons known only to her mother but did seem connected to Teddy's failure to wed elsewhere coupled with the regrettable fact that she wasn't getting any younger, had escalated in recent months. Simon, Mother had argued, was a delightful man and marriage to him would return Teddy, and her mother, to their proper positions in life. Teddy had no desire to marry Simon, although he was indeed nice enough, nor did she wish to marry anyone for purposes other than affection. Love, should she happen upon it, would be ideal. But if these past four years had taught her nothing else, she had learned to be a realist. Love was as elusive as financial security. And marriage was no longer her goal.

She passed by a set of French doors leading to a private, enclosed terrace created when the addition to the building had been constructed. Complete with wrought-iron benches and planters and a small fountain that ran in the warmer months, it was exactly the sort of place to catch a breath of fresh air or have an illicit meeting or escape. A gentleman outside paced the width of the terrace, walking in and out of the pool of illumination cast by a gas lamp mounted on a post. To be expected really. As always at crowded events like this, the ballroom was probably overly warm. He turned and she caught a glimpse of his face. Perfect. This would be far easier in private.

She braced herself, pushed open the door, and stepped out into the cold night air.

"Good evening, Mr. Channing."

He started, then smiled. "Good evening, Lady Theodosia. What a delightful surprise."

She returned his smile. "Life is full of the unexpected."

"You have no idea."

She wrapped her arms around herself. "Good Lord, it's cold out here."

"It is a bit brisk but the building cuts the breeze. Here." He pulled off his coat, moved to her, and wrapped it around her shoulders. "Better?"

"Not really, but thank you." She shook her head. "Now you're going to freeze to death."

He chuckled. "I doubt that. And frankly, the cold feels good."

"What are you doing out here anyway?"

"I just needed a moment. For fresh air."

"Fresh air?"

"And to think," he admitted.

"It's entirely too cold to think," she muttered and pulled his coat tighter about her. "Might I be of some assistance?"

His brow rose. "Are you running this evening too? Do you intend to make certain every guest has a good time?"

"Not tonight." She shook her head. "This sort of event is a far different matter than a private affair. There is no hostess to be held accountable for whether or not one had an enjoyable evening. But yes, I did plan tonight's festivities."

"Another business venture?"

"Another way to fill one's idle moments," she said lightly. "Besides, as this is the Explorers Club, whose purpose is to support and encourage exploration and scientific advancement, we have cut our usual fees. Taking on tonight's gathering was as much in the realm of a favor as anything else."

"You are a supporter of the Explorers Club?"

"Not really although I have attended lectures here on occasion but tonight is a bit out of the ordinary."

"Oh?"

"The wives of the club members refused to organize this year's ball as a form of protest against the club refusing to admit female members."

"How intrepid of them." A thoughtful note sounded in his voice. "Do they want to be club members?"

"Not especially but they are supporting those women who wish to do so, most of whom are extremely accomplished and have a far greater right to be a member than many of their male counterparts." She raised her chin. "And I quite agree with them."

"Of course you do," he murmured. "So the ladies have taken inspiration from Aristophanes' *Lysistrata?*"

"It's not quite as firm a stand as that although I daresay, that would be interesting." In the Greek play, the women of Greece withheld marital relations until their husbands agreed to end the war between Athens and Sparta. Teddy had studied Aristophanes at the very progressive Miss Bicklesham's

Academy for Accomplished Young Ladies. Still, it was a fairly obscure reference. "My, you are well educated."

"You sound surprised."

"Not at all," she said quickly although she had certainly implied otherwise. "Your aunt had mentioned that you had done well in your studies and . . ."

He leaned closer and lowered his voice in a confidential manner. "We do have a few good schools, you know, even in the uncivilized colonies. When we're not fighting the natives or making our way through the wilderness, that is."

"I didn't mean . . ." She winced. "I am sorry. It's just that your aunt has been going on and on about your accomplishments and, well, no one can be quite that perfect. It's nice to know she wasn't exaggerating."

"She wasn't exaggerating about you either."

Heat flushed up her face and she was grateful he couldn't see her blush in the darkness. What was it about this man that made everything he said either annoy her or leave her speechless? "As I was saying, if indeed this was a business instead of a pastime we would not be doing well tonight at all."

"I see."

"And do you still disapprove?"

His eyes widened in surprise. "I don't disapprove."

"Really? I had the distinct impression at Camille's wedding that you strongly disapproved of a woman in business."

"You simply caught me by surprise, that's all. You must admit it is unusual."

She nodded. "I will admit that. But I believe you called taking payment for our services unseemly."

"Surely not. I never would have said such a thing." He shook his head but his eyes twinkled in the lamplight. "You must have misheard me."

"My hearing is excellent."

"Then I misspoke. And for that you have my most heartfelt apologies."

She narrowed her eyes. "Why?"

"Are you always this suspicious?"

"Yes. So again, why?"

"Because if I called your taking payment for your excellent work unseemly it was both rude and unfair. Unfortunately, I am not always as progressive as I would like. Bankers, you see, tend to be both reserved and old-fashioned." He shook his head in a mournful manner. "It's a flaw in my character I'm afraid."

"A flaw." She widened her eyes in feigned disbelief. "How very odd as Lady Briston has yet to mention your having so much as a minor flaw."

He grinned. "I have been on my best behavior."

"No doubt. But please, go on."

"I am engaged in the world of finance and, on occasion, I find myself dealing with a woman, usually a widow, who has undertaken the management of a business she has inherited from a late husband or other relative. Sometimes they have no idea what they're doing."

"This doesn't sound like a reason to apologize."

"I'm not done." He cast her a chastising frown and continued. "As I was saying, sometimes they are not up to the challenge but, in my experience, as often as not they rise to the occasion. Or . . ." He shrugged. "They are clever enough to realize the world of commerce is beyond them and sell their business, ensuring their financial security, at least for a time."

"Then why did you say it was unseemly?"

"Again . . ." He heaved an overly dramatic sigh. "I have no memory of that."

"And yet you apologized."

"Anything to make you like me again."

"It's not necessary." She drew a deep breath. "I owe you

an apology as well. I wasn't at all pleasant to you the morning after the wedding. I jumped to the wrong conclusions and responded poorly and, well, I do hope you can forgive me."

"I imagine I would forgive you anything, Lady Theodosia."

"Teddy," she said, firmly ignoring the rush of pleasure brought by his words.

"No, I don't think so." He shook his head. "If we are going to call each other by our first names, and I suspect Delilah would be more than a little annoyed if we didn't, then I much prefer Theodosia to Teddy."

"I can't imagine why. Teddy isn't at all stuffy and is a great deal of fun. Whereas Theodosia is the name for an ancient spinster, entirely too concerned with propriety, who will die alone surrounded by her needlework in a houseful of cats."

He laughed.

"Although I daresay I am fast approaching that point." She wrinkled her nose. "Fortunately, cats make me sneeze."

"It means 'gift of God,' you know. Theodosia that is."

"I did know that." She narrowed her gaze. "How did you know it?"

"You do ask a lot of questions."

"I always have. Well?"

"Millworth has a vast and impressive library." He chuckled. "You'd be amazed at the information you can find there. Besides Theodosia is a beautiful name." He paused. "It suits you."

"Because I am an adventure?" she said without thinking.

"Absolutely. And a beautiful one at that."

She stared at him curiously. "No one that I know would ever accuse me of being at a loss for words. Are you aware that you say things that quite take me aback and I don't know how to respond?"

"It's not deliberate," he said with a smile. "But yes I was aware of that. I like it."

"It must be the American in you."

"Possibly, because I do find it delightful." His gaze met hers. "Or maybe it's just the man."

Her breath caught. "You are an outrageous flirt. Exactly like your father."

He paused. "That's something at any rate." An odd note sounded in his voice. "Speaking of my father, he's probably wondering where I am."

"And I do need to make an appearance in the ballroom." She nodded toward the door.

"I should escort you in." Still he seemed hesitant to do so.

"It's not at all necessary and our returning together might cause more than a few tongues to wag."

"We wouldn't want that," he murmured but it was obvious his mind was on anything but gossip about the two of them.

"Oh dear." She considered him closely. "Is this another instance of being a fish out of water?"

He grimaced. "Is it that obvious?"

"I'm afraid so, at least at the moment."

"It's, well, it's awkward that's all." He blew a long breath and resumed pacing. "I've never in my entire life felt out of place before. A few weeks ago, there were no questions in my life. I knew who I was, what I was, and where I was headed. Now, I'm not even sure of my own name."

"Jack," she said helpfully. He stopped and stared at her. "Or do you prefer Jackson?"

"Jack," he said and continued to pace. "I've always thought of myself as Jack even if everyone else has always called me Jackson. Jackson is the name of a banker. I don't know who Jack is."

"I can see where that would be difficult."

"You don't know the half of it." He shook his head. "I'm a banker, Theodosia. For much of my life I knew I would be a banker and I've been a banker since I left school. My grandfather is a banker and my great-grandfather founded the bank. Banking defines my family."

"Your *mother's* family."

"Exactly. Now I find myself with a father who is bigger than life. Who has been places I have only dreamed of seeing and done things I have never imagined doing. At least not since childhood. My father is the stuff legends and heroes are made out of. And I'm . . ."

"A stodgy, straitlaced banker." She nodded sympathetically.

He stopped in midstep. "I never said stodgy or straitlaced. I believe I said reserved and old-fashioned."

She waved off his objection. "One in the same really."

"Not . . . yes, I suppose you're right." He returned to pacing. "And tonight, well, ever since we arrived in London, he has been introducing me as his son to these friends and acquaintances of his, all of whom are as adventurous as he and—"

"Don't be absurd, Jack." She scoffed. "Why, I would wager a great deal of money that no more than a handful of those men in that ballroom right now have ever ventured anywhere close to the wilds of Africa or jungles of the Amazon."

"Regardless, they obviously have adventurous spirits or they wouldn't be here in the first place. I don't fit in and worse I don't know how to fit in."

"Come now. I'm sure they're all quite fond of fish. Why, they simply devoured the salmon en croute served tonight."

He ignored her attempt to lighten his mood.

"And as much as you might think we all speak the same language, we don't." He ran his hand through his hair. "Good God, Theodosia, I don't even understand their jokes."

She clapped her hands to her cheeks in horror. "Oh no, not that!"

He stared at her for a long moment. Finally the corners of his lips curved upward slightly. "This is not amusing."

"Of course it is. It's most amusing. You'd see that if you weren't the fish." She shook her head. "Fish have a terrible lack of confidence."

"Do they?"

"Oh my, yes."

"Am I being absurd?"

"Absolutely."

"It's not very heroic, is it?" he said wryly. "Not up to my father's standards."

"Jackson Channing," she said sharply. "I daresay your father has no expectations when it comes to you."

"Oh, that's good to know."

"Now is not the time for sarcasm." She sniffed and continued. "Why, you've barely met after all. Besides, I have known Colonel Channing for nearly a dozen years and yes, he is known for his adventures and certainly he has done any number of things other men have only dreamed of doing but I have never seen him as proud and happy as he is when he looks at you."

"Still, I'm certain he never expected his son to be a stodgy, straitlaced banker."

"A reserved, old-fashioned banker if you please," she said firmly. "In point of fact, he never expected to have a son at all so as far as your not being what he wanted why that's just so much nonsense, rubbish, poppycock."

He raised a brow. "Poppycock?"

"Complete and utter poppycock." She nodded and stepped closer. "Furthermore, it seems to me you have been given an opportunity few other men have."

"And what might that be?"

"Why you can now be whomever or whatever you choose. Although who you are, the man you are, I mean, hasn't changed, not really. But the entire world is open to you. You can follow your heart as it were." She stared up at him. "You can continue to follow in your grandfather's footsteps if that's what you truly want. Or you can choose instead your father's path in life. And eventually of course, you can step into your uncle's shoes. You . . ." She emphasized her words with a poke of her finger. "Can be anything you want. An adventurer. A hero. A banker. An earl. Anything."

"Theodosia—"

"Most people would sell their souls for the opportunity presented to you now. It's a grand adventure you're embarked upon now, Jack."

"I realize—"

"Furthermore, in case you have forgotten, we have already established that I thought you quite dashing and intriguing and mysterious when we first met. All qualities any man of adventure, any true hero would certainly display."

He stared down at her. "Are you finished?"

"No," she said sharply. "Perhaps." She paused. "Yes, I believe I am."

"You're very good at this."

"I know." She cast him a smug smile. "Brides and hostesses are remarkably difficult to manage. I usually tell them to breathe deeply and slowly."

"Does it work?"

"On occasion." Although the effects were usually short-lived. "Let me ask you a question."

He nodded. "Go on."

"If you were in New York, at a gathering of men like the colonel, would you feel ill at ease?"

"Oh, but I would never go to . . ." He paused. "But I would like to. And why shouldn't I?"

"Why indeed?"

He stared at her and she had the distinct sense he wasn't looking at her at all. Even in the faint light she noted a change in his eyes. A realization perhaps or acknowledgement or resolve. "No," he said slowly, "I wouldn't feel the least bit self-conscious. Of course, that's my native environment if you will, and this is completely different."

"Is it?" She studied him closely. "Couldn't one say, as you

are just as English by blood as you are American, you belong in this world every bit as much as you do the other? You simply have to get used to it, that's all. You said it yourself. One step at a time."

"You make it sound simple." A thoughtful note sounded in his voice.

"It is or at least it will be," she said staunchly.

"You barely know me." His gaze searched hers. "How can you be so certain?"

"Probably for the same reason you confided in me, I imagine." Because for one moment at Camille's wedding ball there was something . . . something special that passed between them. Not that it really mattered even if it was nearly impossible to forget.

"Kindred spirits?"

"I suppose that's possible but it's more likely that I was very nearly the first person you met here."

"Yes, I'm sure that's it," he said under his breath and it struck her that he didn't believe that any more than she did.

"I have a feeling about you, Jackson Channing," she said in as lighthearted a manner as she could muster. "Besides, I suspect there's far more of your father in you than merely appearance." She hesitated. "You asked for my help at Millworth and I was not especially gracious about it. But I am now offering you any assistance you might need. With names or titles or the nuances of society here. Do feel free to call on me if you need my help."

"You're being very nice."

"Oh, I am usually nice. Not to you, of course . . ."

"I do appreciate it. You're right, you know." He thought for a moment. "I should have seen it myself. I was comfortable in the life I was leading. I was rarely in a situation new to me. Now, everything is new but while my circumstances have changed, I haven't. Not really."

"Perhaps you should think of it all as a challenge. And

don't the best adventures always include a challenge of some sort?"

"It is a challenge." He nodded. "I've never backed down from a challenge before but then I can't recall ever being faced with one as all-encompassing as this."

"Nonetheless, I daresay, this is one you are more than equal to."

"Am I?" He smiled down at her.

"Well, you are your father's son." She shook her head. "You shouldn't forget that."

"I won't." He paused. "You know I like them. These friends of my father's. They may well be the most interesting people I have ever met."

"Surely not more interesting than bankers?"

"God forbid!" He grinned, then sobered. "Thank you, Theodosia."

"For bringing you to your senses?" She shrugged. "You would have arrived there on your own eventually."

"Probably." He stared down into her eyes for a long moment and she wondered if he were truly seeing into her soul or if it only felt that way.

She swallowed hard. "Well, you should . . ."

"Yes, I should."

She took off his coat and handed it to him. "Thank you, for the coat that is. I'll follow in a moment."

"Very well." He pulled on his coat, stepped to the doors, and opened one. "I will call on you, you know."

"I expect you to." She smiled. "I look forward to giving you any assistance I can."

"After all." He grinned. "I do need all the help I can get."

"I won't help you at all if you throw my words back in my face."

He laughed, stepped into the corridor, and let the door close behind him.

It took her a moment to realize she was still smiling like some sort of madwoman. That had gone well. Better than well, really. They were becoming . . . *friends* was probably the only word for it. She stepped toward the doors.

Abruptly the doors opened and Jack stepped back onto the terrace. "I forgot something."

Without warning he swept her into his arms and kissed her long and hard. Then released her so quickly she had no time to protest. Not that she was able to do so.

Not that she wanted to.

"Now, that was very helpful." He grinned that infectious irresistible smile that had haunted her since their first meeting, turned, and once again disappeared into the building.

She stared after him, the cold completely forgotten.

And wasn't that unexpected? She sank down onto a wrought-iron bench. Although maybe it wasn't. Maybe they had been headed straight toward one another from the moment she had turned around at the wedding ball and looked into his blue eyes. Hadn't her traitorous heart skipped a beat?

This man was everything she'd ever thought she wanted. Everything she'd ever expected to have.

And wasn't that bloody well inconvenient?

Chapter Eight

One week later,
Channing House,
London . . .

". . . and then, of course, the beast, realizing the futility . . ."

Jack smiled and nodded in the appropriate places but his mind wandered from yet another story of adventure from the dozen or so gentlemen his father had gathered for a dinner party at Channing House in London. Most of the men here were longtime friends of his father's, shared common interests, and were his contemporaries in age or older. Thankfully, Gray and Sam were in attendance as well. Jack had become better acquainted with both gentlemen since the wedding. They frequently came into London and Jack had had the opportunity to see their motorwagon for himself. It was indeed remarkable.

". . . nor that my skill has lessened in any way, although I will admit . . ."

Not that each and every story wasn't fascinating. They were the stuff his head had been filled with as a boy. But after hearing several tonight alone about the follies of being inadequately supplied on an African safari or the deadly encounters with predators in the wilds of some jungle or other, or the latest news on who was organizing an expedition to where, even Jack's mind was prone to wander.

And there was only one place it wandered to. Or rather one person.

Try as he might, he hadn't managed to see Theodosia again after their encounter on the terrace at the Explorers Club. And that had been a full week ago. Although he had certainly made an effort.

". . . and, naturally, the gun bearer took it upon himself . . ."

He had planned to dance with her again at the Explorers Club and while he had noted her arrival in the ballroom shortly after his return, the next time he looked for her, the woman had vanished. Deliberately, no doubt. He probably shouldn't have kissed her. It was an irresistible impulse, in and of itself unusual for him, and had surprised him as much as it did her. But he would do it again under the same circumstances. In fact, he fully intended to do it again under any circumstances. There was something between them, he couldn't quite put his finger on exactly what, but something. Something worth pursuing. He certainly liked her; whether there was more than that remained to be seen. But he intended to find out. She was, after all, his first real adventure.

". . . so it did seem to me at the time, although in hindsight . . ."

Jack had managed to call on her twice in the past week but she wasn't home on either occasion. He had left his card the first time and his card with a brief note written on the back the second. But, as he hadn't arranged to meet her, he couldn't complain that he hadn't heard from her although it was annoying. He did hope he hadn't offended her or worse scared her but he wouldn't apologize for kissing her. He wasn't the least bit sorry. And while the kiss had been entirely too short to be certain of her reactions, she hadn't seemed indignant afterward. Of course, he'd given her no opportunity to be. But damn it all, he did want to see her again. The only question was when.

Even finding the time to call on her hadn't been easy; his father had kept him busier than he had ever imagined. The colonel belonged to an endless number of gentlemen's clubs and diverse organizations. Colonel Basil Channing was a man of many and varied interests and was determined to acquaint his son with what seemed like each and every member of each and every organization. That, coupled with showing Jack everything there was to see in London from St. Paul's to Westminster, and Jack had hardly had a moment to himself.

The shuffling of chairs snapped his attention back to the table. He rose to his feet and regretted his lack of attention. The other gentlemen headed toward the door.

His father turned to him. "Jack, are you going to join us in the billiards room?"

"There's nothing like billiards and port after a good dinner," Sir Hugo Tolliver said. He was the director of the Explorers Club and Jack had met him often enough during these last weeks in London to remember the man's name. "I assume there will be cigars as well."

His father scoffed. "Good God, Tolliver, when hasn't there been?"

"I just wanted to make certain," Sir Hugo muttered, and made his way out the door. "I'll need a good cigar if we're going to further discuss the blasted women's issue. Fairer sex my . . ."

Most of his father's friends were already out of the room and a chorus of groans echoed from the hall.

His father chuckled. "Sir Hugo is not what one would call progressive."

"And do you think membership should be given to women?" Jack asked.

"I haven't decided yet. I know any number of women who deserve membership but there's a lot to consider." He thought for a moment. "The world is changing, Jack. More so than ever before, I think. We would be fools to dig our heels in and not change with it. However, there is much to be said for not abandoning long-held tradition."

"Excellent answer, Colonel." Gray joined them, Sam a step behind him. "Are you sure Lionel is the politician in the family?"

"I'd rather face a herd of charging elephants than any single member of Parliament." Father shuddered. "Well, gentlemen, shall we join the others?"

"If you don't mind, Colonel, Gray and I would like to have a few words with Jack," Sam said with a smile. "We have a couple of questions, financial questions, that have come up regarding the, oh, financing of the company we're creating to produce the motorwagon."

Jack narrowed his gaze. Sam and Gray were both successful and accomplished in business and finance. They were far more experienced in matters of an entrepreneurial nature than he was. "I don't think—"

"And who better than a banker to advise us," Gray added quickly.

"Who better indeed." His father nodded. "I assume you'll be chatting in the conservatory then?"

"That was the idea, sir." Gray smiled weakly.

"Grayson, you know where the cigars are?"

Gray nodded. "Yes, sir."

"Don't set the place on fire."

Gray grinned. "I believe you told me the same thing when I was seventeen."

"And?"

"It wasn't me." Gray shook his head.

"Hmph." Father cast Gray a skeptical look and started after his friends, pausing at the doorway. "Tell me one thing, gentlemen. Is it the age of the rest of us, the generation difference and all that, or have you just tired of the stories?"

"Oh, we would never tire of the stories, Colonel," Gray said quickly.

"And this is the first time I've heard them," Sam added.

He looked at his son. "Jack?"

"They are excellent stories, sir." He chose his words with care. "Filled with adventures generally of a perilous nature. They're not the kind of stories you tire of hearing."

"Even if you've heard several of them more than once since you've been in London?"

"Knowing the end just makes them more enjoyable," Jack said staunchly. He would never want to insult his father's friends but if he heard one more story involving a tiger, a head hunter, or even a runaway Indian princess— although he was curious as to why there were so many runaway Indian princesses—he would run screaming through the streets of London himself. Even if that would just provide the older gentlemen one more story to tell.

"That's what I thought. There's a bit of the politician in you as well." Father chuckled. "Don't forget the brandy." He nodded at a decanter on the sideboard.

"We would never forget the brandy," Sam murmured, handing three glasses to Jack and grabbing the decanter.

"Enjoy yourselves, gentlemen," the colonel said and took his leave.

"Come on then, men." Gray led the way toward the conservatory through the maze of the mansion's rooms, one leading directly into the next. An arrangement Jack found extremely confusing. He still didn't have his bearings in the grand London house his family had owned for generations. Fortunately, Gray knew the house fairly well. Jack and Sam trailed behind him.

"Why the conservatory?" Jack asked.

"Cigars are only allowed in the billiards room and your father and his friends are going to be there," Gray said over his shoulder.

"And we thought you could use a break," Sam added

under his breath. "It must be exhausting to be the colonel's son."

"Exhausting is putting it mildly. Not that it hasn't been enjoyable," Jack added quickly. "And it's a new experience, for both of us, this father-son business. We're learning as we go along."

"From what we've heard the colonel is keeping you busy."

Jack snorted. "Between seeing every sight in London and meeting everyone who has ever crossed his path, frantic is a better term for it than merely busy."

Gray pushed open the door to the conservatory. The room was nearly two stories, the outside walls almost entirely glass. The space was filled with an impressive variety of tropical plants, ferns, and any number of foliage Jack couldn't identify. A large palm grew from a huge planter in the center of it all, soaring nearly to the glass ceiling. Jack had been in the conservatory once before to see the rare orchids his father had collected on a trip to South America. Gray circled the palm to a seating area on the far side of the room furnished with cushioned wicker chairs and tables. It was a perfect spot to read a book or contemplate the twists and turns of life, especially if one wanted privacy and didn't want to be seen from the door. A perfect place to escape. Jack made a mental note of that for future reference.

Gray waved for the others to take a seat, then moved to a small decorative chest nearly hidden by a banana plant. A humidor if Jack's suspicions were correct. Gray flipped open the lid, then chuckled. "I must say, I appreciate it when things are exactly where they're supposed to be."

He selected three cigars, a silver cigar cutter, and matches. A few minutes later all three men had a brandy in one hand, a cigar in the other, and were savoring the enjoyment of good cigars, fine brandy, and excellent companionship.

Jack blew a stream of smoke into the air. "I thought you said cigars were only allowed in the billiards room?"

"They are." Gray puffed on his cigar. "This is the colonel's secret supply. You might not have noticed but no one walking by the conservatory can see this spot. And the plants seem to either absorb or dissipate the smoke. Or perhaps they just hide it. I have no idea really. My cousin and I discovered this on a visit here when we were boys." He paused. "It's a good place to escape if one needs to."

Jack smiled wryly. "I'll keep that in mind."

"So what are you thinking, Jack?" Gray asked in an overly casual manner.

"At the moment or overall?"

Gray shrugged. "Whatever you wish."

"Well, at the moment, I'm thinking that Camille and or Delilah with urging from their mother or their father or both sent you here to ask that very question."

Sam laughed. "He's got you there."

"You needn't sound so smug." Gray's eyes narrowed at his friend. "They included you in this. One American to another was how they phrased it, if I recall."

"And didn't I say I had no intentions of spying on anyone?"

"We're not spying." Gray scoffed. "We're coming straight out and asking him what his thoughts are on this new life he's been thrust into."

"Better us than anyone else." Sam turned to Jack and met his gaze directly. "Gray and I have been friends for years. Now we find ourselves in a, I don't know, a brotherhood of sorts or an exclusive club. Membership is limited to Gray and Lionel, who have married into this family, and now to me since I'm about to marry into it."

"I suspected as much," Jack said with a smile. "Congratulations."

"He's given her the most ostentatious sapphire ring." Gray shook his head in a mournful manner. "So American of him."

Jack laughed. "And damned proud of it."

Gray sighed. "He makes the rest of us look bad."

"That was the intention besides . . ." Sam puffed his cigar and blew a smoke ring toward the palm. "It matches her eyes."

"The point is, even though you didn't marry into the family, you have certainly joined it." Gray settled back in his chair. "We know how difficult it is to be the newest member and we're offering our support."

Sam nodded. "And our friendship as well."

"I'd like that." It was only since Jack had left New York that it had dawned on him that, while he had any number of acquaintances, he couldn't name a single friend or confidant. Aside from Lucy, that is. "But I thought your assignment was to ferret out information."

"We can do both," Gray said firmly. "Sam and I have already agreed to this. We won't tell them anything you ask us to keep confidential."

Jack's gaze slid from one man to the next. He knew both men's business reputations and, as far as he could recall, their honor and honesty had never been questioned. He could certainly use a few friends here. Especially men he could trust.

"Agreed then." Jack raised his glass. "Friends it is."

The other men returned his toast and fell into a companionable silence. But only for a moment.

"Now that we are friends," Gray began, "as a friend, we would be appreciative—"

"Most appreciative," Sam added.

"If you could give us something—"

"Anything. Anything at all." Sam gestured with his cigar. "No matter how insignificant."

"As much as I'd like to help you both out I'm not sure what I can tell you." Jack thought for a moment. "It was all somewhat overwhelming when I first arrived and was greeted as, I don't know, a prodigal son or a savior or something of that nature."

"Understandable." Sam nodded.

"I'm not used to feeling out of place."

"Of course not," Gray said.

"But . . ." Jack chose his words carefully. "I am starting to feel, not exactly at home, but more . . . relaxed, I would say." Thanks in part to a spirited talking-to by Theodosia.

"Well, that's something." Gray sipped his brandy.

"So you can tell them that if you wish. And you can tell them my father and I are getting along quite well."

Sam and Gray traded satisfied nods.

"That's that then." Sam reached for the decanter and topped off all three glasses.

"We have what we need." Gray drew on his cigar. "Our work here is done."

"I think he's grooming me," Jack said. "My father that is. As well as trying to give me a basic education in history, art, architecture, and all things British."

"Not surprising." Sam nodded. "Lady Briston mentioned the colonel was showing you around London and introducing you to his friends. She's not overly pleased by it."

Gray chuckled. "She'd be happier if you could stay hidden until the ball. But even she realizes the impossibility of that given your father's excitement."

"I don't want to sound ungrateful, and I'm not." Jack puffed on his cigar, then blew a long stream of smoke. "I want to get to know him as much as he wants to know me. But it would be much easier if we did it, I don't know, one step at a time maybe rather than all at once."

"He's trying to make up for lost years," Sam said mildly.

"I know and I appreciate that."

"Still . . ." Gray tapped his ashes into a nearby pot. "I can see where it might be overwhelming."

Jack nodded. "I've always been a solitary kind of man and I was raised with certain expectations of, oh, independence I suppose. I feel like an ass for saying this but as much as I want to be with my father, I need a little bit of . . .

distance. Don't get me wrong," he added. "As I said, we're getting along together quite well. He's a fascinating man."

"I always thought so," Gray said.

Jack chose his words with care. "But there's such a thing as spending too much time together. From the moment we boarded the ship to New York, we have barely been out of each other's sight. You'd think in a house this size that wouldn't be a problem but it is. We see each other at breakfast and dinner and all the hours in between. We're either going somewhere or meeting someone or seeing some sight." He paused. "Actually, I was seriously thinking about moving to a hotel. For a while anyway. Given this ball Aunt Bernadette is planning, I'll remain in England at least until the New Year."

"You don't plan on staying beyond that?" Gray said slowly.

"I really have no specific plans yet." Jack shrugged.

"You do realize they all expect you to stay?" Sam said.

"I know. And this is something I do wish to keep confidential although my father is aware of it."

The other men nodded.

Jack shook his head. "I don't know what I'm going to do yet. I don't know that I want to go back to New York although I do have certain responsibilities . . ."

"But you now have responsibilities here as well."

"I know." Jack nodded. "Responsibilities to a family I didn't know I had and to a future I never expected or, for that matter, imagined."

Sam studied him curiously. "Sort of like waking up and finding yourself in a whole new world."

Jack grimaced. "Something like that."

"We envy you, you know," Sam said abruptly.

Jack raised a brow. "Because I'm in line to be the next earl?"

"No," Gray said quietly. "Because, against all odds you have found a father you didn't know you had. I lost my father when I was very young and I scarcely remember him at all."

"And mine died thirteen years ago." Sam shrugged. "But at least I knew him."

"I am sorry, for both of you." Jack considered the other men. "All my life I was under the impression that my father was dead, through no fault of his, I might add. Now, to find he's not merely alive but he is this remarkable man. The kind of man you read about in dime novels or stories of adventure . . ."

For a long moment all three men were silent, each caught up in their own thoughts and memories, about fathers lost and found.

"So," Gray said at last. "The idea of being an earl isn't an irresistible temptation?"

"It's hard to be tempted by something that's never so much as crossed your mind. Apparently, I have no choice in the matter. I will inherit the title whether I want to or not."

"The question is whether or not you wish to pick up the reins of the position, as it were. Reside in England, here and at Millworth, accept the traditional seat in Parliament, that sort of thing." Gray studied him thoughtfully. "I imagine it's a difficult decision."

"Maybe it wouldn't be if I'd been dissatisfied with my life. I wasn't. I was content. Now, everything is different. And you're right." Jack nodded at Gray. "There are new responsibilities and concerns. The idea of disappointing my uncle and the rest of this new family of mine and especially my father . . ." Jack blew a long breath. "I'm not an adventurer or explorer or the kind of man books are written about. I'm a banker. The last thing I want is for his newfound son to be a disappointment to him."

Without warning the thought popped into his head: Would he be a disappointment to Theodosia as well? If he decided his life, his future, was in New York? If he turned his back on the title and the family that went with it? Would she care if her minor adventure turned out to be nothing more than a mere dance, a few brief conversations, and a single kiss?

"It's amazing how quickly affection can grow between two people who didn't even know the other existed a short time ago," Sam murmured.

"I know." Jack shook his head. "A few weeks ago, I was practically engaged to a woman I'd known most of my life and now my every waking thought seems to be . . ."

Sam and Gray stared at him.

Jack winced. "And you were talking about my father, weren't you?"

"We were." Sam studied him curiously. "Who were you talking about?"

"It's not important."

"But interesting." Gray blew a perfect smoke ring. "Very interesting."

"A more pressing question is what do I do about my father?" Jack said. "I don't want to offend him. And I'm afraid he might be if I suggest moving out of this house—"

"That will someday be yours," Sam said.

"That he might take your actions as something of a rejection?" Gray nodded. "Of him as well as your heritage?"

"Exactly." Jack shook his head. "Even though this relationship we're forging is going well, it's still tenuous. We're still treading cautiously with each other. I don't want him to think I'm not interested in his life, in his world. I'm afraid if I suggest moving to a hotel he would take it badly."

"Possibly." Gray puffed thoughtfully. "But the colonel is a reasonable man. If you explain to him—"

Jack shook his head. "Nonetheless . . ."

"I have an idea. Why don't you stay at Delilah's house?" Sam said. "She intends to stay at Millworth until after the New Year. Gray and I and Camille, of course, are leaving for New York later this week. I have business to attend to and I'd like to tell my family that I'm getting married before it's an accomplished fact. It doesn't seem the kind of thing you should do in a letter. We'll be back before Christmas."

"We don't want to miss Christmas at Millworth Manor." Gray chuckled. "One never knows what might happen."

"You'd really be doing her a favor." Sam leaned forward. "She was just saying the other day that she hated her house being empty for too long."

"And," Gray continued, "as it is the house of a family member it's not as if you're turning your back on them."

"Still, I don't know—"

"I won't see Delilah until we meet her late tomorrow afternoon to return to Millworth for a few days before we leave for New York," Sam said. "But I can send word to her new butler, a Mr. Beckley I think, something like that, to expect you before we go."

"I'm not certain—"

"Come now, Jack." Gray gestured with his cigar. "Your father is one of the most independent people I have ever met. Which means your desire for a little time for yourself is something you have in common. If anyone would understand how you feel, he would."

"You could move in tomorrow." A tempting note sounded in Sam's voice.

Jack's gaze shifted from one of his new friends to the other. And didn't Gray probably know his father better than he did? Or at least longer.

"Very well then. You've convinced me." He settled back in his chair and puffed his cigar. He'd tell his father later tonight. It was for the best for both of them really. "Because as much as I have grown to care for him . . ." Jack blew a smoke ring into the air. "My father is driving me mad."

Chapter Nine

*The following day,
the Ladies Tearoom at Fenwick and Sons,
Booksellers . . .*

". . . and my mother is driving me quite insane. Look." Teddy held out her hands. "Why, I'm positively trembling."

"Your hands are as steady as a rock," Dee said mildly.

"I hide it well. But inside . . ." Teddy clasped her hands to her heart in an overly dramatic manner. "Inside I am quivering with indignation and fury and resentment." She grabbed a biscuit from the plate on the table and took a vicious bite.

Teddy and Dee sat at a table near the back wall of the Ladies Tearoom at Fenwick and Sons, Booksellers. It was the sort of place one came to see and be seen. The tearoom had become quite popular with ladies of society in recent years. Indeed, gossip had it that a silent partner in the tearoom was a lady of society. Teddy did hope so. It was comforting to think there was another woman in London engaged in business, whether she was doing so of necessity or not.

Teddy drummed her fingers on the table. "I love my

mother, I truly do but she absolutely refuses to accept the fact that I have no intentions of marrying Cousin Simon."

Dee's brow rose. "Is she still going on about that?"

"And she's gotten worse." Teddy heaved a frustrated sigh. "When I'm with her for more than five minutes she brings the matter up. She keeps talking about inviting him for a visit. The only saving grace in all of this is that I'm not sure Simon wishes to marry me although the last time I saw him, the week Father died, he did look at me like a puppy longing for a bone." She shuddered. "I have no wish to be a bone, thank you very much."

Dee choked back a laugh.

"It's not funny. He's really a very nice man. Fortunately, he has not managed to propose but I fear Mother's encouraging him to come to London is to get him to do exactly that. I would hate to hurt his feelings but I have no intention of accepting such a proposal." She shook her head. "Mother refuses to listen to me. It's as if she can't help herself. She has this one thing on her mind." She paused. "No, two things on her mind. One is my marrying someone appropriate—"

"A man with a respected title, or at least good family connections, and a significant fortune."

"Exactly. But as no one fitting that description has stepped forward—"

"Forgive me for bringing it up but you have had no fewer than two proposals since your ill-fated engagement."

"You know as well as I, neither of those were the least bit appealing although admittedly my mother has never understood that." Teddy waved off the comment. "Now, she is concentrating all her considerable energy toward the second thing on her mind."

Dee nodded in sympathy. "Convincing you to wed Simon."

"I can't stand another minute of it, Dee." She refilled her teacup. "Our house is entirely too small to avoid her for any length of time. I find myself doing everything I can to keep from being there at all."

Fortunately, between the events she was planning and those social functions she was obligated to attend, that wasn't at all difficult. Unfortunately, it also meant she was absent on both occasions when Jack had called on her, which was at once annoying and something of a relief. She had no idea what she would say to the man when she next saw him. He had kissed her after all, in a most thorough manner. She still wasn't sure how she felt about that kiss although admittedly, it was quite . . . wonderful. And even though Jack Channing played no role in the new course she had set for her life she couldn't stop thinking about him. It was curiosity, of course. Nothing more significant than that and as such it was most annoying. There was no time in her life at the moment for a man, any man. Still, there was an odd sort of longing when he came to mind . . .

"Why are you smiling?"

"Oh." Teddy stared at her friend. "Was I?"

"Yes, you were."

"It's nothing, really." She waved off the charge. "Just a chance thought . . ."

"You don't have chance thoughts."

She scoffed. "Of course I do. Everyone does. And one certainly can't help it if something springs to mind of its own accord. Without any intention at all on one's part to think about whatever it is that has settled in the back of your thoughts and absolutely refuses to take its leave."

Dee's brow furrowed in confusion. "What are you talking about?"

"Nothing." Teddy adopted an innocent tone. "Not a thing, really."

"I don't believe you." Dee's eyes narrowed. "Out with it, Teddy. What is filling that head of yours?"

"All sorts of things. My mind is a very busy place." She ticked the points off on her fingers. "Why there's Lady Wellby's upcoming soiree. I do so love it when something that was to be a small, intimate gathering grows out of control thus necessitating the need for assistance."

"For you, you mean."

"Exactly." Teddy smirked and continued. "And then there's the New Year's Eve ball at Millworth. Your mother has come to London to discuss the plans with me five times now. Five!"

"My mother can be very nearly as persistent as yours."

"Apparently. And then of course there's my mother and we've already discussed that."

"Indeed we have. However . . ." Dee's eyes narrowed in suspicion. "That smile had nothing to do with your mother."

Teddy considered her friend thoughtfully. It wouldn't hurt to talk to someone about this. Not that it was particularly important. It was of no more than minimal interest really. Why it stayed in her head at all made no sense. "Do I have your absolute promise that you will keep whatever I say confidential?"

"Haven't I always kept your secrets?" Indignation sounded in Dee's voice. "I haven't told a single soul the truth about your finances." She grimaced. "Although I'm fairly certain Mother knows."

Teddy sighed. "Frankly, I'd be surprised if your mother didn't. She has always seemed to know everything."

"She's quite remarkable that way although it can be most annoying." Dee met her friend's gaze. "I don't think even Mother suspects your other secret."

"You mean my having, well, fallen, for lack of a better term?"

"Unless you have another significant secret I don't know about." Dee studied her carefully. "Do you?"

"Certainly not of that nature." She shrugged. "All things considered, this is really quite minor."

"Then tell me."

Teddy pinned the other woman's gaze firmly. "Do I have your promise?"

Dee nodded. "Of course you do."

"Your absolute word of honor?"

"I said so, didn't I?" Dee frowned in annoyance. "This had better be worth the trouble."

"I assure you, it's not."

"Tell me!"

"Very well then." Teddy drew a deep breath. "I saw your cousin."

"Jack?"

"Do you have another cousin?"

"Not that I know of but I didn't know about this one until recently."

Teddy nodded. "It was a week ago. At the Explorers Club ball. He was with your uncle."

"I can't say I'm surprised. Uncle Basil has always been a staunch supporter of the Explorers Club."

"We had a pleasant chat." Teddy said. "I apologized for my rude behavior the day after the wedding."

"That's most appreciated. Thank you."

"He accepted my apology."

"Did he?" Dee slathered clotted cream on a scone.

"Of course." She sniffed. "I was most sincere."

"No doubt." Dee took a bite of her scone. "But there's more, isn't there?"

"I offered him my assistance should he need it. Navigating the treacherous waters of society can be difficult, you know, especially for a newcomer."

"That was quite kind of you. Again, you have my thanks."

"And he kissed me," Teddy blurted and held her breath.

Dee choked and took a quick sip of tea. Her eyes widened, whether from lack of air or surprise, Teddy couldn't be sure, then set down her scone, evidence of just how startled she was. "I wasn't expecting that."

"Nor was I."

"He must have been quite grateful." Dee studied her friend. "For your offer of assistance, that is."

"Well, yes, I suppose." Teddy winced. "And I might have kissed him back."

Dee's brow rose. "You might have?"

"It was difficult to tell." Teddy forced a casual note to her voice. "It happened so quickly."

"I see," Dee said slowly. "So this kiss of gratitude . . ."

Teddy nodded.

"Was this a friendly sort of kiss? The kind of kiss a brother might give you?"

"Good Lord, I wouldn't think so. I don't have a brother but there certainly wasn't anything brotherly about it." She reached for a biscuit and broke it in two. "It quite took my breath away."

Dee stared.

"I do wish you wouldn't look at me like that. Say something."

"I have no idea what to say." Dee shook her head. "I suppose I am wondering what you are going to do about it."

"I'm not going to do anything about it." She shrugged. "It was just a kiss after all."

"A kiss that took your breath away."

"Which I would think is more a testament to his ability to kiss rather than anything of a significant nature. The man has probably kissed countless numbers of women. Why, he's no doubt had a great deal of practice."

"I suppose that's possible," Dee said slowly. "But he doesn't strike me as that sort of man. He seems more the kind to take a kiss quite seriously."

In spite of Teddy's accusation that his comment about her being an adventure was well rehearsed, she had to agree with Dee. He didn't seem the type of man who would go about kissing women without so much as a by-your-leave.

"So he kissed you," Dee said slowly, "and you kissed him back and . . ."

"And?" Teddy drew her brows together. "And there isn't

anything more to it than that." She paused. "He did call on me. Twice actually."

Dee's brow rose. "Oh?"

"There's that suspicious look of yours again." Teddy huffed. "I offered him my assistance, remember? Goodness, it's not as if he came to my house with the intention of having his way with me."

"So he didn't? Want to have his way with you, that is?"

"Of course not." Teddy hesitated. "I assume not anyway. I wasn't at home when he called."

"If that had been his intention—"

"I have another secret," Teddy said abruptly. Dee was like a hungry dog with a tasty bone when she set her mind on a subject. The only way to distract the dog was to offer it a larger bone.

Dee's eyes narrowed. "What?"

"I have decided to seriously pursue being a woman of business." Teddy raised her chin in a firm manner. "A successful woman of business. I am already, really."

"So you're going to throw off this charade that what you and your mother have been doing is nothing more than the innocent dabblings of ladies with too much time on their hands? You're going to reveal the truth?"

"Don't be absurd. I have no intention of allowing anyone to know we are not the dilettantes the world thinks we are." Teddy scoffed. "That would be exceptionally bad for, well, for business."

"And you came to this decision . . . ?"

"At Camille's wedding." Teddy broke another piece off her biscuit. "It simply dawned on me that my life was never going to be as I had imagined it. And it was past time to keep pretending that it was. That this enterprise we're engaged in is nothing more than a temporary solution."

"I know I always thought of it as temporary. Something to make ends meet. Until . . ."

"Until what?"

"Until . . ." Dee shook her head in a helpless manner. "I don't know."

"There are no knights-errant in shining armor that are going to ride to my rescue like those in pre-Raphaelite paintings. Simon is the only potential knight in the foreseeable future and I absolutely refuse to marry him, or any man, simply to have my needs taken care of. Once perhaps but not now. I'm twenty-six years of age and knights riding to the rescue are in short supply. Besides, marriage is no longer of interest. I have other things to do with my life." She shook her head. "No, this endeavor of ours is not a temporary solution, it must be permanent. Because the changes brought about with Father's death are permanent. So the only intelligent thing to do is embrace the life I have now. It's taken me four years but Father's debts are nearly paid off. What better time than now to start anew?" She leaned forward and met her friend's gaze directly. "I want to be the most successful planner of wedding and social events in England. I want to be the one society turns to for a smashing event." Everything she'd been thinking in the past few weeks rushed out, as if her words had a mind of their own. "We've made a good start of it but we need to do better. Or rather I do. Mother's role is relatively minimal. I intend to remain exclusive, of course."

"Of course," Dee murmured, her eyes wide.

"And terribly expensive. If you can't afford the best then you can't afford my services. Expensive and exclusive, exactly what society wants."

"But it's still, well, business."

"Without a doubt but there's no need to bandy the word about indiscriminately. You know as well as I that if anyone knew we actually needed the money, our commissions would be at an end. I need to stand on my own and I need to make my fortune." She blew a frustrated breath. "Why is it that only men can make their fortunes in this world?"

Dee made an odd sort of strangling sound that might have been agreement or objection, it scarcely mattered.

"Men can make their own fortunes but women are expected to marry for theirs. It's yet another example of how this world is entirely unfair to women. Well, I've had quite enough of that nonsense, thank you very much."

For very nearly the first time in the dozen or so years of their acquaintance, Dee couldn't manage to find her tongue. Good. Teddy wasn't finished.

"I'm intelligent, well educated, and socially connected. I am more than capable of succeeding in anything I damn well choose. Do you realize that all the money we've made thus far, after keeping Father's creditors happy of course, has gone toward maintaining the illusion that we don't need money?"

"I had no idea."

"Well, it has." Teddy shook her head. "It takes far more than I had ever expected simply to keep up appearances. Why, the house alone costs a small fortune to run. One never imagines the sort of money it takes to continue the life one has always led until one has to pay for it oneself. I never thought about money until we didn't have any and Mother's no good about budgeting at all."

"I can imagine . . ."

"She cannot get it out of her head that a good marriage is the only solution."

"Perhaps you should try to find a match for her," Dee said weakly.

"Don't think I haven't thought of that," Teddy said sharply. "Unfortunately, most gentlemen of a certain age have no desire for an older woman. The only eligible older man I know who is the least bit charming and dashing is your uncle and he is still married. Believe me, if there was anyone who could entice my mother into marriage I'd be throwing the poor man at her like a virgin into a volcano."

Dee choked back a laugh. "I meant to mention this

before." She leaned forward in a confidential manner. "But if you don't want the entire world to hear what we are discussing, you'd best lower your voice."

Teddy winced. "Is it that bad?"

"Probably not. I am just being cautious." Dee paused, laughter in her eyes. "Although I distinctly noted the ears of a lady at the next table perking up like a good hound's at the word *virgin.*"

Teddy stared for a moment, then laughed. "You did not."

"Perhaps not." Dee smiled and settled back in her chair. "But you do express a great deal of vehemence when the subject turns to your mother."

"I simply find it annoying—no—infuriating that while she's willing to sacrifice my future on the altar of holy matrimony to regain the life we lost, she's far more selective when it comes to her own future."

"What does she think about your newfound determination to be a woman of business?"

"I haven't told her." Teddy drew a deep breath. "Nor do I intend to. At least not yet." She met her friend's gaze. "What do you think?"

"Well, it's most improper, scandalous, really," Dee said slowly. "However, I can certainly understand how losing all your money changes everything. I was fortunate to have my funds restored to me but your circumstances are entirely different." She thought for a moment. "It does seem to me that impropriety and scandal are among those things that are in the eye of the beholder. As you intend to continue to well, deceive society as to the true nature of your endeavor, you have my complete support."

"But only if it remains clandestine?"

"Good Lord, Teddy, you are my dearest friend in the world. I want nothing but the best for you. Certainly being in business is not what I would have chosen for you. And yes, if you were to jump into the Thames naked I would not join you but I would definitely throw you a rope."

Teddy raised a brow. "To hang myself?"

"Whatever you wish." Dee waved off the comment. "The point that I am trying to make is that years and years ago we agreed that we would be good, true friends for the rest of our lives. And I am your good, true friend regardless of what twists and turns either of our lives may take. Regardless of what choices you make. You will always have my support even if some of the decisions you make are not as well advised as others. Even if I disagree with them. Besides . . ." She paused. "You never said a disapproving word when I married my first husband even though I know full well you find the idea of marriage to older men distasteful."

Teddy's eyes widened. "I never . . . that is you . . . and well I mean I . . ."

"It no longer matters." Dee waved off Teddy's words, the sapphire ring Sam had given her flashing in the light. "In fact, it didn't really matter at the time. I did what was best for me just as you will do what is best for you. I will keep my thoughts to myself, as you did, and I shall be here if you need me just as you were there for me."

Teddy stared.

"You had no idea I was quite so, oh, I don't know, wonderful is as good a word as any, I think." Dee smiled and popped a bite of biscuit in her mouth.

"Actually, Dee." Teddy reached out and took her friend's hand. "I have always known that."

"And because I am quite wonderful as well as your good, true friend, I have an idea as to what to do about the problem with your mother."

"Oh?"

"You, my dear friend, need a holiday."

"That's brilliant, Dee." Teddy settled back in her chair. "Why, the south of France is lovely at this time of year."

Dee cast her friend a chastising look. "Sarcasm, Teddy?"

"I am sorry but perhaps you missed that minor point about my lack of funds. I can't afford a holiday. I have neither the time nor the money. Even a day trip to Brighton would be difficult to manage. And every extra bit I have needs to go toward replenishing my wardrobe. I'm afraid I'm beginning to look a touch shabby."

"I didn't want to mention it," Dee said under her breath.

"Again, you mean."

"Haven't I offered to lend you anything in my wardrobe?"

"You're entirely too short for me."

"And haven't I also offered to loan you however much you need to help you replenish your wardrobe? As well as what you need to finish repaying your father's debts?"

"You are a good, true friend."

Dee nodded smugly. "Yes, I am."

"And as much as I appreciate the idea . . ." Teddy sighed. "I can't possibly take a holiday."

"I'm not suggesting you go anywhere. I'm simply suggesting you get away from your mother."

"Excellent idea." Teddy eyed the other woman skeptically. "Do tell me, how you propose that I do that?"

"Well, I intend to stay at Millworth until after the New Year. Mother is very nearly giddy over the thought of everyone at Millworth for Christmas. I'm sure you remember last year's Christmas wasn't quite as traditional as one might have hoped."

Teddy bit back a smile. Last year's Christmas was still something of a sore spot with Dee even though it had worked out remarkably well in the end.

"Quite frankly, since Father's return I haven't seen much of Mother, they've been traveling a lot you know. And I'll be spending at least half of my time in New York when Sam and I marry so who knows how often we'll see each other then. And well, as odd as it may sound, I've missed her."

Dee and her mother had always been close in spite of Lady Briston's eccentricities, or perhaps because of them. Especially since Dee's sisters were older and paid Dee no mind at all when she was young. It was only in the last year that the Channing daughters had become true sisters. In spite of their problems in the past, Teddy couldn't help but envy them.

"And you are always welcome at Millworth, you know. You could certainly come with me."

Teddy shook her head. "There's Lady Wellby's party as well as a few others I have on my schedule. I know Millworth is only an hour by train, and I did manage to do what I needed to accomplish while I was there in the weeks before Camille's wedding, but at the moment, I don't think leaving London is wise."

"I do hate it when you're practical."

"I hate being practical," Teddy said wryly.

"I suspected you'd prefer to stay in London so I propose you simply move out of your house for however long you need to."

"And where would you suggest I go?"

"Why to my house, of course." Dee smiled in a triumphant manner. "I'm not going to be there. Sam has been residing in a hotel and he and Camille and Grayson are leaving for New York in a few days anyway. I would go with them but I have financial matters of my own that still need overseeing and I don't want to be an ocean away should there be a problem."

"I don't know . . ." Although that would be a perfect solution.

"You know how much I adore that house and I hate to have it stand empty. I've managed to rehire my cook and one of the housemaids. The others, including my butler, took positions elsewhere." Dee blew a frustrated breath. "I can't say that I blame them. When I let them go—"

Teddy nodded. "When you were forced to economize."

"Please, I don't ever want to hear that word again." Dee shuddered. "As I was saying, when I let them go, I had no idea if my financial difficulties would be resolved in my favor or not. Now that they have been, I am eager to get my life back in order. Although . . ." She glanced at the ring on her finger and smiled. "There will be a few changes."

"Are you going to keep the house?"

"Absolutely." Determination straightened Dee's shoulders. "Sam and I will need somewhere to live when we are in London. We intend to spend half our time here and half in America."

"How very . . . compromising of you." Teddy stifled a grin.

"I think so." Dee cast the other woman a smug smile. "At any rate, I have hired a new butler but I still need a housekeeper and another maid and an assistant for the cook. If you stayed at the house, you could take care of hiring the rest of my staff for me."

"Still, I'm not sure . . ."

"Besides, I had never considered the financial frivolity of having a house staffed even when I'm not living there." Her brows drew together. "Now, I find it somewhat distressing but at least I haven't reopened Hargate Hall." She took a casual sip of tea. "In fact, I'm thinking of selling it."

Surprise widened Teddy's eyes. "Your country house? I never imagined you'd let that go."

"I didn't admit it at the time, but I never felt quite, oh, right there." Dee shrugged. "It's time to move on with my life."

"Of course." Teddy shouldn't have been surprised. In the last years of their marriage, Dee's late husband, Phillip, spent more of his time alone at their country house than he did with Dee in London.

She leaned forward and met Teddy's gaze. "So you see, you'd really be doing me a great service by staying there. Your mother would surely understand, especially if you point out that I would be forever in your debt." Dee cast her a wicked grin. "And I have always been partial to throwing parties that I will simply be too busy to manage myself in the future."

Teddy considered the other woman for a long moment.

Why not? "I can have a bag packed and be at your house by late this afternoon."

"Perfect." Dee beamed. "I'll have a word with the new butler today before I return to Millworth and tell him to expect you. His name is Mr. Filbeck, by the way."

"Thank you." Teddy nodded absently, already going over the right way to inform her mother about this turn of events. A note seemed best. One her mother would receive after Teddy had already gone.

"Now that that is settled." Dee selected another biscuit. "Tell me what you and my mother have planned for Jack's New Year's ball."

"Well, your mother has not let go of the possibility of a masked ball, not costumes mind you, simply masks. She thinks it would add an aura of mystery."

No, Lady Sallwick wouldn't be at all happy about her daughter residing in a house, any house, alone sans chaperone and would no doubt point out the impropriety of it. And goodness, what would Cousin Simon think then? The last thing Teddy wanted was another confrontation with her mother. Still, if that was the price she had to pay, so be it. If Teddy was truly determined to be independent and stand on her own, this was nothing more than a first step. And it was time—past time—her mother understood it was Teddy's life and she would be the one to decide how it would be lived. Besides, she was perilously close to being an acknowledged spinster already so what real difference did a bit of impropriety make?

"I doubt if Jack or Uncle Basil particularly care about the arrangements," Dee said thoughtfully. "As long as Mother doesn't have him carried in on a gold litter held aloft by Roman slaves like an ancient emperor. Or a sacrifice."

Teddy laughed. "I promise, I won't let her go that far. But she does intend to make this a social event to remember. Why, the guest list alone is enormous."

"And I suspect each and every one on it will attend, out

of curiosity if nothing else." Dee shook her head. "It's not every day a family discovers a lost heir and an American one at that."

"That reminds me, I should tell you." Teddy lowered her voice and leaned closer. "Before you came in, I overheard two ladies talking about how the Earl of Briston has a newfound heir who was raised by natives in the wilds of America."

"Beryl's doing no doubt. The next thing you know we'll be hearing that he was raised by wolves. I don't know why no one listens to me." Dee heaved a long-suffering sigh. "Amnesia was so much more believable."

Chapter Ten

Later that day,
The residence of Lady Hargate . . .

Jack paused in the spacious foyer of Delilah's London house and looked around approvingly. The place was serene and uncluttered with only an upholstered bench against one wall, an ornate mirror hanging above a small table on one side of the door, and a brass coatrack on the other. Not at all what he expected. The tall, red brick building wasn't nearly as grand as he would have thought Lady Hargate would own either but then he didn't know any of them at all really, except for his father of course. Still he liked them. And, better yet, they seemed to like him.

He suspected the rest of society might not be quite so welcoming. He was an American after all. Before coming to England he had always thought the British looked down their noses at their former colonists. Most of the people he had met thus far had been men and friends of his father, not a particularly standoffish group. It was the ladies of society he had to win over. Still, women always did seem to like him. It didn't hurt that he had money and was from a prominent family.

The colonel had taken Jack's desire for a respite from

togetherness extremely well. In fact, the older man had chuckled and said he had wondered when Jack would reach that point. He had given his blessing while admitting they both could use a little time apart. Nonetheless, he reminded his son of an engagement the day after tomorrow and Jack had assured him of his presence.

He handed his coat to the butler who hung it on the rack.

"Where should I put your bag, sir?" the butler asked in an odd manner, as if the servant wasn't sure exactly what to do with this new arrival and was not at all pleased at his presence. But then Sam had said he was newly hired.

"One of the bedrooms will be fine."

"Which one in particular, sir?"

"It doesn't matter." Jack shrugged. "Whatever you think is appropriate."

"My view of what is and is not appropriate makes no difference, sir."

"All right then," Jack said slowly. "The first suitable room will be fine."

"Very well, sir." The butler paused. "Shall I show you to the parlor?"

"Yes, thank you." He followed the butler up the broad stairway to the second floor. First floor here he corrected himself. The butler opened a set of doors off the foyer at the top of the stairs and stepped aside.

Jack strode into the parlor. This room too was well furnished in what he assumed was the latest style with a sofa, a few chairs, and several tables. But the gracious room was not overly crowded with furniture or those annoying little figurines or other odds and ends that women without husbands to restrain them usually had cluttering up the place. Several paintings hung on the walls, portraits and a few landscapes. An empty glass-fronted cabinet, the kind used to display annoying figurines or odds and ends, stood to one side of the tall windows. Why on earth would anyone have an empty cabinet?

"Do you need anything, sir?" the servant said in a manner that might have been disapproving although it was probably just British reserve. Still, their butler in his family's house in New York was English and you never knew exactly what Mr. Edgars might be thinking, good or bad.

"Not at the moment."

"Very well then." The butler sniffed and took his leave.

No, Jack wasn't mistaken, the man definitely disapproved of him or his presence here. Absurd, of course, this was his cousin's house after all. It was already evening, perhaps he disapproved of guests arriving too late in the day. Or it could be that he simply didn't like plans being changed and he hadn't expected anyone to be living in the house for several months yet. Well, he'd have to adjust. Jack was here and here he intended to stay. Delilah's house was the only sanctuary he had and he was not about to let a snob of a butler scare him away.

He wandered around the perimeter of the room, studying each painting in turn. The landscapes struck him as serious works rather than something merely decorative but he didn't recognize the artists.

Raised voices sounded from the hall outside the parlor door. As much as Jack preferred not to eavesdrop, it was impossible to avoid.

". . . and I absolutely refuse to serve in a house where blatant indiscretions are being committed." That was definitely the butler.

A woman's voice responded, too far away for Jack to make out her words. The housekeeper perhaps?

"Ha!" the butler responded. "I am not a fool, my lady."

Not the housekeeper then. But hadn't Sam said Delilah was going back to Millworth?

"Nonetheless, I can certainly see what is going on here," the butler continued, "and I will have no part of it. I have a reputation to maintain. My references are impeccable. Why, my last position was with the Duchess of Mersbury herself!"

Again, the woman's words were indistinguishable but the butler's gasp of indignation was clear.

"She died, my lady!"

He still couldn't make out the words but the woman's tone was unmistakable. Jack winced. He wouldn't want to be in the butler's shoes right now.

"Discharged?" The butler's indignation rang in the hall. "I have never been discharged. I tender my resignation effective immediately!"

Jack couldn't decipher the woman's reply and suspected that was for the best.

A moment later the butler marched by the parlor door in an air of pride and righteous indignation.

"I can assure you, your references won't be impeccable next time!" The woman's voice now sounded just out of sight, irate and very familiar.

Theodosia stalked by the doorway, glanced into the parlor, then continued on. An instant later she returned and stared in obvious disbelief.

"You!"

"Good afternoon, Theodosia," he said cautiously.

"On the contrary, Mr. Channing, it's not the least bit good!" She stepped into the parlor, the fury that had been directed at the butler now aimed at Jack. "What are you doing here?"

He ventured a tentative smile. "We're back to Mr. Channing, are we?"

"You're fortunate that's all I'm calling you!" Her hazel eyes flashed with fire. "Well?"

"Well . . . what?"

"What are you doing here?"

He stared at her for a long moment. She had no reason to be angry with him. He had nothing to do with whatever problem she'd had with the butler. He'd just barely arrived, after all. Now that he thought about it, the blasted woman did seem to be easily annoyed with him more often than not and for very little cause. Well, enough was enough.

"I might ask you the same question," he said coolly. "What are you doing here?"

"I am here at Delilah's, *Lady Hargate's*, invitation," she said in a manner far loftier than necessary. "I'm residing here while she is at Millworth."

"Well then we have a problem." He kept his tone mild. "I too am staying here. At the invitation of Lady Hargate's *fiancé.*"

Her eyes widened. "That's impossible."

"And yet." He shrugged. "Here I am."

"This won't do." She shook her head. "This won't do at all. We can't stay in the same house. Alone. Unchaperoned. Why it's scandalous. It will ruin us both. You may not care but I have a reputation to think of. You have to leave. At once!"

"I'm not going anywhere. But you're right. This is a problem." He narrowed his eyes. "Therefore I suggest you leave."

"Absolutely not." She squared her shoulders. "Delilah is my dearest friend in the world and she, well, she'd be offended if I left."

His brow rose. "Would she?"

"Without question." She nodded. "She would take my leaving as . . . as the gravest of insults. Why, this might destroy our friendship altogether. A friendship, might I point out, that has lasted longer than you have known her."

"Regardless, I'm still not leaving."

She studied him suspiciously. "Why are you here? I thought you were staying with your father at Channing House."

"I was." He shrugged. "And now I'm not."

"Good Lord." Her eyes widened. "They've thrown you out, haven't they?"

"Of course not." He laughed. "Why would they throw me out?"

"I don't know," she snapped. "It was the first thing that came to mind. For a moment I thought, in spite of the resemblance, you weren't Colonel Channing's son after all."

"You thought I might be part of some elaborate dramatic plot to defraud the family out of their money, their home, and their title?" He chuckled. "I imagine there are far less complicated ways to do that than letting the colonel track me down half a world away." He paused. "I can assure you, as my mother is married to Colonel Channing, and was before my birth, and then given the resemblance you've already mentioned, there isn't a doubt in my mind as to my paternity. Or, I might add, in anyone's mind except perhaps yours."

"Not at all." A charming blush washed up her face. "It was just a chance thought and not particularly worthy of me, so I do apologize. Nonetheless." She folded her arms over her chest. "You still need to leave."

He shook his head. "I don't think so."

"But—"

"Give me one good reason why I should."

"Because I promised Dee I would hire a new housekeeper and other staff for her which would be much less difficult if I resided here. And now . . ." Her eyes narrowed. "I have to hire a new butler as well, thanks to you."

"What do you mean—thanks to me?" Jack shook his head in disbelief. "I'm not the one who fired the butler. What was that all about anyway?"

"It was about you," she said sharply, then drew a deep breath. "He thought you were here, at my invitation I might add, for purposes that were, oh, less than honorable."

"Did he?" Jack bit back a smile. "Sam said he'd send a note."

"He obviously failed to do so as your appearance was as much a surprise to the butler as it was to me."

"And he jumped to the conclusion that I was—"

"Yes, yes." She waved off his comment. "We've established that."

"So he was shocked at the possibility of . . . indiscretion."

"He said he had high standards and would not condone a house where blatant improprieties and moral turpitude were acceptable. Moral turpitude—ha!"

Jack stifled a laugh but it wasn't easy. She was so magnificently irate.

"Of course, I had no idea what he was talking about." She rolled her gaze toward the ceiling. "He was making no sense whatsoever and I thought he was quite possibly mad."

"Did you?"

She nodded. "Well, I didn't know you were here and he was far too outraged to make any sense at all although now I understand what he was going on about." She paused. "As he was perilously close to calling me something I refuse to say aloud, I might have lost my temper."

"You?" Jack gasped in feigned surprise. "The nerve of the man."

She ignored him. "And I might have cast aspersions on his ability to, well, differentiate between a portion of his body and a hole in the ground."

Jack laughed.

"This isn't funny." Her lips twitched as if she was trying not to smile. "It's not the least bit amusing. Now I have to find Dee a new butler as well as a housekeeper. And I had planned on his assistance in that regard."

"I'm sure you're more than capable of handling that without assistance."

"That's not the point. The point is your very presence here has added complications to my life that I simply don't need at the moment. Nor do I need to be embroiled in scandal. Which I think is more than enough reason for you to leave."

"I'm afraid that's not good enough." He shook his head regretfully. "You'll have to do better than that."

"Very well then." She stepped closer and met his gaze firmly. "My mother is driving me mad and if I had to stay in the same house with her for another moment, one of us would not have survived another night!"

"Oh?"

"You needn't sound like that. It's not as if I would have smothered her in her sleep." She hesitated, the tiniest hint of a smile curving her lips. "Although admittedly it has crossed my mind." She raised her chin in a determined manner. "And, as I have nowhere else to go, you can see why I must stay here."

"As good as a reason as that is, I'm afraid it's no better than mine." He grinned. "My father is driving me mad as well."

"Colonel Channing." She scoffed. "Why, he's a wonderful, charming man."

"Indeed he is. His character is not the problem." He shook his head. "The problem is that he's a new father. And he's trying to, oh, *indoctrinate* his newfound son into English society, which involves meeting everyone there is to meet and going everywhere there is to go and seeing everything there is to see. Leaving said new son not a moment to himself to so much as catch his breath."

"Oh." She stared wide-eyed. "That is awkward."

"There's such a thing as being together too much, you know."

She nodded.

"As I have no desire to offend him staying here, in my cousin's house, was a suitable solution as opposed to going to a hotel, which might have offended the entire family. As if I were turning my back on them, you see. So." He cast her a triumphant smile. "While I have not entertained the idea of doing my father in, I think my reason for being here is better than yours."

She stared at him for a considerable moment. Finally, she drew a deep breath.

"My mother wants me to marry the cousin who was my father's heir because she thinks that will make life exactly as it's supposed to be, or used to be, and she won't let the matter drop for so much as an instant because, regardless of the fact that I am an adult, and I am not especially interested in marriage at all anymore, she refuses to accept that I am more than capable of making my own decisions about my life and my future," Theodosia said all in one breath as if, now committed to confession, she was going to reveal everything in one fell swoop. She blew a long breath and refused to meet his gaze, obviously realizing she had said more than she had intended or possibly embarrassed by her revelation.

"Well," he said slowly. "I guess you win then."

Her gaze snapped back to his. "Do I?"

He shrugged. "I have a relentless, demanding mother of my own. I had to cross an ocean to escape mine." He smiled wryly. "Moving to another house would have been much simpler."

"You're being awfully reasonable about this."

"I know." But then he had known from the moment he had understood the situation that he would be the one to leave. As a gentleman, leaving was the right thing to do. He wouldn't want to jeopardize Theodosia's reputation and scandal was not the best way to introduce himself to his new family's world. "I'll simply go to a hotel."

"I understand the rooms at the Langham Hotel are very nice," she said helpfully.

"Wonderful," he muttered and stepped into the hall. Still, while there was a certain amount of moral satisfaction in doing the right thing, the proper thing, it was hard to be gracious about it.

"Wait." An apologetic note sounded in her voice.

He turned back to her. "What is it now? Is there some other inconvenient and annoying thing you'd like me to do to make your life easier and complicate mine?"

Her brow furrowed. "You needn't be cross about it."

"Why shouldn't I be? This was the perfect solution for

me. Now, I am going to have to wander London, bag in hand, looking for a place to stay."

"You don't have to sound so pathetic." Her voice was cool but a smile lingered in her eyes. "You aren't, you know. Pathetic, that is."

"That will certainly keep me warm in the streets."

She frowned. "I really don't understand why you can't stay at Channing—"

"Because I don't want to," he said sharply. "Because I feel smothered with . . . with expectations and unspoken pressure. Because being there implies a commitment I am not ready to make. Because I don't have any time at all to consider the changes in my life and decide what I want to do about them. Because I have no idea at the moment as to who I am or who I want to be!"

"Oh, well, do tell me how you truly feel," she snapped. "Don't think it's necessary to restrain yourself because I am practically a stranger."

"I have been restraining myself my entire life!"

"Ha." She scoffed. "I doubt that."

He narrowed his eyes. "You know nothing about me."

"I know a man who restrains himself doesn't go around randomly kissing women he barely knows."

"I don't go around randomly kissing women I barely know."

"You kissed me," she said in a lofty manner.

"Well that . . ." Abruptly the thought struck him: What would his father do in a situation like this? He smiled slowly. "There was nothing random about that."

"Oh." She stared at him for a long moment. "Well . . . then . . ."

"Then what?" he snapped.

"Then . . . I don't know. You've made me feel quite dreadful about this which is deeply annoying as I have just as much right to be here as you do." She glared at him. "So before you go, would you care to join me for dinner? It's the least I can do as I am throwing you out."

"You are not throwing me out, I am choosing to leave. And yes, I'd like that very much!"

"Good!" She nodded. "I shall inform the cook. You passed the dining room on your way in. I shall meet you there in a few minutes."

"Excellent." He started down the stairs.

"Mr. Channing. Jack." She appeared behind him at the top of the stairs.

"What is it now?"

"Do you intend to do it again? Kiss me, that is."

"I haven't decided yet."

"Oh." She paused. "Why not?"

"Because as much as I enjoyed kissing you, every time I encounter you, you are either delightful and any number of things men only dream about or you are snippy and annoyed with me for reasons that are not my fault. You may well be the most confusing woman I have ever met." He continued down the stairs. "I'm not certain you are worth the trouble, Lady Theodosia!"

There was a long silence in response but he was sure it wouldn't last.

"On the contrary, Mr. Channing," she called after him. "I am more than worth the trouble."

He was right and she was absolutely wrong. There was nothing to be done about it except apologize. Again.

"Mr. Channing. Jack," Teddy said the moment she joined him in the dining room. "I have been unaccountably unpleasant to you on more than one occasion and I do hope you will see your way clear to forgive me."

"There's nothing to forgive," he said in a cool tone that belied his words. Apparently, he did indeed have a sense of restraint when it came to forgiveness. It scarcely mattered;

starting this very instant she was going to be as pleasant to him as possible.

He held a chair out for her and she took her seat, then folded her hands in her lap and waited for him to sit down. Try as she might she couldn't figure out why Jack Channing seemed to bring out the worst in her. Why, she was usually so pleasant and even-tempered. Certainly, her finances were on her mind but then they always were. She'd also been thinking a great deal lately about how to build her business. Still, that was exciting and not at all something that would put her in a foul mood. Of course, her mother had been pushing Simon's case with renewed vigor of late. It was enough to make any rational woman more than a little out of sorts. All in all, this was not the best time to further her acquaintance with anyone.

Jack himself really hadn't done anything. The problem with the butler hadn't been his fault at all. Nor was it his fault that when she found out his true identity it immediately brought to mind the deceit of her late fiancé. Cyril Goddard had been handsome and charming, which completely hid the fact that he was vile and dishonest as well. Something Teddy hadn't discovered until it was too late. Yes, she had been deceived by one man but she knew better than to paint all men with the same brush. It certainly wasn't fair, especially not to Jack.

And it was neither his fault, nor his problem that she couldn't seem to get him out of her head. Her thoughts inevitably strayed back to him in her most unguarded moments. Particularly in those moments before sleep. Try as she might, those . . . thoughts and the dreams that had followed were unrelenting and more than a little, well, intimate. It was annoying and confusing. She had no desire to be involved with him or any man at the moment. She cleared her throat. "Mrs. Tully is Dee's cook and has been with her forever. She is wonderful. She'll be serving tonight as Mr. Filbeck has now taken his leave."

Jack's brow furrowed. "Who?"

"Mr. Filbeck. The butler?"

"I thought Sam said his name was Beckley?"

"Sam was wrong," she said in a dismissive manner, then caught herself and adopted a pleasant tone. "I'm sure it was just a bit of confusion. Now then." Her hands tightened in her lap. "I have a, oh, a proposal of sorts for you."

He glanced at the door. "Then I gather Mrs. Tully doesn't take the same view of moral turpitude as the butler?"

And wouldn't that be delightful? She ignored the unwanted thought and allowed her smile to slip just a bit. "I suspect you know full well that is not the nature of the proposal I have in mind."

"Go on." His polite tone matched hers.

Thankfully, the door to the back hall opened and Mrs. Tully bustled in with mock turtle soup. Smells and tastes were duly commented on and the cook returned to the kitchen.

"I'm sorry," Jack said the moment the cook was out of earshot. "You're right. I did know what you meant. I don't know why . . ." He shook his head. "You make me say the damnedest things."

She stared at him. This was going to be much easier than she thought. *And much more enjoyable*, the annoying voice in the back of her mind whispered.

She cleared her throat again. "What I was going to suggest was that you and I start over. We could pretend we just met . . . oh . . ." She shrugged helplessly. "Now."

He studied her thoughtfully.

"Perhaps?" She held her breath.

"I can't tell you how delightful it is to finally meet you in person, Lady Theodosia." He leaned forward slightly and gazed across the table at her. And the oddest thing happened to her insides. "I've been wanting to meet you."

"What a lovely thing to say, Mr. Channing."

"It's nothing more than the truth," he said in an offhand

manner. "I met someone once who looked vaguely like you but she was unpredictable and temperamental in character. You never knew when you happened to cross paths with her if she was going to be delightful, the kind of woman you wanted to get to know better. You understand."

She nodded.

"Or if you were going to wish you had run in the other direction." He raised his glass to her and took a drink.

She resisted the urge to wince. "I'm sure she had her reasons."

"Possibly. Although if she did she never made me aware of them."

"Perhaps she didn't know you well enough?"

"Perhaps." He nodded. "It is a shame though, I had thought we were going to be friends."

"Let us suppose for a moment, that she had jumped to the wrong conclusions and was then rather embarrassed to admit how absurd those conclusions were as they were based on past experience and had nothing whatsoever to do with you. Under those circumstances would you be willing to revise your opinion of her character?"

"Possibly. Go on."

She chose her words carefully. "Then let us further suppose that her penchant for jumping to conclusions, which is not at all like her I might add, was perhaps a result of undue anxiety brought on by a variety of problems including her mother's relentless tirade on the subject of marriage as well as financial concerns and, well, other matters."

He nodded. "I can see where that might make someone less pleasant that they might otherwise be."

"And I suspect she apologized on more than one occasion, Mr. Channing."

"Jack," he said firmly.

"Oh, but that's terribly improper. Still . . ." She cast him her most flirtatious smile. "My friends call me Teddy."

"And are we going to be friends?" His gaze meshed with hers.

She stared at him. "I do hope so."

"So do I." He shook his head. "But I won't call you Teddy."

"Why not?"

"Because I would much rather call you Theodosia. I like the way it sounds on my tongue and in my head. Theodosia is a beautiful name for a beautiful woman."

"Why, Mr. Channing, Jack, you will quite turn my head."

"Good." His eyes glittered with amusement. "Did you know Theodosia means 'gift of God'?"

She paused, her soupspoon halfway to her mouth. "You said that the last time we met."

"But we've never met before, remember?" He sipped his soup. "You must have dreamed it."

She stared at him. She had dreamed any number of things. How on earth did he know? "Did I?"

"If we've never met, you did. Furthermore you liked it. In your dream, that is."

She started to protest, then realized how silly and pointless that was. "Yes, I did." She smiled. "In my dreams, of course."

"And you liked the fact that I had made the effort to ferret out that bit of information."

"One likes all sorts of things in dreams," she said in an offhand manner. "Which certainly doesn't mean one likes the same things when awake."

"On the contrary, Theodosia," he said smoothly. "I'd say a person's fondest desires are those they only acknowledge in their sleep."

"And what do you dream about, Jack?" she said without thinking.

He stared at her for a long moment, then smiled a private sort of smile as if deciding something or confirming something to himself. It would have been most annoying had it not been such a nice smile. Had it not made her breath catch and her heart thump.

This was absurd. She drew a deep breath. "You do realize that flirtatious banter wasn't exactly what I had in mind when I suggested pretending we had just met."

"I assumed as much but given the possibility that I was wrong and that might annoy you I decided to choose the most prudent course." He smiled in an overly pleasant manner. "What did you have in mind?"

"Oh, I don't know." Was he deliberately making this difficult? "I thought we could talk about the usual things people talk about when they have first met. Likes and dislikes. Literature, art . . . banking."

"Banking?" He stared at her.

"Yes. How is banking?" She cast him her most brilliant smile.

He stared at her for a moment, then laughed. "Good God, Theodosia, you needn't try so hard."

"I wasn't," she said staunchly. "I am extremely interested in banking."

"Come now, I'm a banker and I don't find banking interesting." He paused and his brow furrowed, as if he had just realized what he had said.

It was obvious that man had had some sort of revelation but she suspected now was not the right time to ask him about it.

"Literature then?" she said brightly.

"Literature." He nodded in an absent manner, his mind definitely anywhere but on literature.

"Books?" she prompted.

"Yes, of course." He thought for a moment. "I have always appreciated the humor of Mark Twain. I like a story that can make me laugh. But I also like the works of Jules Verne, Robert Louis Stevenson, and Alexandre Dumas. And I recently read *King Solomon's Mines* and I enjoyed it immensely."

"Novels of adventure then?"

"I hadn't thought of it that way but yes, I suppose you're right."

"I would imagine you share that with your father."

"I only read about adventures, Theodosia," he said. "My father lives them."

She studied him for a moment. "You're rather hard on yourself, aren't you?"

"Aren't we all? Harder on ourselves than others are, that is." He smiled. "I would imagine even the competent, capable, lovely Lady Theodosia Winslow is her greatest critic."

"Possibly. But then, Mr. Channing . . ." She adopted an overly sweet smile. "You haven't met my mother."

He laughed and reached for his wine. "You haven't met mine."

She scoffed. "I would match my mother against yours any day."

"I wouldn't if I were you." A warning sounded in his voice. "You may have won when it comes to who stays here but your mother can't possibly be as . . . oh . . ." He sipped his wine, then set the glass down. "Devious as mine."

"Ha." She smiled in triumph. "My mother wants me to marry someone I don't want to marry to ensure her position in society."

"My mother didn't tell her husband they were still married and he had a son for thirty years. My mother let her son believe his father was dead. My mother—"

"Wait, that's enough." She raised her glass to him. "You win."

"Imagine my delight," he said wryly. "But we were talking about literature, a much less annoying subject. I suspect you are fond of novels of a romantic nature."

"Because I'm a woman?"

"No, of course not." he said quickly, shaking his head. "I know any number of men who like romantic novels."

"Do you?"

"Of course." He hesitated. "None that I can think of at the moment but I'm sure I know some."

"Or one?"

"Hopefully." He grinned.

"Well, I won't ask you to name him." She laughed at the relieved expression on his face. "And yes, I do love a good romantic novel but I must confess I share your appreciation of Mr. Verne's works."

"You do?"

"Oh my yes." She widened her eyes. "Why, I can't think of anything more exciting than the idea of spending five weeks flying in a balloon. Or racing around the world in eighty days."

"Although traveling to the center of the earth or twenty-thousand leagues under the sea has a certain appeal as well."

"Or to the moon? Or streaking across the skies on a comet?"

"It seems we have this in common." He smiled. "A fondness for stories of adventure."

"Perhaps that's because I am an adventure." The words were not as lighthearted as she had intended them.

"Indeed you are."

His gaze locked with hers and for a long moment something crackled in the air between them. Something bright and electric and inevitable. Something that took her breath away. Her heart thudded hard in her chest and she wondered if he could hear it. Wondered if his heart was thudding as well.

"I thought we were forgoing flirtatious banter in favor of literature?" he said at last.

"Was I being flirtatious?" She forced a casual note to her voice. "Why, I hadn't noticed."

He smiled at her again, in that way he had of making her feel he could see right through her.

"Finish your soup, Mr. Channing." Teddy tried to concentrate on the mock turtle but it was nearly impossible. She was far too conscious of being alone with him. Far too aware of him. "Mrs. Tully will be most annoyed if the rest of dinner gets cold while she waits for us to finish."

"And we wouldn't want that." He chuckled.

"No, we would not," she said in a prim manner and tried to ignore the annoying voice in the back of her head that was anything but prim.

What exactly did she want?

Chapter Eleven

"Excellent dinner," Jack said after Mrs. Tully had cleared away the dishes from their meal of roasted beef and replaced them with a platter of cheese and fresh fruit. "Did you know this is Thanksgiving Day in my country?"

"I had no idea." Theodosia studied him. "Dare I ask what you are thankful for today?"

"Any number of things. I am an extremely fortunate man. Finding my father is probably at the top of my list. But at the moment . . ." He raised his glass to her. "I am simply thankful for good food in good company."

"Thank you, Jack." She smiled. "It's been quite an enjoyable evening."

"Do you think anyone who might see me leave the house will think the worst?" He wasn't entirely sure how he felt about that but the idea was vaguely exciting. "Will we be embroiled in scandal?"

"Honestly, Jack, I have no idea. Probably." Theodosia picked up an orange and scored it with a knife. "Sometimes, I get so dreadfully tired of obeying all the rules. All the time."

"Do you? Obey all the rules, that is?"

"I'm afraid so." She hesitated. "For the most part I always have."

"Do you? Then having dinner alone, unchaperoned, with a gentleman is not considered against the rules for an unmarried lady here in London?"

"Good Lord." She stared at him. "That hadn't even crossed my mind."

"I believe you were too busy being irate with me."

"That does explain it. And I did say I followed the rules for the most part." She grinned in a decidedly mischievous fashion. "When I remember."

"I've never given rules much thought really, simply done what was expected." He shrugged. "But I have always followed the rules, I suppose. I have no misspent youth. No questionable reputation to live down. No scandalous secrets in my past." He grimaced. "Rather boring, don't you think?"

She scoffed. "I don't believe you for a minute."

"You think I'm just trying to make myself look good in your eyes?"

"Yes."

"I doubt that confessing the dull nature of my past is the best way to go about that." He shook his head. "It's been my observation that women are intrigued by men who refuse to follow the rules."

"Men who break rules end up in prison," she said in a prim manner.

He laughed. "Men who break laws perhaps, but men who break rules, those are the kind of men who tend to have adventures rather than read about them." He paused to slice a piece of cheese. "I wish I was more like him, you know."

Her brows drew together in confusion. "Who?"

"My father."

"Oh." Theodosia peeled the sections she had scored, curled them, and tucked them into the base of the orange. She glanced at him. "What makes you think you aren't like him?"

He snorted. "I think that's fairly obvious."

"Not to me."

"For one thing, he's done all sorts of things I stopped dreaming about years ago. He's seized opportunity when it presented itself to venture into the unknown. He's traveled the world, had grand adventures, seen things not everyone does." He shook his head. "Until I came to England, I'd never left American shores."

"Anyone can travel, as you said it's opportunity more than anything else. Besides, he never had any sort of real responsibilities to hold him back. When you think about it, he's never had to concern himself with anyone other than himself."

"That's one way of looking at it, I suppose."

"As for dreams of adventure, it seems to me, until one dies, there's still the possibility of adventure. One simply has to seize it. Carpe diem and such."

He raised a brow. "Latin?"

"Miss Bicklesham's Academy for Accomplished Young Ladies was very progressive."

He chuckled. "Apparently."

"Although I am scarcely one to talk about seizing the day." She studied the orange that now looked more like a work of art than something to eat. "But then I am female and adventures for women in this world tend to leave them ruined and abandoned. Unless . . ."

"Unless?"

"Unless they have a great deal of money. Then they are able to do exactly as they please." She smiled. "And that, Jack, is my observation."

"Very astute."

"I can be quite astute." She considered him thoughtfully. "But I thought we had agreed you can be anyone or anything you want to be."

"That's all very well and good on a terrace under a full

moon but in the light of day . . ." He shook his head. "What I am is a thirty-year-old banker."

"A banker who doesn't find banking particularly interesting." She separated the orange segments and set them on her plate.

"I did say that, didn't I?" Odd, he'd always thought his work at the bank was useful and fulfilling. His life was solid and content. It was only since he'd met his father that he'd come to suspect there was little difference between useful and dull, and no difference whatsoever between content and boring. How was it that a few months ago he had thought his life was just fine and now it didn't seem to suit him at all?

"Yes, you did." She broke the orange segments apart. "I've always thought your father was a remarkable man."

"When I was a boy and wondered about my father, the colonel is exactly the kind of father I wanted to have. The kind of man any little boy would like to be when he grows up."

"The kind of man any young girl would dream about."

"Really?"

"Oh my, yes." She chuckled. "When I first met the colonel, I thought he was a most heroic figure. Bigger than life. Quite exciting." She picked up an orange segment and took a bite. "He was the kind of man one could imagine riding up on a stalwart steed to rescue a fair maiden."

"And you were the fair maiden," he said slowly.

"Absolutely." She smiled at the memory. "I was thirteen and it was my first visit to Millworth. The colonel was just back from Egypt, or perhaps he was just about to leave, I don't remember now. No." She thought for a moment. "He had just gotten back. I remember because he gave both Dee and me carved scarabs, for luck. Oh, I was quite smitten with him. He was a hero from a romantic novel come to life."

"I see." Well, this was awkward. She was smitten with his father? *His father?*

"When Dee and I returned to school, I wrote him a long letter professing my undying love."

"Did you?" How could he ever compete with his father?

"Fortunately, Dee discovered my missive of everlasting devotion and explained to me, quite firmly as I recall, that the colonel had no interest in a thirteen-year-old girl." She wrinkled her nose. "Especially a thirteen-year-old girl who was entirely too tall and gangly, had no bosoms to speak of, and hair reminiscent of a burnt orange."

"You changed," he said mildly.

"Thank goodness." She took another bite of orange; juice trickled down her long fingers.

He had the almost irresistible urge to pull her fingers to his mouth and lick the juice away. He ignored it.

"She also said the colonel had long ago given his heart away and there would never be room in it for someone else."

"My mother?"

"I'm afraid not." She wrinkled her nose. "Dee confessed to me years later that she had made that up. Although in hindsight, given that he never married, I suppose it's possible. I didn't see your father again until Dee's wedding." She thought for a moment. "He was still handsome and dashing and heroic. But as fascinating as his life was, in spite of Dee's confession, he struck me as, well, a bit sad I thought."

"Sad?"

"There was a moment, an expression on his face when he looked at Dee and her sisters. Regret I thought at the time as if, in spite of the exciting life he had chosen, there was something missing." She shrugged. "As I said, it was only a fleeting instant and I certainly could have been mistaken. It was a very long time ago."

"And are you still smitten?" he asked in as casual a manner as he could muster.

"Why, Jack Channing." Her eyes widened with delight. "If I didn't know better, I would think that was the question of a jealous man."

"Not at all," he said smoothly, reached across the table and took an orange segment. "It was simple curiosity. Nothing more than that."

"Of course." Disappointment flashed in her eyes so quickly he might have been mistaken. For a long moment she pulled the segments of orange apart, then looked at him. "How much do you know about your cousins' history?"

"I know that Delilah, Camille, and Beryl were widowed." He shrugged. "Is there more?"

"Your uncle left when they were very young. According to what Dee has told me, he apparently wanted his brother's more carefree, adventurous life than the life of responsibility he had. It's only been since last Christmas that Lady Briston has allowed him back in their lives and even then he was pretending to be his brother. She raised her daughters to marry well and they did. All three married older gentlemen, with healthy fortunes and respectable titles."

He nodded.

"It's not the least bit uncommon, you know. Older men marrying pretty young women."

"It happens all the time."

"But, and I wasn't really aware of this until Dee married Phillip, her first husband, I find it . . ." She thought for a moment. "Distasteful, I suppose."

"Do you?"

"I do." She nodded. "It seems to me such a marriage is nothing less than a trade, if you will. Beauty and youth for money and position. It makes marriage more of a, I don't know, a business proposition than it should be."

"I see." He studied her thoughtfully. "But then hasn't marriage always been a kind of business proposition? Historically anyway. The alliance of two families for profit or position or politics?"

For the first time it struck him that that was exactly the kind of marriage he and Lucy had been willing to enter into. Perhaps the reason they had put off their engagement so often was because, deep down inside, they both knew it wasn't what either of them really wanted. Which made Lucy even smarter than he had realized.

"That doesn't make it right, especially now." She shook her head. "Goodness, Jack, we're on the verge of a new century. Progress is in the very air we breathe. This isn't the Middle Ages. Women are not chattel. We should be able, indeed, encouraged to pursue our own desires."

"You mean running a business or membership in the Explorers Club?"

"Indeed I do."

"You probably think women should vote as well."

"Absolutely." She raised her chin in a defiant manner. "I daresay we couldn't do a worse job of running the world than men have done."

He laughed. "You have a point there."

"Of course I do." She studied him sharply. "Do you think women should vote?"

"Oh no you don't." He shook his head. "It's been entirely too pleasant an evening to spoil it now with talk of social upheaval."

"It's a simple enough question."

"There's nothing simple about that question but to be perfectly honest, I haven't given it much thought." He paused. "But I will admit that you're right. Women couldn't do a worse job of it than men have."

"I shall take that as a yes." She cast him a triumphant grin. "However, that was a most evasive answer, Jack, and you well know it."

"An evasive answer is better than none." He chuckled. "You still haven't answered my question."

"About being smitten with your father?"

He nodded and held his breath.

"Colonel Channing is a fascinating man and I shall always

be fond of him but no." She shook her head. "I put that infatuation behind me years ago. Besides, as I said, I have no desire to marry a man old enough to be my father. Nor will I marry simply to better my position in life." She wrinkled her nose. "If I wanted that I could marry my cousin and be done with it."

"What kind of man do you want to marry?" he said without thinking.

"As we're being so honest with one another I have to admit, I really don't know. I suppose I want what all women want." She shrugged. "As I have already discarded the notion of marriage for many of the usual reasons—"

"Social position and financial security?"

"Don't misunderstand my words. I quite like the idea of wealth and position, I simply think there should be more if one is going to spend the rest of one's life with someone." She thought for a moment. "I suppose I want a man who will, I don't know, slay dragons for me. Figuratively, of course. Sweep me off my feet. That sort of thing."

He raised a brow. "You want a hero?"

"What woman doesn't? Unfortunately, heroes are in remarkably short supply these days."

"Then it's a good thing you're not especially interested in marriage."

"Indeed it is. Knights on white horses riding to the rescue of fair maidens may well be the stuff of poetry and romantic novels but real life is a far different matter." She laughed, then sobered. "He wouldn't have to be a hero in the strictest definition of the word, as the world sees such men." She smiled into his eyes and the oddest thing happened to his heart. "He would only need to be a hero to me."

For a long moment their gazes locked. He resisted the urge, the need, to reach out, pull her across the table into his arms, press his lips to hers . . . sweep her off her feet.

"Goodness, Jack," she said with a self-conscious laugh.

"I am being fanciful tonight. I don't know what's gotten into me."

"Obviously too many romantic novels." He drew a steadying breath. For a moment . . . What had gotten into him as well?

"Yes, that's it," she murmured.

"I should probably be going." Now, before he acted on impulses he'd never known before. He got to his feet. "It's late and I still need to find a hotel."

"I don't know where the time went." She shook her head and stood. "I have to confess, I've never talked to anyone, well, to a man that is, the way we've talked tonight. But then I've never had dinner alone with a man before either." She smiled. "You're remarkably easy to talk to, Mr. Channing."

He grinned. "It's a gift, Lady Theodosia."

"It must come in handy for a banker."

"Oh yes, we bankers are a talkative lot," he said in an overly somber manner.

"Really?"

He chuckled. "No."

She laughed. "I'll see you out."

She took his arm and his muscles clenched beneath her touch. Good Lord, what was this woman doing to him?

They stepped into the front entry, his bags still beside the door. He took his coat from the rack and pulled it on. An envelope lay on the table beneath the mirror. He hadn't noticed it earlier. Theodosia picked it up, glanced at the name written on it, then smiled.

"This is no doubt Sam's note." She waved the envelope at him. "It's addressed to Mr. Beckley. Which is why Mr. Filbeck wouldn't have opened it."

"Then I am eternally grateful for the mistake."

"Are you?"

He nodded. "If Sam hadn't written the wrong name, Mr. Filbeck would have read the note. He wouldn't have been so outraged and you wouldn't have blamed me."

She winced. "Not my finest hour."

"Everything would have been calm and civilized and I would have left hours ago." He smiled into her emerald eyes. "And I would have missed a lovely evening with a beautiful woman."

She stared up at him. "You do say the most charming things."

He stepped closer. "Are you charmed?"

"No." She scoffed. "Perhaps . . . Yes."

"Good."

She drew a deep breath. "I don't think you should go, to a hotel that is."

"I can't stay here," he said in a tone a shade harsher than expected. "And you won, remember?"

"I'm not suggesting you stay here." Her brows drew together. "We agreed that would be most inappropriate."

"Then—"

"I think you should go back to Channing House." She met his gaze firmly. "Your father now understands your feelings and I would suspect he will be much less . . . overwhelming."

"It might be easier to return, at least tonight. It is late after all."

She nodded. "Entirely too late to go looking for a hotel. I would feel quite dreadful to think of you wandering the streets, bags in hand, searching for a place to stay. Why, the guilt alone would be unbearable."

"We wouldn't want that." He grinned.

"No, we would not," she said firmly.

"I should go then." Although he made no move toward the door.

"Yes, you should." Although she made no move to step away. She was close enough that with the barest effort, he could pull her into his arms. And why not? What harm would a simple kiss do? He drew a deep breath.

"I'm going to kiss you again, you know."

Her gaze locked with his, her eyes reflecting his own desire. "Yes, well, I suspected as much."

"You should also know, there's nothing random about it. I have been thinking about it . . ." His gaze dropped to her lips and back to her eyes. "Since we last kissed."

"Have you?" She forced a light laugh.

He nodded and stepped closer. "Have you?"

"No, of course not . . ." She swallowed hard. "Well, perhaps . . . Yes."

"The first time, you kissed me back."

"Don't be absurd, I was . . . I was simply surprised, that's all." It was obvious she didn't believe her words any more than he did. She sighed. "Yes, I suppose I did."

"And this time—"

"For goodness' sake, Jack." She huffed. "Do all bankers have to go on and on about a simple kiss before—"

He pulled her into his arms and pressed his lips to hers with a firm but gentle touch. Her lips were soft and pliant beneath his and his stomach tightened. And all his intentions about a simple kiss vanished the moment her arms slipped around his neck and her mouth opened beneath his.

She tasted faintly of orange and wine. Of summer and light and everything he'd ever loved, everything he'd ever longed for.

At last he raised his head and gazed down into her eyes, shadowed with passion and a need that reflected his own. He had kissed women before of course, but never had he felt a kiss that seemed to sear into his very soul.

"Oh my." Her voice was breathless. "That was . . . there was . . ."

"Nothing simple about that?"

"Dear me, no." Her chest heaved against him and she struggled to catch her breath. "You should probably, well, I should probably . . ."

"Yes, we should. Probably." Reluctantly, he released her,

an immediate feeling of loss washing through him along with the oddest sense that she was meant to be in his arms.

She took an unsteady step back and it was all he could do not to grin with satisfaction. She was as affected by their *simple* kiss as he was.

"I fully intend to see you again soon," he warned. "Very soon."

"Good Lord, I hope so," she murmured, then her eyes widened as if she had just realized what she had said.

He laughed, grabbed her hands, and raised them to his lips. "You are indeed a gift, Theodosia. Tomorrow then."

"Tomorrow?" She gasped in surprise, then nodded. "Yes, indeed." She cast him a brilliant smile. "Tomorrow."

He grinned in return, released her hands, stepped back, and picked up his bags. She moved to the door and her scent drifted around him. Gardenias perhaps?

She grabbed the door handle, then paused and looked at him. "I too had a lovely evening, Jack. I'm not sure I have ever had an evening as, well . . ."

"Promising?" It was the first word that came to mind.

She stared at him for a long moment, then slowly nodded. "Yes, I do believe you're right."

She smiled and pulled open the door. Cold air flooded in and with it a female voice.

"Oh, good. We were just about to ring the bell."

Theodosia sucked in a sharp breath and her face paled. "What are you doing here?"

"Good Lord, Theodosia, is that any way to greet your mother?" An older lady swept into the entry followed by a man of about Jack's age juggling several pieces of matching luggage. "Do hurry with those, Simon," Lady Sallwick said in a commanding tone. "It's far too cold outside to linger and I don't wish to catch a chill."

"Wouldn't want that," Simon muttered and hurried through the door, managing to shut the door behind him with his foot.

"Simon?" Theodosia stared. "What?" Her eyes narrowed. "Mother, explain yourself."

"It's really very simple, dear." Lady Sallwick began pulling off her gloves. Of indeterminate age she was an attractive, petite blonde with delicate features. It was obvious that at one time she must have been truly beautiful. She was shorter than Theodosia, and the resemblance to her daughter was vague but evident nonetheless. Especially in the determined set of her shoulders and the glint of annoyance in her eyes. "Simon came for a visit. Aren't you going to greet him properly?"

"Of course." Theodosia nodded at the other man. "Good evening, Simon. Lovely to see you again." Her tone was polite enough and just shy of being curt.

"Theodosia," Simon said with a smile. He set the bags down and took a step toward her.

She ignored him and turned toward her mother. "Simon's presence was not an explanation."

"I daresay I am not the one who should be explaining herself." The older woman's gaze flicked over Jack as if she was assessing his worth and found it lacking. "He is handsome enough, I'll give you that." Her gaze shifted to the bags in his hands. "I dearly hope this isn't as bad as it looks. Why, what will poor Simon say?"

Poor Simon looked as if he wanted to say any number of things but was wise enough to keep his mouth shut.

"Well?" The countess's brows drew together in a forbidding manner. "Go on, Theodosia, explain yourself. Who is he and what is he doing here?"

"Good evening," Jack said in as pleasant a manner as he could muster and set down his bags.

The older lady gasped. "And he's American!"

"This is a matter of a simple misunderstanding, nothing more significant than that," Theodosia said through clenched teeth. "Mother, allow me to introduce Mr. Jackson Channing. Jack, this is my mother, Lady Sallwick."

"A pleasure to meet you, Lady Sallwick," Jack lied.

"Hmph." Lady Sallwick was a good half-foot shorter than Jack and yet was still able to somehow look down her nose at him.

"And this is Mr. Simon Winslow. Or rather . . ." A pained expression crossed Theodosia's face. "Lord Sallwick. My cousin."

"Mr. Channing." Sallwick nodded.

"Lord Sallwick." Jack nodded in return.

So this was the cousin Theodosia's mother wanted her to marry. Not at all the ogre Jack had expected. In fact, he seemed a nice enough sort and might well be considered somewhat handsome. He was a few inches shorter than Jack with dark brown hair and regular features. Still, even though the man had scarcely opened his mouth, Jack took an immediate dislike to him.

"I'll ask you again, Mother." Theodosia's eyes narrowed. "Why are you here? And why is Simon carrying your luggage?"

"Not just mine, Simon's are in the carriage." The countess glanced around the entry. "A bit stark to my liking but it will do, I think."

"What will do?" Theodosia glared at her mother.

"There was something of a problem at the house," her mother said coolly.

"A fire," Simon said.

"A flood," Lady Sallwick said at the same time, then cast an annoyed look at Simon. "First, there was a fire, and in putting out the fire, there was a flood. It was quite dreadful, especially as it happened shortly after Simon arrived."

"Shortly after you received my note saying I was staying at Lady Hargate's house, I suspect."

"One in the same, dear." Her mother smiled in a satisfied manner. "Needless to say, the house is uninhabitable for the time being."

"You could have gone to a hotel." Theodosia's hands

clenched at her sides. "There are any number of suitable hotels where you would be quite comfortable."

"Goodness, Theodosia, and what would you have said then?" Lady Sallwick shook her head in a chastising manner. "Good hotels are not cheap. And I am trying my best to watch what I spend."

Theodosia snorted in disbelief.

"Besides, I knew Lady Hargate would be most hospitable to the family of her dearest friend so we came here." She raised a brow. "You're not going to throw us out, are you?"

The look on Theodosia's face said she would like to do exactly that. Instead, she drew a deep breath. "No, of course not."

"I didn't think so. In spite of evidence to the contrary"— she slanted a sharp look at Jack—"I did raise you properly. Besides, Simon has something to ask you." She cast an annoyed glance at the other man. "Go on, Simon, ask her."

The other man's brow furrowed. "Now?"

"Yes, now," the countess said sharply. "There's no time like the present and apparently"—she nodded at Jack—"no time to lose."

"This is not how I wanted to do this." Simon glared at the countess. "I don't think it's at all approp—"

"Oh, don't be a ninny." Lady Sallwick huffed. "Just do it."

"Mother." Apprehension sounded in Theodosia's voice. "I warn you. Do not push me too far."

The countess ignored her. "Go, on Simon. Do it. Now."

"Very well then," Simon snapped. He squared his shoulders and met Theodosia's gaze. "Theodosia Winslow, would you do me the very great honor of becoming my wife."

"Excellent," Lady Sallwick murmured with a smug smile.

Theodosia stared at her cousin. For an endless moment silence hung in the entry.

Jack hadn't known her for long but he already knew her well enough to know she would not wish to hurt this man's feelings. And he knew as well she would not be forced into a marriage she didn't want. Still, her mother had pushed her into an awkward spot and escape seemed impossible. Surely, someone should do something . . .

What would his father do?

Sympathy and regret mingled with resolve in Theodosia's eyes. She drew a deep breath.

At once the answer struck him.

Theodosia Winslow needed a hero. A knight, a man to ride to her rescue. Well, by God, if a hero was what she needed, a hero is what she would have.

"Simon," Theodosia began in a firm but gentle manner. "I don't think—"

"Lord Sallwick," Jack interrupted. "What Lady Theodosia is trying to tell you, in as kind a manner as possible, is that she can't marry you."

"Jack!" Theodosia stared at him. "What are you doing?"

"Yes." Lady Sallwick glared. "What are you doing?"

He ignored the older woman. "I'm saving you from an awkward situation."

"Mr. Channing." Simon frowned. "I daresay this is none of your concern."

"On the contrary, this is very much my concern," Jack said in his best vice-presidential voice. "You see, Lady Theodosia cannot accept your proposal because . . ." He flashed Theodosia a triumphant smile. "She has already accepted mine."

Chapter Twelve

Theodosia's eyes widened and her mouth dropped open, then promptly shut as if she was about to say something but thought better of it.

Lady Sallwick gasped. "She what?"

"Your daughter has agreed to be my wife." Jack stepped to Theodosia's side and took her hand. "And we have never been happier."

"Ecstatic," Theodosia said, her eyes glazed with shock.

"She doesn't look ecstatic. She looks . . ." Lady Sallwick's eyes narrowed. "Surprised."

"Of course she's surprised," Jack said smoothly. "I only proposed a few minutes ago."

"And . . ." Theodosia drew a deep breath. "We hadn't planned on telling anyone quite yet."

Her mother's suspicious gaze slid from her daughter to Jack and back. "I don't think this is at all—"

"Congratulations," Simon said with a genuine smile and what might have been a touch of relief. "To both of you." He stepped forward to shake Jack's hand. "Well done, Mr. Channing. You should know you are getting a wonderful woman."

"Thank you. I am well aware of that." Jack shook the other man's hand. He might like Simon after all.

"Theodosia." Simon turned toward her. "I can't say I'm not disappointed. I have always been more than fond of you and I thought we would have suited well together." He took her hand and raised it to his lips. "I do wish you all the best."

"Thank you, Simon," she said with a weak smile. "I am sorry."

"Don't be," he said. "Things have a tendency of working out the way they are supposed to in the end."

"Not in my experience." Lady Sallwick glared. "Aren't you going to fight for her?"

"No, Aunt Adelaide, I'm not," Simon said firmly. "Theodosia has made her choice and it's obvious to me that she is indeed happy."

Lady Sallwick scoffed. "There's more to life than happiness, young man."

Simon met his aunt's gaze directly. "Pity." He turned to the others. "Now, as my bags are still in the carriage, I shall take my leave and head for a suitable hotel."

"And perhaps you can find a footman to bring my bags to my room." Lady Sallwick heaved a resigned sigh. "Although, it does now seem pointless."

"Pointless, Mother?"

"Well yes," She smiled in an innocent manner. "You see, I packed all these bags thinking repairs would take a very long time but, just as we were leaving the house, I was informed that all would be set to rights in no more than three days."

"Informed by whom?"

"By the butler, of course. Jacobs managed to hire additional help to take care of the problem."

"Then the damage was not as bad as it sounded?" Theodosia asked.

"It certainly could have been much worse. And believe me, I am thanking God that it wasn't. Now then," her mother said in a brisk, no-nonsense tone. "Which room should I take?"

"Whichever one you want, Mother. Although it seems you did not fully read my note. I said I was staying here to facilitate the rehiring of Lady Hargate's staff." Theodosia smiled pleasantly. "So I'm afraid there are no footmen."

"No footmen?" Lady Sallwick stared in disbelief. "Why, we might as well be staying in a hovel in the forest."

"It's not as bad as all that, Mother. And it's only for three days remember."

"I'll take her bags up," Simon said abruptly, obviously realizing the sooner he had Lady Sallwick settled, the sooner he would be free. He collected the luggage and started up the stairs.

"Thank you, Simon." Lady Sallwick raised her chin in a haughty manner and followed him.

Theodosia waited until the footsteps and voices faded up the stairs, then turned to him. Her voice low and intense, her eyes blazing. "What have you done?"

He grinned. "Why, I believe I have rescued you from an exceptionally awkward situation."

"You *rescued* me?" She could barely choke out the words.

"You may thank me later." Although he suspected she wouldn't.

"I am not going to thank you at all." She stared in disbelief. "I didn't need to be rescued."

"On the contrary." He shook his head. "It seemed obvious to me that you did."

"So you took it upon yourself to . . . to . . . to *interfere?*"

"I prefer *intervene*. And most successfully I might add."

"I don't care what you call it, it was not necessary," she said sharply. "I was perfectly capable of handling Simon without any assistance from you."

"Were you?" He raised a brow. "And what precisely did you have in mind?"

"I didn't have anything specific in mind." She waved off his question. "I was simply going to say that while I did appreciate his offer, I had no desire to marry him." She paused. "As nicely as possible of course."

"I doubt that there's any nice way to tell a man you don't want to marry him."

"I would have thought of something," she snapped. "Short of telling him I was engaged, that is."

"While you might have thought of something, I doubt that something would have been up to the task of avoiding hurt feelings. Which I assume, you wished to do."

"Of course." She sniffed. "Simon is not only a relation but a very nice man as well. Even though I have no desire to marry him, I certainly don't want to offend him."

"Let me tell you what would have happened had I not stepped forward."

"Oh, yes, Mr. Channing." She folded her arms over her chest and glared at him. "Do tell me what would have happened had you not taken it upon yourself to complicate my life."

"Had I not rescued you, you mean."

"That's not at all what I mean but please go on." Her eyes narrowed. "I can't wait to hear your assessment of what might have happened."

"Very well." He clasped his hands behind his back and slowly circled the perimeter of the foyer.

"What are you doing?"

"I always think better when I pace." He paused in midstep. "Does it bother you?"

"Yes! I'm not at all comfortable with someone circling me like a hungry tiger stalking his dinner."

"Sorry," he said and resumed pacing. "It seemed to me that, while you might well have thought that at some point

Simon—" He glanced at her. "Do you mind if I call him Simon? Or should I refer to him as Lord Sallwick?"

"I don't care what you call him!"

"Simon it is then." He was annoying her but he couldn't seem to help himself. It was a great deal of fun. Especially as it made her eyes flash and her cheeks flush. He wondered if she knew how magnificent she was when she was angry. And damn near irresistible. Odd, he'd never imagined an angry woman would be either magnificent or irresistible but perhaps passion was passion, no matter what its source. "After all I am engaged to his cousin."

She scoffed.

"As I was saying, Simon's proposal, here and now, took you completely by surprise. Did it not?"

"Well, yes," she admitted reluctantly. "My mother's doing entirely, really. It was obvious that the moment she saw you . . ." Her voice hardened. "The moment she saw you she realized there might be another man on the horizon so it was imperative that Simon act immediately."

"Stake his claim as it were?"

"I'm not at all sure I like that analogy but it does seem accurate. Furthermore, one could say this was entirely your fault."

"Simply because I was here?"

"Yes." In spite of the vehemence in her voice, the look in her eyes said even she knew her charge was not on solid ground.

"I disagree that I am to blame . . ." He circled her slowly. "However, if I was, it would be up to me to remedy the situation, don't you think?"

"Not necessarily."

He cast her a skeptical look.

"Perhaps. I suppose." She sighed. "Possibly."

"As I was saying, Simon's proposal was unexpected and

unless I'm wrong—" He stopped and smiled innocently at her. "And do tell me if you think I'm wrong."

"Oh, you may count on it."

"No matter how hard you tried to be kind, you were about to say something that would have wounded the man's pride at the very least. His heart at the very worst."

"I don't think—"

"There is no good way to tell a man you don't want to marry him." He shook his head. "No, indeed. Regardless of the reasons behind a proposal, it's far better to let him think your affections lie elsewhere than to lead him to believe the objection wasn't to marriage but to him."

"And you know this because you have been in this situation?"

Had he? Lucy had never actually turned down his proposal because he had never actually proposed. With the not-so-subtle encouragement of their parents they had both simply assumed . . . Good Lord. Had Lucy realized this long before he had? And why hadn't she mentioned it to him?

"No, Theodosia, I haven't. But I don't have to fall from the roof to know that even if it doesn't kill me, it's going to hurt like hell."

"Well, yes, I imagine it would." She thought for a moment. "What are we to do now?"

"What do you mean, now?"

"I mean now that my mother thinks we're engaged?"

He paused. "I hadn't considered that."

"You hadn't considered it?" Her voice rose.

"Not really."

"Don't you think you should have?" Astonishment widened her eyes. "Shouldn't you have thought this through? Wouldn't it have been better to have a plan rather than boldly leaping forward?"

"In hindsight perhaps but I liked boldly leaping forward," he said firmly. "I don't think I've ever done anything before without giving it due consideration. Although I did decide to come to England on little more than impulse—"

"Jack!"

"There was no time to consider the consequences, Theodosia. Simon proposed. You were about to break the poor man's heart—"

"I doubt that."

"You might say I rescued him as well."

"Let's *not* say that."

"Immediate action was called for." He set his chin in a determined manner. "And action I took."

She stared in disbelief. "You're proud of what you just did, aren't you?"

"Yes, I am." He grinned.

"Don't you understand—"

"I understand that I hear your mother and Simon returning." He shook his head. "And I understand this will be even more complicated should they suspect you and I are not the blissfully engaged couple we appear."

She choked.

Lady Sallwick led the way back down the stairs. "I have a few questions for the two of you."

"Yes, Mother." Theodosia heaved a long-suffering sigh. "I imagine you do."

"As much as I would like to hear the answers," Simon said, edging toward the door. "I think it's best if I took my leave."

A few minutes later, Simon escaped for lack of a better word. Jack envied the man. But apparently if one was going to rescue a fair maiden, one was going to have to face the consequences. And the dragon.

"Now then," Lady Sallwick began the moment the door closed behind the other man. "Where did you meet? Who is your family? How long have you known one another? What is your income—"

"Mother!" Horror sounded in Theodosia's voice and a blush washed up her face.

"It's quite all right, Theodosia," Jack said. "Your mother has only your best interests at heart."

Theodosia scoffed. "*My* best interests?"

"Of course I do." Lady Sallwick paused. "Why, I know nothing about this man aside from the obvious. He's an American. His apparel is of good quality. He's not unattractive—"

Jack flashed her a grin. "I believe you said I was handsome enough a few minutes ago."

Amusement shone in her eyes but her expression remained cool. "Did I?" She shrugged. "I don't recall."

He laughed.

"There is nothing amusing about this, young man," the older woman said in a hard tone. "You intend to marry my daughter and there are any number of assurances I need before I . . ." Her brow furrowed. "Channing, did you say?"

"Mother." A warning sounded in Theodosia's voice.

Lady Sallwick ignored her. Her eyes widened with realization and she gasped. "You're the American everyone is talking about. You're Basil Channing's son, aren't you?"

"You needn't make it sound like an accusation, Mother." Jack nodded. "I am."

"The one raised in the wilderness by wolves?"

Theodosia groaned.

"You've met my mother then?" Jack said lightly.

Lady Sallwick ignored him as well and continued to stare. Jack could almost see the cogs and flywheels of her mind turning like a fine Swiss watch. "Then you're the Earl of Briston's heir."

"So it would appear."

"I see." Her eyes narrowed slightly, her perusal ongoing although Jack was fairly certain she was no longer seeing an American caught in what might be considered a compromising situation with her daughter but rather the future.

Theodosia was right. He hadn't thought this through. "How . . . perfect."

Theodosia stared at her mother. "Perfect, Mother?"

"Yes, of course." Her mother nodded firmly. "This is a brilliant match, Theodosia. In spite of the circumstances we find ourselves in at the moment." She cast a chastising look at her daughter. "Which I am willing to believe are completely innocent despite appearances."

"Completely, Mother," Theodosia said in a resigned tone.

"He is exactly the kind of man you should marry. Well connected, heir to a respectable title, and even if one didn't know the financial resources of his family, one can tell just by looking at him that he is not lacking for funds."

Jack's brow rose. "Then I meet with your approval?"

"Oh my, yes." Lady Sallwick beamed and held out her hands to him. He promptly took her hands in his. "Welcome to the family, Mr. Channing."

Jack grinned. "Thank you, Lady Sallwick."

"You have my heartiest congratulations and my blessing."

"Thank you." Jack tried to pull his hands away but the older woman held fast.

"I cannot wait to announce your engagement."

"No." Panic shone in Theodosia's eyes.

"Not quite yet," Jack said quickly.

Lady Sallwick frowned and dropped his hands. "Why on earth not?"

"Well . . ." Theodosia nodded at her mother. "Explain it to her, Jack."

"Very well." Explain what? "It's really quite simple." He struggled for an acceptable reason. Or any reason.

"Yes?" Lady Sallwick's brow arched upward.

"An announcement at this time would be, oh, premature," Jack said.

"I assumed that much. What I don't understand is why." Suspicion sounded in the older woman's voice.

"It just seems best to me . . ." he began. "To us that is . . ."

"Yes?" Lady Sallwick prompted.

"Well . . ."

"Out with it, Mr. Channing."

"Yes, Jack." Theodosia's tone was pleasant enough but there was a distinct gleam of revenge in her eyes. "Out with it. After all, my mother deserves to know the truth."

"And I wouldn't dream of keeping it from her." At once the answer struck him. "Or any mother, for that matter. Lady Sallwick, as a mother, surely you can understand why we don't want to announce our engagement to the world until I am able to inform my own mother and the rest of my family. As she and my grandfather reside in New York, and given the slow nature of mail between our two countries, it will take several weeks. So you can see why I am reluctant to announce our engagement publicly until I hear from my family."

"Very good, Jack," Theodosia said under her breath and favored him with an admiring smile. "Nicely done."

"You do have a point, I suppose," Lady Sallwick said.

"Beyond that, my aunt, Lady Briston, is planning a grand ball on New Year's Eve to, well, introduce me to their friends and society as a whole I suppose. In fact, Theodosia is handling the arrangements."

"A coming-out party of sorts." Lady Sallwick nodded. "Excellent idea." She glanced at her daughter. "Why didn't you tell me about this?"

"My apologies, Mother." Theodosia shrugged. "I thought I had."

"I would have remembered if you had. Goodness, it isn't every day a new heir—"

"And it did seem to *us*," Jack continued, "that there would be no better time than that to announce our engagement."

"Yes, I can see that." Lady Sallwick thought for a moment, then nodded. "That would be most appropriate and completely unexpected. It would add a lovely element of surprise to the evening. People would talk about it for months. It would certainly go a long way toward everyone's acceptance of you as well. Why, I think it's a splendid idea. Simply splendid."

"Thank you," Jack said modestly. "But it was Theodosia's idea."

"Excellent plan, my dear girl." Lady Sallwick cast her daughter an affectionate smile. "But then I always knew you were a clever child."

"Thank you, Mother," Theodosia said wryly.

"Now then, I believe I shall retire for the evening." Lady Sallwick heaved a weary sigh. "It's been a most exhausting day what with all the surprises, good and bad."

"Oh, then Simon's visit was a surprise?" Theodosia asked.

"Of course it was." Her mother shrugged. "Oh certainly, I've been inviting the man to come for some time but I had no idea he would make an appearance today."

"That together with the fire," Jack began.

"And don't forget the flood," Theodosia added.

"I would never forget the flood." Her mother sniffed. "The flood was the worst of it. All that . . . water."

Theodosia glanced at Jack and he resisted the urge to grin. It was obvious neither of them believed her mother.

"Ah well. If Simon had come when I first invited him perhaps things would be different now but I can't say I'm disappointed. And he may well be right." Lady Sallwick cast them a brilliant smile. "Perhaps things do have a tendency to work out the way they are supposed to in the end after all." She nodded and started back up the stairs. "I shall leave the two of you to say good night." She glanced back at them over her shoulder. "You are leaving now are you not, Mr. Channing?"

"I was on my way out the door when you arrived."

"See that you remain on that path." She continued up the stairs. "Good evening, Mr. Channing."

"Good evening, Lady Sallwick."

Theodosia's gaze followed her mother. "She didn't used to be like this," she said softly. "Before Father died she was really quite pleasant and oh, easygoing I suspect is the right term for it, even a bit flighty. She never seemed to have a care in the world. Now, she feels the need to control everything around her, especially me."

"*Extremis malis extrema remedia,*" Jack said quietly.

"Extreme remedies for extreme ills? Desperate measures for desperate times?" Theodosia nodded, then her eyes narrowed. "What do you mean by desperate times? Our times are certainly not desperate."

"Maybe they are for her, with your father dead and the loss of the family title. Her life, her expectations changed entirely. That would be enough to scare anyone, I would think." He shrugged. "Perhaps all she wants is for her life to return to the way it was."

"Unfortunately, the only way to get what she wants is for me to make an appropriate match." Her tone hardened. "I have no intention of marrying at all let alone simply to better our lot in life. Nor am I a prize to be auctioned off to the highest bidder."

"Oh, but you are." He took her hand and raised it to his lips. "A prize, that is."

"And I thought I was a gift."

"You are both a gift and a prize."

"Goodness, Jack." She pulled her hand from his. "Don't think you can charm your way out of this."

He gasped in feigned dismay. "I would never . . ." He grinned. "Is it working?"

"Perhaps a little." A reluctant smile tugged at the corners of her mouth.

"Ah well, then." He shook his head in a mournful manner. "I shall have to do better."

She laughed, then shook her head. "At least you have bought us some time."

"Time?"

"To come up with a way out of this mess and do it without gossip and scandal. I have managed to avoid scandal thus far in my life but it hasn't been entirely easy." She shuddered. "And I really would prefer not to lose another fiancé, thank you very much."

"Another what?"

"It's not important at the moment." She waved off his question. "What's important is that the New Year is still five weeks away."

He drew his brows together. "I'm not sure I like my fiancée calling our engagement a mess."

"Nor would I if it was a real engagement preceded by a genuine proposal. As it is not . . ." She shrugged.

"Of course not." He ignored an immediate stab of something that might have been disappointment. Or regret. "I shall see you tomorrow then."

"Tomorrow? Oh no." She shook her head. "That will never do. Not with my mother here. She'll be watching us like a bird of prey ready to pounce on a field mouse."

"Then I shall play the dutiful fiancé," he said staunchly. "We do have to decide on a course of action. Perhaps we could go for a stroll in the park?"

"It is dreadfully cold and wet for a walk in the park."

"Well then . . ." He thought for a moment. "An inside stroll at the British Museum perhaps. Or a gallery."

"Not a bad idea, really," she said thoughtfully. "It's not at all unusual for me to go to a gallery or museum in the afternoon without benefit of a chaperone. But I don't know . . ."

"We do have to convince your mother we are a legitimately engaged couple."

"I suppose but . . ."

"Besides, you did promise me your assistance and I still don't know my dukes from my counts."

"England has no counts," she said dryly.

"See? I need your help."

"Apparently." She nodded. "Very well then, Jack, tomorrow it is. And tonight I shall try to come up with a way to dissolve our engagement before it all gets out of hand."

"And we wouldn't want that."

"No," she said firmly, "we would not."

He leaned closer and spoke softly in her ear. "I would kiss you again if I wasn't concerned that your mother might appear at the top of the stairs at any moment and demand that I marry you at once."

"Why, isn't that the most interesting thing, Jack." She turned her head and gazed into his eyes, her lips close to his. "Even with my mother at the top of the stairs, I am fairly certain I would kiss you back."

His gaze slipped to her lips and the memory of how delicious they felt against his washed through him. "I do hate to miss that."

"As do I."

"I should go."

"I believe you said that earlier this evening and yet here you are."

"I know." He studied her for a moment. "It appears I find it remarkably difficult to leave you."

"Oh." The word was little more than a sigh. "My . . ."

"And yet . . ."

"And yet . . ." She drew a steadying breath and took a step back. "Good evening, Jack."

"Good evening, Theodosia." He smiled and again picked up his bags.

She opened the door and he stepped out into the night.

"Jack."

He turned back to her. "Yes?"

"I didn't need to be rescued but thank you for doing so nonetheless."

He grinned. "It was entirely my pleasure."

"I know." She smiled and closed the door.

Jack inhaled the cold, sharp air and grinned. Try as he

might, he couldn't keep what was obviously a ridiculous, self-satisfied grin off his face. Why, one might think he was actually engaged to the magnificent Lady Theodosia Winslow.

In truth, he was practically, almost engaged to Miss Lucinda Merryweather. His step faltered. No, given all she said to him he had every right to consider himself free. Still, he should make certain he had not misunderstood. He would write to Lucy at once.

In the meantime, he was the fraudulent fiancé of the most fascinating woman he'd ever met. She was an intriguing mix of stubborn self-reliance and concern for propriety. She was indeed an adventure and for one moment, whether she admitted it or not, he'd been her hero. It was enough to make any man grin like an idiot. Even though they were now both in an awkward situation fraught with all sorts of complications and the possibility of scandal, he didn't care. He was thoroughly enjoying himself and he would be her hero again if necessary. There was something about coming to the rescue of the fair Theodosia that was exhilarating and exciting and . . . right.

He did indeed have a great deal to be thankful for tonight.

Even if some of it wasn't entirely real.

Chapter Thirteen

The following day,
The British Museum . . .

". . . and so," Teddy continued, "I do think this is the best course. We continue this farce of an engagement until after Christmas and then—"

"Christmas?" Jack slanted a thoughtful look at her. "I'd almost forgotten about Christmas."

"Nonsense, how can you possibly forget about Christmas?"

"I don't know." He smiled and turned his attention back to perusal of the sculpture of some Egyptian deity or king or a rat catcher for all Teddy knew or cared. She suspected he hadn't forgotten at all. He struck her as the kind of man who would use Christmas as the perfect excuse for extravagant and delightful surprises. Even if she wasn't really his fiancée, it was a lovely idea.

She and Jack had been wandering the Egyptian galleries at the British Museum for a good half an hour now but it was nearly impossible to drag the man's attention away from remnants of a long-dead civilization to discuss the very pressing matters of the here and now. She had no idea bankers were so fascinated by antiquities but then she suspected Jack was not a typical banker. No, he was the son of the dashing, adventurous Colonel Channing and with every passing day, the similarities in mannerisms and character between father and son grew stronger. She had no idea if Jack was actually changing or if his father's influence was bringing a part of himself long buried at last to the surface.

"Christmas is a month from today, Jack, and you do need to give it some attention."

"Do I?"

"Of course you do." She huffed. "You are staying in England for Christmas, unless you've changed your mind."

"No, I intend to stay until the New Year." He moved away from a huge granite torso of Ramses II, according to the placard, to a black granite seated figure, apparently also of Ramses II.

"Have you given any thought to gifts for the family? Or at least for your father?"

"I have no idea what to give a father for Christmas." He shook his head. "Do you?"

A thought struck her and she stared at him. "Have you written to your mother that you'll be here for Christmas?"

"I think so." He shrugged. "I really can't recall."

"Jackson Channing." She resisted the urge to stamp her foot. "What on earth is wrong with you today?"

"Nothing that I can think of. Why? Have you noticed something?"

"Yes! You haven't paid a bit of attention to anything I've said. Furthermore, you're not behaving at all like the rational, responsible banker that you are."

"You mean the stodgy, straitlaced banker that I am."

She ignored him. "Instead you're acting like a—"

His brow rose. "Like a what?"

"I don't know exactly but it's most disconcerting."

He chuckled. "My apologies then." He paused. "I'm

simply in excellent spirits at the moment. My father tried to hide it but it was obvious that he was pleased by my return last night." He glanced at her. "I have you to thank for that."

"You're quite welcome."

"And he has promised not to occupy my every waking moment. I have yet to hear from my mother." He cast her a chiding look. "And while I haven't written to her directly, I have written to my grandfather as is the responsible thing to do."

"Good."

"Furthermore, as you have reminded me, Christmas is only a month away. I have always loved Christmas."

"Everyone loves Christmas, Jack. I would be quite disappointed in you if you didn't."

They moved to the next ancient sculpture, yet another depiction of Ramses II.

"I used to write to him at Christmas. My father, that is."

She started. "But you thought he was dead."

He nodded. "I know."

"I thought it was Father Christmas children wrote to."

"No, in that you English are wrong. They write to Santa Claus," he said firmly, then paused as if debating whether to continue. "When I was very young I began writing to my father at Christmas instead of Santa Claus. No one ever talked about my father, you see. He was never mentioned. In my mind, he was every bit as mythical and magical as Santa. So I started writing to him." He chuckled. "Even as I grew older and knew how silly it was, I would write, one letter a year. Telling him about my life, what I had done in the past year, what I was thinking, what I wanted. I would catalog an entire year in that letter. It became my own private Christmas tradition. My life is chronicled in those letters." A self-conscious smile quirked a corner of his lips. "I said it was silly."

"It's not the least bit silly. It's quite touching and very sweet," she said softly. Her heart twisted for the little boy who wrote to a father he never knew. "And this will be your first Christmas together."

"I am both looking forward to it and a little apprehensive. As a boy, I always wanted to have a father for Christmas. Now that I do, well . . ." He blew a long breath. "I've never told anyone about those letters." His brow furrowed and he considered her curiously, as if she were a puzzle he was trying to solve. "You do make me say the oddest things."

She stared at him for a moment, then grinned. "Excellent."

He laughed. There was something about the way the man laughed that melted her heart and warmed her soul. Utter nonsense, of course.

"Now then, Jack, we need to—"

"I am well aware of what we need to do but at the moment, I am thoroughly enjoying the lost treasures of one of the greatest civilizations man has ever known." He took her hand and tucked it in the crook of his arm. "With my beautiful fiancée by my side. What man wouldn't be in excellent spirits?"

"I am not your fiancée," she said firmly, but smiled all the same. "And about that, we do need to decide on a plan."

"Do we? And I thought you already had." He chuckled and they moved to the next granite statue of Ramses II.

"Goodness, Jack." She frowned at the ancient work. "Is Ramses II the only king worthy of acknowledgement?"

He laughed. "No, but he is regarded as one of the greatest rulers in Egyptian history. Didn't they teach you that at Miss Bicklesham's?"

"Probably, but it's obviously slipped my mind. I am far more concerned with what is happening in London today than in Egypt thousands of years ago. And I do wish you would be more concerned about it as well." She cast him an accusing frown. "You haven't paid the least bit of attention to anything I've said."

"On the contrary, my dear Theodosia." He directed his words to her but continued to study the figure of the dead king before them, as if Ramses II had the answer to questions Jack had yet to ask. "You said we should continue to behave as if we are engaged until Christmas. You further said I should give you a Christmas gift that is entirely wrong for you, which would be the beginning of the end as it would indicate we scarcely know each other well enough to marry." He glanced at her. "Quite shallow of you really to discard me simply because I choose the wrong gift."

"I can be extremely shallow or at least I used to be," she said. "Besides, I can't think of anything else. In very many ways you are perfect for me. If I was interested in marriage," she added quickly.

"So . . ." He glanced at her. "What exactly might I give you that would be entirely wrong?"

"Anything to do with birds." She shivered. "I realize it makes no sense but all that flocking and gathering and watching. I find them rather . . . ominous."

"Birds?"

"Yes," she said firmly. "And I detest feathers, specifically peacock feathers. I know they're very popular on hats and fans and whatnot but I can't abide them." She leaned close and lowered her voice. "When I was very young, I got the absurd image of a featherless peacock in my head, I'm still not sure how. A large, angry, featherless peacock. I swear whenever I see one of those birds it looks as though it is plotting revenge on all those women foolish enough to wear feathers they have no right to."

"Peacock feathers it is then." He grinned. "So to continue on with your plan, in the days after Christmas we begin with little disputes, small disagreements, minor things that build until, the day of the ball, we tell your mother we have had a change of heart and have decided we do not suit after all."

She stared. "You were listening to me."

"Every word." He chuckled. "But I do have a question. It might even be a flaw in your plan."

She scoffed. "I doubt that."

"What happens then?"

"When?"

"After you and I end our engagement, won't your mother still try to convince you to marry Simon?"

"Probably." Her jaw tightened. "But I have no intention . . ." She turned and met his gaze firmly. "You told me your secret."

"Did I?" Caution sounded in his voice.

She nodded. "About the letters to your father."

"Yes, of course," he murmured.

"May I tell you a secret of mine?"

"I can't think of anything I'd like better than to hear your secrets." A wicked twinkle shone in his eye.

"No doubt," she said under her breath and led him to a marble bench along one wall of the gallery. She sat down and gestured for him to join her.

"When my father died . . ." This was harder than she'd thought. Dee was the only other person who knew this and even she didn't know all the details surrounding her father and her late fiancé's illicit financial dealings. There were some things one didn't tell even one's closest friend. But Jack was remarkably easy to talk to and it seemed, well, right to confide in him. She wasn't sure why she knew that and preferred not to question it. Still, it wasn't easy. She clasped her hands together in her lap. "After his death, I discovered he had been deeply embroiled in something rather unsavory. An investment of sorts that went horribly awry. Exposure was apparently imminent. If his heart hadn't failed when it did . . ." She shuddered. "He might well have gone to prison. If there was anything fortunate about his death it's that it ended any further investigation and any possibility of scandal." She smiled weakly. "But then Father always did appreciate a twist at the end of a play."

Father hadn't been a bad sort, a villain, as far as she knew but then she hadn't really known him as anything other than a kind but distant figure. Of course, it would have been different had she been born male. How very ironic that the girl her father seemed to have little use for was now responsible for cleaning up the mess he had left behind. And wouldn't he have loved that particular twist?

She drew a calming breath and continued. "I'm not sure if he had financial difficulties before his involvement or if his situation was the end result. It scarcely matters now, I suppose. There were debts as well. The consequences of all this are that . . . well . . ." She drew a deep breath. "We were left, not entirely penniless, we did keep the house in London, but other than that . . ." She wrinkled her nose. "Penniless is as good a word as any and more accurate than most."

"I see."

"So, my mother's and my little enterprise is indeed a business but one that would never survive if society realized that we needed the income. That we weren't just dilettantes playing a game of commerce in our spare moments. Our commissions would vanish." She shook her head. "Poverty, Jack, is a very great sin here among people with titles and power, even greater than scandal. But scandal too would destroy us."

He nodded.

"While my mother has yet to face the fact that our world as we knew it is gone forever, I have recently accepted that life will never be as I expected it. And I believe it's time to embrace my new life." She raised her chin. "I am a woman of business, Jack. An independent woman of business. And while it wouldn't be at all wise for me to acknowledge that publicly, I have at last acknowledged it to myself. I intend to stand on my own two feet and make my fortune with my business. And I further intend to be the most exclusive and successful planner of wedding and society events in England."

"To prove to the world that you can?"

"No, to prove it to myself." She searched for the right words. "A woman like myself is raised with certain expectations. That ultimately she will be a good wife, a good hostess, a good mother, a good Lady Whomever. Her training and education is with those goals in mind. No one, including herself, imagines for even a moment that she might deviate from the course set for her. So she does tend to question if that which is expected of her is all she is able to do. And . . ." Her tone hardened. "I need to know that I can indeed accomplish what I have set out to do."

"I see." He nodded. "There's more though, isn't there?"

She nodded. "Last night I gave this a great deal of thought along with our predicament. Given the events I have scheduled between now and the end of the year, and including my fee for coordinating your aunt's ball, I shall finally be able to pay off the last of Father's creditors. Fortunately, those who lend credit or money to the aristocracy in this country are quite patient and discreet as long as one makes regular payments. You have no idea what a sense of freedom just the thought brings to me."

"I can imagine."

"I don't believe you really can but thank you for the sentiment. Once Father's debts are no longer hanging over us, my mother might give up her quest to find me a perfect match. Or at least temper it. I have accepted that our lives have changed. Now she has to. And then, while I still have no intention of allowing the world as a whole to know the truth of my business, I intend to put my foot down with my mother. About marriage and my future." She cast him a wry smile. "I'm not sure one can be an independent woman without standing up to one's mother."

He considered her thoughtfully but didn't say a word.

"Well?" she said at last.

"Well," he said slowly. "I was wondering if you were going to tell me."

She narrowed her eyes. "You don't seem surprised."

"I suspected something of the sort although you do hide it well."

"Thank you." She paused. "How did you know?"

"Small details, minor things that probably go unnoticed for the most part to most people. But I am a banker and as such, I'm well used to dealing with people whose finances aren't quite what they want the world to believe."

She sighed. "Go on."

"Are you sure?"

"Better to know than not to know, I think."

"As you wish." He studied her for a moment. "No woman of means would allow her clothing to be anything other than pristine and your gowns are just a shade worn. Not shabby, mind you, but definitely not perfect."

She nodded. "And?"

"And your mother has an air of desperation about her that has nothing to do with securing a good marriage for you. And you chafe at any suggestion that your life might not be as it appears." He leaned closer and met her gaze firmly. "Furthermore, you work entirely too hard for someone who is simply playing at business."

"Oh." His comments weren't at all easy to hear but she couldn't deny the truth of them. Maybe it was indeed time to set aside her pride and borrow some of Dee's clothes, at least until she could replenish her own wardrobe. As for the rest of it, there was nothing to be done about her mother although for the first time in a long time this morning her mother had seemed somewhat less tightly laced than usual. "Thank you, Jack. I shall do better in the future."

"I'm sure you will." He chuckled. "As for our charade . . ." He reached into his waistcoat pocket and pulled out a small jeweler's box. "You should probably wear this."

"Jack!" Her gaze skipped from the box to his eyes and for an instant her heart stuttered at the look she saw. Obviously, she was mistaken. As he'd said, this was only a charade.

"Take it."

"I couldn't possibly."

"Of course you can." He opened the box, and took out a gold ring adorned with a large opal encircled by diamonds.

"Jack!" She stared at the ring and he slipped it on her finger. "It looks so . . . so . . ." She held out her hand and the diamonds flashed in the light, the opal shimmered like crystal fire. "Perfect." She fairly sighed the word.

"You don't think it's too large? Too pretentious?"

"Goodness, Jack." She scoffed. "Did your mother teach you nothing? A quality gemstone can never be too large. And, as long as it's real, it can never be considered pretentious."

He chuckled. "I bought it this morning and I can assure you, it's real."

"Still . . ." Reluctantly, she pulled her gaze away from the flashing brilliance on her hand. "This really wasn't necessary."

"If we're to carry off the deception and fool your mother it is. She might get suspicious if there was no ring, no token of my affection."

"And God knows what she might do then. At least she has agreed to abide by our request not to say anything until we're ready to announce our engagement."

"A lot can happen in five weeks." A warning sounded in his voice.

"I know."

"However, I can think of nothing I would like better than to play the role of smitten fiancé."

"You don't have to be smitten you know," she said with a smile. "Attentive will do."

"I can be both. Besides, being with you is a legitimate reason why I am not with my father."

"Oh dear." She drew her brows together. "I hadn't thought of that. What will you tell your father?"

"The truth, of course. That I am spending time with the

enchanting Lady Theodosia in an effort to assist her on matters of a financial nature regarding her . . . hobby."

"He's certain to suspect something."

"Possibly." Jack shrugged. "But I doubt that he would say anything. I don't think my father is who we should be concerned about. Should my aunt or my cousins or anyone other than my father learn of this engagement—"

She shuddered. "We'd be trapped."

He raised a brow.

"Not trapped exactly," she said quickly. "But it would be extremely difficult to explain. And there would be a certain amount of scandal should our ruse become public."

"I suppose one never thinks of the possible repercussions when one performs an act of heroism," he said somberly but laughter lurked in his eyes.

"Obviously one of the downfalls of being a hero." She cocked her head to one side and considered him. "Still, it does seem to suit you."

"Yes, indeed. Nothing like a stodgy, straitlaced hero." He grinned, got to his feet, then offered his hand to help her up.

"You're not, you know." She stood up and met his gaze firmly.

"What?" He smiled. "Stodgy and straitlaced or a hero?"

"You certainly aren't stodgy and straitlaced and in spite of what you've said, I don't think you ever were." Without thinking, she reached out and straightened his necktie.

He caught her hand and at once she realized how shockingly intimate her gesture was. And realized as well it had seemed completely natural.

"You don't?" He stared down at her.

A voice in her head urged caution. She had decided upon a course for her life and he played no part in it. Nor did she want him to. They had become friends and friends was all they would be, in spite of dreams late in the night when he was so much more than merely a friend.

"No, I don't. A man doesn't change who he is deep down inside. I think stodgy and straitlaced was no more than a chapter in your life you are now moving past. And whether I wished it or not, you were indeed my hero." That annoying, rational voice of reason faded, overcome by the louder thud of her heart. "And I suspect, if we were truly to be married . . ." Her gaze locked with his. "You always would be."

Chapter Fourteen

One week later,
The residence of Lady Hargate . . .

"I have a confession to make." Jack smiled down at Theodosia in the foyer of his cousin's house where he was just about to quite properly take his leave.

"Oh good, another confession." Theodosia grinned up at him. "I have grown quite fond of your confessions."

"Have you?" His brow rose. "I wasn't aware I had made enough confessions for you to have grown fond of them."

"You, Jackson Channing, are a veritable treasure trove of secrets all waiting for you to confess. Or . . ." A wicked smile lurked in her eyes. "For me to uncover."

"I suspect we all have secrets, Theodosia. Even you."

"Oh my, yes, Jack." She pulled off her gloves and tossed them onto the table by the front door. "I too am filled with secrets just waiting to be revealed. Although, as you are the one confessing at the moment, I shall say no more. I will only tell you that my secrets are extraordinarily ordinary."

"I can't imagine anything about you being ordinary," he said in an overly gallant manner, even if it was nothing but the truth.

At his insistence, he and Theodosia had seen each other

every afternoon for the past week, with the exception of two days when she was preparing for a party for Lady Someone-or-Other. After all, if they were to play the part of a happily engaged couple, they should make a good show of it. They agreed afternoons were best for their purposes. If they appeared together in the evening, there was bound to be talk about the two of them. What had begun for her mother's benefit had evolved into something entirely different, even if Jack wasn't sure exactly what that was. They were friends certainly but beyond that . . .

"Now then, your confession?"

The problem was he wasn't sure what he wanted them to be. But with every passing day he was more and more convinced a mere friendship with the lovely Theodosia Winslow would soon not be nearly enough.

"I would never want my father to know this." He lowered his voice in a confidential manner. "But seeing the sights of London with you has been far more enjoyable than seeing them with him."

"You're right," she said solemnly but her eyes twinkled. "The colonel would be most humiliated to know that he has failed as a tour guide."

"I wouldn't say failed exactly. He is extremely knowledgeable about history and the significance of assorted monuments and statues as well as the architectural influences on nearly every important structure in the city. You, on the other hand . . ." He shook his head in a chiding manner. "I didn't want to say it but you might want to brush up on your knowledge of the important sights of London."

"I can't believe you would make such a comment." She gasped in mock indignation and pulled off her cloak, absently handing it to the new footman. "Why, I've shown you all sorts of things most visitors to London never so much as hear about."

"I suspect there's a reason for that."

She ignored him. "Tell me, Mr. Channing, did I or did I not

point out to you the very fountain where a marchioness and her friends, who really should have known better, frolicked wearing little more than their underpinnings to win a wager?"

"Indeed you did."

"And did I not indicate the gallery window where a highly provocative painting of a duke, sans clothing and dignity, was displayed albeit with appropriate draping?"

He nodded. "You did."

"And did I not show you the public corner where a well-known opera singer declared his love in song for a long-married countess? Or the bookstore where a famous poet threatened to shoot himself if the object of his affections—and his poetry—did not return his love?" She paused. "Although admittedly, he wasn't nearly as famous before his public declaration of affection and threat of suicide as he was after. I have always been rather surprised that any number of little-known poets didn't try their hand at spectacular yet stupid similar feats simply to increase their notoriety."

"All right, you win. Again." He laughed. "A tour of the scandalous sights of the city was every bit as interesting as the more usual places."

Her brow arched upward. "Only every bit?"

"I stand corrected." He grinned. "Anything of prurient interest is always far more intriguing than, well, than anything else."

"You are a wicked man, Mr. Channing."

"Thank you, Lady Theodosia. I suspect you have a distinct wicked streak as well."

"Simply one of my secrets," she said in a lofty manner. "Yet another is that I can be quite persistent."

"That's really not a secret."

"You must admit, places of mild notoriety have not been the sum of our sightseeing. Didn't we also go to the Crystal Palace? As well as the Grosvenor and the Society of Lady Artists galleries? Did we not climb to the top of St. Paul's?" She crossed her arms over her chest. "Well?"

"And don't forget the Tower of London and Soane's Museum."

"Oh, I would never forget them. Being the excellent tour guide that I am," she added primly.

"That, my dear Theodosia, is only one of your charms."

"I know." She grinned, then shook her head. "I must say, I never imagined how fun it would be to see the sights of my own city through the eyes of someone who has never been here before."

It had been fun, every minute of it. And informative in ways he never would have expected.

Amidst paintings of pastoral settings or churning, storm-tossed seas at one gallery, he discovered she enjoyed the peace of the country but much preferred the excitement of the city. And he confided there was nothing he liked better than standing on the shore of an ocean and gazing out into forever. At which point she had accused him of being alto-gether more romantic in nature than any banker had a right to be. At an exhibit of ancient coins, she mentioned that she and her mother had discreetly disposed of nearly all their valuable jewelry. He had then sworn to himself that, at the end of their *engagement,* he would not allow her to return his ring. And he had admitted to her that he had once invested a considerable amount of money in a scheme to raise a sunken Spanish galleon laden with treasure in the West Indies. It was not the sort of responsible investment expected of him, which was precisely why he had never told anyone about it. His rev-elation only strengthened her charge that he did indeed have a romantic nature.

With every passing day they grew closer and it grew harder to keep in mind that there was nothing real about their relationship except friendship. It was particularly hard when she took his arm and the heat of her body by his side urged him to pull her into his embrace. It was especially difficult when the faint scent of gardenias wafted around him when she leaned close to share an observation and he'd wonder if her lips tasted as good as he remembered. Nor was it easy to remember when they were not together and the vaguest sense of something missing lingered in his mind or possibly in his heart. It was a sensation at once enticing and daunting. And confusing.

"I do believe I have a new appreciation for it all," she said. "And I thank you for that."

"Perhaps someday I can return the favor," he said casually. "Show you everything there is to see in New York."

"I'd like that."

"So would I." He gazed down into her eyes. He should take his leave for the day but each day he was more reluctant to do so. He spent evenings alone with his father at Channing House or at one of his clubs or at some gathering of his father's friends and acquaintances. She attended to her business pursuits in the evening as well as those social events she was obligated to appear at as part of keeping up the pretense that her father's death hadn't changed her financial circumstances.

Today, as he had everyday they'd been together, he wanted nothing more than to kiss her again. He hadn't done so since the night they had become embroiled in their fake engagement, her mother's fault entirely. Before Lady Sallwick returned to her own house, she took it upon herself to make certain Delilah's residence was fully staffed once again. The end result being that, even now, there was a footman in the foyer and a new butler probably lurking just out of sight.

Jack would have given a great deal to be completely alone with Theodosia, if only for a minute. After all, how could he possibly be expected to sort out his feelings if they didn't have the chance to be by themselves now and then? He tried to ignore the memory of how her lips had felt pressed against his, how her body had molded and melted into his as if they were halves of a never before united whole, as if it was . . . right.

Silly, absurd thoughts, of course. What had gotten into him? They were friends, nothing more.

He cleared his throat. "And what famous or infamous sights of London do you have in store for me tomorrow?"

"I shall have to check our list." She paused. "I do realize what you're doing, you know."

"Aside from fulfilling my responsibilities as a dutiful fiancé?" He shook his head. "I have no idea what you're talking about."

"Goodness, Jack, I know your father has taken you to many of the same places we have been together. I know you're just feigning interest so as not to offend me as I am trying very hard to be an excellent guide."

He laughed. "And you are succeeding admirably."

"I'm glad you're enjoying yourself, especially since you're only doing this to keep my mother's suspicions at bay." She smiled up at him. "I'm enjoying myself as well. Jack, I—"

"Yes?" he said, trying to hide a distinct note of eagerness in his voice.

She glanced at the footman standing by the door, tactfully pretending not to notice them, and sighed. "Nothing."

Vague disappointment stabbed him and he forced a pleasant smile. "I shall see you tomorrow then."

"Tomorrow." There was a faint hint of wistfulness in her voice. His heart ached in recognition.

"Good day, Theodosia."

The footman opened the door and Jack stepped over the threshold.

"Good day, Jack." Theodosia's voice drifted after him and then the door closed with a firm snap.

Damnation, it seemed he was always saying good-bye to her. And he didn't like it. Not one bit.

Perhaps, a voice that sounded suspiciously like his father's murmured in the back of his head, he needed to do something about that. Perhaps he needed to decide if indeed friends was all he wanted them to be. Perhaps he needed to determine exactly why the woman lingered in his mind and in his dreams.

Regardless, he had time. Until he came to England he couldn't remember ever putting off a decision before. But there was no need to decide anything about the future until the New Year. Between now and then, he could simply enjoy learning about his father's world and relish the delightful companionship of the charming Theodosia.

Still, even though every day spent in each other's company drew them closer, there did indeed remain secrets between them.

She never mentioned the fiancé she had referred to once in passing and he never worked up the courage to ask. And he never managed to tell her about Lucy or that he wasn't sure if he wished to take up the reins of the Earl of Briston and stay in England permanently. Apparently he didn't have the courage to do that either.

What kind of hero refused to reveal his greatest dilemmas to the woman who was becoming more and more important in his life?

And what kind of fair maiden had secrets?

Teddy smiled at the young footman and made her way up the stairs. It was far better to smile than to succumb to the urge to scream in frustration.

Jack wanted to kiss her, she could see it in his eyes. But the man was far too, well, polite perhaps to simply grab her and do the deed. Which made no sense whatsoever. He'd done it before, after all. Twice! And both times it had been . . . unforgettable.

It wasn't as if she didn't want him to kiss her. Surely he realized that. Why, hadn't she given him every signal imaginable save perhaps throwing herself bodily into his arms? She would do so if it came down to it. Admittedly, there had been no real opportunity. No moment when they weren't in public or there weren't servants about. Her mother had seen to that.

No, that really wasn't fair. Teddy sighed and turned into the parlor. Her mother had, for once, been trying to make Teddy's life a bit easier. It was both unusual and thoughtful. And touching as well. There had been a time when she and her mother had been quite close. But then Father had died and Teddy's fiancé had been killed soon after and they had discovered the disastrous state of their finances and, well, Mother had changed. They both had, really. Lady Sallwick and her daughter had once been content and carefree. If they worried about anything at all it was the color of a new gown or which invitation to accept. They never concerned themselves about such things as debt repayment and ledger sheets and bank statements.

Perhaps her mother's newfound thoughtfulness was because she no longer seemed so frightened. Odd, that Teddy hadn't realized it before Jack had raised the idea. But Teddy had now lived up to expectations and snagged a future husband who was everything her mother had ever wanted. And was once everything Teddy had ever wanted as well.

She stepped into the parlor and crossed the room to the cabinet where Dee kept her favorite Scottish whisky. Teddy poured a healthy glass and took a long sip. The spirits burned her throat and took her breath away. Her eyes watered and she coughed twice, then drew a deep breath. A liking for good Scottish whisky was, to Teddy's way of thinking, not an entirely bad thing.

She sank down onto the sofa, her glass in one hand, and studied the opal ring on the other. And what if he did kiss her? Where might that lead? Jack was not the kind of man who would seduce a woman and then not expect her to marry him. And marriage was not what Teddy wanted. Not now.

But why couldn't *she* seduce him? She took another sip of her whisky. She certainly wouldn't expect marriage if she seduced him. It was definitely something to consider although she'd never seduced a man before. Nor did she have a great deal of experience with seduction. Of course she had succumbed to Cyril's seduction, not the wisest moment of her life. How hard would it be to turn the tables? To be the seducer instead of the seduced? Still, given Jack's honorable nature, who knew what might happen then. Nonetheless, it was something to consider.

Voices echoed up from the front entry and a moment later determined steps sounded on the stairs. Obviously those of a woman. Teddy braced herself. She wasn't at all sure she was up to talking to her mother this afternoon. Nor did she wish for her mother to find her with a glass of hard spirits in her hand. Besides, weren't they supposed to attend a play together tonight? Why she was here now did not bode well. Her mother wasn't—

Dee burst into the room. "What have you done?" she demanded waving a newspaper at Teddy. "And why wasn't I the first to know?"

Chapter Fifteen

At very nearly the same time,
Channing House . . .

"Is something wrong?" Jack settled back on the leather sofa in the library and studied his father.

"I wouldn't say wrong exactly." The colonel swirled the whisky in his glass.

Jack and his father had taken to meeting in the library before dinner for a glass of whisky or brandy, depending on the day and their respective moods. Tonight it was good Scottish whisky. Since they had been spending more time apart, their time together had become more meaningful. Jack was completely at ease in his father's company now and was fairly certain his father felt the same, especially as his overwhelming enthusiasm at having a son had mellowed. Jack wondered if the older man had at last realized his new-found son was not going to vanish into thin air.

It had turned into a pleasant ritual, this daily meeting of father and son. In the dim light cast by the low-burning gas lamps, surrounded by books and ancestral portraits, the spacious Channing House library was warm and intimate. Here it was easy to forget that the bonds between child and parent were still tenuous. That this tradition of sharing a drink in the evening was new and hadn't grown between father and son through the years. There was something about the smell of ancient volumes and aged leather and freshly polished wood that had always soothed Jack's soul and eased his spirit. Indeed the libraries of the London house and Millworth Manor were the places where Jack felt most at home, as though he truly belonged. In those rooms a man could embrace the past while still looking toward the future.

Theodosia would look right in this room, natural and at ease. He could almost see her here. Standing near the fireplace, with a glass of wine in her hand, the room lit with the glow of the fire, low and seductive, wearing little more than a wicked look in her eyes and a smile—

"However, there is a matter I do wish to discuss." His father seated himself in one of the supple leather wing chairs that flanked the sofa.

Jack's attention jerked back to his father. Where on earth had that vision of Theodosia come from? Not that it wasn't an extremely interesting image . . . He cleared his throat. "I suspected as much."

"Did you?" His father's brow rose. "Have we grown to know each other that well already?"

"So it would appear." Jack smiled. "And you have the definite look of a man who isn't certain how to proceed with whatever it is he is determined to do."

His father scoffed. "No I don't."

"Oh, but you do. Besides . . ." Jack nodded at his father's hand. "You absently tap your finger against your glass or on a table or whatever is handy when you're apprehensive."

The colonel stared at his hand. "Bloody hell." His gaze shifted to his son's. "Remind me never to play cards with you. Again. Is that how you beat me the other night?"

"No, I was just better than you." Jack grinned. "And oddly enough, you don't do it when you play cards. Or chess."

"Well, that's something." He took a deep swallow of his whisky. "You're very perceptive."

"I have to be." Jack shrugged. "I'm a banker. I need to be every bit as attuned to a man's character as I am to his accounts and balances and debts. I also have to be as alert to what he doesn't say as what he does. If you can't tell a genuine story from something completely fabricated then you will fail in the financial world. When it comes to both profits and, well, morality, for lack of a better term."

"I didn't realize morality was a requirement in banking," his father said idly.

"We're not all Ebenezer Scrooge, you know." Jack chuckled. "Although admittedly it is hard to admire those in a profession where the assets of men fallen on hard times are routinely seized for back payments." He shook his head. "It's not an easy thing to do, putting the interests of an institution over those of an individual. At least it's never been for me. However, I know any number of men in my profession who seem to have no difficulty with that aspect of it at all. It's part of the responsibility of the position. You do what's expected of you, even if it's something you don't particularly like. And you try to make it less painful for all concerned." He paused. "I always thought it was in my blood, you know. It was what I was expected to do and I never really questioned it. Now, I wonder. My grandfather is president of the bank and my great-grandfather one of its founders. But at this point I'm no longer sure if it suits me at all."

"Did you ever think of pursuing another profession?"

"When I was a boy, I wanted to be a pirate." Jack grinned. "Or a treasure hunter."

His father chuckled. "It's something to consider, not being a pirate of course, but whether you wish to resume your position with the bank."

"I do seem to have choices." And hadn't Theodosia said he could be or do anything he wanted?

"I've always thought of myself as being fairly good at taking the measure of a man." A casual note sounded in his father's voice. "I thought you and I were getting on well together."

Jack frowned. "We are."

"Good." The older man got to his feet and crossed the room to refill his whisky, returning with the decanter to top off Jack's glass. "Do you think it's odd that a man in his fifty-fifth year would still live in his family's house?"

"I think it's odd that such a question would come to mind."

"Its just something that has occurred to me of late."

Jack sipped his drink. "It's a very big house."

The colonel smiled. "And that was a very diplomatic answer." He set the decanter on the table by the arm of the chair, settled back into his seat, and glanced around the room, affection in his gaze and his words. "Between this house and the manor, I never saw a need for a separate dwelling. Through the years, I've never stayed in England for more than six months at a time I think. I've spent more of my life in other countries than I have here. There's much to be said for returning to a place you've considered home for all of your life. I might have felt differently had I had a family of my own."

"And a wife?"

"As it turned out that I had a legal wife all these years, another would have been awkward." He paused. "Do you think your mother really would have had me arrested if I'd married again?"

"I'd like to say no but . . ." Jack shrugged. "If I've learned nothing else since meeting you, I have learned that I don't really know my mother at all. So I wouldn't put it past her."

"You should write to her, you know."

"How do you know I haven't?"

The colonel raised a skeptical brow. "Have you?"

"Not directly. Quite frankly, I don't know what to say."

"Are you still angry with her?"

"I'm not as furious as I was initially." Jack thought for a moment. "In some ways I can almost understand why she didn't tell me about you." He glanced at his father. "I might well have tried to find you, you know."

"Thank you, Jack." His father smiled.

"And I can see why she wouldn't have told you about me. That doesn't excuse it, of course. I do think she was truly scared of losing her only child. But . . ." Jack shook his head. "I haven't been a child for some time. I'm not sure I can ever forgive her for this." He met his father's gaze. "Can you?"

"I don't know." He thought for a moment. "I do know that I have many regrets when it comes to your mother."

"That you married her or that you let her leave you?"

"Mostly the latter. I never would have let her leave if I had known about you." Father raised his glass to his son, then took a sip of his drink. "Seeing her again, well, it makes one think."

"Oh?"

"How different our lives might have been. Why I never found another woman I wished to marry, that kind of thing. Don't misunderstand me," he added firmly. "I have never believed in the concept of soul mates or one true love or any of that sort of balderdash. Or at least I didn't."

"And now?"

He considered the question. "Plato wrote that originally men and women were one creature but their strength threatened the gods. So Zeus split them in half and each half spends its life tying to find its mate. To become complete once again." He shook his head. "Rubbish of course. Still, it is something to ponder."

"Do you think Mother is your soul mate?"

"I just said the very idea is absurd."

"But the thought has crossed your mind."

"I suppose it has. Just one of many things that have filled my head recently. Another is your future, of course." A deceptively casual note sounded in his voice. "I gather you have doubts about returning to the bank."

"On the contrary, Father, I'm fairly certain my banking days are over." Even as he said the words he realized the truth of them and a weight lifted from his shoulders. He had been content enough as a banker, he'd never questioned his role in life or his future. Upon reflection it now seemed that he had been doing little more than marking time, waiting for something to happen even if he hadn't realized it at the time. Now his entire life had changed. And content was no longer enough.

"But you've made no decision yet about whether you might stay in England and accept all that goes along with the title of earl?"

"Not yet." He studied his father. "Does it matter? When I decide, that is?"

"I suppose not." His father shrugged. "I would imagine Nigel has a good number of years left in him, as do I. No need to decide anything at the moment." He swirled the liquor in his glass, then adopted an overly casual tone. "It is entirely up to you, of course."

"And I do appreciate that you haven't pressured me about this. Even though I know what you would prefer."

"I won't lie to you, Jack. It's been bloody hard not to try to press my case. But I do realize this is not a simple matter of choosing between a life as a banker and a life as an earl. In many ways, it's also a choice between countries and between families."

"My mother would neither understand nor accept a decision on my part to stay in England." He smiled wryly. "Nor would she accept that it's not her decision to make."

"You do realize it doesn't have to be either or?"

"I realize that." He paused. "She won't."

"The last thing I want is for you to make a choice that isn't right for you." His father shook his head. "I'd rather have a son who is happy with his life, whether that life is in America or here, than one who feels trapped by circumstances beyond his control."

Jack met his father's gaze. "I never doubted it for a moment."

"And I am here for any sort of, oh, I don't know, guidance or advice. Sage wisdom if you will. I have learned a few things along the way, you know."

Jack laughed.

"Particularly about women. Not your mother admittedly," he added quickly, "even though I suspect I learned a great deal from her. But rather about women in general."

"Good to know."

"Still, as I said, your decisions are yours and yours alone although . . ." His father hesitated and again Jack had the distinct impression that something was wrong. "You might want to talk it over with Lady Theodosia first. It's been my experience that women don't like a man to make decisions that affect his future without even mentioning it to them."

"True enough," Jack said slowly. "But it really doesn't have anything to do with her."

"Not this minute, of course, but in the future."

"The future?"

His father nodded. "After you're married."

Jack choked on his whisky. "After we're what?"

"After you're married," his father said. "Which is exactly what I wanted to talk about." He rose to his feet and paced. "You're older than I was when I married your mother and hopefully wiser."

Jack stared. Did he know about the engagement or was this just speculation on his part? According to Sam and Gray, Lady Briston had brought up the idea of a match between Jack and Theodosia more than once.

"God knows I'm not one to give advice on marriage. And Theodosia is a lovely young woman but don't take this step unless both of you are completely certain."

"I shall keep that in mind," Jack said cautiously.

"And, well, I know we haven't known each other for long and I know I have no particular right to ask for anything but . . ."

He drew his brows together in annoyance. "I would be most appreciative if the next time you decide to do something significant in your life, I was not the last to know. I felt like a complete idiot today when I ran into an acquaintance and he congratulated me on your engagement."

Jack winced. That was that then.

"And I don't even want to think what Bernadette will do when she discovers you have upstaged her grand gala."

"I thought it was my gala."

"You, dear boy, are little more than an excuse." His father scoffed. "There is nothing my sister-in-law likes better than having a legitimate reason for a social gathering of outrageous proportions that will serve to heighten her reputation as a hostess and make all her friends jealous."

Obviously, he was going to have to tell his father the truth.

"Father, there is something—"

"And it's no good thinking that she hasn't heard about this. I daresay everyone in the country knows by now."

Jack stared. "How would everyone in the country know?"

The colonel stared back. "It was in the *Times,* in one of those society notices. I never read that kind of drivel myself but apparently in that I am quite alone."

Jack stifled a rising sense of doom. "There was an announcement in the papers?"

"Not an official announcement, more of a knowledgeable mention." The colonel studied his son. "You look surprised."

"Shocked, actually." Jack shook his head. "No one was supposed to know about this."

"I daresay someone would have noticed about the time you reached the altar."

"We're not reaching the altar." Jack drew a deep breath. "We've only been playing the part of a happy couple. Theodosia has been showing me around London in the afternoon to make our relationship look genuine. We thought by avoiding evening appearances as a couple we could avoid any speculation about the two of us."

His father shook his head. "I'm completely confused."

"Our engagement isn't real, Father. I told her mother we were engaged to save Theodosia from an uncomfortable dilemma."

"I can't imagine anything uncomfortable enough to spur a feigned engagement."

"The man who has inherited her father's title asked her to marry him, prompted by her mother. Theodosia has no desire to marry him."

His father frowned. "So she's marrying you instead?"

"No." Jack shook his head. "I simply rescued her from an awkward situation."

"Let me see if I understand this," his father said slowly. "You saved Theodosia from an awkward situation by putting her in an even more awkward position?"

"I wouldn't have put it quite that way."

"Is there a better way to put it?"

"None that I can see," Jack said under his breath. "I'm afraid I didn't think about the consequences. I simply acted. She needed help, or at least it seemed to me she did, and so I did what I thought needed to be done."

His father stared at him for a long moment.

"Well?"

"I'm not sure what to say." His father's forehead furrowed. "On one hand it was very gallant of you."

Jack nodded. "I thought so."

"On the other . . ." His father chose his words carefully. "You do realize that there is the very distinct possibility you could actually end up married?"

"No." Jack scoffed. "I doubt that this will . . ." He widened his eyes with realization. "I could, couldn't I?"

The colonel studied him closely. "You don't seem overly concerned about the prospect."

Was he? He certainly hadn't considered that possibility.

Could he really end up married to the beautiful, intelligent, independent Lady Theodosia?

"Jack," his father said thoughtfully. "Do you realize you're smiling?"

Jack's gaze jerked to the other man's. "No, I hadn't but . . ."

His father's eyes narrowed. "Dare I take this to mean you are not opposed to the idea of marriage to the lovely Lady Theodosia?"

"I hadn't really considered it but . . ." Jack grinned. "I guess I'm not opposed to it. Not at all. In fact, I like the idea."

"And does she?"

"She says she's not interested in marriage but every woman wants to marry," Jack said staunchly. Except perhaps a woman who was determined to prove she could succeed on her own.

"I've known Theodosia since she was a girl. I would say she is not at all like every woman."

"No, she's not."

"Which is exactly what makes her so . . . special?"

"Only one of many reasons, Father," Jack murmured. And hadn't he already noticed? Hadn't the woman already invaded his dreams and, even tonight, crept into his waking thoughts as well?

He certainly could use their situation to his advantage if indeed he wished to marry Theodosia, although he'd never be a party to forcing her into marriage. That was not the way to start a life together. And, regardless of what he might want, there was the question of what she wanted. The resolve in her eyes when she'd confided about her financial difficulties and her determination to build her little business enterprise was not something he suspected she'd willingly give up. Still, he had time. They had told her mother they'd announce their engagement at the New Year's Eve ball and that was still four weeks away. And who knew what might happen in a month?

"So what do you intend to do?"

"Nothing." Jack shook his head. "Not a thing."

"Don't you think you should do something?"

"Probably but as nothing comes to mind doing nothing seems like the most prudent course." He sipped his whisky and thought for a moment. "It seems to me almost anything I do is going to be wrong. It might be best to let Theodosia guide this farce. At least for now."

"Do you intend to keep playing the part of the smitten fiancé then?"

"Absolutely." He grinned slowly. "I'm enjoying it."

"I can see that." His father paused. "And then?"

"Then . . ." He shrugged. "I have no idea."

"I suspected as much." His father studied him for a moment. "And here I thought you were the sort of man who never did anything without due consideration and a great deal of thought."

"Apparently I've changed. I like the idea of letting things unfold as they will, at least for now."

His father shook his head. "You'll never win the hand of the fair Theodosia by letting things simply unfold."

"Perhaps not." He grinned. "But I might win her heart."

"Possibly but no battle was ever won without a certain amount of preparation. Even fate needs a helping hand on occasion. And what you need, my boy . . ." Father grabbed the decanter and refilled both glasses. "Is a plan."

"You're going to have to have some sort of plan, you know," Dee said thoughtfully, sitting beside Teddy on the sofa in her parlor. "Short of actually marrying him, that is."

Not that marrying him would be such a bad thing. The thought sprang unbidden to her mind and Teddy firmly ignored it.

"I had a plan. I had an excellent plan." Teddy poked her finger with disgust at the newspaper Dee had brought. "We specifically asked my mother not to say anything about this."

"How do you know this was your mother's doing?"

Teddy rolled her gaze toward the ceiling.

"You're right, of course." Dee sipped her whisky thoughtfully. "She probably thought if the engagement was publicly announced, Jack wouldn't be able to get out of it."

"Well, she thought wrong," Teddy said firmly. "And Jack's getting out of it is not what I am concerned about."

"All things considered, the man is quite a catch," Dee said in a casual manner. "He's wealthy, his family on both sides is more than acceptable, and he is the heir to a respected title. Besides that, he's not at all unattractive. You could certainly do far worse."

"Thank you." Teddy stared at her friend.

"He really is everything you've ever wanted."

"He's everything I used to want." She paused. "Or rather everything I thought I wanted. Everything I was expected to want."

"He's perfect for you," Dee said mildly.

"My plans do not include a husband."

Dee shrugged. "Plans change."

"Yes, I suppose," Teddy murmured and sipped her drink. Oddly enough, even though the women were on their second glass neither seemed to feel any particular adverse effects. In fact, Teddy felt surprisingly alert. No doubt anger at one's manipulative mother soaked up inebriating spirits like a proverbial sponge. "He does make an excellent fiancé." And wouldn't he make an excellent husband? She glanced at her friend and braced herself. "We've been spending every afternoon together."

"Oh?" Dee's brow rose.

"It's part and parcel of convincing my mother of the veracity of our engagement. There's nothing more to it than that." And there wasn't really. Except for that annoying desire of hers to kiss him again. And the idea of seducing him that had taken root in her head and simply refused to let go.

"No, of course not."

"Don't look at me like that, Dee." Teddy huffed. "I have no intention of marrying your cousin."

"Intentions, like plans, change."

"Not mine," Teddy said staunchly.

Dee smiled a knowing sort of smile.

"Stop that this instant."

"Stop what?" Dee's eyes widened innocently.

"Stop looking like you know something I don't."

"I daresay I know any number of things that you don't." Dee smiled smugly.

"Do you wish to share?"

"I do so adore sharing."

Teddy sighed. "What do you think you know that I don't?"

"I know that you like Jack."

Teddy snorted. "That's not something I didn't know. He's a very nice man. Only a fool wouldn't like him. He's clever and amusing and extremely thoughtful."

Dee glanced at the ring on Teddy's finger. "So I see."

"And very, oh, interesting, I would say."

"You like him a lot."

"Of course, I like him a lot. I said he was a very nice man but there's far more to him than meets the eye. And he's going to a great deal of trouble to help me even if this whole mess was his fault." She cast an annoyed look at the other woman. "There's no reason not to like him."

"You didn't like him at all when you first met him."

"Actually, when I first met him I liked him well enough." Indeed, there was an element of something that might well have been magic upon their first meeting. "It was after I discovered who he really was that I felt somewhat, I don't know, deceived I suppose."

"I see."

"That was more my fault than his." Teddy sighed. "He's

not Cyril and it wasn't at all fair of me to react the way I did. I don't think Jack would ever deliberately lie to me."

"Then you trust him?"

"Yes," Teddy said thoughtfully. She hadn't realized it before but she did indeed trust him. There was something about the man that was most trustworthy. "I suppose I do."

"How very interesting."

"And?"

"And nothing." Dee sipped her drink. "I just think it's interesting that you're willing to trust him. I didn't think you'd ever trust another man again."

"It's as much trusting myself as it is trusting him."

"Well, there are worse ways to begin a marriage than with trust."

Teddy laughed. "I'm not going to marry him."

"So you've said." Dee paused. "What are you going to do now?"

Teddy considered the question for a moment, then shook her head. "Nothing."

"What do you mean nothing?"

"I mean we had a perfectly good plan. I see no reason to change it simply because my mother has mucked it up."

"Then you will continue your engagement until the ball?"

Teddy nodded.

"And call it off before the announcement?"

"Exactly."

"You do realize while losing one fiancé to death is acceptable, there will be a certain amount of talk when you lose a second."

"There's no way to avoid that."

"You could marry him."

Teddy cast her friend a long-suffering look.

"Oh, I have also been instructed to invite you, and your mother as well, to come to the country next week and stay at the manor through Christmas and the New Year."

"Instructed by whom?"

Dee raised a brow.

Teddy groaned. "Your mother knows."

"My dear friend, perhaps you weren't listening. Everyone knows."

"Christmas is still three weeks away and I am committed to one event each week before then." She shook her head. "I can't cancel, not at this late date. It would ruin my reputation and beyond that, well, it would be a problem, that's all."

Dee studied her closely. "What aren't you telling me?"

Teddy blew a long breath. "These parties, plus your mother's ball, will give me what I need to finally finish repaying Father's debts."

Dee's eyes narrowed. "I thought you had finished with those years ago."

"Precisely what I wanted you to think."

"If I had known, I would have—"

"I know what you would have done and I am eternally grateful to you for that." Her jaw tightened. "But this was my responsibility."

"It was your father's responsibility."

"When he died, it became mine. Tell me, Dee, if I were a man wouldn't I have been expected to pay off my father's debts?"

"Yes, I suppose but—"

"There is no but about it."

"You should have been honest with me."

"If I had you never would have let the matter drop. Every time I saw you, you would have insisted that I allow you to loan me what I needed."

"And you would have put this behind you that much sooner."

"And I would have had to repay you even though you would have resisted that. No." She shook her head. "This was the best way to go about it. And now it's very nearly over and done with."

"Still, you should have told me."

"You didn't tell me when you were in financial difficulties."

"No, but I should have."

"Yes, well, you didn't tell me and I didn't tell you. I would say that makes us even." She smiled. "I know how you are when you get something in your head. You, Lady Hargate, can be extremely stubborn and you would have driven me quite mad."

"Probably," Dee said with a smile and took a sip. "Might I point out no one is as stubborn as my mother. If she wants you at the manor for Christmas, at the manor you will be."

"You simply have to explain to her—"

"Absolutely not." Dee scoffed. "You want to refuse my mother's invitation, you shall have to do it yourself. Besides, she's not merely my mother but she now believes she is your future aunt."

Teddy groaned. "Good Lord."

"Come now, Teddy. Millworth is only an hour by train from London. You can come back whenever you wish to take care of what you need to do. Might I point out, you did exactly that when you stayed at the manor for Camille's wedding?"

"Well, yes."

"And you have always loved Millworth, especially at Christmas. Why, didn't you once tell me there was no better place to spend Christmas than at the manor?"

"I've always felt terribly disloyal about that."

Her own family's country estate, Sallwick Abbey, was ancient, its origins dating back to a fifteenth-century monastery. In spite of rebuilding through the centuries, it still retained a somber, dark presence. Even when she was a child, the abbey had seemed more forbidding than welcoming, whereas Millworth had always felt more like a home than a monument to history. It was little wonder that, when given the opportunity,

Teddy had chosen to spend her holidays with Dee at Millworth rather than at her own family's ancestral home.

"You do realize that Jack will inherit Millworth someday," Dee said in an overly casual manner.

"I was aware of that, yes, but thank you for pointing it out."

Dee grinned. "I do what I can." She sobered. "You know, as a strictly practical matter, this is not a bad time to remove yourself from London." Dee shook her head. "It's not particularly safe at the moment and Lionel fears the unrest is not at an end."

"Don't be absurd. I feel completely safe." Teddy waved off the comment although admittedly Dee had a point.

Teddy was well aware of the rioting last month in Trafalgar Square that had begun as a protest against the appalling state of unemployment. Hundreds had been arrested, scores injured, and there had been at least one death as a result of the clash between protestors and police. She and Jack had discussed it at length and they were in agreement that men who wanted to work should have that opportunity. Jack had a very firm view of that subject, which struck her as unusual for a banker. But then he was an American after all and Americans did seem to have a different way of looking at things.

"And you did agree that you could use a holiday."

"Yes, I did, although deceiving your entire family morning, noon, and night was not exactly what I had in mind."

"Don't be absurd." Dee scoffed. "There is nothing my family likes better than a good farce."

"I don't know . . ."

"Sam and Camille and Grayson will be back next week as well. We shall all have a grand time."

"I don't doubt that but . . ."

"Very well, then. Don't come. Stay in London and manage other people's parties. Alone, comforted only by the knowledge that your obligations to your late father are nearly at an end. I must say it doesn't sound at all like Christmas to me."

Dee heaved an overly dramatic sigh. "Still, I should mention that your intended—"

"He is not—"

"And his father are expected to return to Millworth next week as well. It won't look good if you aren't with him."

"Dee," Teddy said in a warning tone.

"How long did you say Simon was going to be in London?" An innocent note sounded in Dee's voice.

"I didn't." Teddy clenched her teeth. "But you have made your point."

"And rather well, I thought." Dee cast her a smug smile. "I knew you'd come."

"Hmph." Short of confessing all to her mother, did Teddy really have a choice? Now that their engagement had been made public, there would be a great deal of talk if she and Jack were not seen together. In fact, they should now start appearing as a couple in the evening as well. She shook her head. "I had no idea a pretend engagement would be even more effort than a real one."

"But well worth it, don't you think?"

"I suppose I would do nearly anything to avoid continuing conflict with my mother. And she will not rest until I'm married to Simon or someone else." Teddy blew a long breath. "Hopefully, she will see reason when the specter of Father's debts no longer hangs over our heads."

"One can only hope."

"I'm more than hoping, Dee, I'm counting on it."

"I knew you'd see reason." Dee cast her a smug smile.

"However, if I am going to spend the next few weeks at Millworth, I am going to allow you to do something you've wanted to do for a long time."

"And what is that?"

"I'm going to allow you to loan me some of your gowns. And to make you feel even better . . ." Teddy grinned. "I'm going to let you pay for the alterations."

Chapter Sixteen

Teddy sat on the upholstered bench in the corridor outside her usual room at Millworth and paged through her notebook, patiently waiting until the maid assigned to her needs finished unpacking her bag. Although patient wasn't entirely accurate. It was all she could do to sit still. Patience had never been one of her virtues.

She and Jack and Colonel Channing had arrived at the manor an hour or so ago. Her mother would not be arriving until next week, which was something of a relief. It was one thing to carry on her charade of an engagement in front of Jack's uncritical family and quite another under the sharp eyes of her mother. Camille, Grayson, and Sam were expected to dock today and should arrive at Millworth at any time.

As soon as she was able to get into her room she intended to spend a good hour alone going over the plans for Sir Malcolm Hodgett's dinner the week before Christmas although dinner was not as appropriate a term as banquet. The older gentleman had invited no fewer than twenty-three of his closest friends to join him. Elderly, well-connected, unmarried gentlemen were proving to be some of her best clients and as her reputation grew, so did her commissions. Teddy knew full well they were employing her services as much to have a suitable hostess of sorts as anything else. She suspected this particular aspect of her business would not be as successful if she wasn't pretty. Hopefully, by the time her looks had faded, her business would be solid and her appearance would no longer matter.

"Lady Theodosia?" The young housemaid appeared in the door carrying one of Dee's gowns. "Everything is put away. I thought if you wished to wear this for dinner tonight, I would press it for you."

"It's a perfect choice, thank you," Teddy said gratefully.

Teddy and her mother had shared a maid in recent years in an effort to trim expenses and Teddy hadn't had the services of a lady's maid at all since she'd been staying at Dee's house.

"I thought it would go nicely with your hair, my lady."

"Indeed it will." But then Teddy and Dee had carefully selected those gowns that showed Teddy off to best advantage. Not that she wished to impress anyone. It was simply always a good idea to look one's best. "It's May, isn't it?"

"Yes, my lady." May nodded. "If there's anything else you need, please send for me."

"I will." While there was certainly something to be said for fending for yourself, having a maid to help one get ready for an evening was a luxury Teddy missed. "Perhaps you could help me dress for dinner?"

"I'm very good with hair, my lady." May lowered her voice in a confidential manner. "I do hope to be a lady's maid one day, Lady Theodosia."

"I'm certain you'll succeed admirably." Teddy nodded. "I shall see you later then, May."

"Thank you, my lady." May bobbed a curtsy, then hurried off down the hall. It struck Teddy that here was another woman determined to succeed in life. On her own.

She stepped into her room, closed the door, and breathed a sigh of relief. This particular room with its ivory drapes and coverlet, pastel Aubusson rug, and windows that looked out over the back garden had been hers from her first visit to Millworth as a girl and always made her feel as if she had come home. Silly of course. This wasn't her home and never would be. *Unless she married Jack*, an annoying voice that sounded suspiciously like Dee's murmured in the back of her head. She ignored it and sat down at the lady's desk near the window.

If she was going to stay at Millworth, she was going to have to be more organized than usual. Fortunately the plans for the last two events on her schedule before Christmas, Sir Malcolm's dinner and Mrs. Hendrickson's evening of music and dancing next week, really a small ball, were already well in hand. However, as experience had taught her, the success or failure of any social gathering was in the details.

She opened her notebook and spread out her notes and lists on the desk. It took her no time at all to realize she had indeed thoroughly prepared. Aside from some minor odds and ends that she would take care of when she went into London in a few days, both events were under control. But even with her mother's questionable help, Teddy could not manage more than one affair in any given week. She settled back in her chair and gazed out the window, tapping her pen absently on her notebook. After the New Year, when her father's debts were no longer an issue, she could put the money she usually set aside for repayment back into her business. Then she could hire an assistant or two, someone socially connected who needed either distraction or a relatively steady income. Widows perhaps. Just off the top of her head she could think of several widows who had been left with far less than they'd anticipated although they were all excellent at keeping up appearances. With more help, Teddy could handle more events.

Teddy smiled. It was actually Jack's idea. He had suggested

a number of ways to increase her business. The man had an excellent head for figures. But then he was a banker after all.

He was also an excellent fiancé. In the week since their engagement had become horribly public he had gone out of his way to prove what a perfect match they were. Accompanied by her mother or his father or on occasion both they were together nearly every evening that she was not otherwise occupied. They had gone to a rather dreadful play, the title of which mercifully escaped her the moment they left the theater. They had attended a lecture that had held Jack spellbound on the lost treasure of some South American country. There was indeed a lot of the colonel in his son. And even at Lady Wellby's soiree, he had appeared at precisely the moment Teddy had been about to make her obligatory appearance to act as her escort. He was charming and amusing and clever and she couldn't have asked for more in a fiancé—false or true. The man was most impressive. She overheard more than one lady comment on how he certainly did take after his father and wasn't Lady Theodosia fortunate to have snatched him up before the rest of the world even knew of his existence?

Fortunate indeed, even if their engagement wasn't real. The more time she spent with the man, the more she liked him. The more she wished . . . Utter nonsense. She had a purpose for her life and silly romantic notions had no place in it.

Still, she did wish he would kiss her again. And who knew where a kiss might lead?

A sharp knock sounded at the door. It opened at once and Dee burst into the room.

"Please come in." Teddy twisted in her chair to face her friend. "Don't let silly things like a closed door stop you."

"Sam and Camille and Grayson are here!" Dee gasped for breath, shut the door behind her, and leaned back against it, as if to keep something horrible out.

"How . . . nice?"

"Yes, of course." Dee waved off the question. "I'm delighted to see Sam. I can't tell you how much I missed him. And I have promised myself the next time he travels to New York, he shall not be going alone."

"Shouldn't you be with him now?" Teddy asked carefully.

"Without question but you are my dearest friend in the world." Dee raised her chin in a gallant manner. "And I should think by coming to you now, by thinking of your best interests rather than welcoming Sam properly, as both he and I would much prefer, I have proved what a worthy friend I am."

Teddy drew her brows together. "Whatever are you talking about?"

"I'm not entirely sure," Dee said under her breath. "Fortunately neither Mother nor Father is here at the moment, which gives us some time." Dee straightened and met Teddy's gaze firmly. "You, my dear friend, are going to need a new plan."

"What on earth—"

"A real plan, something more substantial than your last plan. *Nothing.*" She huffed. "What kind of plan is *nothing?*" Dee paced the floor. "Mother will be the problem or one of them. Father won't be difficult to manage once Uncle Basil talks to him." She paused. "Does he know?"

"Does he know what?"

"Does Uncle Basil know that your engagement isn't legitimate?"

Teddy nodded. "Jack told him when it became public."

"That's something anyway. It will certainly help."

"Help what?"

Dee stared at her for a moment, then drew a deep breath. "We have visitors or at least we will. They're spending a few days in London before they come here. A surprise visit, Camille said. She told me all this. They met them onboard their ship."

"What are you talking about? Who met whom?"

"Camille, Grayson, and Sam of course."

"And?"

"And . . ." Dee paused, obviously reluctant to continue. "And they met Uncle Basil's wife. Jack's mother. Mrs. Channing."

"Good Lord." Teddy gasped.

"She's apparently come for Christmas. Or to reclaim her son. Camille didn't wish to speculate on that possibility although given some time, I'm certain she will."

"That will certainly complicate matters. Does Jack know?"

Dee shook her head. "He and Uncle Basil are off riding. They weren't here when Camille and the others arrived."

"I should probably find him. He should be warned." Teddy pushed back from the desk and stood. "I would hate for him to be taken unawares. I can't imagine . . ." She narrowed her eyes and stared at her friend. "But you said *them.*"

"Yes, well, Mrs. Channing is not alone."

"Did his grandfather come as well?"

"I don't think so." Dee shook her head. "It's possible I suppose but Camille didn't mention a grandfather. I daresay she wouldn't overlook a grandfather."

"Then who?"

"Mrs. Channing was accompanied by a young woman, a Miss Merryweather. She was introduced as . . ." Dee winced. "Jack's fiancée."

"His what?" Shock coursed through Teddy and her stomach twisted. "His fiancée?"

"Apparently," Dee said weakly.

"His fiancée," Teddy repeated. Surely not. "Perhaps Camille misunderstood?"

"I don't think Camille would misunderstand something like that."

"His fiancée," Teddy said again. Try as she might she couldn't quite grasp the concept of it. Jack had a fiancée? "How could he?"

"How could he have a fiancée?" Caution sounded in Dee's voice. "Or how could he not tell you?"

"Both," Teddy snapped. Anger swept through her along with a stunning sense of sheer betrayal. She turned and paced, fury fueling her steps. "How could he?"

"You said that."

"It bears repeating!"

"I know this complicates the fake engagement between the two of you. And I can certainly understand why you might be annoyed." Dee studied her closely. "But you are far angrier than I expected."

"Of course I'm angry. I'm furious." A voice of reason somewhere in a part of her mind not simmering with rage whispered that Dee was right. Teddy shouldn't be nearly as angry as she was. She ignored it. "I can't remember ever being this angry with a man before in my life."

"Yes, I can see that," Dee murmured.

"Even when I discovered the truth about Cyril, I wasn't this angry." But then hadn't she always suspected that Cyril Goddard was not quite as he appeared? But Jack, Jack was a good man. The kind of man a woman could trust. With her secrets. Or her heart. Or so he had seemed. "The man has two fiancées, Dee. Two!"

"One of them is not exactly—"

"I thought Jack was one of the most responsible men I'd ever met. And trustworthy as well, the cad!" Her jaw clenched. "Obviously I was wrong!"

"I'm not sure that—"

"Bloody hell, Dee. The man's a banker! Shouldn't a banker be a bit too stuffy to have two fiancées?"

Dee stared. "You do realize you're actually not—"

"And an honorable banker at that. Why, he should be entirely too straitlaced and stodgy for this sort of thing."

"He doesn't really have—"

"Two fiancées! Two! What was he going to do? Marry us both?"

"I didn't think marriage—"

"One in America. One in England." She narrowed her gaze. "What if he has one in every country? Who knows how many fiancées he has!"

"Don't you think you're being a bit irrational?"

"You're right." She waved off the question. "He's not well traveled, he's admitted as much. Not that what he says can be taken as the truth."

"Teddy, I—"

"I wonder if he rescued her as well. He does that, you know," she said darkly. "He rescues women who have no need or desire to be rescued. No need or desire for a . . . a hero!"

"I—"

"But then we all need a hero, don't we? Or at least we all want one. Deep down inside where we are weak and vulnerable." She moved to the wardrobe and flung open the door. "Are there still swords hanging over the fireplace in the billiards room?"

"As far as I know."

"Good!"

"Why?"

"Just a thought, nothing important." She grabbed her cloak and slammed the door shut.

"Teddy, this might not be the best time—"

Teddy pulled on the cloak, then realized where she'd heard that name before. "Did you say Merryweather?"

Dee nodded.

"Isn't the name of Jack's bank, Graham, Merryweather and something?"

"I don't remember." Dee stared. "I don't think I've ever seen you so—"

"I daresay it's not a marriage as much as it is a business arrangement." She buttoned her cloak and started for the door. "Which he thinks is perfectly all right. Marriage, he said, has always been a business proposition."

"Does that make it better or worse?"

"I haven't decided yet." Teddy stalked into the hall, Dee right behind her.

"Where are you going?"

"I am going to find Jack."

"What are you going to do?"

"I haven't decided that yet either."

"You're not going to hurt him, are you?"

"Probably not." Teddy reached the top of the stairs and drew a calming breath. "Your family would never forgive me if I did away with the newfound heir to Millworth Manor. And I am fond of your family."

"Do keep in mind that we like him," Dee said. "It would really be such a shame—"

"He'll be fine." Teddy started down the stairs. "I promise not to hurt him. Much," she added under her breath.

"Are you sure this is the right time—"

"I told you, Jack should be warned that his mother and his . . ." She could barely choke out the word. "*Fiancée* are on their way here."

"Yes, of course," Dee called after her. "But who is going to warn him about you?"

"He doesn't need warning about me." She grit her teeth. "He's my bloody hero!"

Jack had known any number of crafty men before but he could now put Colonel Basil Channing at the top of the list. Rather than point out the benefits of being the Earl of Briston as the men rode around the estate, the older man chose instead to concentrate his comments on life at Millworth, on the importance of heritage and family, and how one generation passes on responsibilities to the next. Jack realized his father consistently, but oh so subtly, brought up these particular themes whenever he and his son wandered the estate. Oh, he was indeed a crafty devil.

It was just cold enough today to be invigorating without being frigid but by the time father and son had turned over their horses to the stable hands, both men agreed it was time to share a steaming cup of tea or coffee by a warm fire.

"Isn't that Theodosia?" his father said when they left the stable and started toward the manor.

A female figure strode toward them in a determined manner. Even from a distance, the set of her shoulders and the length of her stride said she obviously had something on her mind.

His father leaned closer and lowered his voice. "I don't want to borrow trouble but . . ."

"I suspect you won't need to borrow it," Jack said under his breath although he had no idea what it might be. He thought all was going quite well between them.

In spite of the fact that there had been no official announcement, their engagement did seem to be universally accepted as fact. Everywhere they went, someone remarked upon what an excellent match they were. He couldn't have planned a better way to be more quickly accepted into English society although he was decidedly uncomfortable with the deceit. Still, as it meant spending more time with Theodosia, it was well worth what was really little more than a white lie.

He was fairly certain his feelings toward her went far beyond friendship even if hers did not. At least not yet. But the more time they spent together, the greater the chance that he could indeed win her heart.

Not now, of course. The closer she came, the more apparent it was that she was not happy about something.

"Did you know there is a distinct flash of copper in your eyes when you're angry?" Jack said with a grin. "It's very becoming." And frightening.

"Excellent," his father said under his breath. "Disarm her before she has a chance to attack."

"I'm not angry," she said sharply, then paused. "Although, I will say, a few minutes ago, I was completely irrational. I have now thankfully come to my senses, perhaps because it's so bloody cold out here."

Jack and his father exchanged glances.

"That's good to know," the colonel said cautiously.

"It's always good when you come to your senses," Jack added.

"I think so." She nodded. "Admittedly I was a bit taken aback when I first heard."

"Were you?" Jack had no idea what she was talking about but he had learned with Theodosia it was wiser to let her say whatever it was she had to say rather than plunging ahead and making a mess of it. Inevitably, he would be wrong.

"Well, furious, really." She drew a deep breath. "But then I realized I have no real claim on you."

He studied her closely. "Perhaps this would be the right time to tell me exactly what you're talking about."

"I'll leave you to it then," Father said. "It's too blasted cold to stand around chatting." He started toward the house.

"I'm afraid this involves you, too," Theodosia said.

His father stopped, a wary look on his face. "Oh?"

She nodded. "It appears we are about to receive some unexpected guests."

"Unexpected guests?" The colonel's eyes narrowed. "Out with it, Theodosia. Who are these unexpected guests?"

She hesitated, then met his father's gaze. "Your wife for one."

Jack stared. "My mother is here?"

"Elizabeth?" His father shook his head as if to clear it. "Are you sure?"

"Unless you have another unknown wife, I would say yes, Elizabeth, Mrs. Channing." Theodosia huffed. "And no she's not here yet. She's in London but is expected to arrive here in a few days. It's a surprise."

"She's never been to Millworth," Father murmured.

Theodosia's expression softened. "Then Christmas is an excellent time for a visit. There are few places lovelier at Christmas than Millworth."

"I should . . ." Father started toward the manor, then

paused. "Thank you for warning me. I would hate to be caught unawares."

She cast him a weak smile. "I thought you should know."

He nodded and again started off.

"She's not here yet, you know," Jack called after him. "Where are you going?"

"To prepare," he said over his shoulder. "Spruce up the place, select the right room, talk to the cook, that sort of thing, whatever is necessary, you know . . ."

"Well, isn't that interesting." Jack chuckled. "My father wants to impress my mother."

Theodosia watched the older man's brisk walk back. "Do you think he still cares for her?"

"Stranger things have happened, I suppose. Although she's certainly not done anything to endear herself to him. She could be coming to apologize, or make amends, but I wouldn't bet on it. My mother rarely acknowledges when she is wrong."

"Perhaps she's coming to drag you back to America."

"I'm not a child, Theodosia." He drew his brows together. "She cannot *drag* me anywhere."

"Perhaps she can't." A deceptively casual note sounded in Theodosia's voice and Jack braced himself. "But perhaps Miss Merryweather can."

Jack's breath caught. "Miss Merryweather?"

"Your fiancée?"

"Lucy is with my mother?"

Theodosia folded her arms over her chest. "Awkward, isn't it?"

He studied her for a long moment. A dozen thoughts ran through his head. This was obviously what Theodosia was so upset about. She had no need to be. Even if he and Lucy had once planned to marry, her parting words made it very clear she considered him under no obligation to her. Of course, he'd had no response yet from the letter he'd written to her but unless he was terribly mistaken he was free to do as he wished.

"Well?"

"Well . . ." No, Theodosia had absolutely no need to be angry and yet it was obvious from the look in her eye and the set of her chin that she was. For a fake fiancée to be so angry at the sudden appearance of a heretofore unknown almost fiancée struck him as, well, delightful. No one was that furious unless she cared more than she wanted to admit. He resisted the urge to grin. Theodosia would not take that well at all.

"Aren't you going to say something?"

"There's really nothing to say." He took her arm and started toward the manor. "You'll like Lucy. She's very intelligent and—"

"And." Theodosia jerked out of his grasp and glared. "She's your fiancée."

"No, she's not." He took her arm and again started off.

Again she pulled free. "Your mother seems to think she is."

"My mother is confused about a great many things. I would certainly not take her word on a matter of even minute importance." He met her gaze firmly. "Now, are we going to go back to the house and discuss this in a sane, rational, *warm* manner or are we going to stay out here and freeze?"

"I'm not cold," she said in a lofty manner.

"Well then. Good day, Lady Theodosia." He tipped his hat, turned, and strode toward the manor.

An indignant gasp trailed after him. "Are you going to leave me here?"

"I'm not leaving you," he called back to her. "You're choosing to stay."

"Oh, for goodness' sake."

He tried not to grin but it wasn't easy. A moment later she was by his side.

"Then you're not engaged?"

He shook his head. "Not to my knowledge."

"But your mother thinks you are?"

"Probably." He stopped and turned toward her. "It was assumed that Lucy and I would marry eventually. We assumed it ourselves. But we never managed to make it official. I never proposed, she never accepted. There was no ring, no announcement. In that respect you and I are more engaged than Lucy and I ever were."

"Go on."

"That we kept putting it off never seemed to bother either of us. Which now, in hindsight, does seem to indicate that we both knew it wasn't right for either of us. When I left with my father she released me from any obligation, real or assumed."

"I see," she said thoughtfully.

He glanced at her. "Feeling foolish, are we?"

She ignored him. "If you're not engaged why would your mother bring her here?"

"The actions of my mother become more incomprehensible with every passing day. As I suspect do the actions of yours."

"We're not talking about my mother." She paused. "And really, my mother's actions make a fair amount of sense if you understand how uncertain her life has become. You made me see that."

"I am wise beyond my years." He gestured toward the manor. "Shall we?"

She nodded and this time took his arm. They walked on in silence for no more than a few seconds.

"Do you love her?" Theodosia said abruptly.

He slanted a glance at her. "Why do you want to know?"

"It just seems to me that is the kind of thing a fraudulent fiancée should know." She paused. "It's simple curiosity, I suppose."

"I have always loved Lucy and I always will."

"Oh." A vague but definite note of disappointment sounded in her voice.

"She has always been my closest friend."

"Oh." Her tone lightened. "Still, you should have told me about her."

"Why?" He glanced at her. "You haven't told me about your fiancé."

"That's different." She shrugged. "He isn't going to show up when you least expect him. He is dead after all."

"Did you love him?"

"Why are you asking?"

"I could say curiosity, just as you did."

She shrugged. "Admittedly, it was not a good answer."

"No, it wasn't." He forced a casual note to his voice but held his breath. "You asked about Lucy, it seems only fair that I ask about your fiancé, that's all."

"I thought I loved him at the time." She sighed. "Then, shortly before he died, I realized I was wrong. He had, well, deceived me. What we had, or what I thought we had, was built on lies."

"I have never lied to you."

"Probably but—"

"No probably about it. Did you ever ask if I was engaged? If I'd ever been engaged?"

"Perhaps not but—"

"There are all sorts of things about me that you have not inquired about. Yet, I suspect, when they surface you will be annoyed that I didn't feel it was necessary to mention them."

"Don't be absurd." She paused. "What things?"

"Nothing that I can think of at the moment but I'm certain I have done any number of things in the past and I shall do any number of things in the future that will annoy you. But this time, you have no legitimate reason to be annoyed with me."

"I wasn't annoyed," she said indignantly, "I was furious."

He laughed. "You're magnificent when you're angry."

She pulled up short and stared at him. "There you've done it again."

"Done what?"

"You've gone and left me speechless."

He grinned and pulled her into his arms. "You make me say things I never thought I'd say aloud."

She smiled with satisfaction. "Do I really?"

"Yes, you do." His gaze slipped to her lips, then back to her eyes. "I have never been a man of action or adventure."

She scoffed. "I don't believe that."

"I know. I find that remarkable." He shook his head. "But believe this, Theodosia Winslow." He gazed into her eyes. "You make me want to be a man of action and adventure."

She stared up at him. "Oh . . . my."

"Although you haven't asked, you should also know, I would very much like to kiss you again."

"Goodness, Jack." Her breath puffed in the cold air. "That's not a secret."

"And if we were not within sight of the manor, where anyone might see us, I would do exactly that."

"Oh, they're very discreet at the manor. Besides, what kind of adventure would it be without an element of risk?" Desire flashed in her eyes. The woman wanted him as much as he wanted her. Good.

"Excellent point, however . . ." He cast a last look at her delectable lips, then blew a long breath. "When this is over and done with, I don't want you left with a shattered reputation."

"I am most appreciative," she murmured but the look in her eyes said otherwise.

"Other than wanting to kiss you, which you pointed out was not a secret . . ." He released her, then stepped back, took her arm, and firmly steered her toward the house. "I have no deep, dark secrets. Do you?"

"No, of course not," she said quickly. Too quickly. "But I do owe you an apology."

"Again, not a secret."

"I was, well, hurt. I thought you had, not exactly lied perhaps but . . ." She heaved a frustrated sigh. "Honestly, Jack, I'm not sure why I was so angry but the fact remains that I was."

"Because I didn't tell you about a fiancée I didn't actually have?"

"Something like that."

"You are the most confusing, irrational woman I have ever met."

For a long moment she didn't say a word, then she smiled. "Thank you, Jack."

Chapter Seventeen

If Teddy had known how thoroughly delightful it would
be to have a fake fiancé whose sole purpose was to show the
world how utterly perfect they were for each other, she would
have acquired one years ago. Jack was so good in the role,
even she had a hard time remembering it was all a show for
his family. Admittedly, both of them had more than a twinge
of guilt at their deceit but it couldn't be helped. And of course
it would end with the New Year. Exactly as she wanted it.
Still, she would miss him. Miss the way he laughed, and the
way she would catch her breath at some of the things he
would say and even how he delighted in annoying her.

Teddy sat at the desk in Dee's parlor and finished the list
of final details to be seen to for Mrs. Hendrickson's party
tonight. She'd returned to London yesterday and as much as
she loved Millworth, it was something of a relief to be back
in London. There was an air of equal parts anticipation and
apprehension hanging over the manor what with not knowing exactly when Jack's mother and his dear friend Miss
Merryweather would arrive. Camille had been thoroughly

chastised by both Dee and Lady Briston for her failure to find out in which London hotel the ladies were staying.

Lady Briston had sprung into action in a flurry of nervous energy, directing the manor staff in the cleaning and polishing of everything from doorknobs to chandeliers. She said she had no intention of allowing her sister-in-law and the mother of the man who would one day inherit the house to see it looking anything other than its very best. Colonel Channing's preparations were more personal in nature and Teddy had noticed his hair trimmed as well as a visit to his tailor. Jack, on the other hand, was cool and calm and even slightly amused by all the fuss. It was rather soothing to see him so at ease. His nature was much more complicated than she had suspected.

Voices sounded from the front entry and she replaced her pen in its holder. Her heart sped up. She hadn't expected Jack so soon but he had said he would be coming in to London while she was there because he couldn't bear the thought of being away from her for long. Of course, he said it in front of his family. Even so, there was something in his eyes that was quite—

"There you are." Her mother swept into the room with her usual aplomb but something seemed oddly off. "I'm so glad you've come back to London. We have a great deal to discuss."

"And here I thought you had come to assist me with the plans for Mrs. Hendrickson's party."

"Goodness, Theodosia, you don't need my help." She scoffed but that too struck Teddy as half-hearted. "You never have."

She studied her mother carefully. "What's wrong, Mother? You're never out and about at this time of the morning."

Indecision washed across her mother's face coupled with something that might well have been fear, then she clasped her hands together in front of her and drew a deep breath. "Is there something you've been meaning to tell me?"

"Not that I can think of," Teddy said slowly.

"About your fiancé perhaps?"

Good Lord, she knew. That was that then. Still, experience had taught her never to make assumptions when it came to her mother. "About Jack? Nothing comes to mind. The man is really something of an open—"

"Not that fiancé."

Teddy narrowed her eyes. "What fiancé are you talking about?"

"This came to the house." Mother held out a letter, her hand trembling slightly.

Teddy stood and crossed the room to take the letter from her mother. The handwriting on the envelope was vaguely familiar but she couldn't place it.

"It was addressed to me but it concerns you." Mother paused. "It was slipped under the door late last night or early this morning, Jacobs didn't know. Something about it struck me as, well, wrong even before I opened it."

Teddy stared. Her mother was decidedly uneasy. It was not at all like her.

"Read it."

"Very well." Teddy opened the envelope and pulled out a single sheet. She read the first line and sucked in a hard breath. "This is impossible."

"That's what I thought."

Teddy looked at her mother. "But he's dead."

"Not as dead as one might have hoped." She paused. "You're not pleased by news of his resurrection then?"

"Dear Lord, no!"

"Thank God." Mother wrung her hands together. "Go on, finish it."

Teddy scanned the brief note. "It's nice of him to apologize for being alive although I daresay he didn't mean it as an apology." She looked at her mother. "It says he will pay a call on me the day after tomorrow."

"You can imagine how shocked I was to receive this." Mother turned and paced. "The man's supposed to be dead. If one can't count on the dead staying dead, one can't count on anything in this life."

"This makes no sense." Teddy studied the letter. "Cyril was lost at sea when his ship sank. But obviously, he wasn't on the ship he was supposed to be on."

"Or he was found." Her mother shook her head. "I don't understand. Why would he let the world believe he was dead? How could he have done this to his family? To you? Especially coming right on the heels of your father's death."

To escape the consequences of his actions. Teddy chose her words with care. "Perhaps he saw no other choice."

"Understandable, I suppose. The man was not as he appeared. Of course, I had no idea until . . . He and your father . . ." Mother drew a deep breath. "How much do you know about your father's financial interests?"

Teddy stared. "How much do *you* know?"

"More than I wish." She sank down onto the sofa and gestured for Teddy to join her. "I didn't know anything at all until a few days before he died. It was the stress, you know, that killed him."

Teddy nodded.

"Your father was a charming man but not overly clever when it came to matters of money. I don't know all the details, I've never been good with numbers or money either, aside from the spending of it. In that, your father and I were well matched." She paused to pull her thoughts together. "He invested heavily in an enterprise, the name escapes me. What was it?" She thought for a moment. "The Argentine Atlantic Trading Company, that was it. It was involved in development of some South American country—primarily Argentina I think but I'm not sure. It was Cyril who brought the company to his notice, around the same time he started calling on you."

"Yes, of course," Teddy murmured.

"At first, your father's investments proved to be quite lucrative but returns diminished rather quickly. When your father questioned what was happening, he was told this was simply the market adjusting itself."

Teddy frowned. "What does that mean?"

"I have no idea. I suspect neither did your father. Nonetheless, he was made a member of the company's board of directors and, unfortunately, increased his investments. To show his confidence in the venture, he said."

"So, even though this wasn't proving profitable, he put more money into it?"

"I said he wasn't good with numbers. Which was not your father's greatest fault."

Although, given the circumstances, it did seem a rather significant fault. "Then what was?"

"He trusted far too easily. He believed what he was told without question. He never imagined others would deliberately lie to him. As it turned out, that was his, and our, undoing." Mother sighed. "In an effort to make up for what he had lost, he took to gaming more than usual. He'd always been a bit of a gambler, you know, but even in his youth, he was never serious about it. He never gambled more than he could afford to lose and through the years won as much as he lost. It was an amusing game to him, an innocent enough pastime, nothing more than that. At least until that last year. I was blissfully unaware of any of this until shortly before his death although it was obvious to me that he was greatly worried. He tried to deny it but eventually he told me everything. How he'd lost our entire fortune, his involvement with the trading company, and the gambling. And then . . ." She blew a long breath.

"Then, amidst charges of bribery and corruption and fraud, an official investigation began and Father feared he would go to prison," Teddy said bluntly.

Her mother's gaze snapped to hers. "You knew?"

"Not until after he died."

"I never wanted you to know about any of this. I had no idea the kind of man Cyril was. When your father confessed everything, I planned to urge you to break it off with him but then your father died and Cyril left and, well, *died* and it seemed the less said the better. How did you find out?"

"I overheard Cyril talking to another man the day we buried Father. I didn't see the other man but I heard . . ." Her jaw tightened. "I heard enough. Everything really. How Cyril had not only encouraged Father's initial investments, but kept him putting his funds into the company. It was Cyril who introduced him, and accompanied him, to those high-stakes games of chance where Father was obviously out of his depth. I didn't know anything about the gambling at all until then."

"Yes, well, your father was nothing if not discreet." Mother's brow furrowed. "It was desperation that drove him, I think. The hope that with one more spin of the dice or turn of a card he would recoup his investment losses. Obviously, he didn't and you know as well as I how far in debt he was at the end. Why, we didn't fully realize how dreadful it was until nearly a year after he died."

"From what I heard, it was obvious Cyril was deeply involved in this trading company and could well go to prison, depending on the outcome of the investigation." Teddy paused to gather those unpleasant memories. "I confronted him of course."

Mother smiled wryly. "I'd expect no less of you."

Teddy's brow rose. "Was that a compliment?"

"Very much so. You have the sort of courage I've never had. You confront problems head-on. I much prefer to sweep them under the rug and ignore them in the hope that they will take care of themselves or disappear." Mother nodded. "Go on."

"Cyril tried to deny it, all of it, but I refused to accept what

I could now see were lies. But then one doesn't expect the younger brother of a viscount to be involved in something dishonest. He had an honorable reputation after all. And he was very convincing. But . . ." She shuddered. "There was something about the look in his eyes and the tone of his voice . . ." She drew a deep breath. "He was a desperate man, Mother, at least at the end, and I think he'd do whatever he thought necessary to protect himself."

"Up to and including pretending he was dead."

"So it would seem. I still can't believe I never noticed."

"Some men are quite good at hiding their true nature."

"Apparently." Teddy shrugged. "Upon reflection, there were hints here and there, an odd moment on occasion, tiny irregularities in something he said or the look in his eye that should have struck me as troubling but . . ." She smiled at her mother. "I ignored them."

"My apologies," Mother murmured.

"Naturally, I broke it off with him. He urged me to reconsider or at least wait until he had returned from his trip to Argentina. If you recall, he was scheduled to leave a few days after Father's funeral."

Mother nodded.

"He claimed his trip might well clear up everything. I didn't believe him. I had overheard entirely too much and had, at last, put all those little pieces together that I had tried very hard not to see. Then of course, his ship was reportedly lost at sea."

"And you and his family received solicitous telegrams from the trading company informing you of his death."

"I don't know what other names might have been connected to all this but I had some discreet inquiries made after Cyril's death. Or alleged death now, I suppose. The company simply disappeared so the investigation was at an end." Teddy shook her head. "It seemed with both Father and Cyril dead, the authorities had no thread of inquiry to follow."

"Your father was barely past his fifty-second year," Mother said quietly. "But his heart couldn't take the threat of scandal and prison and all that went with it. His father died in much the same way at very nearly the same age. I suppose it was only a matter of time really." She studied her hands in her lap. "I know it sounds dreadful, it is dreadful, but it did seem the timing of his death was somewhat fortuitous. I have never quite forgiven myself for thinking that."

"I felt the same way about Cyril's death."

"Ah, but you didn't love Cyril, did you?"

"I thought I did but . . ." Teddy shook her head. "No, I didn't."

"Your father was the one true love of my life." Her mother stared unseeing, as if looking back over the years. "But he never would have survived prison or disgrace. The scandal alone would have destroyed him. He wasn't nearly as strong as he appeared. I think, as long as I had him, I could have survived anything. Without him . . ."

Teddy stared. She couldn't remember ever having shared such intimate confidences with her mother before.

"I'm glad you found yours." Her mother's gaze met hers.

"My what?"

"Your one true love."

"You mean Jack?"

"Of course I mean Jack. And I am sorry about my efforts to throw Simon at you but . . ." She shook her head. "Poverty is a dreadful thing, Theodosia, and I thank God we were able to avoid it. I am well aware that is not to my credit. If you were not as clever as you are, we would have had to sell the house and we would be begging Simon or some other distant relation to take pity on us. Now, however . . ." Mother squared her shoulders. "You are to be the next Countess of Briston and your future is assured."

This was probably not the best time to mention to her mother that her engagement wasn't real or confide her own plans for her future. No, *their* future.

"As much as I would like to believe that, Mother, there is the awkward matter of a late fiancé who isn't apparently late at all."

"That is a problem." Mother considered her thoughtfully. "Do you think you should tell Mr. Channing about this?"

"Absolutely not," Teddy said sharply. "He is the last person I want to know about any of this. Jack is a good, honorable man. While I'm certain he wouldn't hold Father's misdeeds against us, he would feel compelled to, well, rescue me. No, I think it's best not to say anything about this to him."

"Perhaps that is best," Mother said slowly. "At least until we know what Mr. Goddard wants."

"I must admit the very fact that he wants to meet with me is, well, disconcerting."

"Disconcerting? I find it terrifying." Mother paused. "I suppose doing away with him and throwing his body into the river would be wrong."

Teddy stared. "Mother!"

"What?" Mother raised a brow. "You think I'm going to let some man who doesn't have the decency to stay dead harm one hair on my daughter's head." She scoffed. "I should say not."

"There's no way around it. I have to meet with him. His note says it's a matter of urgency regarding Father."

"I've been thinking about that." Mother rose and paced the parlor. "My first impulse is to insist you return to our house, I hate the thought of your being here alone and I would feel much better if you were where I could keep an eye on you."

"I can't imagine I'm in any particular danger. Cyril would never hurt me."

"Come now, Theodosia." Mother pinned her with a firm look. "Are you really willing to trust a man who has deceived you? A man desperate enough to allow even his family to think he's dead? The man who led your father to ruin and ultimately his death? Besides, you know his secrets. You may think he would not hurt you. I am under no such illusions."

"You do have a point," Teddy said under her breath. "So, you're going to protect me?"

"Don't think the irony isn't lost on me either given that you've been the one taking care of me since your father died." She studied her daughter closely. "Do you know how to use a pistol?"

"No." Teddy widened her eyes in surprise. "Do you?"

"As a matter of fact I do. Indeed, I was quite good with a pistol in my youth and I've made it a point through the years to keep my skills sharp."

Teddy stared. "I had no idea."

"I daresay there are any number of things about me that would surprise you."

"Apparently."

Mother smiled and continued. "However, as Mr. Goddard doesn't know you've been staying here at Lady Hargate's, I think it's safer for you to remain. Unless you'd prefer to return to Millworth?"

"I can't. At least not yet. Mrs. Hendrickson's party, remember?"

"Very well." Mother nodded. "I shall have Jacobs stay here every night for the time being. He too is very good with a pistol."

"Jacobs?" The tall, thin, morose butler who had been with their family for as long as she could remember?

"Jacobs was not always in domestic service, dear."

"I see," Teddy murmured. Apparently this was the day for revelations. "I suppose there is the possibility that Cyril wants nothing more than an innocent reunion."

Mother's brow arched upward. "Do you believe that?"

"Not for a moment." Teddy sighed. "Especially given the way we parted. But, no, I imagine there is something he wants." She considered the possibilities but nothing came to mind. "Although I can't imagine what it might be. I want nothing more to do with the man, dead or alive."

"Good." Mother nodded. "I was afraid, when I received the note that . . ."

"That I would welcome him with open arms?" Teddy scoffed. "Not bloody likely."

"Theodosia." Mother frowned.

"Sorry." For a moment, Teddy was a child again being chastised for improper behavior.

"No, I'm sorry," Mother said. "You're an adult and far more responsible than I ever was. But then I didn't have to be. There was always someone to look after me. My family and then your father and then you. I was lost for a while when he died."

"I didn't realize . . ."

"Nor did I want you to. You had enough to deal with." She heaved a resigned sigh. "Past time I became the woman my daughter already is. Through no fault of my own I might add."

"Nonsense, Mother," Teddy said staunchly. "I am precisely who you raised me to be."

"You, my dear girl, are independent and rational and competent. You are well able to chart your own course and manage your own affairs. None of that is my doing." Mother shrugged. "I wish it was." She met her daughter's gaze directly. "I have never said it, and my behavior certainly hasn't shown it, but I am extraordinarily proud of the woman you have become."

Teddy's throat tightened. "Mother, I—"

"It's of no importance now however." Resolve rang in her mother's voice. "There are other matters to be dealt with." She paced for a moment, obviously lost in thought. "I've been wondering why the man has chosen now to reveal himself." She glanced at Teddy. "Are you aware that Viscount Nottwood died a few weeks ago."

"Cyril's brother?"

Mother nodded.

"No, I hadn't heard."

"That might have something to do with why this little cockroach has come into the light."

"Mother!" Teddy bit back a grin.

"You needn't take that tone with me, Theodosia." Her mother folded her arms over her chest. "Cockroach is the kindest name that came to mind and even in that, I am insulting cockroaches."

"I had no idea you could be so . . ." Teddy choked back a laugh. "Adamant. Determined."

"I couldn't save my husband from that man but I will do everything necessary to save my daughter." A determined glint sparked in her mother's eyes. "Right now, I am at your disposal to help you prepare in whatever way you need for Mrs. Henrickson's event."

"Thank you, Mother."

"And the day after tomorrow, promptly at three—and if the man can't stay dead let us hope he can at least be prompt—you shall meet with your late fiancé and find out what he has to say." Mother's lips pressed together in a firm line and her eyes narrowed. She looked at once terrifying and magnificent and Teddy was more than a little proud herself. "And why in the bloody hell he's still alive."

Chapter Eighteen

Theodosia circled Mrs. Hendrickson's ballroom stopping to chat with an acquaintance here or direct a waiter to refill an empty glass there. She was the epitome of grace and confidence and Jack's pulse sped up just looking at her.

It did appear tonight was yet another social success. The ballroom floor was crowded with dancers. Music and laughter hung in the air. Gaslight had been abandoned tonight for the flickering glow of hundreds of candles in chandeliers and sconces. Festive swags and garlands created an impression of a lush, evergreen garden of Christmas and magic.

Jack had become quite adept at slipping into an event at just the right moment to serve as Theodosia's escort. As he had no interest in anyone else there, it worked quite nicely for both of them. Besides, as soon as he took her in his arms to dance, it didn't matter if half the population of London was in the room. He had eyes only for her.

Theodosia caught sight of him and she nodded slightly in acknowledgement. She made her way toward him, a smile lighting her lovely features. He hadn't seen her for two days.

Two full days! It was the longest they had been away from each other since their *engagement* had begun and he didn't like it one bit. Admittedly, she did appear in his dreams, and in any number of passing thoughts while awake, but the simple fact was that he missed her.

It was probably time to face a truth, a realization, that grew stronger every day. He didn't want to be Lady Theodosia Winslow's pretend fiancé and he certainly didn't want to go their separate ways after the New Year's ball. He wanted Theodosia in his life for the rest of his days and he was certain she felt the same. Although he suspected winning her heart wouldn't be as difficult as getting her to admit it. She had a plan for her life and he had no place in it. Still, plans change. Wasn't his own life a perfect example of that?

"Have I ever told you how the red of your hair gleams like burnished gold in candlelight?" He took her hand and drew it to his lips.

"Goodness, Jack." A hint of impatience sounded in her voice but she smiled up at him. "No one can hear us. You needn't waste your efforts."

"Oh well, in that case." He kept hold of her hand and leaned closer. "Your eyes sparkle in the candlelight as well."

She pulled her hand from his. "You are incorrigible, aren't you?"

"I do try." He drew his brows together. "Are you—"

"Am I what?" she said sharply.

He studied her carefully. The faintest lines of worry showed at the corners of her eyes. "You look, I don't know, tired."

"Thank you, Jack. That's exactly what a woman wants to hear."

"I'm sorry I just—"

"No, you're right." She sighed. "I haven't been sleeping."

"Well, I can understand that." He nodded in a sage manner. "Can you?"

"Absolutely." He nodded. "It's been two days since you left Millworth and I haven't slept a wink myself."

"Oh?"

"My head is too filled with thoughts of you." He shook his head in a mournful manner. "It's ruining my rest."

A genuine smile lifted the corners of her lips. "Did I mention you were incorrigible?"

"I know. You like it."

"Yes, I suppose I do."

"Shall we dance, Lady Theodosia?" He offered his arm.

"I would love to dance with you, Mr. Channing." She took his arm and he escorted her onto the dance floor.

The small orchestra was playing one of her favorite waltzes and there was nothing he liked better than watching the enjoyment she took in the music and the dance. But something was definitely wrong tonight. She danced as flawlessly as ever, as perfectly in step with him as if they had danced together always, but her heart wasn't in it. She was entirely too quiet and obviously preoccupied.

He chose his words carefully. "You do know that you can confide in me. If there is something that has upset you—"

"No, there's nothing." She forced a smile that didn't fool him for a second. "As I said, I'm simply tired."

"Have I done something to annoy you?" He chuckled. "Something new, that is?"

"No, of course not." Her tone softened. "You have been all I could have asked for in a fake fiancé." She paused. "And in a friend."

"We are friends, aren't we?"

She nodded.

"I was thinking, perhaps . . ." He drew a deep breath. "You and I . . . well, we—"

"I am sorry, Jack," she said abruptly. "But I am in no mood to talk tonight. I am tired and I would much prefer if we simply concentrated on the dance and the music."

"All right." He smiled down at her and she smiled back but there was an absent look in her eyes, as if she were simply going through motions.

He had seen her angry or annoyed, irate or terse, but he had never seen her like this before. He might not be really engaged to her but he knew her well enough by now to know there was definitely something wrong. That she refused to confide in him could only mean it was something of significance, something important, and possibly something very bad.

The music ended and she stepped out of his embrace at once. That too was an indication of her state of mind; usually she lingered in his arms. It was one of the best parts of dancing with her. They walked off the floor in silence. Yet another bad sign. Theodosia was never silent.

He turned to her. "Theodosia, I—"

"My apologies, Jack," she said. "I am unusually weary tonight and I think it would be best if I took my leave now."

He narrowed his eyes. "You never leave this early."

"Tonight I will." She drew a deep breath. "To be perfectly honest, I have been feeling a bit under the weather. I fear I am coming down with something. I spoke with Mrs. Hendrickson's staff and they are more than capable of handling the rest of the evening."

"Well then, I shall escort you home."

"It's not necessary. My mother is here and she has her carriage." She paused. "Has your mother arrived at Millworth yet?"

"No. I suspect she's waiting for that moment when we least expect her."

"When are you returning to the manor?"

"In the morning."

"Good," she murmured.

He studied her for a moment. She looked more worried than tired, more preoccupied than ill. Still, he couldn't force the truth out of her. Theodosia might well be one of the most stubborn women he'd ever met. "But perhaps I should stay—"

"No!" she said sharply, then paused. "You really should be at Millworth when your mother arrives."

"But if you're not well—"

"I'm sure I'll be fine," she said quickly. "You don't want your father to have to deal with her without you, do you?"

"No, I suppose not." He stared down at her. "When do you plan to return to Millworth? Christmas is fast approaching, you know."

"Oh, I shall be there long before Christmas." She cast him a brilliant smile that struck him as not quite right, as forced rather than legitimate. "I shall see you there soon."

"I hope so." His gaze met hers. "I have missed you. It's difficult to be a hero if there is no fair maiden about."

"Then it's fortunate you're a banker and not a hero," she snapped.

He stared at her.

"I'm sorry." She pulled her gaze from his and shook her head. "That was uncalled for."

"And yet entirely accurate."

"No, it isn't. I'm just . . . I have a great deal on my mind."

"And you're not feeling your usual self."

"Yes, that's it." She paused. "But I have missed you, too," she said, a catch in her voice. She cleared her throat and smiled. "Good evening, Jack." With that she nodded and disappeared into the crowd.

He stared after her for a long moment. The blasted woman was trying to get rid of him. She never would have made that comment about his being a banker otherwise, at least not in the way she did. It was a continuing joke between them but there was no humor in her words tonight. She was definitely worried, even scared, about something. He didn't imagine anything could scare Theodosia Winslow. The very idea was cause for concern. He turned and made his way through the crowd toward the door.

He didn't like the idea of leaving her alone in London. It was possible, he supposed, that he was jumping to conclusions. That she really wasn't feeling well. He could certainly be mistaken and whatever was on her mind was of little consequence. No, he had always been able to trust his instincts about people and instinct was telling him now that something was very, very wrong.

Still, if she wouldn't confide in him, there was one person who knew all of Theodosia's secrets. One person she had always confided in. And the only person he knew who cared about Theodosia as much as he did.

"Is Lady Hargate here?" Jack handed his overcoat and hat to Clement the moment he crossed Millworth's threshold.

He had planned on taking the first train back to the country this morning but had been delayed thanks to his grandfather. There had been a letter waiting for him at Channing House yesterday requesting that he meet with an official from the Bank of England regarding what turned out to be a minor matter. It did seem little enough to do as he had yet to tell his grandfather he would probably not be returning to his position at the bank. Yet another discussion he was not looking forward to.

"She's in the main parlor, sir."

"Thank you, Clement." Jack headed for the parlor.

"She's not alone, sir," the butler called after him.

Jack pushed open the door and spotted Delilah seated in one of the chairs flanking the sofa along with his aunt, Camille, and two other ladies whose backs were to the door.

"I beg your pardon." He forced a polite smile. He really had no time for niceties. "I am sorry to interrupt but I need to speak to Delilah." He met his cousin's gaze. "It's a matter of some importance."

"Of course." Delilah stood at once, an uneasy expression on her face.

"Aren't you going to greet your mother, Jackson?" His mother rose to her feet, as did Lucy beside her.

"Sorry, Mother, I didn't see you." How clever of his mother

to finally appear just at the most inopportune moment. Well, he had no time to deal with her now. He strode toward her and kissed her proffered cheek. "You're looking well."

Her gaze swept over him. "As are you."

"Jackson." Lucy beamed and held out her hands. "She's right, you do look wonderful. England must agree with you."

"I think it might, Lucy." He smiled and took her hands. "And how do you like your first trip abroad?"

"I love it, I simply love it. It's so enlightening." Enthusiasm rang in Lucy's voice. "London was all I ever thought it would be and more. What a fascinating city. It's all so grand and ancient and . . . and royal."

"I thought you would like it." He smiled and released her hands. "I expect you to give me all the details of your travels later."

"Oh, I will. I've been noting everything in a journal so as not to forget anything important." She leaned close and spoke softly for his ears alone. "We need to talk as soon as possible."

"I look forward to it," he said quietly. It wasn't like Lucy to be so clandestine but whatever was on her mind would have to wait. He glanced at Delilah. "But at the moment, I need to have a word with Delilah."

"Jackson." His mother frowned. "We have only just arrived and as it's been over a month since you left I do think—"

"Later, Mother," he said firmly and nodded at Delilah. "This is important."

"Of course." Delilah smiled at the other women. "If you will excuse me." She led the way out of the room.

The moment Jack closed the door behind them she turned to him. "Thank God, you're back."

He raised a brow. "Should I take that to mean this meeting between both sides of my family is not going well?"

"I can't say it's not going well exactly. Everyone is on their best behavior. It's been extraordinarily polite thus far."

Delilah shuddered. "But there are undercurrents, Jack. There is more not being said in that room than is being said."

"And that's a problem?"

"Yes, it's a problem." She stared at him as if he were a complete idiot. "You must understand, all those years my father was gone, Uncle Basil was here for us. My mother and Uncle Basil have always been close. She is very protective of him and she feels your mother treated him quite badly."

"Because she never told him about me."

"Among other things. Mother is convinced Uncle Basil never married, or rather never married again, because your mother broke his heart."

"That's possible, I suppose," Jack said slowly. "I suspect there are a lot of unresolved issues between them."

"Frankly, I don't want to be in the room when the past raises its ugly head, even though I am dying to see what happens next. Mark my words, Jack." An ominous note sounded in her voice. "Between my mother and your mother, we are headed toward a confrontation the likes of which would put the ancient games in the coliseum at Rome to shame."

"I'd actually pay to see that."

She stared at him. "You really do take after your father." She rolled her gaze toward the ceiling. "And if all that wasn't enough, I am having a devil of a time trying to keep the conversation away from the subject of your engagement."

Jack winced. "Good Lord, I hadn't thought of that."

"I'm assuming, and do correct me if I'm wrong, that your mother knows nothing about this."

"Frankly, I hadn't considered her one way or the other. It didn't seem necessary to tell her."

"Jack," Delilah said as if he were a small child and unable to understand even the most fundamental basics of civilized behavior. "It might not have been necessary to mention your engagement when your mother was an ocean away but, at any moment, someone is going to say something. And then, I suspect, there will be hell to pay."

"Probably." He shrugged.

"You don't seem overly concerned."

"I'm not."

"Oh. I didn't expect that." Delilah studied him. "It's an excellent, if perhaps short-sighted, attitude. But if you're not worried then I suppose I won't worry either. After all, it's not my mother or my life. I am nothing more than a spectator. So I shall simply watch and enjoy the upcoming . . ." She smiled in a wicked manner. "Spectacle."

"I'm glad you find my life so entertaining."

"Oh I do and I am most grateful for it."

"Good, because there is a price to pay for your amusement. I need your help." He drew a deep breath. "It's Theodosia."

"What's wrong?" Delilah's eyes widened with concern.

"I don't know." He shook his head. "I saw her last night and she's not herself."

"What exactly do you mean?"

"She's preoccupied, she's terse, and she's unusually quiet." He shook his head. "I realize this all sounds minor but—"

"But it's not at all like her," Delilah said thoughtfully.

"Exactly. She said she wasn't feeling well but . . ."

"You don't believe her?"

"No, I don't." He paused. "I thought she and I had grown quite close. As friends if nothing else."

"Friends?" Delilah's brow arched upward.

"That's a subject for another time," he said firmly. "But whatever is bothering her is too immense or too personal or too awful for her to share with me. It's obvious, at least to me, that she's worried and maybe even scared."

"You don't think you're jumping to conclusions?"

"No, I don't. I was thinking that if she won't tell me what the problem is maybe—"

"She'd confide in me." Delilah nodded. "I have an appointment with my solicitor in London tomorrow, I'll see Teddy as soon as I'm done with that."

"I'll go with you."

"No, Sam is going to accompany me."

"But I—"

"Jack." Delilah laid a hand on his arm and met his gaze directly. "If this is indeed something of a serious nature, and she doesn't want you to know, your presence might do more harm than good."

"Possibly, but—"

"Besides . . ." She nodded toward the closed parlor doors. "I daresay you're going to have enough on your hands right here."

"Probably."

"Probably?" She snorted. "Oh, you are a foolish man."

The door to the parlor opened and Aunt Bernadette joined them, Camille a step behind.

"Jack," his aunt said the moment Camille closed the door. "Your mother would like a word with you."

He chuckled. "I'm certain she would."

Aunt Bernadette's eyes narrowed. "I must say, I find her quite—"

"Interesting," Camille said quickly. "She's a very interesting woman, Jack. Don't you think so, Mother?"

"Oh my, yes." The hard tone in his aunt's voice belied her words. "Although that's not exactly the word I would use. I would more accurately describe her as—"

"We needn't go into that now," Delilah said with a stern look at her mother. "She is obviously concerned about her son's future, Mother. You of all people should understand that."

"Yes, well I—"

"Thank you, Aunt Bernadette." He took his aunt's hands. "For being so gracious as to welcome her to Millworth."

"She is your mother after all." The older woman's expression softened. "And it is Christmas."

Delilah cast a grateful glance at Jack, then addressed her mother. "We really should leave them to their reunion."

"And I do like Miss Merryweather," Aunt Bernadette said thoughtfully, "although I am a bit confused as to—"

"Now, Mother." Delilah took her mother's arm and attempted to lead her away. "We have a great deal to do, what with new guests and—"

"Nonsense, everything has been ready for days now." Aunt Bernadette stood her ground. It was obviously going to take more than a bit of prodding from Delilah to get her to leave. "Perhaps we should stay here in case Jack needs . . . assistance."

"I'm sure Jack knows exactly what he's doing." Camille took her mother's other arm. "And we should allow him to greet his mother properly. *You* would expect no less."

"Perhaps." Aunt Bernadette's gaze shifted from one daughter to the other. "Not that it appears I have any choice."

"It's for the best, Mother," Delilah said in a soothing manner.

"Very well," His aunt pinned him with a firm look. "Jack, you have my deepest—"

"Wishes for a happy reunion," Camille blurted. "Come along now, Mother." The two sisters fairly pulled the older woman away from the door.

"It's going to be an interesting Christmas," Aunt Bernadette said under her breath.

"It always is, Mother." Delilah sighed. "It always is."

Chapter Nineteen

Jack drew a deep breath and reentered the parlor.

"I thought perhaps you weren't planning on returning." An annoyed frown creased his mother's forehead.

"She thought you might have escaped," Lucy said. The innocent note in her voice did nothing to disguise the laughter in her eyes.

"I would like to see Jackson alone, Lucinda." Mother cast Lucy her most imperious look. "So, if you would be so good as to take your leave . . ."

"Oh, I couldn't possibly." Lucy sat down on the sofa, settling back as if she fully intended to stay for a while.

Jack stared. Defying his mother wasn't at all like Lucy. But then hadn't he noted a change in Lucy on the night he had first met his father? He wasn't sure how or why but then, and now, she seemed, well, stronger. A bit defiant, a touch independent, but certainly not the more docile Lucy his mother had thought so perfect for him. Of course that was before Jack knew the truth about his father. Before Lucy had urged him not to consider himself under any obligation to her. Before their lives had changed irrevocably.

His mother's eyes narrowed. "Of course you can, my

dear. Simply direct those little feet of yours out the door and close it behind you."

"I do know how to exit a room, Mrs. Channing," Lucy said in a pleasant manner. "But I have no intention of leaving at the moment as you are about to question Jackson regarding his plans for the future. Which makes this talk my business as well."

"I'm certain Jackson would prefer—"

"Lucy can stay," Jack said. "I've never kept anything from her in the past and I see no reason to do so now." Lucy was, after all, his dearest friend. Even so, he was not especially eager to tell her about Theodosia.

"As you wish." Mother shrugged. "I was simply trying to spare your feelings, Lucinda."

"How very thoughtful," Lucy murmured.

Mother cast her a sharp look, then turned to her son. "When do you plan to return home?"

"Straight to the point, Mother? No idle chatter about the weather or your voyage?"

"No." She clasped her hands together in front of her. "But I would appreciate an answer."

"I'm not sure I have one." He shook his head. "I'm not sure I know where home is at the moment."

"Don't be absurd." She sniffed. "Your home is New York. It has been from the day you were born."

Jack met his mother's gaze firmly but didn't say a word.

"You needn't look at me like that. I have already admitted that I made, oh, a mistake by not telling your father about you and you about him." She drew her gaze from his but not before a flash of guilt showed in her eyes. "But the past is the past, Jackson, and now we should move on from here."

"Agreed."

Her gaze shot back to his. "Really?"

He nodded. "I think that's best, all things considered."

"Then you forgive me?"

"I didn't say that." He shook his head. "I'm not sure I can ever forgive you."

"But you did agree to put the past behind us?"

He nodded. "I did."

His mother studied him for a long moment. "Very well then. In the spirit of moving forward, I should like to know if you've made any decisions about your future."

"A few." He glanced at Lucy and she nodded her encouragement. "I don't plan on returning to New York anytime soon."

"Surely you're not serious." Mother scoffed. "You have responsibilities. Obligations. To the bank and your grandfather."

"The bank is a well-run institution, manned by gentlemen whose abilities far surpass those of a man whose prime qualification is that he was born to the position. Gentlemen who want to be bankers. As for Grandfather . . ." Jack thought for a moment. "I suspect he already knows what I am finally coming to realize. Banking was never in my blood."

"You're going to stay here? In England?" Mother stared in disbelief. "You're going to give up everything you've ever known to assume an insignificant, antiquated title in a country that is so firmly entrenched in the past that its people refuse to see the benefits of something as elemental as decent plumbing?"

"Oh, we see the benefits of decent plumbing, Elizabeth." His father's voice sounded from the doorway. "But all that past we're entrenched in prevents us from sacrificing heritage for the sake of comfort."

His mother glared at his father. "What are you doing here? I wished to speak to my son *alone.*"

"Yes, I can see that." Father peered around her. "Good day, Miss Merryweather."

"Good day, Colonel." Lucy beamed at the older man. "How very nice to see you again."

"You're looking even more lovely than when last we met."

"Oh my, Colonel, you will quite turn my head—"

"Stop it. Both of you," Mother snapped. "This is not the appropriate moment for . . . for idle flirtation!"

His father's eyes widened innocently. "Was I flirting? I certainly hadn't intended to flirt."

"I didn't think he was flirting," Lucy said. "In my opinion, he was simply being charming. Most charming. Didn't you think so, Jackson?"

"I thought he was charming." Jack nodded.

"*Most* charming," Lucy pointed out.

Father chuckled. "Thank you, my dear."

"Yes of course." Jack grinned. "Most charming and not the least bit flirtatious."

"I see what you're doing." Mother huffed. "All of you. You're trying to drive me mad. That's it, isn't it?"

"I don't think so." Jack glanced at his father. "Are we?"

"Not at all." His father paused. "It's just an amusing consequence."

She ignored him. "You never used to be like this, Jackson."

"Actually, I think I've always been like this, whatever that means." Jack shrugged. "I simply kept it to myself."

"It's your influence, no doubt." She glared at his father.

"Do you really think so?" Father asked.

"You needn't look so proud about it, Basil. You're a bad example, you've always been a bad example."

"I have not." Indignation rang in his father's voice.

"Hah! You've never stayed in one place for any length of time at all. You have no roots, no ties, and certainly no stability. All you've ever done is wander the world."

"I did serve in Her Majesty's—"

"And after that your life has been nothing more than one . . . one *exploit* after another." Mother's gaze slid between Lucy and Jack. "The two of you might think this man-of-adventure nonsense is exciting and romantic and heroic. I, however, do not. As for you, Jackson." Her voice rose and her words came faster. "I did not raise you to follow in your father's footsteps, to wander the world in an aimless quest for the next thrilling encounter regardless of whom you might leave behind. Nor did I intend for you to disregard those people who have entrusted their faith in you. I did not bring you up to be the kind of man a girl throws away everything sensible and rational and practical for in exchange for the promise of romance and adventure and excitement!"

"I'd rather like to be the kind of man a girl throws away everything sensible and rational and practical for in exchange for the promise of romance and adventure and excitement," Jack said mildly. "And I see nothing wrong with following in my father's footsteps."

"Very good, Jackson," Lucy said under her breath.

Mother continued as if he hadn't said a word. "I raised you to face your responsibilities and accept your obligations, unlike your father. You"—she turned back to her husband—"have spent your life with no particular purpose and certainly no responsibilities and—"

"And whose fault is that?" His father's voice sharpened. "Had I known about my responsibilities, about my son, about my *wife,* my entire life would have been different."

"Would have, Basil?" His mother stared at his father. "Or might have?"

"Thanks to you, Elizabeth." His gaze locked with hers. "We shall never know."

A myriad of emotions crossed her face. At last she drew a deep breath. "I have given this a great deal of thought since our last encounter and . . . and I am sorry, Basil. Truly sorry. About all of it."

"You can't undo the past, Elizabeth." Father shook his head. "You can do no more than make amends for it."

"Can I?" His mother's gaze locked with his father's for a long silent moment. Questions unasked and unanswered hung in the air. Jack suspected his parents had forgotten they were not alone. "Is that even possible?"

"Perhaps," his father said quietly.

As much as Jack hated to interrupt whatever was going through the minds of his parents it obviously had nothing to do with him and he would prefer not to be a witness to it.

He cleared his throat. "Why are you here, Mother?"

"To talk some sense into you, of course. Obviously, in that I am too late." Resignation sounded in her voice. "Certainly, I knew that was a possibility. I have known since you were a little boy and wanted to be a treasure hunter. I knew then that you were your father's son regardless of what I wanted for you. Your grandfather knew. He warned me but . . ." She drew a deep breath. "Of course, I didn't listen."

That was as close as Jack had ever come to hearing his mother admit there was a chance she was wrong.

"Regardless, there are other matters to attend to at the moment." She studied him coolly. "Jackson, do you agree that as your mother I have certain rights when it comes to your life?"

"I don't know whether I can agree to that, Mother, as I have no idea what you are referring to."

"I am referring to . . ." Mother heaved an exaggerated sigh. "Poor, poor Lucinda."

Lucy's sigh echoed his mother's even if it didn't strike him as quite as genuine. "Poor, poor me."

He narrowed his eyes. "What are you talking about?"

"I had hoped to speak privately to you before your mother did but we saw you, Jackson," Lucy said. "Last night."

"Last night?" he said cautiously.

"Last night," Mother said firmly. "We were invited to accompany the American ambassador and his wife to a social event. We saw you but you left before we could approach you. You should be aware, Jackson, that you are the center of a fair amount of gossip and quite a bit of speculation."

"I'm not surprised." He chuckled.

"This is not amusing." Mother's eyes flashed. "Grahams have never been the topic of rumor and innuendo."

"Pity," Lucy murmured.

"Channings tend to be rather frequently." His father glanced at him and shrugged.

"While I was not surprised to hear you being hailed as something akin to a prodigal son . . ." Mother rolled her gaze toward the ceiling. "I was shocked to learn you were also engaged."

Jack considered his mother thoughtfully. This wasn't how he wanted Lucy to learn about Theodosia but apparently that ship had sailed. At this point, he had several choices. He could deny it, which seemed pointless. He could pretend he had no idea what they were talking about, which also seemed pointless as they had obviously seen him dancing with Theodosia last night. He could tell them the truth about his fake engagement, an option he discarded immediately, or he could admit that he did indeed intend to marry Lady Theodosia Winslow. A truth he hadn't fully realized until this moment.

He nodded slowly. "I can see how you might have been surprised by that."

"Surprised?" Mother's eyes widened. "I was stunned. To think that you would take such a step without so much as a note to me. And poor, poor Lucinda of course," she added quickly.

"Poor, poor me." Lucy shook her head in a mournful manner.

"I didn't know I needed your approval."

Mother hesitated. "It's not that you need my approval but I don't even know this young woman. She could be, well, wrong."

"Although everyone does speak quite highly of her," Lucy said helpfully.

Mother ignored her. "And even if you pay no heed to my feelings, what about her?" She gestured at Lucy. "Have you considered her feelings?" She shook her head. "Poor, poor Lucinda."

Lucy heaved an overly dramatic sigh. "Poor, poor me."

"Lucy?" Jack studied her closely. Was she really upset? He'd thought she was just playing along with his mother but perhaps he was wrong. And if he was wrong about that, was he wrong about everything when it came to his good friend? Had she meant to release him from any commitment to her or had he misunderstood? His stomach lurched. The last thing he would ever want to do was to hurt Lucy. "Are you—"

"I really would prefer not to talk to you about this in front of your parents, Jackson." Lucy rose to her feet. "Perhaps, we could speak elsewhere."

He nodded slowly. "Yes, of course."

"Jackson, I don't believe we've finished." Indignation sounded in his mother's voice.

"I'm not sure there's anything more to say. At least not between the two of us. Although I suspect Father has a great deal to say to you."

His father nodded. "And past time too, Betty."

Mother's jaw clenched.

Jack resisted the urge to grin and cast his mother an affectionate smile. In spite of her faults and misdeeds, she was still his mother and in her own misguided, self-centered way had done what she'd thought was best. "I assume you're still staying for Christmas."

She stared at him for a moment, then sighed. "If you will have me."

"I've been wanting to have you here for Christmas for thirty years," Father said gallantly.

"I doubt that." Mother scoffed. "I daresay you haven't given me a second thought in, well, longer than I care to say."

"You'd be surprised, Elizabeth." Father paused. "You were not the only one to make mistakes." His gaze met his wife's. "Obviously, you and I have a great deal to talk about as well."

"Obviously." She paused, then cast him a hopeful look. "I don't suppose my earlier comment, well, promise really—"

Father raised a skeptical brow.

"—about making amends is enough on this particular subject?"

"It's barely even a beginning." Father grinned.

"Yes, I was afraid of that."

Father chuckled. "Would you care for a brandy?"

"Good Lord, yes," Mother said with relief. "I was afraid you were going to offer me more tea."

Lucy caught his gaze and nodded. Jack moved to the door, opened it, and allowed Lucy to slip out a step in front of him.

"While I like tea," Mother continued, "I never realized before that I don't like quite so much—"

Jack closed the door behind him. "We could speak in the library if you'd like."

"All right."

Jack led the way to the Millworth library. He couldn't recall ever in his entire life feeling the least bit uncomfortable around Lucy yet, at the moment, he was distinctly uneasy.

Lucy gazed around the grand room. "Oh my, this is wonderful." She wandered around the perimeter of the library. "It's very much like your grandfather's only larger and older. And filled with the history of your family and the past. Are all these portraits ancestors?"

"I think so." He smiled. "I'm still trying to sort it all out myself."

She stopped before a painting of a woman and three young girls. "Is this your aunt?"

He nodded. "The twins are Camille and Beryl, you've met Camille, and the other girl is Delilah."

Her gaze fixed on the painting but she directed her words to him. "You've changed your mind, haven't you?"

"About what?"

"Whether you wish to be the next earl or not. When you left, you said you had no intention of accepting the title. But then you also intended to return to New York. Now, however . . ." She glanced at him. "It's apparent, at least to me, that everything has changed. You have changed."

It was pointless to deny it. He wasn't the same man who had said good-bye to her less than two months ago.

"To be honest, I haven't decided about the title yet."

She continued around the room, pausing to study another portrait. This one of a man in the garb of the last century.

"Do you have any idea how I felt when you wished to postpone our engagement yet again to go to England?" she asked abruptly.

A heavy weight settled in his stomach. "I am so sorry, Lucy. I would not have hurt you for anything."

"Goodness, Jackson, don't be so dramatic." She cast him a wry smile. "I'm not the least bit hurt. When I told you not to consider yourself under any obligation to me, I meant it. I should have said it a long time ago. Perhaps you haven't noticed but I have gone through a great deal of trouble in recent years to avoid marrying my best friend."

He drew his brows together. "You what?"

"You needn't look so indignant although I suppose I would be a tiny bit offended if you looked relieved."

"What I am is confused."

"For the moment perhaps but . . ." She turned and met his gaze firmly. "We have always been honest with each other, at least about everything but this. In all honesty, Jackson, you must admit you don't want to marry me any more than I want to marry you."

"I was perfectly prepared to marry you."

"Exactly the kind of declaration a girl wants to hear."

He grimaced. "I didn't mean it the way it sounded."

"I know that, I know you. I have known you my entire

life. You are my closest friend in the world. Which is probably why I don't really want to marry you."

"That makes no sense," he said slowly.

"It makes perfect sense. It seems to me if one is going to be married for the rest of one's life, it should be at least a tiny bit of an adventure. And knowing absolutely everything about the other party sounds frightfully dull."

"Are you saying I'm dull?"

"Not anymore." She studied him for a considering moment. "I said you've changed and I wish I could tell you how but I can't quite put my finger on it. There's a look in your eyes that wasn't there before. You're more, I don't know, solid than you've ever been. More complete perhaps. I know that makes no sense."

"Probably not but I understand."

"You're more exciting as well."

"Would you marry me now then?" He grinned.

Her brow rose. "Is that a proposal?"

"More a matter of curiosity," he said cautiously.

"Good, because my answer is absolutely not." She smiled. "But even if I would consider it, I could never marry you after seeing you with Lady Theodosia."

"Oh?"

"Even from across the room, it was obvious, at least to me, that you and she belong together. There's something between you, something, I don't know . . ." She shook her head. "I don't think you and I ever looked quite that . . . *right* together. Silly romantic nonsense of course but there you have it. Besides, you have never looked at me the way you looked at her."

"And how is that?"

"As if she is everything you ever wanted and never knew you wanted before you met her." A slight wistful smile curved her lips. "I would be quite jealous if I weren't so happy for you."

"I am sorry, Lucy. About you and me, that is. And not

looking at you . . ." He shook his head. "You have my deepest apologies."

"Don't be absurd." She scoffed. "I never looked at you the way she does either."

"She looks at me in a certain way?"

"Good Lord, yes. The woman is quite head over heels for you. Anyone can see it."

He blew a long breath. "Not anyone."

"You haven't noticed?"

"No." Jack shook his head. "Worse than that, neither has she."

Chapter Twenty

The next day,
The residence of the Countess of Sallwick
and Lady Theodosia . . .

"Are you certain you wish to see him alone?" Mother's gaze searched hers.

"I don't wish to see him at all." Teddy cast her mother a weak smile. She and her mother had grown closer than they'd been since before her father had died, thanks to Cyril's letter. Which almost made up for lying to Jack.

She had hated lying to him. Hated the look on his face the other night that said more than words that he knew she was lying. And worse, that he knew there was something she was keeping from him, something she didn't trust him enough to share. Still, it wasn't all a lie. She did feel awful. A heavy weight had settled in the pit of her stomach the moment she read Cyril's letter and realized the man she had believed was out of her life forever was back.

And now she had to face him. "But he did ask to see me alone."

"Very well." Mother's lips pressed together in a firm line.

"But I fully intend to press my ear to the door the moment it's closed. And I shall be right here should you need me."

Teddy narrowed her eyes. "Please tell me you don't have a pistol hidden in your skirts."

Mother hesitated, then smiled in an overly sweet manner. "I don't have a pistol hidden in my skirts."

"Are you lying?"

"I would never lie to you about a thing like that." Mother raised her chin. "And I'm really quite offended that you think I would."

Teddy studied her. "If I phrased the question differently, if I left out the part about where the pistol is perhaps, would your answer be different?"

"It seems to me it would be better for all concerned if you simply didn't ask."

Teddy stared. "Who are you?"

"I thought you understood, dear." A determined smile lifted her mother's lips. "I am your mother."

"Well then." She met the countess's gaze and nodded. "We have nothing to worry about." Teddy stepped to the parlor doors, adjusted her skirts, squared her shoulders, and swept into the room in as cold and heartless a manner as she could muster. It wasn't hard.

"Theodosia." Cyril's face lit with alleged delight, but his eyes said something altogether different. "Good God, I have always loved your hair."

"How very kind of you to say, Cyril. Might I mention that I hate the fact that you are apparently alive and well."

His brow arched upward. "You'd rather I'd be dead?"

"Yes."

"What? No polite hesitation? No moment to ponder the question?"

"It seemed pointless." She shrugged. "I had no need to ponder that particular question."

"Come now, Theodosia." He clasped his hand over his

heart. "You wound me deeply. Is that any way to greet your resurrected fiancé?"

"You are not my fiancé."

"In the eyes of the world I am."

Unfortunately, he had a point. He had died before anyone knew she had broken off their engagement. "In the eyes of the world you are, oh, how shall I put it?" She narrowed her eyes slightly. "Dead."

He grinned. "But remarkably spry for a dead man."

"What do you want, Cyril? Why are you here?"

He gasped in mock dismay. "Shouldn't you first, as the loving fiancée that you are, ask how is this possible? What miracle has brought me back to you?"

"Very well." She crossed her arms over her chest. "You're supposed to be dead. Why aren't you?"

"Any number of reasons I suppose. Fate. Destiny. Brilliant planning." He shrugged. "I'd be happy to give you all the details if you wish. Don't you want to know where I've been?"

"Not especially. My curiosity is not nearly as great as my desire to remove you from my life forever and as quickly as possible." She forced a tight smile. "So again—why are you here?"

"If you insist on being rude."

"I would think you would be grateful that I am merely rude."

"I see." He studied her curiously. "So my sins were not forgiven with my death?"

Her jaw tightened. "As you are not dead, no."

"And when you thought I was dead?"

"No."

"You are a hard woman, Theodosia Winslow." He shook his head in a mournful manner. "I never suspected it. I had hoped you would have gotten over the misdeeds of your late fiancé by now."

"Misdeeds?" She raised a brow. "You led my father to

lose his fortune and ultimately his life. I would scarcely call those *misdeeds*."

"Mistakes then." He shrugged. "Errors in judgment."

"Crimes?"

"Such a harsh word." He shook his head. "And, as no charges were brought, no evidence presented, it's inaccurate as well."

"The investigation ended when you and Father died. Although now that you're alive . . ."

"Ah, but any examination of my activities would trigger a closer look at your father's. I can't imagine you'd want that."

Yet another point.

"So I think it's best to avoid any renewed inquiry. As much as it might pain you to agree with me about anything surely you can agree on that."

She resisted the urge to scream in frustration. "What do you want, Cyril?"

He frowned. "That is getting tiresome."

"My apologies. I shall try to think of another way to ask what you want."

"A man has a great deal of time on his hands when the world considers him dead, Theodosia." Cyril slowly meandered around the perimeter of the room and Teddy had to turn to keep him in sight. The last thing she wanted was this vile creature where she couldn't see him, even for a moment. "More than enough time to consider what he has done with his life. To reflect, if you will. On his mistakes and errors in judgment."

"Are you trying to say you've repented?"

"Indeed I have." Sincerity rang in his voice but didn't quite reach his eyes.

"So are you here to ask my forgiveness?"

He hesitated, then nodded. "Forgiveness would be a beginning. If you could find it in your heart—"

"My heart?" She scoffed. "I wouldn't appeal to my heart if I were you."

"We meant something to each other once." He picked up a figurine and examined it.

"Come now, Cyril, you know as well as I you never had any real feelings for me. I was nothing more than a way to get to my father."

Pity she hadn't figured that out until after Cyril was, well, dead. She'd been a fool not to have seen it long before but she had thought herself in love. Cyril was a blond-haired, blue-eyed handsome figure of a man, charming and dashing and very nearly irresistible. On a list of everything she had thought she wanted in a suitor, in a husband, he'd had it all. Not the title but everything else. There were clues, of course, as to his true nature through the time they were together. Little things she paid no attention to until it was too late. Now, she knew there was no greater fool in the world than a woman who believes herself in love.

"I still remember the first time I saw you." He set down the figurine. "You were stunning, Theodosia, in a white gown if I recall, with all that red hair, like molten mahogany I thought, and those eyes that sparkled even in the moonlight." His gaze slid over her and she resisted the urge to shudder.

"You're wasting your time, Cyril. And your questionable charm."

"You used to like my questionable charm." He chuckled. "You used to like a great many other things as well."

Heat washed up her face. The last thing she wanted was a reminder of how he had seduced her and how she had allowed him to do so. No, she hadn't allowed him. She'd encouraged him and on more than one occasion. Still, regrets were pointless. One learned and moved on. Cyril Goddard was a mistake she would not make again.

"I never noticed how calculating the look in your eyes is," she said coolly. "I can't believe I didn't see it before. It's really quite remarkable."

His eyes narrowed. "Do you know how easy you were, Theodosia?" He smiled a slow, nasty sort of smile. "You were twenty-two. Not quite irredeemable in terms of a good match."

"Are we sharing fond memories now?" She stared at him, determined to avoid even an iota of anything other than disgust on her face. "I really have more important things to attend to."

"Oh you were pretty enough," he continued. "Really quite lovely, just not as, oh, fresh as the newest crop of debutantes. Not desperate by any means. Not yet."

She sighed in an exaggerated manner. "Do you have a point to this, Cyril?"

"Yes." He smiled slowly. "I want you back."

She stared at him for a long moment, then laughed. "You're mad if you think I want anything whatsoever to do with you. If that's all then"—she nodded toward the door—"this reunion is at an end."

"Actually, it's just beginning." He settled down on the sofa as if he intended to stay for a while. "Sit down."

"I'd prefer to stand."

"As you wish." He considered her thoughtfully. "But you may want to sit for this. I'm about to answer your question. Why I am here."

"Imagine my delight," she muttered and took a seat in the chair farthest from him.

"I don't know if you're aware of this but my brother died a few months ago."

"Permanently?" she said with a polite smile.

"As they buried him, I would assume so. I am his only heir."

He paused obviously to let the significance of his statement sink in. "Which means I am now Viscount Nottwood."

"My condolences on the loss of your brother."

"My brother was far more clever than I had ever suspected, as is my mother. She and he never especially trusted me." He heaved a heartfelt sigh. "He made certain, if he died without another heir, I might well get the title and the estates but the money remains firmly under my mother's control."

"How very farsighted of them."

"That, in my opinion, is debatable. Suffice it to say, my mother was delighted when you and I were engaged. You were the perfect match, you know. In spite of your advanced age, you were quite a catch. Excellent family connections, substantial dowry. I am sorry about that by the way."

She shrugged. Her dowry had gone the way of the rest of her family's fortune.

"My mother thought I was finally on the right path. I was mending my wicked ways as it were."

"I have to compliment you, Cyril, I never realized you had wicked ways. You hid it quite well."

"I did, didn't I?" He smirked. "I worked very hard to make certain my reputation, as far as the world knew, was, while not exemplary, no worse than most men I know."

"But your family knew?"

He shrugged. "It's hard to hide one's more nefarious activities from those you rely on for financial rescue."

"Go on."

"You can imagine my mother's delight when I appeared a few weeks ago, fresh from a watery grave and scarcely even wet." He cast her a chastising look. "She was much more pleased to see me than you were."

"She's your mother." In spite of herself, Teddy was fascinated by Cyril's tale, even if every word made her feel more like an idiot. She should have known what kind of man he was. "What did you tell her? Where did you say you've been for the last four years?"

"Oh, you know. Shipwreck, native tribes, amnesia, the usual sort of thing."

"I gather none of that is true?"

He scoffed.

"But she believed you?"

"As you said, she's my mother." He paused. "And she wanted to believe."

"So," she said slowly, "what does this have to do with me?"

"That's the sticking point in all this. As much as I have sworn to her that my close brush with death has changed me, that I am an entirely new man ready to take up the mantle of family responsibility and respectability, she's still, oh, the tiniest bit suspicious. Even though she does want to believe me she has doubts." He met her gaze directly. "Renewal of our engagement will go a long way toward alleviating those doubts."

"Renewal?" She scoffed. "Are you suggesting we pick up where we left off?"

"Not the exact point obviously."

"No, because if I recall correctly, the exact point, the last time we were in the same room together, I said I detested the very ground beneath your feet. I said I never wanted to see you again. I said I—"

"Really, there's no need to go into everything you said. You were upset at the time. Your father had just died and you had jumped to some rather unsettling conclusions."

"Conclusions that were, nonetheless, completely accurate."

"Regardless . . ." He waved off her comment. "I did ask you to wait, to reconsider ending our engagement until I returned."

"I never agreed—" She stared in disbelief. "And you never returned. You died, remember?"

"And now I have returned. Although, you can imagine my

dismay when I discovered you were engaged to someone else. And, I don't care whose heir he is, an American, Theodosia? I thought you had better taste than that."

"Perhaps you're right about my taste in fiancés, given my first fiancé, that is."

"You really should stop being so clever, it's not at all becoming. Nor am I fond of clever women," he said sharply. "Needless to say, Mother is quite distressed." He shook his head. "So you can see why it's necessary to break it off with him."

"I see nothing of the sort."

"It's best for all concerned that you do so."

"I can certainly see where you might have a problem, particularly with your mother. I, however, do not."

"Ah, but my problems are your problems, my dear."

"On the contrary, Cyril, your problems stopped being my problems when I learned the truth about what kind of man you really are and ended our engagement."

"I'm afraid you're still not seeing the entirety of our circumstances. Allow me to explain." He smiled. "First of all, it would be most awkward if upon my return from the grave, my fiancé did not welcome me back into her loving arms. What would people say?"

She smiled tightly. "I don't care."

"Don't be absurd, of course you do." He scoffed. "Your public acceptance of my resurrection would go a long way toward alleviating any suspicion regarding my story as to where I have been these last years as well as convince my mother I am worthy of trust. After all, if Lady Theodosia Winslow puts her faith in me, my mother can do no less. She would certainly loosen her grips on the family purse strings if she knew you were to be her new daughter-in-law."

"Then it would appear the next time you go to your grave you will be unwed and penniless."

He laughed. "I have missed your wit, Theodosia. But I have no intention of returning to the grave anytime soon. Indeed, I plan to live a long and happy life with my beloved wife by my side."

"I wish her all the best. I, however, have no intention of becoming your wife."

"Intentions often change with circumstances or necessity, my dear. And here's where it gets really interesting." He leaned forward and met her gaze. "I have in my possession documents that clearly show the depth of your father's involvement in our ill-fated venture. They paint him in the poorest of lights. Should those be made public, his name and reputation will be destroyed. As will yours, your mother's, and that of the relative who inherited your father's title. Anyone even distantly related to you will be ruined. And this little hobby of yours, yes, my dear, I have heard about that." What might have been genuine admiration shone in his eyes. "It's quite enterprising of you especially as the world seems convinced you don't need the money. That endeavor will be at an end." He smiled and settled back on the sofa. "Of course as your future husband it would be in my best interest to make certain such documents never see the light of day."

Her stomach churned and she struggled to keep her tone level. "I can't imagine that anything that would incriminate my father wouldn't point a finger at you as well."

"Come now, surely you don't think I would be that stupid. Actually, my evidence makes me look fairly good. Oh certainly, I might appear a bit of a fool, taken in by the duplicity of an older man, the father of the woman I love but no worse than that." He smiled. "It wouldn't take much you know. Documents delivered anonymously to the right official. Or perhaps a whisper into an eager reporter's ear. Even if nothing came of it, gossip and rumor alone would be enough to destroy everyone you care about."

She narrowed her eyes. He was right of course. The scandal would be enormous. Her father's name would be dragged through the mud and everyone else in the family along with it. Her mother would never survive the disgrace. She did not deserve this, nor did Simon. There had to be some way to escape Cyril's clutches.

"I'll consider it." She rose to her feet.

"Consider it?" He chuckled and stood. "My darling, Theodosia, I'm afraid you misunderstand. There is nothing to consider. You have very little choice."

He was right, at least for now. What she really needed was time to come up with a plan.

"I refuse to ruin Christmas and a New Year's Eve gala my fiancé's family is planning with the kind of gossip that ending our engagement will cause." She thought for a moment. "However, I will break it off with him on the day after."

"I'm afraid I can't agree to that." He shook his head. "Mother is growing impatient and I am perilously low on funds. We have kept my reappearance circumspect thus far but Mother would like to announce to friends and family and the rest of the world the resurrection of her lost son on Christmas Day. I want you by my side when she does so."

"On Christmas?" She stared at him. Christmas was a scant nine days away.

"It seems appropriate given it isn't every day one returns from the dead."

He had her exactly where he wanted her, at least for now. Helpless rage swept through her and her fists tightened by her sides.

"As I have no choice." She shrugged. "Fine."

He studied her closely and she resisted the urge to squirm. "Do keep in mind that, should you renege on our agreement, I would not hesitate to do whatever is necessary to remove Mr. Channing from your life."

"Am I to take that as a threat?"

He smiled. "Yes."

"Very well then. I do not expect to see you again until Christmas." She nodded at the door. "Good day."

"Now, now, Theodosia." Without warning, he grabbed her and yanked her into his arms. "I love it when you try to act as if you don't want me as much as I want you."

She clenched her teeth and ignored the frisson of fear that skated up her spine. "Release me at once."

"You were always very good at saying no when you meant yes. You liked it, you liked this." He tightened his hold and murmured against her neck. "And you will like it again."

She pushed against him but he was surprisingly strong for a dead man. "I wouldn't wager on it, Cyril."

"Nor would I." Mother's cool tone rang from the doorway. "I suggest you unhand my daughter at once."

"Lady Sallwick." Cyril released Teddy in the unhurried manner of a man who knew he had the upper hand. "How delightful to see you again."

"You're looking well, given your death," Mother said pleasantly. "Now would you like to explain why you were grappling my daughter."

He slanted an annoyed glance at Teddy, then returned his attention to her mother. "My apologies, Lady Sallwick, I was simply overcome with joy at being reunited with my beloved. You understand."

"I understand far more than you imagine, Mr. Goddard."

"Lord Nottwood, if you please."

"Very well, Lord Nottwood." Mother's eyes narrowed. "Now, get out of my house."

"Come, come, is that any way to talk to the man who is going to marry your daughter?"

Mother didn't allow so much of a flicker of surprise to show on her face but then she had said she'd be listening at the door. "It's the way I speak to the man who ruined my husband and, quite frankly, I thought I was being more than civil."

"This is not the welcome I expected from you." Cyril shook his head in a disappointed manner. "You used to like me. You were delighted when I asked Theodosia to marry me."

"Well, I'm not known for my cleverness, Lord Nottwood. Ask anyone." Mother smiled sweetly. Too sweetly and Teddy wondered exactly where her pistol was.

"Good day, Cyril," Teddy said firmly.

"Until Christmas then." He smiled. "And afterward, we shall plan our wedding. Mother will enjoy that. I think a grand affair is called for as befits our union. Good day, ladies." Cyril nodded and took his leave.

Mother stepped to the doorway and waited until Jacobs saw him out. She closed the parlor door and leaned her back against it. "I am so sorry, Theodosia. This is my fault." She shook her head. "I encouraged that man. I had no idea."

"It's as much my fault as it is yours." Although most of the blame could be laid at her father's feet. "I have always considered myself intelligent but apparently in this matter I was sadly lacking."

"I won't let you marry him." Mother straightened. "I would rather face ruin than allow that."

"Oh, I have no intention of marrying him."

Mother ignored her and paced. "We could sell the house. That would give us enough money to leave London, leave England altogether. Oh, we'll certainly have to continue to be frugal but we could travel the world or start a new—"

"Mother," Teddy said sharply. "I said I will not marry him but I might have to be his fiancée. At least until I can find a way out of this."

"What if there isn't a way out?"

"There must be." Teddy paced in opposition to her

mother's steps. "Did Father tell you anything that might be helpful?"

"Nothing that I can recall, he was always rather vague about details, and it was four years ago." She paused. "You know, your father never disposed of anything. He was something of a collector, although of nothing in particular. There might—"

A knock sounded at the door and it opened before they could respond. Jacobs blocked the opening as if he was trying to keep someone out. "I am sorry to interrupt you, my lady, but—"

Dee pushed her way passed him. "I told you this was no time for formalities. This is obviously a crisis!"

Mother's eyes widened. "Good day, Delilah. How pleasant to see you again."

"Lady Sallwick." Dee nodded at Mother, her gaze shifting between the two women. "It is a crisis, isn't it?"

Teddy and her mother traded glances.

"Crisis?" Mother said innocently. "Why, Delilah dear, we have no idea what you mean."

"I mean I just saw Teddy's fiancé, her *dead* fiancé not her current, *living* fiancé, leave this house not five minutes ago." Dee glared. "I should think the fact that a dead man was here, apparently alive and well, would certainly be a crisis given the villainous nature of this particular dead man."

"She knows, Mother." Teddy sighed.

Mother winced. "About everything?"

"Most of it, I suspect," Dee said.

Teddy nodded. "I'm afraid so."

"Obviously, Delilah, you are excellent at keeping confidences," Mother said. "I thank you for that."

"Think nothing of it." Dee waved off the thanks. "Teddy has kept more than a few secrets for me. Now, tell me everything. Why is he alive and what does he want?"

"It appears Mr. Goddard—Lord Nottwood—thought it best if the world considered him dead to avoid legal consequences of the scheme he had embroiled my husband in."

"And what he wants now . . ." Teddy blew a long breath. "Is me."

Dee's eyes widened. "You? What do you mean?"

"He wants me to resume our engagement. He thinks it will give him respectability, especially with his mother who apparently controls the family fortune."

"Yes, I can see that." Dee nodded. "Then this is what had you so worried last night. Jack was concerned—"

"You can't tell him about this," Teddy said sharply.

Dee's brow furrowed. "Why not?"

"Because he'll want to help. He'll want to be my hero. He's very endearing that way but I neither need that nor can I allow it." Teddy shook her head. "Cyril is dangerous and if I don't do what he asks he'll expose documents that detail Father's less than legitimate activities. I don't want Jack involved."

"And Nottwood threatened Mr. Channing," Mother said in an ominous manner.

Dee stared, then scoffed. "You can't possibly be serious."

"I tend not to doubt a threat coming from a man ruthless enough to let his own family think he is dead for four years!" Teddy glared. "Do you think I'm being overly cautious?"

"Yes, well, when you put it that way, probably not." Dee thought for a moment. "You need a plan. Everything always goes much better when you have a plan."

"I realize that." Teddy's jaw tightened. "I simply don't have one."

"Well then, it's a good thing I'm here. I have always been excellent when it comes to plans." Dee pulled off her cloak and hat and tossed them onto a chair. "Now then, you said Nottwood has documents?"

Teddy nodded.

"Documents . . ." Her mother's brow furrowed in thought. "Papers." Her eyes widened. "There is a trunk in the attic with all the papers from your father's library, everything in his desks, at the abbey and here."

"And it would seem to me . . ." The idea formed as Teddy spoke the words. "Cyril couldn't possibly expose Father if he was threatened with exposure himself. If there is something in those papers of Father's . . ."

"You could blackmail him!" Delight sounded in Dee's voice.

Mother frowned. "I am not fond of the word *blackmail.*"

Dee stared. "But surely you can see how your blackmail makes his blackmail useless?"

"Oh, I'm not opposed to the practice of it, I simply don't like the word. I much prefer . . ." Mother smiled. "Retribution."

Dee glanced at her friend. "I don't believe I have ever seen this side of your mother."

"No one has, dear." Mother smiled and called for Jacobs to have the trunk brought down from the attic.

Jacobs was quicker than expected and in no time at all the trunk was opened in the parlor. It was filled nearly to the top with assorted papers, documents, and correspondence.

Dee looked at the trunk skeptically. "Do either of you have any idea what we're looking for?"

"Something to do with stocks, perhaps," Mother murmured.

"That's at least a place to start," Teddy said with far more confidence than she felt.

The women started pulling papers out of the trunk and within a few minutes decided it would be best to stack everything into piles according to topic and then go through it one stack at a time. A few minutes after that, they realized the project was entirely too large for the small table in the parlor and moved to the dining room table. Mother remembered a cache of correspondence she'd seen in a bureau drawer and went to fetch it. And a few minutes later, Dee sank back into a chair with a sigh. "It seems to me, this would be easier if we had any idea what we were looking for."

"Just keep looking," Teddy murmured, her eyes beginning to blur. As much as she knew this didn't have to be accomplished today, the sooner they found something, the sooner she would be rid of Cyril once and for all. Especially as she couldn't rely on death to do that for her.

"You know," Dee said in an offhand manner, "on occasion, when I have what is for the most part an excellent plan, I find I need help of a more specialized sort. An expert, perhaps, something of that nature. In this particular case, I think someone with financial knowledge—"

"No!" Teddy snapped.

"Someone who is well versed in monetary matters—"

"Absolutely not!"

"Someone who might have a hereditary background in bank—"

"Delilah Hargate, if you so much as breathe a single word about any of this to Jack, I will never forgive you." Teddy glared. "I don't want him near this. It's bad enough that Mother and I are involved. I don't doubt that Cyril is dangerous but more so to Jack than to us. Besides, if this all goes horribly wrong, the scandal will be enormous. I don't think the future Earl of Briston should be embroiled in scandal of a financial nature especially given his connections to a prominent American bank. Do you understand?"

"Yes, but you know that my family is not averse to scandal. We have certainly weathered scandal and gossip before. Not me, of course, but everyone else in the family."

"Promise me you won't say a word to him."

"Fine," Dee snapped. "I think it's completely shortsighted and really rather stupid of you not to ask him for his help but I promise I won't say a word to Jack." She got to her feet.

"I'm supposed to meet Sam to return to Millworth but I will be back first thing in the morning to continue this . . . quest."

"Thank you." Teddy breathed a sigh of relief and cast the other woman a weak smile. "You are indeed my good, true friend."

"I am and I always will be. And might I say you were right. You don't need a hero. What you need, my good, true friend . . ." Dee met her gaze firmly. "Is a banker."

Chapter Twenty-One

"Well, this looks daunting." Jack's cool tone sounded from the dining room doorway.

Teddy clenched her teeth and prayed for strength. She should have known Dee wouldn't be able to keep her mouth shut. Still, she had promised not to say anything to Jack and, at least for the moment, Teddy should give her the benefit of the doubt.

"This?" Teddy adopted a pleasant smile, pushed her chair back from the table, and stood. "Mother and I thought it was past time we went through Father's records, put everything in order, that sort of thing. It's something we should have done years ago but she was never quite up to it. You understand. And you're right." She heaved an overly dramatic sigh. "It is a daunting task."

A task Teddy had been dealing with since she arrived home shortly after daybreak. At her mother's insistence, Teddy had slept at Dee's house although sleep was not an entirely accurate description of the tossing and turning that had plagued Teddy through the long night. Now, after hours of sifting through the seemingly endless pages, it did appear futile, especially since neither she nor her mother had any idea exactly what to look for. Teddy assumed anything with Cyril's name on it would be significant. Her mother was currently searching other rooms in the house in hopes of finding anything else Father might have hidden away.

"So have you learned anything of interest?"

"Learned anything?" She raised a shoulder in a casual shrug. "Except for the fact that my father was exceptionally disorganized, which came as no surprise, no, nothing of particular interest."

He studied her for a long moment. "Would you care to hear what I've learned?"

"What you . . ." She narrowed her eyes. "You know, don't you? Dee told you, didn't she?"

"I do and she didn't," he said, his tone harder than she expected. Almost annoyed. "While you did secure her promise not to tell me, you did not forbid her to tell anyone else."

"Well, that was stupid of me." Teddy should have known better. "She told Sam everything, didn't she?"

"The words were out of her mouth the moment she saw him." He scanned the table, no doubt hoping to find an element of organization amidst confusion. The neat stacks of papers she and her mother had spent hours sorting last night had somehow rearranged themselves into a chaos of indecipherable bits and pieces.

"And he told you."

"Without so much as a moment's hesitation." He picked up a random document and studied it. "She also told Sam she wouldn't be here to assist you today. I suspect she doesn't want to face you."

"Wise of her," Teddy muttered. "Damn it all, Jack. You shouldn't be here and I don't see why you are. I do appreciate it, really I do, but I don't need your help. This has nothing to do with you and I would much prefer to keep you as far away as possible. It's messy and awkward and . . . and . . ."

"Keep me as far away as possible?" He stared at her in disbelief. "You may be the most intelligent woman I have ever met but unfortunately, you're the most stubborn as well." He threw the document in his hand back on the pile, then circled the table toward her. "And at times, you haven't a brain in your head."

"That's exactly what I want to hear right now, thank you very much. I am well aware of any number of stupid mistakes I have made in the past." She glared and brushed a persistent strand of hair away from her face. "And there's absolutely no reason why you should be quite so annoyed with me. All I was—"

He grabbed her, pulled her hard into his arms, and gazed into her eyes. "And you don't *see* anything."

She stared up at him and her breath caught. "What do you mean?"

"Good God, if I have to explain it to you . . ." Without another word he pulled her tighter against him and pressed his lips to hers in a kiss demanding and possessive and utterly wonderful.

Shock held her still for the barest moment, then desire and need and something quite remarkable filled her. She clung to him, the scent of cold wool and vague spice that was completely Jack surrounded her and swept into her soul. And when at last he raised his head from hers she marveled that she could still stand. Dear Lord, what was happening to her? This wasn't the first time he had kissed her after all. Still, it felt like a first kiss. It felt like a revelation. Or a beginning. Or forever.

"Why did you do that?" she said with a gasp.

"Because I've wanted to do that again since the last time I did that. Entirely too long ago." His gaze slipped to her lips then back to her eyes. "I want to kiss you every minute I'm with you and most of the time when I'm not."

"Oh." She stared up at him and struggled to catch her breath. "That really wasn't at all fair of you, you know."

"I do know and I'm delighted that I thought of it." He smiled. "Besides, it seemed the best way to shut you up."

She smiled reluctantly. "I suppose it was effective."

"Only for a moment apparently."

Her gaze searched his. "Is there any way I can stop you from becoming involved in this?"

He leaned in and brushed his lips against her forehead. "What do you think?"

The oddest feeling of awe washed through her and warmed her soul. She regretfully ignored it. "Have you considered the possible repercussions if this becomes public? For you and for your family? On both sides of the Atlantic I might add."

"I'm more than aware of that. We shall just have to make sure it remains a private matter." He kissed her again, fast and hard and again it took her breath away.

"Yes, of course."

He released her and turned his attention back to Father's papers. "Although I suspect we don't need to worry about that. In spite of what he told you, I doubt your Lord Nottwood wants this matter made public any more than you do. If he did carry through with his threat to release the evidence he claims to have against your father, it might not incriminate him but it would definitely adversely affect this new image he wants to present to the world. And it would destroy any benefit he would gain from marrying you."

"Then you don't think we need to worry about him," she said slowly, hope rising for the first time since she'd met with Cyril.

"I didn't say that." He sat down and began sorting the papers. "Rationally, it makes no sense for him to expose your father but then it's obvious your Lord Nottwood is not especially rational."

"He's not my Lord Nottwood and I do wish you would stop referring to him as such."

"Sorry." He pulled out a pair of spectacles from his waistcoat pocket and put them on.

She raised a brow. "Glasses, Jack?"

"Only when I have a lot of fine print to go through."

"I like them." Whereas Teddy had appreciated his boyish good looks before, the man in the spectacles looked not merely handsome but distinguished and resolute. The kind of man in whose hands you could put your future. And your heart.

"One less thing to worry about then." He smiled but it was apparent his thoughts had already turned to the work ahead. He selected another paper and perused it. "As I was saying, a man willing to go to the lengths he has gone to in order to avoid prosecution is not a man to whom normal considerations of rational, sensible behavior would apply."

"I suspect you're right there."

Jack's gaze stayed on the paper in his hand. "There was no shipwreck."

"What?"

"The ship Nottwood was allegedly on, the one lost at sea . . ." He glanced up at her. "It didn't exist."

She sank down into the nearest chair. "What do you mean?"

"Then it appears you do want to know what I have learned after all," he said under his breath.

"Bloody hell, Jack, stop being so smug. I am not fond of games at the best of times. Now tell me what you're talking about."

He leaned back in his chair and met her gaze. "Sam and Gray and I have been in London since early this morning. Gray especially has a wide variety of sources of information. There is no record to be found of a ship being lost anywhere in the world during the period Nottwood's *death* was reported."

She stared. "So it was all a lie?"

He nodded. "Quite a detailed one from what we've been able to gather. There might even have been bribery involved in order to make this lost ship seem legitimate. Sam and Gray are still looking into it. Didn't you wonder why there was no notice of a wrecked ship in the newspapers?"

"No, I was preoccupied what with my father's recent death and my mother's grief and my belief that my former fiancé was at the bottom of the ocean." She huffed. "I had a great deal on my mind and verifying the letter I received from the company never so much as occurred to me." She thought for a moment. "It should have though, given what I had learned about Cyril."

His eyes narrowed thoughtfully. "Do you still have it? The letter, that is."

"I think so. Why?"

"It might point us in a particular direction. It certainly couldn't hurt. Now . . ." He studied her closely. "Tell me everything you know about the Argentine Atlantic Trading Company."

"It's not much, I'm afraid." Briefly, she explained all they knew about her father's business dealings.

When she finished he stared at her for a long moment. "You didn't understand one word of what you just said, did you?"

"Of course I did." She scoffed, then grimaced. "But only one. As much as I hate to admit it, all this . . ." She waved at the table. "It's as indecipherable to me as if it's a foreign language. I understand profit and loss and what I need to do to balance expenditures with charges but as a matter of business, that's minor. What Father was involved in, what you understand so easily, it's quite beyond me."

"Precisely why you need an expert." He sifted through the papers in front of him. "Make no mistake, Theodosia, even if you needed help with something I had no knowledge of or experience with, I would give you my assistance whether you wished me to or not."

"Oh?" She smiled. "Would you save me from a fire-breathing dragon?"

"Absolutely," he said and began sorting the papers on the table.

"Rescue me from kidnapping pirates?"

"Without question." He glanced at her. "Are you involved with pirates, too?"

"Not that I'm aware of."

"Good. I know nothing about pirates that didn't come from a children's book or a novel of adventure." His gaze returned to the task in front of him. "It appears these were in some sort of order once."

"We tried to sort it all out but it quickly became pointless," she said. "Would you also—"

"I would risk my fortune, my future, and my very life for you should it be necessary," he said absently, his attention already back on the documents strewn over the table. "Now then it appears this is a stock . . ."

Jack continued explaining what various papers were and why they might or might not be important, more to himself than to her. She was too shocked by his declaration to pay any attention at all, even if she had understood any of it. While she nodded and made appropriate comments, she couldn't pull her mind away from his pronouncement.

Was it just something he said without thinking or would he truly risk everything for her? After all, he wasn't really her fiancé. He didn't actually plan to marry her. And he certainly wasn't in love with her. Although he did sound like a man in love. And he definitely kissed like one. But Jack was the sort of man for whom love would lead directly to marriage. And marriage was not in her plans. But then neither was love.

It was a silly thought and she tried to dismiss it. Jack was simply trying to be like his father. He was trying to be her hero. There was nothing more to his comment than that. Why the man wasn't even really paying attention. The realization was at once comforting and the tiniest bit disappointing.

Through the long day and well into the evening, she sat by his side and watched him study, arrange, and rearrange the papers left by her father, offering her assistance in any way she could. She supplied him with paper and pen and he'd jot notes periodically or pause to ask a question. Usually one she had no answer for. Mother popped into the dining room off and on. Unfortunately, she had discovered nothing that might prove worthwhile, which she found most distressing. All three of them agreed it was best if Mother absented herself from the proceedings as she wasn't of any help anyway.

There were long stretches when he would study something that appeared promising and Teddy would study him. The man wielded intelligence like a sword, carried it like a warrior. His features strong and determined, he was obviously at home in the world of finance and figures. She noticed the tiny lines of concentration that furrowed his brow and the way his spectacles would slide down his nose and he'd absently push them back in place in a most endearing way. On more than one occasion she had to resist the impulse to reach out and smooth away an errant strand of hair. She noted the way his lips pressed together when his eyes narrowed and he focused on something that might be significant. She watched his hands shuffle through papers, strong and virile and knowing, and wondered in passing how they would feel sliding over her hips or her breasts. It was as intriguing and exciting a thought as it was improper. She tried in vain to vanquish that and other persistent thoughts.

They took a brief break for a light supper with her mother and Jack seemed determined to charm her. And he did. By the end of the meal Mother was taken with far more than his prospects and his future title. When they finished eating, she said she had a few other places her husband might have left papers, cast an approving look at her daughter, then took her leave.

"I think that's it for tonight," Jack said a few hours later. He leaned back in his chair and blew a weary breath. "We've gotten through nearly a quarter of it." He shook his head. "Your father didn't believe in throwing anything away. Receipts, notations, half-written letters . . . To our benefit, really."

"Except that there's so much of it." Teddy cast a disgusted look at the now neatly stacked piles of her father's financial life. "Why couldn't my father have been smart enough to have hidden evidence to incriminate Cyril in a secret drawer or slipped between the pages of a book or something of that nature."

Jack chuckled. "It would have made this easier."

"Although I suppose if Father had been farsighted and clever enough to do that, perhaps he wouldn't have been in the position he was."

"Theodosia." Jack leaned forward and took her hand. "Everything I've seen so far tells me that your father had no idea what he was involved in, at least not until the end."

She drew a deep breath. "There was no company, was there?"

"As far as I can tell, there was something." Jack hesitated. "But it appears to have been built on stock certificates, questionable bonds, paper, and promises without anything solid or substantial to back it up."

"It was all a fraud, Jack, wasn't it?"

Again he paused, then nodded. "That's how it appears. Looking at it all, and admittedly we're nowhere near finished, there are indications that your father was not the only one to lose a fortune in this. It's not surprising really when you consider that currently the largest group of investors in Latin America—especially in Argentinean interests—are British. And a lot of them have made a lot of money. But as

I said, it looks to me that your father had no idea what he was involved in."

"Stupidity is not really a good excuse, is it?"

He smiled in a half-hearted manner. "Probably not." He got to his feet. "Are you staying here tonight?"

"I hadn't planned to but it is late." She pushed her chair back and rose to her feet. "Mother thinks I'm safer at Dee's than here because Cyril has no idea I've been staying there. She's insisted on having Jacobs stay at Dee's as well. For protection."

He raised a brow. "The butler?"

"Apparently he wasn't always a butler." Yet another mystery she'd like to delve into. She heaved a weary sigh. "It's shocking how exhausting it is to do nothing but watch you try to unravel this mess."

He paused as if choosing his words. He'd done a lot of that today but then it was no doubt awkward to tell even your fake fiancé all the details of her father's fraudulent financial dealings. "You needn't worry about safety. There are men watching your house as well as Delilah's."

She narrowed her eyes. "What?"

"It's futile to protest," he said firmly. "Sam and Gray and I agreed it was a reasonable precaution. My father knew of a reputable agency that provides such a service."

"Your father?" She stared at him. "Does everyone in your family know about this?"

"Not everyone." He chuckled. "I doubt that my mother knows."

"Good Lord." She buried her face in her hands. "How humiliating. I didn't want anyone to know about Father's—"

"Stop that." He pulled her close and enfolded her in his arms. "Everyone at Millworth thinks of you as another member of the family. They would do anything to help you. And while Sam and Gray and my father and Uncle Nigel do know about your father's difficulties, some of which came as no surprise by the way, no one else is aware of that part of it, except Delilah of course. Aunt Bernadette and Camille only know that your dead fiancé has returned from the grave." He chuckled. "It was all I could do to keep my aunt from coming into London with the rest of us."

She smiled against his coat. "Between your aunt and my mother, Cyril wouldn't have a chance."

"About your mother . . ."

Reluctantly she lifted her head. "Yes?"

"There's something different between the two of you. You seem, well, to like each other?"

"If there's any benefit to this mess with Cyril, it's that it's brought us together."

"Facing a common enemy will do that."

"We've talked a great deal in the last few days." She thought for a moment. "I think we've found something we had lost."

"So . . ." His gaze searched hers. "That's good?"

"Very good."

"We'll figure this all out, you know." Confidence rang in his voice. "There is no possible ending that leaves you married to him."

"Are you sure?"

"There isn't a doubt in my mind. Besides . . ." He smiled in a wry manner. "What kind of hero would abandon the fair maiden to the villain?"

"I don't need a hero, Jack." She smiled up at him. "But I am quite grateful to have a banker."

"That's all this banker needs to hear." He bent to brush his lips across hers in a kiss warm and slow and infinitely perfect. A kiss that fueled a fire deep within her, an ache that grew with every moment in his arms. At last he released her with a reluctant sigh. "I'll be back first thing in the morning."

"Until then." She cast him a half-hearted smile.

"Try not to worry."

"I'll try. But I doubt that I'll succeed." She shook her head. "It's going to take a miracle, Jack."

"This is the right time of year for it then. We will find something," he said firmly. Not even a flicker of doubt shone in his eyes and as much as Teddy feared there was nothing to find, his confidence lifted her spirits.

"Sleep well, Theodosia, gift from God."

"Good evening, my banker." *My hero.*

He smiled, nodded, and took his leave.

For a long time she stood in the dining room doorway and stared after him, too tired to summon the energy to move, too filled with unanswered questions crowding her mind.

Was he in love with her? Or was he just trying to ride to her rescue?

She didn't know and, given her experiences with Cyril, no longer trusted her own judgment about such things. She was afraid to assume anything. About Jack or about herself.

Because as much as she didn't know if he was in love with her, she had absolutely no idea if she was in love with him.

The days quickly fell into a pattern. Jack would arrive somewhere around late morning to begin the arduous task of trying to find something to incriminate Cyril. Quite often he would report some new bit of information that Grayson or Sam had ferreted out but nothing of any real worth. Teddy quickly realized there was little she could do to assist Jack but offer her encouragement. Regardless, she was reluctant to leave his side even if he had no idea she was there most of the time. It struck her as an intimate sort of silent companionship that was at once comforting and exciting and . . . right.

Still, she wished she could be of more substantial assistance. But Father's papers were incomprehensible to her. There was something about the enormity of the task that fogged one's mind and deadened one's soul. At least when it came to Teddy's mind and soul. Jack, on the other hand, reveled in it. He was obviously invigorated by this financial conundrum whereas she felt both helpless and stupid. He assured her she was neither but he didn't seem quite as sincere in his assurance as one might have hoped.

On the second day, in the desk in her rooms, Teddy found the letter informing her of Cyril's demise. On the third day, Grayson told Jack he might have uncovered something significant. On the morning of the fourth day, the day of Sir Malcomb's dinner, the first miracle of the Christmas season occurred when Teddy's mother volunteered to handle Sir Malcomb's gathering on her own. Mother insisted Teddy's time was better spent helping Jack and took over all the final arrangements with a shocking display of confidence and an equally astonishing level of competence. By late afternoon she had wished them luck, confided that she was quite looking forward to seeing Sir Malcomb and his cronies, most of whom she'd known for years, and sailed off with all the poise and self-assurance of someone who did indeed know what she was doing. Which could certainly be called another miracle. Or at least part of the first.

The second miracle was far more subtle but remarkable nonetheless and occurred late in the evening after the servants had retired. Teddy and Jack agreed they needed to clear their minds and talk about something entirely different from the matter at hand. Teddy spoke of the plans for the New Year's ball. As she'd had so much of the arrangements already well in hand before Cyril's appearance she was not especially worried about the event's success. The gala was still more than a week away after all. Neither of them mentioned the possibility that if they failed to find what they needed, she might not be there at all.

Jack talked of his meeting with his mother and his hopes that she and his father were at least speaking to one another. He was surprisingly optimistic about that. And he told her about speaking with Miss Merryweather and how they had agreed they were meant to be nothing more than good friends and how much she was enjoying travel and so on and so forth. Indeed, he did go on for rather a long time about the intrepid Miss Merryweather and her sea voyage and how much she loved traveling by ship and . . .

It struck them both at almost precisely the same moment. Their gazes met and they realized, regardless of actual proof, that they'd had the answer very nearly all along. Which, by anyone's reckoning, could definitely be called a second miracle.

And when Teddy threw her arms around Jack's neck and he picked her up and twirled her around the room, their laughter echoed through the house. It wasn't a miracle that their lips would meet in the rush of victory. Indeed, it was to be expected really. He had kissed her good-bye every night since they'd begun. But while this particular kiss started innocently enough it flared quickly to something powerful and overwhelming and altogether irresistible. Something Teddy never imagined she'd feel. A feeling she never imagined she'd trust.

Certainly a purist in the matter of miracles would most assuredly disdain this particular miracle given its sinful nature. After Cyril she had vowed intimacy with a man was not a mistake she would make again. But this was different. This desire gripped not merely her body but her heart, her soul.

This was different. This was no mistake. This was Jack.

Her banker.

Her hero.

And regardless of what might happen in the future, what plans she had made for her life, what path he might ultimately choose for his, here and now she wanted nothing more than to be with him.

And that might have been the greatest miracle of them all.

Chapter Twenty-Two

"This could be a dreadful mistake, you know," Jack murmured against her neck, his voice ragged with urgency and desire.

Her back was flat against her closed door and she groped with one hand to turn the key in the lock. Thank God the lamp in her room was lit. "Yes, I do know. But . . ."

He raised his head and gazed into her eyes. "But?"

"But it isn't." She swallowed hard. "I know that too."

His gaze searched hers for an endless moment; then he nodded and pulled her close. "Good." And his lips again claimed hers.

Teddy had no idea how they'd managed to get up the stairs and into her rooms. The last few minutes were a blur of hands and lips and passion too long denied. Nor was she at all sure how she came to be clad only in her corset and chemise and drawers and where exactly he had lost his shirt. Details were insignificant, lost in the fog of arousal that enveloped her.

He fumbled with the fasteners on the front of her corset and she tugged at the buttons on his trousers. It struck her that she was not being at all retiring in this, wasn't even feigning reluctance. But then why on earth should she? She was already ruined after all. One couldn't be more ruined. And dear Lord, she wanted him with an intensity she'd never so much as suspected could burn within her. Bloody hell, she was a tart. A tart ruled by lust and passion and all those things she'd been told would doom her to hell. Not that it mattered. Nothing mattered at the moment but him.

Her corset loosened and slipped to the floor. His hands slid under her chemise and touched her naked flesh and she shivered. His buttons popped open beneath her fingers and she slid his trousers down his hips until his erection pressed hard against her. And he groaned.

Heat pooled between her thighs.

She wrenched her lips from his. "I really should tell you. I am not exactly, that is to say, well . . ." She drew a deep breath. "I have done this before."

"Oh?" He cleared his throat. "Do you think now, this particular moment, is the right time to mention that?"

"It didn't occur to me to mention it before."

"And it occurred to you now?" His hands skimmed over her waist and his fingers found the ribbon of her drawers and pulled it free. The undergarment slid to the floor. "Now?"

"I just thought you should know," she said weakly, her attention centered on the feel of his, well, his *cock,* for lack of a more appropriate term, hard against her. She never would have used the word aloud. Cyril had used it, had indeed been quite proud of using it, and it had always struck her as coarse and vulgar. Yet another detail about her late fiancé she had ignored. But here and now, with Jack, its very sinful sound was exciting and arousing. There was something to be said for being a tart.

"I did always think I would marry a virgin." His hands splayed over the small of her back and drifted lower to cup her bottom.

"Excellent." She moaned softly and pressed against him. "As we are not discussing marriage."

"Well then, you should know." He smiled a slow, wicked

smile and shifted to pull her chemise off over her head. "I am not a virgin either."

"Thank God." She sank forward into his arms and he swept her up and carried her to the bed. Like a prize. Or a gift.

They fell onto the bed together and were at once a tangle of arms and legs, of lips and mouths and tongues, of exploration and discovery.

Without warning he paused and raised his head. "Although, as we are confessing, I suppose you should know I am not, oh, exceptionally experienced."

"What do you mean by *exceptionally experienced?*" Now was probably not the most opportune time for this discussion either. "You did say, or implied, that you had done this before."

"I have done this before." The slightest edge of indignation sounded in his voice. "But I'm not the sort of man who finds it necessary to bed every woman I meet."

"I never thought you were."

"I do have experience. I am simply not *exceptionally* experienced."

"Well then, Jack." She shifted her head and nuzzled that delightful masculine curve where his neck met his shoulder. "It seems we are well matched."

"I wouldn't want you to be, well, disappointed."

"I can't imagine you being disappointing." He tasted of spice and man and promises. "In anything."

"I have been told I have a certain natural ability."

"We shall see," she murmured.

"Indeed we shall." He turned, caught her tight against him, and rolled her onto her back.

He trailed kisses down her throat so lightly she wasn't sure he was touching her at all and she arched upward to meet his lips. His mouth drifted over her breasts and he tasted first one then the next. He teased and toyed until her breath came faster and his mouth traveled lower.

And she ached for more.

She ran her fingers through his hair and caressed the hard muscles of his shoulders and his back. And reveled in the feel of his naked body against hers. In the heat of him and the passion that arched between them, wrapped around them, bound them.

His hand slipped between her legs to fondle and stroke, his fingers sliding over her, slick with her own arousal. He explored her with tongue and fingers, worshipped her. Molded her into a being of pure sensation until she existed only in the touch of his hand and the brush of his lips. And the ever-increasing yearning that threatened to rip her apart.

She relished the heat of his flesh beneath her fingertips, the heat she shared. A fire within them, growing hotter, consuming all in its path. She took pleasure in the learning of him, exploring the hard planes of his body, discovering the smattering of hair that drifted over his chest and trailed down his stomach. She marveled at the hard, hot length of him and gloried in the way his body surged toward hers when she stroked him.

He groaned. "Theo . . ."

Every whisper of his lips across her throat, her breasts, her stomach wound her tighter and tighter. With every touch of his, every caress of hers, she lost herself more and more into a world of absolute sensation. A world raw and electric. Dimly, she noticed a soft moaning echoing the pleasure gripping her senses and realized it was coming from her. And that too was arousing and erotic and intoxicating.

Some semblance of rational thought still lingering in the back of her mind noted that this was not at all how her intimacies with Cyril had been. She did not recall this intensity of feeling, this all-consuming desire as if the forces of nature itself possessed them. And surely she would remember. No, this was new. And all the more powerful for the newness of it.

Her awareness shrank to nothing save him. The taste of

him. The feel of him. The scent of him. Nothing existed but the need for him, unrelenting and immediate. She hooked her leg around his and guided him up her body. She clutched at him and urged him on.

"Jack," she murmured, his name no more than a breath or a prayer on her lips.

Her hips rolled toward him as if of their own accord. He positioned himself between her legs and slid into her with a measured stroke that brought a low cry from somewhere deep within her. She moaned with the sensation of their joining and the joy of being one with him.

She met his thrusts with hers, rocking her hips against him harder and faster, in an ever-increasing rhythm that tore at her soul. She claimed him for her own and belonged to him in return.

She was, they were, one. For now. Forever. Until at last her body tightened around his and release flooded through her in waves of sheer ecstasy. And that too was new.

Dimly, over the roar of blood in her ears, the thud of her heart in her chest, she heard him cry her name and felt him thrust deep into her and his body quake against hers.

This was so much more than she had imagined or expected. But then this was Jack.

And wasn't he more than she had expected as well?

"You were right." Jack stared unseeing at the ceiling above them, struggling to catch his breath.

"Oh?" The breathless note in her voice matched his own.

"You were worth the trouble."

Beside him, Theodosia paused. Then giggled. "As were you."

She rolled onto her side and smiled at him. "I'm not sure what to say now. This was, well, really quite . . . wonderful."

"I was going to say unexpected." He grinned. "But all the

more wonderful for its unexpected nature. Of course I am not exceptionally experienced."

"But you do have a certain natural ability."

He laughed.

"Whereas I am, well . . ." She sighed. "A tart."

He sobered and nodded solemnly. "Yes, there is that."

She stared at him. "Do you really think so?"

"No, I really don't." He chose his words with care. "I think you were deceived by a man you trusted and—"

"Three times," she said abruptly and sat up, clutching the covers around her.

He drew his brows together in confusion. "Three times what?"

"Three is how many times . . ." She winced. "I was, well *deceived* by Cyril. It was a mistake, Jack," she added quickly. "One that I shall always regret. But I alone am to blame." She paused. "Although I suppose one could say once was a mistake and three times was becoming a habit."

He sat up, rested his back against a pillow, and pulled her into his arms. "You don't have to tell me this."

"I know. It's really none of your concern but oddly enough I feel that I do need to tell you. That not telling you would be somewhat deceitful."

"They do say confession is good for the soul."

"Oh, I'm not especially worried about my soul but I would hate for you to think poorly of me."

"I would never think poorly of you." He pulled her tighter to him and brushed a kiss across her forehead.

"I was young, well, *younger,* and foolish and believed myself in love and thought I was going to spend the rest of my life with him. So it didn't seem especially wrong."

"I think we can agree, as he duped you on so many things, this too can be accredited to that." He thought for a moment. "From what I understand, the man was an expert at maneuvering people into getting what he wanted. It's not surprising that he managed to seduce you."

"It wasn't altogether difficult for him. I . . . I allowed him to seduce me." She flicked an invisible piece of lint from the blanket. "I should have been smarter, Lord knows I was with other men. But I was engaged and I wasn't getting any younger and, well . . ." She shifted in his arms, twisted to meet his gaze directly. "I didn't want to die a virgin."

He choked back a laugh.

She glared at him. "This is not amusing."

He grinned. "Yes it is."

"It's different for men, you know. Why, you're expected to sow wild oats and all that. Women have to wait, quietly, patiently, and seemingly forever. Some of us are simply not that patient."

He laughed.

"Stop that." She pulled away and folded her arms over her sheet-covered bosom. It was an enticing sight and arousal once again rippled through him. "Now you think I'm the worst sort of tart."

"Oh, I do hope so." He tugged her sheet down and leaned forward to run his tongue over her nipple. "I have always loved tarts."

"Have you?" she said with a gasp.

"Oh my, yes." He cupped her breasts with his hand and sucked until her head fell back on the pillow and she moaned softly.

"So . . ." Her voice was breathless. "It doesn't bother you? My fallen nature, that is."

Obviously, no matter how much effort he put into it, she was not going to be distracted. He heaved a resigned sigh, readjusted her sheet, and sat back against the pillow. He wanted nothing more than to make her promise right here and now that she would never again be in anyone's bed save his but he was fairly certain this was not the right moment to declare his intentions. "How honest do you want me to be?"

"I don't know." Her brow furrowed in concern. "I suppose, given that I worked up the courage to ask, I would prefer you be completely honest."

"Very well." He thought for a moment. "I would be lying if I were to say I don't mind not being the first, the only, man in your bed. Not being the first to taste your luscious flesh. Not being the first to feel the heat of your body surrounding me."

Her eyes widened. "Oh my, Jack, I had no idea you were so . . . *descriptive*."

"I can be very descriptive." He grinned in a wicked manner. "As I was saying, I am entirely too selfish not to mind not being the only man ever to share your bed. I do mind, quite a bit really, that you didn't wait for me to come into your life before you allowed yourself to be *deceived*."

She winced.

"But that was long before we met. He was your fiancé after all and I suspect we'd be surprised by how many engaged couples find themselves unable to wait until the wedding to . . . know each other better."

"Oh, that sounds much better than *deceived*," she said under her breath.

"It's not as if you then set out on a career of promiscuity and endless affairs." He narrowed his eyes. "You didn't, did you?"

"Jack." She gasped and smacked his arm.

"I didn't think so." He chuckled.

"You're awfully progressive for a banker."

"What I am is a realist. The past is past and cannot be changed. Besides, I would be the worst sort of hypocrite to condemn you for behavior I have indulged in."

"That's right. Although you are not exceptionally experienced." She studied him curiously. "Still, I assume you indulged more than three times with one woman."

"Well, I didn't want to die a virgin."

"Jack." She huffed. "Do be serious."

"That's the problem, isn't it? I don't feel particularly

serious, I feel . . ." He leaned over and kissed the tip of her nose. "Quite delightful, somewhat euphoric, and in an astonishingly good mood."

She waved off his comment. "Yes, well, so do I but . . ."

"But you now expect me to reciprocate and confess my past transgressions."

"No, no, of course not."

"Because I am not about to give you a list of the names of women I have been with, regardless of how long or short that list might be."

"I would be disappointed in you if you did," she said staunchly, then paused. "Although I do admit to a bit of curiosity regarding you and Miss Merryweather—"

"Good Lord, Theodosia, absolutely not. The thought never crossed my mind." Odd, he had never before realized that in spite of how much he had always cared for Lucy, he had never actually wanted her. "Which really should have been an indication as to our true feelings for each other."

"And it did cross your mind with me?"

"Given our current state of undress, I would think you know the answer to that."

"Well, yes." A delightful blush washed up her face. He had no idea a blush could be quite so erotic.

"But if you must know, yes, it crossed my mind. Immediately and constantly. Even worse, you, Lady Theodosia, invaded my dreams."

She widened her eyes in an innocent manner. "Did I?"

"You can be quite persistent in dreams." He chuckled. "And extremely wicked."

"Really? In what way?"

"Let me think." He shifted to face her, pulled her sheet lower, then ran his finger lightly around her nipple, noting with satisfaction how it tightened at his touch. "In my dreams you were most demanding."

"Oh?"

"Indeed, you insisted I do any number of things. Like

this." He leaned closer to graze her nipple with his teeth, then flicked it lightly with his tongue.

She shivered. "Did I?"

"You found it delightful."

"I can see where I would." A wicked light shone in her eyes. "What else?"

"Oh, all sorts of things." He grabbed her hips and slid her down the bed, then clasped her wrists in one hand and held them over her head, pinning her to the bed. She was nothing short of delicious, an offering to the gods, or a gift from them. "You did like this."

"Yes, well, I can see why I would." Her breasts rose and fell with every breath, a feast for him alone. He wouldn't have thought it possible but he grew harder with every breath she took. "I feel quite at your mercy. It's most . . . um . . . exciting."

"I know." He smiled down at her. He might not be exceptionally experienced but those experiences he'd had taught him well. "You found this delightful too." He ran his fingers lightly from the side of her breast down the length of her.

She swallowed hard. "Oh, my."

"And this." He leaned over her and trailed his tongue over her stomach. Her muscles tightened and she gasped.

He slipped his hand between her legs and nudged them open. Her legs widened for him without hesitation. His fingers parted her and slid over her slick core.

"Oh . . . my . . ." She moaned and the sound nearly undid him. Still, he could wait.

"You especially liked this," he murmured. He bent close and replaced his finger with tongue.

She gasped and her back arched. "Oh, my God, Jack!"

He turned his head and looked up at her. "Of course, that was in my dreams. If, awake, you don't find that especially—"

"Good Lord, Jack, if you stop now . . ." She rocked her hips upward. "I would be forced—"

Somewhere in the recesses of the house, a clock chimed and she stilled. "What time is it?"

"It's only midnight."

"My mother could be home at any minute." Panic widened her eyes.

"That would be awkward."

"Awkward is the least of it." She squirmed in an effort to escape his grip. "Jack! Release me at once."

He heaved a frustrated sigh. "If you insist."

"It does seem best at the moment!"

"Not for me," he muttered but released her wrists nonetheless.

"Don't think this is any easier for me than it is for you." She sat up and glanced around the room for her clothing. "I was quite, well . . ." She cast him a wicked smile. "I shall expect you to finish what you started at some point."

"My pleasure." He returned her grin, got to his feet, and held out his hand to help her up.

"If my mother were to discover us it would be more than merely awkward." She took his hand, slid out of bed, and began collecting her clothes. "She'd demand you marry me at once."

"Extremely awkward then." Still . . . He grabbed her from behind, settled back on the bed, pulling her back onto his lap and back into his arms, where she belonged. "But well worth the risk."

"Oh God, Jack, we can't . . ." Her protest was weak and she struggled against him in a half-hearted manner that belied her feeble objection.

"Are you sure?" He nuzzled the back of her neck.

"I'm not sure of anything when you . . ." She wiggled her bottom slowly against his erection in a most seductive manner.

"I like it when you're unsure . . ." he murmured against her neck.

He held her tight with one hand, slipped the other around

her and between her legs. She was again wet with desire and he stroked her until she whimpered and her head fell back on his shoulder.

"Although, I suppose if you think we should get dressed . . ."

"You are a wicked, wicked man." Her voice was thick and she could barely get out the words. She rocked slowly against his hand. "And I am a wanton tart."

"I told you." He clasped her waist, lifted her up, and turned her around to face him. She straddled him, his cock wedged hard between them. "I like tarts."

She drew a deep shuddering breath. "Good."

She lowered herself onto him, her gaze meeting his in challenge or acknowledgement. Her green eyes darkened with desire. She encompassed him, surrounded him, drowned him in her heat. He groaned with the feel of him seated deeply inside her.

She rose up on her knees then slid slowly down, the sensation shooting through him. And he shuddered. "Good God, Theodosia . . ."

"This . . . this changes nothing . . ." Her head fell back, and her breasts jutted forward, her hips rolling against him. "I have no intention of marrying you."

"I don't recall asking." He buried his face between her breasts and thrust upward deeper into her.

"You're the kind of man . . ." She struggled for breath. "Who thinks something like this . . . calls for marriage."

"Am I?" Cupping her breasts with his hands, he lavished attention on one, then the next. Tugging gently with his teeth, sucking at her nipples, flicking the responsive flesh with his tongue.

"You know you are. Oh God yes. . ." Her breath caught. Her nails dug into his shoulders. "Are you trying to distract me?"

"That's not my sole purpose . . ."

She rocked her hips against his, riding him faster, harder. "We were talking . . . about marriage."

"You were talking about marriage." He gripped her waist, guiding her up and down. Every movement pure pleasure. "I have other things . . . on my mind . . . at the moment."

"My plans do not . . . include marriage." She panted, riding him harder.

"I am well aware of that."

"As long as you know . . ."

"Know this then. Plans . . ." He thrust up into her. "My dear Theodosia . . ." God, the feel of her enveloping him nearly drove him mad. He thrust again. "Change."

"Not . . . mine." Her breath came faster.

"Mine . . . have . . ."

Her muscles tightened. Her eyes were closed, her mouth slightly opened, the expression on her face as close to pain as pleasure. Beautiful and wondrous. She moaned and shuddered around him, pushing him over the edge of oblivion. He stroked hard again and surrendered.

And knew, as the world again exploded around him, he could never let her go.

It was much more difficult to help Theodosia back into her clothes than it had been to get her out of them. And not nearly as much fun. But fairly quickly, they returned to the dining room.

"I should go."

She nodded. "I'm afraid so."

He took her hand and raised it to his lips, his gaze locked on hers. "You're reluctant to see me go, aren't you?"

She smiled slowly. "Why yes, Jack, I believe I am."

"Good." He pulled her into his embrace. "Are you ready to face Nottwood?"

"When?"

"Tomorrow?"

She cringed. "So soon?"

He nodded. "Now that we have a plan, I see no reason to put it off. Do you?"

"Other than the fact that I'd prefer never to set eyes on him again, no I suppose not."

"Send him a note the first thing in the morning asking for a meeting." His gaze bored into hers. "I won't let you see him alone."

"I don't want to do this alone but I would very much like to be the one to tell him."

Jack nodded.

She hesitated. "You do realize this might not work."

"It's a risk but we have enough, I think." He studied her. "But it's your family that's at stake. If you don't want to take the chance—"

"No, let's do it." She smiled. "I believe I could face anything with you by my side."

"When that's done, we'll return to Millworth, along with your mother, of course. Christmas Eve is only a few days away and we've been gone far too long. God knows what my parents have been up to in our absence."

"There is that."

"Besides, I have no intention of leaving you alone in London once we confront Nottwood. I want you where I know you'll be safe."

"Very well."

He narrowed his eyes. "You're not going to protest? Claim you can take care of this on your own?"

"Absolutely not. I agree with you."

He studied her closely. "You agree with me?"

"Certainly." She grinned. "On this particular point."

"I suppose I'll take what I can get." He pulled her into his embrace and kissed her, then reluctantly released her.

"Tomorrow then?" A slight breathless note still sounded in her voice. If he didn't leave now, he never would.

"Oh, you're still here, Mr. Channing. How nice." Lady Sallwick's voice rang from the corridor.

"How was Sir Malcomb's dinner, Mother?" Confidence sounded in Theodosia's voice but Jack noted a slight tensing in her shoulders.

"Delightful, just delightful." Lady Sallwick beamed. "Everyone had a wonderful time. I daresay, there are any number of gentlemen in attendance who will be calling on us for dinner parties of their own." Satisfaction gleamed in her eyes. "And I wouldn't be at all surprised if at least one, or more, called on me privately."

"Mother!" Theodosia's eyes widened.

"Oh don't look at me that way, dear. I'm not dead yet. I still have a few good years left and I wouldn't mind spending those years with an appropriate gentleman."

"This does strike me as a conversation that should remain strictly between a mother and a daughter." Jack grinned and edged toward the door. "So, until tomorrow then—"

"Not so fast, Mr. Channing." Lady Sallwick's voice was abruptly somber. "I'm almost afraid to ask and obviously the two of you have put in a great deal of effort as you both look a bit disheveled but have you and Theodosia found anything of worth?"

Theodosia glanced at him and Jack nodded. "We think so. In fact, I'm fairly confident of it."

"Thank God." Relief washed across the older woman's face. "And thank you, Mr. Channing."

"You could call me Jack, you know."

"I could but I would prefer not to," she said in a lofty tone. "However, I wouldn't be at all averse to Jackson."

He chuckled.

"Jackson and Theodosia," Lady Sallwick said in a musing manner. "It has a lovely ring to it."

"Doesn't it though?" he said and glanced at Theodosia. Her eyes narrowed slightly but she held her tongue. "I was thinking the very same thing myself."

"We shall see you in the morning, Jack," Theodosia said firmly. "Good evening."

He grinned. "Good evening, Theodosia. Lady Sallwick."

"Good evening, Jackson." Lady Sallwick smiled.

Jack turned and took his leave, the ladies' conversation trailing behind him.

". . . to Millworth tomorrow."

"Oh, I can't possibly. I would hate . . . On second thought, that's a splendid idea. One doesn't want to be too available . . ."

He chuckled to himself. Theodosia was right. He was the sort of man who expected marriage to accompany an intimate encounter with the woman he loved. But he had no intention of arguing the point with her. Not now anyway.

A vague plan was forming in the back of his mind about his future but until he had it much more in hand, it was pointless to say anything. Regardless, all his plans included her at his side, as his wife. He would have it no other way.

Jackson Quincy Graham Channing, youngest vice-president in the history of Graham, Merryweather and Lockwood Banking and Trust, had never especially had to pursue anything he wanted. There had never been any particular need. He had been given very nearly everything. He was rich and he was privileged and life had been fairly easy. Nor had he taken advantage of his position. He had lived up to all that was expected of him, he had followed the rules laid out for him by his family, society, and even the bank. He'd never been the subject of scandal or gossip. He had trodden a path that was acceptable, respectable, and possibly dull. No, he had never really had to fight for anything but then there had never been anything he had wanted that he didn't have.

Jack Channing, son of Colonel Basil Channing, wasn't sure about his future or his destiny but he did know whatever the future held for him, he wanted to face it with Theodosia Winslow's hand in his. And he knew as well, whether she was ready to admit it or not, Theodosia felt the same way.

Convincing her would be the hard part but this was a battle he had no intention of losing.

Jackson Quincy Graham Channing might well have taken no for an answer and accepted loss graciously.

Jack Channing would not give up without a fight.

Was that the difference between a banker and a hero?

Or the difference between a man who thought he knew who and what he was and a man still trying to figure it all out?

Chapter Twenty-Three

"I must say, I was surprised to get your note but delighted that you have accepted the inevitable. I was afraid this might be awkward otherwise." Cyril strode into the parlor with the confidence of a man who had no doubt of his victory. "Although, as I am trying not to be seen, it was not at all easy to . . ." He caught sight of Jack and her mother and pulled up short. "Theodosia?"

"I'm so glad you could come, Cyril. You know my mother but I don't believe you've met my fiancé." Teddy forced a pleasant smile. "Cyril, this is Mr. Jackson Channing. Jack, this is Lord Nottwood."

"Nottwood." Jack nodded politely but his eyes were cold and hard and positively frightening.

Cyril ignored him. "I don't have time for nonsense today, Theodosia. What is the meaning of this?"

"The meaning of this? Oh, let me think." She pulled her brows together thoughtfully. "I know. It simply slipped my mind for a moment." Her voice hardened. "As much as I am, oh, *flattered* isn't quite the right word, let's say *repulsed* shall we, by your charming insistence that we renew our engagement I have given it a great deal of thought and the answer is no."

Cyril's eyes narrowed. "Perhaps you have forgotten our little talk."

"I've forgotten nothing." She cast him her sweetest smile. "Fortunately, neither did my father."

Cyril's face paled but he held his ground. "What do you mean?"

"Well, it was an odd quirk of my father's. He was quite concerned about discarding anything that might prove to be of value someday. He rarely disposed of something that came into his possession. Including, oh, stock certificates, varied and assorted documents, correspondence." She shrugged. "That sort of thing. We've been going through some of Father's papers and it's really astonishing how very often your name appears. Some of it quite, oh . . ." She winced. "Well, *incriminating* is probably the word for it."

She held her breath. Cyril couldn't possibly know they had found nothing to implicate him among Father's papers but she and Jack had agreed this was the best way to begin. Besides, if they could find nothing regarding Cyril, the chances were better than ever that he really had no evidence against her father. It was a gamble but it was all they had.

Cyril studied her for a moment, then laughed. "I don't believe you. Besides, it would be the word of a dead man against mine."

"A man who pretended to be dead." Mother shook her head in a mournful manner. "Really, Lord Nottwood, it wasn't as clever of you as you thought."

For the first time, unease shone in Cyril's eyes. "What do you mean?"

"What she means, Nottwood, is that it takes a great deal of effort to make the world believe you're dead," Jack said coolly. "It's a complicated endeavor, this business of faking a lost ship. It involves forgery of things like shipping manifests and customs registries and a myriad of other documents. Misdeeds I believe Her Majesty's government takes rather seriously."

"My goodness, Cyril, you really should be more cautious about the company you keep. Why what would your mother say?" Teddy cast him a chastising look. "When one deals with the type of men required to orchestrate such a ruse, men who apparently do not come cheap, they are also the sort of men more than willing to sell what they know. And put it in writing. For a price, of course."

"Perhaps, but you have no money," Cyril said with a smirk.

"But I do," Jack said. "It appears what you paid was not enough to ensure their silence or their loyalty. Pity really. One never knows whom to trust."

"Oh, and don't forget the bribery, Jack," Teddy added. While Grayson and Sam had uncovered a suggestion of bribery, they had yet to find the officials involved. Still, Cyril didn't know that. "That's really the best part."

Cyril's gaze slid from one face to the next, a calculating look in his eyes. "You have proof of this?"

"We wouldn't be here if we didn't." Jack's voice was cold. The man was positively magnificent.

"I want to see this proof," Cyril demanded.

"Don't be absurd." Jack scoffed. "Did you expect us to wave it in your face? We aren't foolish enough to have it here where you could get your hands on it. It is safely in the keeping of a trusted officer at the Bank of England." He paused. "Still, we could certainly go together to look at the documentation at the bank although that could be awkward." He shook his head regretfully. "One never knows where the loyalties of even a trusted bank officer lie. And should we be overheard, well . . ."

"Even if it didn't lead to prison, although I suspect it would . . ." Mother leaned forward in a confidential manner. "You, of all people, are well aware of the damage to one's reputation, and the reputation of one's entire family, if so much as a hint of all this were to become the fodder for

gossip and idle talk. Your mother would be beside herself."
Mother sighed deeply. "It would be most distressing for her."

"I see." Cyril glanced at Teddy. "Well played, my dear."
Teddy smiled.

Cyril thought for a moment. "I assume that if I relinquish
any claims to Theodosia, this evidence of yours will remain
our secret?"

"As long as the documents you have incriminating Lord
Sallwick never see the light of day, I believe we can agree to
that. Although . . ." Jack's brow furrowed thoughtfully. "It
might be better for all concerned if we simply trade what we
have. That way we'll all feel much more confident."

Cyril's brow rose. "You don't trust me?"

"Not for so much as a moment," Teddy said coldly.

"Are we agreed then?" Jack said. "Your evidence for
ours?"

"Yes, well, about that." Cyril grimaced. "The documents
I had apparently went down with my ship."

Cyril's threat had been nothing but bluster? Exactly as
Jack had suspected. Relief swept through her. "You didn't
have anything, did you?" Her voice rose. "You lied to me?"

"Come now, Theodosia. You needn't sound so shocked.
As if I'd never lied to you before." He scoffed. "One plays
with the hand one is dealt after all. And I have always been
excellent at games of chance. The odds were on my side in
this."

"Bastard," Mother said under her breath.

"Come, come, Lady Sallwick." Cyril adjusted the cuffs at
his wrists. "I assure you I am quite legitimate." He glanced
at Jack. "I assume it's pointless to ask for your documentation."

"It will stay where it is." Jack smiled. "Let's call it insur-
ance against any further difficulties, shall we."

"Very well then." Cyril sighed. "I do so hate losing but,
what is it they say? Ah yes. At least I have my health." He
turned to Teddy. "I can't say I'm not disappointed. I really

did like you, you know." He glanced at Jack. "You'll like her too, Channing. Especially the little moaning noises she makes when—"

Teddy had never seen anyone move as fast as Jack. In two quick strides he was at Cyril, his fist connecting with the man's chin. Cyril's head snapped back, his feet left the floor, and he flew a few feet backward to land smack on his behind. He stared in astonishment and rubbed his chin. "Really, Channing, was that necessary?"

"I thought it was," Teddy said.

"I quite liked it," Mother added.

Jack glared down at him. "I would suggest you leave now."

"I was going." Cyril picked himself up, dusted off his trousers, and started for the door. He paused, then turned back. "I know you won't believe this, Theodosia, but I do regret how things turned out. About your father and, well, everything."

"Get out," Teddy said.

Cyril shrugged and a moment later Jacobs snapped the front door behind him.

"Well, that was . . ." Mother began, then sank into the nearest chair.

"Mother!" Teddy rushed to her side. "Are you all right?"

"Perfectly." She waved off Teddy's concern. "That was . . ." She grinned up at them. "Positively exhilarating. I'm not sure when I last felt quite so invigorated. We should take on evildoers everyday. Jackson, you were wonderful and terrifying and most heroic. Why, you made me want to confess all my sins."

Teddy bit back a laugh. "Mother."

"And atone for them." Mother smiled a distinctly wicked sort of smile.

Teddy stared. She really didn't know this woman at all. But she did like her.

Jack grinned. "Thank you?"

Mother stood and took his hands in hers. "No, Jackson,

thank you. If you hadn't taken a hand in this and gone through Charles's papers . . ." She shuddered. "It's fortunate you found what you did."

Someday, Teddy would tell her mother everything. Certainly, they had uncovered a little regarding his scheme to play dead but not enough to send him to prison. But Jack had been confident that a man smart enough to do all that Cyril had done wouldn't be so foolish as to keep any evidence that could be turned against him. For the most part, they had been playing the same game Cyril had. The only difference was that they had won. But then they'd had so much more to lose.

"Now, if we are going to catch the train we want for Millworth, we should gather our bags together and be on our way." Mother paused. "I think it would be best if we put all this behind us and did not mention this incident again. I know I intend to."

Teddy blew a relieved breath. "I would like nothing better, Mother."

"Which means I have no desire to know exactly what Nottwood was referring to when Jackson hit him." Mother met Teddy's gaze firmly. "Ever."

Teddy nodded weakly. "Agreed."

Mother started for the stairs. "Excellent punch, by the way, Jackson. Really most impressive," she said over her shoulder. "I would have done it myself but I don't have the strength for fisticuffs. I much prefer a bullet . . ."

Jack stared after her. "What did she say?"

"It doesn't matter." Teddy shook her head. "We're free, Jack, and we have you to thank for it."

"It seems to me it was a mutual effort. I only examined your father's papers. What happened today was as much to you and your mother's credit as it was to mine. I had no idea you were such an excellent actress."

"Oh, I have any number of talents you would not suspect," she said in a lighthearted manner.

He smiled a slow, wicked sort of smile and her heart fluttered. "Although, I must admit Nottwood was right about one thing."

"Oh?"

He leaned close and spoke softly into her ear. "I do like those little moaning noises."

Chapter Twenty-Four

Later that day,
Millworth Manor . . .

It was, as it always was, good to be back at Millworth Manor.

They'd arrived in the midst of a decorating frenzy with Lady Briston explaining that there was entirely too much to do to let it wait until the day before Christmas. Furthermore, as this was such a significant Christmas, it did call for an excess of Christmas cheer.

They had scarcely handed over their bags when Mother was enlisted to help in the decoration of Millworth's grand stairway. The invitation to assist was no doubt due to Mother's initial observations, which might have been construed as compliment or criticism depending on the sensitivity and nature of the listener.

The colonel appeared within moments of their arrival and ushered Jack away for a talk. Judging by the look on his face, it must have concerned a matter of some importance. And a minute later, Dee hurried Teddy into the parlor.

"I am so glad you're finally here. Lord knows I don't believe in such things but . . ." Dee glanced from side to side as if afraid they might be overheard. "The manor has always seemed, well, special at Christmas—"

Teddy nodded. "Magical."

"Magical then but this year . . ." Dee shook her head in disbelief. "It really is."

Teddy laughed. "Really?"

"Oh my, yes. I can't believe it myself. It's not what I expected once Uncle Basil's wife appeared." Dee grimaced. "Mother was not at all taken with Mrs. Channing when she arrived, although she quite likes Miss Merryweather."

"I can't wait to meet her," Teddy murmured.

"You'll like her too but then I didn't think she would be the problem although one really never knows. You see, Mother blames Mrs. Channing for ruining Uncle Basil's life." Dee paused thoughtfully. "Although it does seem to me he's had the life he wanted. Regardless, I did think the two of them would come to blows, Mother and Mrs. Channing that is, and believe me there were some tense moments but . . ."

"But?"

"I don't know." Dee's eyes widened in amazement. "There have been no particular problems, no clashes of unyielding natures, and no embarrassing outbursts. I think . . ." She lowered her voice. "It's some kind of Christmas miracle."

"How . . . perfect."

"And there's more. Jack's parents . . ." She paused dramatically. "They've been spending a great deal of time together, deep in conversation apparently. Why, one can barely go anywhere in the house without running into them with their heads together."

"They do have thirty years to catch up on."

"And it all seems quite cordial, even friendly. Certainly there have been a few moments when there have been raised voices but for the most part it's been . . ." She shook her head. "No one knows what to make of it."

"Jack will be delighted that all is going so well. Of course, now my mother is here."

"I'm sure it will be fine," Dee said staunchly. "Oh certainly, your mother has always thought my mother was more than a little eccentric, not to mention the fact that two of her three daughters were often the subject of gossip and in Beryl's case, scandal, through the years."

"And your mother has always thought mine entirely too stiff and proper but then she doesn't really know her at all." Teddy paused. "I've discovered there's far more to my mother than I ever imagined."

"Really?"

Teddy nodded. "I shall tell you all about it later."

"And Nottwood?" A worried frown creased her friend's forehead. "Is he taken care of?"

"He won't be bothering us again."

"Thank God." Dee winced. "I am so sorry I betrayed your confidence although I didn't actually say anything to Jack. Well, not directly—"

"All is forgiven, my good, true friend." Teddy embraced the other woman. "You did what you thought was best although I will watch my words when eliciting a promise from you in the future. But, as it turned out, you were right. I did need a banker." She smiled. "And a hero."

"And what about Jack?" Dee's gaze searched hers.

"Jack is . . ." Teddy shrugged. "Jack is wonderful."

"He's everything you ever wanted, you know."

"He's everything I used to want. Everything I expected to have one day. Now . . ."

"Now, you want something different," Dee said slowly.

Teddy nodded. "I have spent my entire life being exactly what I was expected to be. There was a time when I expected the rest of it to be exactly what I was raised for—wife, hostess, lady of the manor, that sort of thing. I never imagined I would want anything else. I'm not sure how to explain it." She shook her head. "I've tasted what it feels like to provide for myself. In spite of the difficulties, independence, Dee, is a powerful potion. I can't go back to being what I was expected to be, I won't. It seems too much like giving up." She thought for a moment. "Do you remember your mother once telling us most of her regrets were about those things she didn't attempt? That wondering *what if* was what would drive you mad?"

"Vaguely. But you've already been quite successful. You needn't prove anything to anyone, you know."

"Only to myself."

"And you have always been exceptionally hard to please." Dee paused. "So you still intend to end your engagement to Jack before the New Year?"

"I don't have an engagement to Jack, remember? And yes, that's still the plan."

"Is he aware of that?"

"We haven't discussed it lately." Teddy frowned. "But nothing has changed."

"What a pity as the two of you are so clearly in love."

"Nonsense." Teddy raised her shoulder in a dismissive shrug. "We are simply playing a part."

Dee studied her closely. "Is proving something to yourself worth the risk of losing him?"

"I don't have him to lose," she said firmly.

Dee raised a brow.

Teddy sighed in surrender. "I don't know. I only know if I don't try to succeed on my own, I'll never know if I could. To thine own self be true and all." She shook her head. "I don't want to spend my life wondering *what if*. It's not fair to me and it wouldn't be fair to him."

"I suppose you have to do what you feel you must." Dee studied her for a long moment. "I only hope, my dear friend, you won't find the price for the life you're choosing to be too high. Or too lonely."

"Goodness, Dee, this is an altogether too serious discussion to be having at the moment." Teddy forced a light note to her voice. "After all, Christmas is nearly upon us and there are all sorts of far more delightful topics to be considering."

"Sugarplums and stuffed stockings and the like, you mean?"

"Exactly." Teddy nodded, took her friend's arm, and started back for the stairway. "Now then, tell me what you have in mind for Sam . . ."

It was far easier to distract Dee from the topic of Teddy's future than it was to keep her mind off it herself because as much as she might try to deny it, Teddy was afraid she had indeed fallen in love with Jack.

And didn't that just complicate everything?

"I like her, Jack." Father paced the width of the library. "I didn't expect that."

"Why not?" Jack sat on the library sofa and watched his father with a certain amount of amusement. He would have bet nothing could put his father in such a state. But apparently his mother could. "You liked her once."

"Well yes but that was different." Father waved off the comment. "We were both young, swept away by the impetuousness of first love. We hadn't known each other for long. It was all very romantic and passionate and intense. I've always credited the rashness of our marriage to impulse even though I've never been an especially impulsive man. We were in love and promised to love each other forever. Now, I can't help but wonder . . . He paused and met his son's gaze. "Did we keep that promise?"

"Oh." Jack stared at his father. "I don't know what to say."

"Neither do I." His father ran his hand through his hair. "When I learned about you and set off for New York I was furious with her. And well, frankly, I was hurt. Deeply hurt. Not merely by her deception but by her lack of faith in me. Of trust if you will. I thought I had put her behind me years ago but the pain I felt when I learned what she had kept from me all those years was as sharp as it was the day she left me."

"I see," Jack said slowly.

"It makes you wonder, doesn't it? Why she never sought a divorce. Why I never married again. Or rather, why I never again found someone I wished to marry." He resumed pacing. "We've spent a great deal of time together since she arrived at Millworth. She's far more interesting now than she was when we first met but then I suppose so am I. And quite passionate, too, in her opinions about any number of things." He shook his head. "There's a great deal we disagree about but . . ." He stopped and looked at his son. "Oddly enough, I enjoy arguing with her. It's rather a lot of fun. I find it most invigorating as, I suspect, does she."

"As neither of you has done the other in, you might be right."

"I know I said the whole idea of soul mates was absurd—"

"Balderdash." Jack nodded. "You called it balderdash."

"I'm beginning to think I might have been wrong." His brow furrowed. "Don't misunderstand me, I haven't spent the last three decades thinking about her, longing for her, or missing her although now, upon reflection, I wonder if she was ever far from my mind. Oh, not consciously of course but there nonetheless."

Jack studied the older man for a moment. "What are you trying to say?"

"I don't know." The colonel stared in astonishment. "I have no idea. I'm completely confused. We have gone our separate ways, lived our separate lives and it's absurd to think we can find what we once had. We're completely different people after all. I'm not sure we can go back. Or that we want to, either of us. Still . . ."

"Still?"

"One does wonder . . ."

"Yes?"

"No, we can't go back. I'm certain of that. But perhaps . . ."

Even though his father was addressing Jack, it was obvious he was trying to work out the answer in his own head. "Perhaps what?"

"Perhaps we can go forward from here. Start over, that sort of thing." He lowered his voice in a confidential manner. "I don't mind telling you I still find your mother a most attractive woman. Most attractive."

"That's nice," Jack said weakly. While it was gratifying that his mother still held a certain appeal for his father, it was more than he really wanted to know.

"I've always believed when you find what you want in life, your heart's desire I suppose, you should let nothing stand in your way." Father shook his head. "Admittedly I did not follow that precept when I first met your mother . . ."

"But you were much younger then and not nearly as wise."

"I'm not sure I'm wise now but I am smart enough to know second chances are rare in this life. One would be a fool to ignore an opportunity when it comes along."

"It sounds to me as if you have made up your mind."

"It does, doesn't it?" Father thought for a moment. "I suppose I have. I'm certainly not ready to let her go again." He glanced at his son. "I think you should forgive her, you know."

"Why?"

"Because as wrong as she was, I believe her actions were prompted by fear and love."

"Even so—"

"Because she's your mother, Jack," Father said firmly. "And because it's Christmas. This is the one time of year when one tends to realize what is truly important in life. Friends, family, love."

"Have you forgiven her?"

"One makes mistakes in this life one can never make up for. I do think your mother regrets her actions." He shook his head. "Although I can't say she wouldn't do the same thing again given the same circumstances. Nor can I say I wouldn't make the same mistakes again. But she is my wife and I wouldn't at all mind taking a crack at being a husband." His brows drew together. "Do you think I'm too old for that?"

Jack laughed. "I wouldn't think so."

"What about you and Theodosia?" He studied his son closely. "Wasn't your original plan to end this engagement before the New Year?"

"That's still the plan but . . ."

His father chose his words with care. "But you'd like to make it real?"

Jack nodded.

"You're in love with her, aren't you?"

"I'm afraid so." Even as he said the words, he realized they were true.

"And does she share your feelings?"

"I think so but . . ." Jack blew a long breath. "I'm not sure she would admit it. She has set a course for herself that does not include marriage and unfortunately does not include me."

"I see." Father thought for a moment. "Have you told her how you feel?"

"Not yet."

"Perhaps that would be the place to start."

"Perhaps." Jack arched a brow. "And have you told Mother how you feel?"

His father winced. "I suppose this is a case of do what I say not what I do, isn't it?"

"So it would appear." Jack chuckled.

"Very well, then I shall make you a bargain." Father squared his shoulders. "I shall tell your mother no later than January first exactly how I feel and you shall do the same with Theodosia."

"I can agree to that." Jack paused. "And if this doesn't end as we wish, what then?"

"You mean if they don't throw themselves into our arms and vow their undying love?"

"Something like that."

Father thought for a long moment. "The benefit of growing older is that one has hopefully learned a lesson or two along the way. I failed to fight for your mother once." He shook his head. "I will not make the same mistake again. Even if the only one I have to fight is the lady herself."

Jack grinned. "That should be interesting."

"I don't intend to lose." Father eyed him firmly. "And neither should you."

"Theodosia has plans for her life that don't include me."

"Change them." Father nodded. "Love is a powerful force, Jack. You have that on your side."

"It might not be enough."

"I have faith in you, my boy." Father studied him for a moment. "As I said, when you find your heart's desire, you should let nothing stand in your way."

"Even the lady herself?"

Father grinned. "Especially the lady herself."

Jack laughed. His father was right, of course. But Theodosia was a stubborn woman. While he was fairly certain her feelings for him matched his for her, there was always the possibility he was wrong. Just because he had fallen in love for the first time in his life didn't mean she had. Her affection for him might go no further than friendship.

No, Jack had always been able to judge the nature of a man. He was not wrong about this. The woman loved him whether she realized it or not.

Now, he just had to convince her.

Chapter Twenty-Five

". . . and then, of course, the solicitor, being a solicitor," Lionel continued, "could do little more but arrive at the obvious and yet completely far-fetched . . ."

Teddy surveyed the faces gathered around the table for Christmas Eve dinner, all focused at the moment on Beryl's husband regaling them with a humorous legal tale of a man discovered to have more than one wife.

". . . needless to say, wife number two was not at all amused by the . . ."

As entertaining as Lionel's story was, Teddy's mind wandered. In all the years she'd known this family, she never would have imagined one day they would all share a convivial Christmas Eve together. Of course, there had been a few trying moments in the last few days.

In spite of Dee's observation as to the unexpected lack of friction at the manor, all was not perfect among the older ladies of the party. The first night of their arrival, there were tentative undercurrents among the three mothers. Silly of course. They were all of a comparable age and background and should have gone on quite well together. But as much as her mother and Lady Briston knew many of the same people and had similar interests there were still years of vague distrust to overcome. And while Mrs. Channing was cordial enough to Teddy, she had the distinct feeling that she was being evaluated and found wanting. It was obvious Jack's mother preferred the annoyingly delightful Miss Merryweather as a more appropriate match for her son. Miss Merryweather—who had insisted Teddy call her by her given name—was as charming and lovely as everyone had said. Mrs. Channing's preference for the young woman did not sit well with either Teddy's mother or Lady Briston, not merely because Lady Briston was fond of Teddy but because Mrs. Channing's preferences seemed something of a slap against the entire British Empire.

Jack found it all most amusing. During the first night of their stay, while they were gathered to sing Christmas carols in the parlor, he'd nudged Teddy with his elbow when a politely phrased, but no less deadly, barb was thrown between the three ladies. One would have thought they were natural enemies confined together against their will. The other men seemed to find it amusing as well especially given that it was all Teddy, Dee, and Camille could do to keep them singing along. It was very nearly impossible to snipe at one another while singing one of the glorious carols each and every lady knew and loved.

It might indeed have been the spirit of Christmas, or possibly each mother had decided, in the interest of the season, to make a concerted effort to get along with one another, but by the second day, overly polite comments had eased into genuine conversation. The ladies took part in an afternoon of skating on the frozen Millworth pond, admittedly with a fair amount of mutual trepidation. They put aside any reluctance to cooperate and worked together in finishing the decoration of the manor. And in an odd twist of fate that had the other members of the household holding their breaths, all three mothers ended up on the same team for an evening of games in the parlor. By the time they had soundly beaten the others at charades and tableaux and lookabout, their individual competitive natures had forged some sort of bond or at least an alliance. Now, one would have thought they'd been friends forever. Perhaps it was the inevitable result of compromise for the sake of their offspring. Or perhaps the ladies had at last recognized in each other kindred spirits. Or possibly it was indeed a true miracle of the season.

By the time Christmas Eve was upon them Teddy had decided to simply enjoy the revelry and enjoy Jack's company as well. It wasn't much of a plan as plans went but it was all she had. She refused to consider the question of whether or not she was in love with him, although it did seem that her heart leapt whenever he was in the room, and her pulse quickened when he so much as brushed her hand, and the thought of living her life without him lay like a heavy weight in the pit of her stomach.

". . . and then of course wife number four—"

"I thought you said there were only three?" Surprise rang in Camille's voice.

"Only in the beginning." Lionel chuckled. "Our Mr. Benson was a bit of a traveling man, you see—"

Lucy gasped. "And did he have a wife in every port?"

"Very nearly." Lionel chuckled. "And when wife number four was discovered, well, it led to . . ."

Dinner was a festive affair with spirited debate, much mirth, and the kind of good-natured teasing that can only occur when people care for one another. Teddy marveled that this family that had spent years celebrating Christmas apart now seemed completely comfortable in each other's presence. In the midst of laughter over a recollection of Christmas past when Lady Briston had typically filled the house with acquaintances and even strangers who had nowhere else to go for Christmas, Jack's amused gaze met hers and for a moment . . . for a moment it was hard to remember that they weren't really engaged. They weren't planning to spend the rest of their lives together. And they weren't in love. A twinge of what might have been regret or remorse or sorrow stabbed Teddy and she tried to ignore it. But every time his gaze met hers, the oddest thing happened to her heart.

It was fitting that she and her mother were here, given Lady Briston's history of welcoming those who had nowhere else to go to Millworth at Christmas. They had no family save Simon but they would not be here next year. While Teddy had spent a few Christmases here through the years, and was always made to feel like a member of the family, as were all the wanderers Lady Briston collected, she suspected they might not be welcomed back after she and Jack ended their engagement.

Still, Teddy and her mother had each other now thanks to Cyril. Cyril's threat had wrought an unexpected change in Lady Sallwick, and Teddy's engagement appeared to have given her mother a measure of serenity as well. This was not the mother she'd known for the last four years nor was Mother the woman she'd been before their lives had altered irrevocably with her father's death. No, this woman had a strength about her and a determination Teddy had never before seen, and she realized they were more alike than she had ever imagined. While Teddy was certain Mother would not be happy when she broke it off with Jack, nor would she be pleased about Teddy's plans for her future, she suspected her mother would be far more accepting now.

". . . and of course, the rest of us agreed." Lionel flashed an affectionate smile at his wife. "One wife was more than any man should have to handle."

The table erupted in laughter and Teddy joined in, even if she had no idea how the story had ended.

Laughter and stories and the sharing of fond memories continued until at last Lady Briston declared dinner at an end. In the spirit of the evening, the gentlemen agreed to forgo their usual brandy and after-dinner cigars and joined the ladies in the parlor. Lady Briston's special Christmas Eve punch was passed around and Lord Briston got to his feet.

"It has been a long time, a very long time, since this family has been together under one roof for Christmas Eve. And of course this is Jack's first Christmas at Millworth." His gaze passed over the gathering, over all three of his daughters and their respective spouses or, in Dee's case, fiancé, and settled on his wife. "I am most grateful to be here and most thankful for all of you." He nodded at his brother.

The colonel rose to his feet. "In the years my brother was away, Christmas was celebrated here without him and in spite of the sometimes crowded nature of the manor, thanks to Bernadette's hospitality, there was still something missing. I suspect there always is when family isn't together." He paused for a long moment, then smiled wryly. "My brother knew what he was missing in the years he was not with us and tonight, for the first time, I know as well what it's like to have your child and your wife together at Christmas. And our company is only enhanced by the addition of our very good friends, our dear Theodosia and Adelaide and Lucy. Thank you all for making this a Christmas Eve I will never forget." He raised his glass. "To family and friends."

The toast and the sentimentality echoed around the room and Teddy suspected she was not the only one with a tear in her eye.

The colonel cleared his throat. "Nigel and I would like to renew a Christmas Eve tradition we had as boys here at Millworth."

"Dear Lord, not a tradition," Beryl said under her breath.

"When we were children," the colonel continued, "Christmas Eve was spent in the telling of tales of those who had gone before." He paused in the manner of a master storyteller. "Those who are still with us."

Dee groaned.

"Ghost stories?" Camille's eyes lit with excitement. "I love ghost stories."

"As do we all, dear," Lady Briston said with a smile. "Go on, Basil."

"Actually, we thought I'd begin," Lord Briston said. "And we shall start with the story of lovers torn apart."

"Thomas and Anne?" Dee brightened.

"Of course." Her father chuckled and launched into the story of the star-crossed lovers, one from Millworth, the other from a nearby estate, who had to wait for death to be reunited, and the various times they had been seen at the manor and on the grounds.

Teddy had heard the story before and spent most of the time watching Jack listen to his uncle although she thought he had heard it before too. Someday he would probably tell this story to his children. Children with dark hair and blue eyes who had their father's intelligence and sense of responsibility and his laugh. Children he would have with some other woman. Her throat tightened and she ignored it.

When the story of the long-ago lovers had ended, Colonel Channing launched into another, this one about spirits he and his brother had seen as children who were substantially more frightening than poor Thomas and Anne.

Midway through the story, Jack caught her gaze and nodded toward the hall, then he quietly left the parlor. She waited another moment and then slipped out to join him. He met her by the grand tree that, as always, had been set up and decorated in the gallery.

"You should be listening to this, Jack," she said in a hushed tone. "After all it's your heritage."

He chuckled. "I suspect I'll have more than enough time in the future to catch up on all the spirits inhabiting Millworth but right now, I have something else I wish to do."

"Oh?" She gazed up at him.

"I'm afraid I've made a dreadful mistake."

She raised a brow. "Have you?"

"I have." He nodded. "I—"

"I am sorry to interrupt." Mrs. Channing's voice sounded behind Teddy. "But I'm not sure if I'll have another chance."

"Perhaps I should leave the two of you—"

"No dear, stay," Mrs. Channing said firmly. "I'll only be a minute. Besides, you're the most important woman in his life now which is as it should be."

"What is it, Mother?" Jack asked with a smile.

"I know you'll never quite forgive me but you did say we could move on from here."

He nodded. "I did."

"Your father and I, well . . ." She drew a deep breath. "We have decided, as we both made mistakes in the past, and yes I do realize the most egregious of those were on my part," she added quickly. "At any rate, we've decided to try to start over. As friends initially and see where that might take us."

Jack's eyes narrowed. "And Uncle Dan?"

"He and I had a long talk after you left New York. Several actually." She clasped her hands together. "I owed him as great an apology as I did you and your father." She paused. "Oddly enough, Daniel had always suspected that my true affections lay elsewhere. He had always thought it was lingering grief and in a way I think it was." She shook her head. "I suppose I never truly got over your father although I did try. For thirty years I tried but . . ."

"Mother—"

"You're so very much like him. Which is probably why I never wanted to share you." She studied her son for a long moment. "I can't make amends for the past but there is one thing I would like to do." She stepped away, bent down, and pulled a small, wrapped parcel from under the tree. "I brought something for you. I can't give you back the lost years but I thought you might want to have these." She handed Jack the package.

He hefted it in his hand. "What is this?"

"These are the letters you wrote to your father at Christmas."

A lump lodged in Teddy's throat.

Jack stared. "How did you know? I never told anyone about these."

"I'm your mother." She shrugged. "I know everything. I thought you might want to give them to your father."

Jack stared at the packet for a long moment, then met his mother's gaze. "Thank you."

"It's little enough . . . I . . ." A slight smile lifted the corners of Mrs. Channing's lips. "I should be returning to the others. I would hate to miss the ghost of Christmas past or whoever the next story might be about." Her gaze shifted between her son and Teddy. "I assume the two of you will be in momentarily."

Teddy nodded.

"Good." She turned to go, then turned back. "Merry Christmas, son."

"Merry Christmas, Mother." He stepped toward her, kissed her cheek, then murmured something in her ear.

Her eyes widened slightly, then she sniffed, nodded, and started back to the parlor.

Jack stared at the packet in his hand. "Well, that was . . . unexpected."

"And quite wonderful."

"Yes, it was," he said softly. "It doesn't really change anything but . . ."

"But I do think she's trying."

"Then I can do no less." He shook his head. "I had no idea . . ."

"You forgave her, didn't you?"

"Well, she is my mother." He tucked the packet of letters in his waistcoat pocket.

"You're a good man, Jackson Channing." Without thinking she laid her hand on his cheek and gazed into his blue eyes. "It's been an honor and a privilege to be your fiancée, even if it wasn't real." She drew a deep breath and stepped back. "We should really return—"

"Not yet." He smiled. "I had a confession, remember?"

"I have always been fond of your confessions." She tilted her head and studied him. "It was something about a mistake, wasn't it?"

"A huge mistake." He bent down, reached under the tree, and picked up a small, black velvet box tied with a red ribbon. He handed it to her. "Which is why I wanted to give it to you in private."

"You don't want to wait until tomorrow? When everyone can see what a huge mistake you made and we can begin to disagree and start our journey toward ending our engagement?"

He hesitated. "No, I want you to have it now."

"Very well." She pulled off the ribbon and slowly opened the box. A small, delicate pendant on a gold chain lay nestled in the box. She sucked in a sharp breath. "Oh my, Jack." She looked up at him. "It's a peacock."

"I'm afraid so."

"It's . . ." The pendant was no bigger than the last two joints of her little finger and perfectly proportioned. The peacock's body was gold filigree, its sweeping tail feathers encrusted with pearls and sapphires. "It's exquisite."

"I am sorry." He shook his head in feigned regret. "I tried to find something repulsive with feathers and almost purchased a truly revolting hat." He shuddered. "But I couldn't bring myself to do it. So I thought a peacock, with all its feathers intact, might vanquish the image of an angry, naked bird. I am sorry. I did try to get something you would hate."

"In that you failed. I love it, Jack." She stared at the peacock in her hand. "It's perfect."

"We shall have to come up with another way to show everyone how mismatched we are," he said slowly.

"Yes, we will," she murmured.

"Theodosia."

She raised her gaze to his.

"A minute ago, it sounded like you were saying good-bye."

"Don't be silly." She forced a smile. "We have a week until the ball. We certainly have time to come up with another idea for dissolving our engagement. I would hate to ruin everyone's Christmas." She glanced at the pendant. "Will you help me put this on?"

"Of course."

She handed him the pendant and turned around. He fastened it around her neck, his fingers barely brushing her skin.

She turned back to him. "How does it look?"

He stared into her eyes. "Perfect."

The moment between them stretched. Lengthened. Endless. Forever. And she realized what she hadn't wanted to think about, what she hadn't wanted to face.

She drew a deep breath and the moment shattered. "I wanted to give you something as well." She stepped around the tree and found the small package she had hidden. "It's just something I thought you might like."

He opened it and stared.

"It's the scarab your father gave me when I was a girl. I thought since it was a keepsake from his travels that perhaps you might like to have it."

"Thank you." His gaze again met hers. "This too is perfect." He shook his head. "All in all, this is turning out to be an extraordinary Christmas."

"As it should be, Jack. You're with your father and your entire family. Exactly as it should be, as it always should have been." She ignored the rush of emotion that swept through her and adopted a brisk tone. "Now then if we don't return, someone will surely be sent—"

"Theodosia." He took her hand, her ring catching the light. "We have a great deal to talk about."

"Well, yes, we need a new plan—"

"I don't."

She drew a deep breath. "Nothing has changed, Jack."

His gaze bored into hers. "Everything has changed."

"No," she said in a hard tone. "It hasn't." She pulled her hand from his. "Are you going to accompany me back to the parlor?"

"I'll be there in a minute." He nodded. "You go ahead."

"Very well." She smiled pleasantly and took her leave. It was all she could do to walk toward the parlor and resist the urge to turn and run back into his arms. Or sprint up the stairs to her room and fling herself across her bed and weep.

What a fool she had been. She should have realized what was happening, what had been happening since the first moment they'd met in the Millworth ballroom. Of course she loved him. She would always love him.

Even when she said good-bye.

He stared after her for a long moment, turning the scarab absently over in his hand.

That hadn't gone as planned but then he hadn't expected her to say good-bye to him. His heart had thudded in his chest at her words because, regardless of her denial, it had been good-bye just as surely as if she had said the words aloud. But that he would not allow.

He raised his chin slightly. Jack was his father's son and there was no time like the present to begin following in his footsteps. Obviously Father had already lived up to his end of their bargain and declared himself to Mother. Theodosia would not be so easily won. He ignored the fact that one could say winning over his mother had taken his father some thirty years.

The New Year's Eve ball was a week from today. He had a full week to . . . to what?

He needed some sort of plan. He needed to offer her something more than what she had planned for her life. Something she couldn't resist. Love would not be enough, not for this woman. And she did love him, even if she was not ready to acknowledge it to him or to herself. He would not let her walk out of his life. Not now that he had found her.

It had taken his father thirty years to finally be with the love of his life but then his father had lost sight of what he really wanted. Of his heart's desire.

Jack might well decide to follow in his father's footsteps. But he absolutely refused to repeat his father's mistakes.

Chapter Twenty-Six

If Teddy had been trying to avoid Jack in the week between Christmas Eve and the ball, she no doubt would have run into him every time she turned around. As she wasn't, she scarcely ever saw the man.

Not that it wasn't to be expected. Even though the New Year's gala was in many ways a repeat of Camille's wedding ball, there were still endless arrangements to be finalized. Arrangements that wouldn't be quite as all-consuming if Lady Briston hadn't taken it into her head to make changes, admittedly most of them minor, on a daily, sometimes hourly, basis. There was something to be said for planning an event when one was not living on the premises and was not therefore within easy reach of the hostess.

Difficulties weren't limited to those already residing at Millworth. Quite a few of the guests traveling from London had written to ask if lodging could be provided for them. Millworth would be filled with relatives so Teddy had arranged with the inn in the village to house those needing overnight accommodations. While one would think guests were capable of finding their own places to stay, Teddy's previous experiences had proved that false. Fortunately, for very nearly the first time, her mother was providing more than competent assistance. She really had changed.

Those distant family members staying at Millworth had begun arriving as soon as two days after Christmas and all but two were expected. Jack's grandfather and his uncle Daniel, Mr. Lockwood, who apparently wasn't an uncle at all, had arrived from America to join in the festivities, which added yet another layer of unintentional drama to the proceedings. Mr. Graham, who was obviously trying his best to be pleasant and cordial, just as obviously had not overcome a certain amount of distrust of the colonel. On the other hand, Mr. Lockwood's ill-fated affection for Mrs. Channing seemed to vanish the moment he laid eyes on Teddy's mother, which did tend to irritate Mrs. Channing but put a definite sparkle in Mother's eyes and an unquestioned spring in her step. Teddy had no idea her mother could be quite so flirtatious.

Teddy had decided to enjoy this final week as Jack's fiancée. To savor it and take pleasure in it as one did a rare, special sweet. Their time together was drawing to a close and she wanted to remember every minute of it. They had, as yet, still not come up with a way to dissolve their engagement although she suspected they might simply have to confess the truth. That might indeed make it easier for everyone and she and Jack could part friends. Even though she wasn't sure she could bear to be his friend.

While she knew he had decided not to return to New York, she had no idea what his plans were for his future although it did seem obvious that he would become the earl, after his father and uncle were gone, of course. She knew it was inevitable that they would run into one another on occasion and knew as well it would be awkward and uncomfortable. The man's feelings for her were obvious. Every time he looked into her eyes she knew and she tried very hard not to let him know his feelings were returned. In that, she suspected she failed. Still, it would be best if he never knew. With every minute spent in his company she was terrified he would declare himself and ask for her hand. Regardless of her feelings for him, that would never do.

But oh, it would be so very easy to admit that she loved him and abandon her own future for his. He was, after all, everything she'd ever wanted and more. So much more. But letting go of her own dreams would eventually destroy them both. Her regrets would only grow through the years and ultimately she'd blame and resent him. The joy she now felt in his arms would fade and love would die a slow, horrible, bitter death. His life and hers would be ruined. No, as hard as it would be to live without him, following the course she had set for herself was best for both of them even if it meant shattering both their hearts.

Pain would surely ease in time, regrets would only grow.

Dee was not the only one to try to convince her of the error of her ways. The day before the ball, Lucy asked to speak with her privately in the parlor. She closed the door behind her and studied Teddy for a long moment.

"I do hate to be impolite, Lucy, but I have a great deal yet to accomplish today," Teddy said with a pleasant smile. "So I really don't have time to—"

"I'm sorry you're so unhappy," Lucy said abruptly.

"I'm not the least bit unhappy," Teddy lied.

"Come now, Teddy. I'm not the only one who has noticed a slight but distinct air of melancholy about you."

"Nonsense, I am simply busy," Teddy said staunchly although her spirits had been low since Christmas Eve.

"Delilah says you are never downhearted." Sympathy shone in Lucy's eyes. "I've never experienced heartache myself but I can certainly recognize it when I see it."

"I have no idea what you mean," Teddy said slowly.

"Jackson told me everything."

Teddy's brow rose. "Everything?"

"Well, perhaps not everything." She shrugged. "But he did tell me that your engagement isn't real." She paused.

"Even though he wants it to be. He's in love with you, you know."

Teddy started to deny it, then sighed. "I was afraid of that."

"And you're in love with him." Lucy considered her closely. "Are you afraid of that, too?"

"Not afraid exactly but . . ." She shook her head. "It just won't work, that's all."

"Because you want to be independent and make your own fortune and that sort of thing?"

Teddy smiled weakly. "It sounds rather foolish when you say it that way."

"Oh, but it's not. I quite admire you. And any woman willing to forgo what she is expected to be for what she wants to be is most impressive," she said firmly. "It takes a great deal of courage and conviction. Why, you are an inspiration and I fully intend to follow in your footsteps."

Teddy stared. "You do?"

"I most certainly do." Lucy crossed the room to the sofa, sat down, and gestured for Teddy to join her. In spite of the endless number of details she had to see to today, Teddy couldn't resist hearing what the younger woman had to say.

"So." Teddy settled on the sofa. "You intend to plan weddings and parties and other events?"

"Oh no, nothing like that." Lucy scoffed. "I would be dreadful at that sort of thing. I am not the least bit organized or efficient and details often slip right by me. But I do have a new plan for my life that has nothing to do with what I am expected to do." She leaned closer in a confidential manner. "I have a tidy fortune left to me by a distant relative, a very independent female relative, and it's time I put it to good use. If I'm no longer expected to marry Jackson, well, I'm free to do as I wish, you see."

Teddy stared. "What are you going to do?"

"I haven't finalized my plans yet but I will." Confidence

shone in the American's eyes. "However, we are not here to talk about me, we're here to talk about you and Jackson."

"There really is nothing to say."

"It is a quandary, isn't it?" Lucy heaved a heartfelt sigh. "When there are two things you want so very much and you can't have them both."

Teddy smiled. "*Quandary* is putting it mildly."

"As much as I admire you, Teddy, Jackson is my dearest friend in the world." She squared her shoulders. "And I feel it my duty to lay out his case."

Teddy drew her brows together. "Does he know this?"

"Don't be absurd. He would never ask me to speak on his behalf." Lucy folded her hands in her lap. "First of all, Jackson Channing is intelligent and handsome and has a good head on his shoulders. He is the best man I have ever known."

"Indeed he is."

"You'll never find anyone even half as good."

"Probably not, but—"

"But?"

Teddy chose her words with care. "Once, he was everything I ever wanted. Now, I want something different."

"Still—"

"I don't want to spend my life wondering what might have been." She shook her head. "I don't want to live my life with regrets."

"Won't you regret not being with Jackson?"

Teddy met the younger woman's gaze directly. "Every minute until I breathe my last."

"Oh." Lucy stared. "I was right. You do have courage."

"Or I'm a fool." She shrugged. "There's apparently a fine line."

"Apparently. Although I suppose I'm a bit of a fool myself." Lucy wrinkled her nose. "I let him go after all."

"Why did you?"

"Well, I suppose it's because I didn't really want him. Not

for my husband that is. I've known Jackson all of my life and I really think if you are going to spend the rest of your days with a man, it should be at least a little bit of an adventure." She shook her head. "I can tell you what he will usually order in a restaurant. I can tell you what song he can't resist dancing to when an orchestra plays. I can tell you his favorite color, book, play. There's nothing left to discover about Jackson. And as truly wonderful as I think he is, I find it all rather, well, dull."

"And I find it all fascinating."

"That's because he is your adventure." Lucy smiled. "Not mine."

"Well, adventures do come to an end you know." Teddy forced a light laugh. "It's the very nature of adventure."

"Nonsense, I don't believe that at all. Why, life itself is an adventure or at least it should be." Lucy cast her a chastising look. "Surely you realize, Teddy, the very best adventures are only a beginning."

Lady Briston was beside herself with delight as were her new dearest friends Lady Sallwick and Mrs. Channing. All three women agreed the New Year's ball organized by the simply brilliant Lady Theodosia Winslow was the event of the year.

The Millworth ballroom had been transformed into a winter fairyland with hundreds of twinkling candles and garlands of sugared evergreen. Red roses overflowed from every nook and cranny and silvered half-masks were tucked into every arrangement. Even though Lady Briston had abandoned her idea of a masked ball, she had insisted on the masks as part of the decoration and Teddy had to admit she was right. The overall effect was breathtaking and nothing short of magical.

Teddy and Jack managed to convince the daunting trio that the ball was not the time to formally announce their engagement as they pointed out it would overshadow the true purpose of the evening, which was, of course, to introduce Jack to their world. Oddly enough, all three ladies, even Teddy's mother, agreed. Teddy wondered if Lady Briston had already learned the truth from Dee. Mrs. Channing, who had seemed to accept Teddy, probably hoped there was still a chance Lucy would become her daughter-in-law. As for Teddy's mother, well, she had firmly met her daughter's gaze and said this was a decision best left to Teddy and Jack. It was as shocking as it was delightful.

It was indeed a night to remember. Once the ball began, Teddy turned over her duties to Clement to oversee. The butler accepted that as his due but broke from his usual proper demeanor and urged her to have a wonderful evening. Perhaps he too had noticed her manner wasn't quite as cheerful as usual.

Jack hadn't said a word about her low spirits but she had caught him studying her thoughtfully in those rare moments this week when they were in the same room together.

He was as brilliant tonight as the ballroom. Handsome and dashing, he danced with the dowagers and charmed the younger ladies. He joked with his father's cronies and debated in a good-natured manner with his uncle's friends. It struck her that, in spite of his apprehension, he fit in as surely as if he had lived his entire life here. There's was no evidence of the ill-at-ease American she had met at Camille's wedding, no sign of a fish out of water. And why should there be? Millworth, and all it meant, was in his blood.

And when he took her in his arms to dance, her resolve melted and she wanted nothing more than to stay in his arms forever.

"Have I told you how beautiful you look tonight?" He smiled down at her.

"Why, no, you haven't." She heaved an overly dramatic sigh. "A grave oversight on your part, I would say."

He laughed. "Absolutely. One I should rectify at once.

Unfortunately . . ." He studied her for a moment. "Words are not enough."

"As charming as that is, I'm not letting you get away that easily."

"Oh, I could say your eyes sparkle like emeralds, your skin glows in the candlelight, your hair gleams like liquid fire, your lips are as irresistible as ripe cherries."

"Come now, Jack, surely you can do better than that," she teased.

"You are a dream, Theodosia, a gift from God. You are truly an adventure." His gaze locked with hers. "My adventure."

Her heart lodged in her throat. "See," she said weakly. "I knew you could do better."

"I think we should tell the family about our engagement tomorrow," he said abruptly. "Delilah says the guests staying at the manor all plan on leaving first thing in the morning. We can do it at breakfast after they depart."

"Breakfast will be later than usual," she murmured.

"And then . . ." His eyes narrowed. "We need to talk."

"We really have nothing to talk about. Not once we confess our deception."

"We have a great deal to talk about," he said firmly. "On a matter of some importance, I would say."

She frowned up at him. "What?"

He ignored her. "The dining room is apparently where all matters of importance are discussed in this family so it does seem appropriate to make our confession there. Once that is settled, I have another announcement to make as well."

She stared up at him. "What?"

"You do ask a lot of questions."

"I always have." She huffed with impatience. "I should warn you, I have never been fond of surprises."

"Nor are you particularly patient. Tomorrow, Theodosia," he said in what was obviously his best vice-presidential tone. "We shall discuss what needs to be discussed. Tonight . . ."

He smiled down at her. "I have the most beautiful adventure in the world in my arms and I don't intend to allow anything to spoil it."

"But—"

"For once, just for once, simply smile and agree with me."

She stared at him, then sighed and smiled. "Very well then."

"I knew you could do it if you tried." He grinned.

"Well, it's not easy."

"It's not supposed to be." He pulled her slightly closer and smiled into her eyes. "After all, where would be the challenge in that? Or the adventure?"

". . . and there you have it." Jack stood at the head of the table, his father on one side, Teddy on the other. "Lady Theodosia and I were never actually engaged."

Teddy held her breath. The entire family had gathered around the dining room table. The twins, Grayson, Sam, and Lionel as well as Lord and Lady Briston, Jack's mother and grandfather along with Teddy's mother and Mr. Lockwood all stared in stunned silence. The expressions on their faces ranged from shock to acceptance. Dee, Lucy, and the colonel simply kept their mouths shut.

"How very . . . heroic of you, Jack," Camille said at last.

"Admittedly it's rather extreme simply to save someone from an awkward situation," Beryl said. "But no less gallant for the absurdity of it. It's quite impressive when one thinks about it."

"I can't say I'm not disappointed." Lady Briston sighed at Teddy. "I was quite looking forward to having you as a member of the family."

Teddy glanced at her mother. "Mother?"

"I . . ." Mother hesitated, then drew a deep breath. "I owe you my apologies, Theodosia. I should never have put you in such a position. I am truly sorry."

Teddy swallowed hard. "Thank you, Mother."

Almost at once everyone launched into their own opinions and for a minute the air was filled with expressions of surprise or disappointment

"One moment if you please." Jack's mother stood up. "I have something to say to my son."

Jack's brow rose. "Yes?"

"What do you mean? You're not going to marry this woman?" Mrs. Channing glared at him. "Feigned engagement or not, and, as much I might hate to admit it, she is so obviously perfect for you. Do not make the same mistakes I did of disregarding something simply because it's completely unexpected. You belong together." She glanced at Lucy. "It's no more than the truth, Lucinda. Why, anyone can see it. I am sorry but there you have it."

"Poor, poor me." Lucy grinned, then sobered. Her gaze shifted between Jack and Teddy. "She's right, you know."

"Thank you, Lucy." Jack nodded. "Sit down, Mother."

"But—"

"Sit down, please. There's more."

The colonel frowned. "More?"

"Yes, Father." Jack drew a deep breath. "When I came to England I had no intention of staying. I had simply thought it was the opportunity to get to know my father and meet the rest of my family. I felt quite out of place here at first. All that has changed."

Lord Briston beamed. "Excellent."

"In the beginning, I assumed I would return to New York to resume my position at the bank." He looked at his grandfather. "I am sorry, Grandfather, but that is no longer my intent."

"Not a surprise to me," Mr. Graham said gruffly. "I never thought banking was really in your blood."

"I'm glad you understand."

The older gentleman shrugged.

"As for the rest of it." Jack turned to Lord Briston. "I

understand the way this sort of thing, inheritance and titles and the like, works in this country. That, regardless of any decision I make, I will someday be the Earl of Briston. The question is do I want to accept all that goes along with it." He glanced at Lionel. "I'm not under any obligation to take on the responsibilities of the earldom, am I?"

Surprise washed around the room. The colonel winced. A startled expression crossed Lionel's face. "No, I suppose you're not."

"I could conceivably return to America, live the rest of my life there, and have nothing to do with Millworth or Parliament or any of it?"

"I've never considered that before." Lionel nodded. "But yes."

Lord Briston's brow furrowed. "Now see here, Jack—"

"Wait, Uncle." Jack held up a hand to quiet the older man. "I'm not saying that's my intention but my life, even how I see myself, has changed enormously in the last few months. I feel as though I have barely begun to live and I'm not ready to decide how I want to spend the rest of my days."

"Nonetheless, Jack," his uncle began.

"Uncle Nigel," Jack said. "Do you intend to die anytime soon?"

Lord Briston huffed. "I do not intend to die at all although I suspect I cannot avoid it forever."

"I wish you a long and happy life, Uncle." He turned to the colonel. "Father, you look like a healthy sort. How do you feel?"

His father chuckled. "Never better, Jack."

"Well then, as both of you would have to depart this world before I would inherit the title, it seems to me any decision on my part would be premature and completely unnecessary. Besides, I'm tired of having my entire future planned and plotted and expected."

Delilah stared. "What do you intend to do?"

"Actually," He glanced at his mother. "It was something

you pointed out, although the idea has been growing for some time. I intend to travel the world. I intend to see all those places and try all those things I wanted to do and see as a boy." He grinned. "I intend to follow in my father's footsteps."

His mother stared in disbelief.

The colonel leaned closer to her and lowered his voice. "I would strongly suggest, Betty, that you force a brave smile to your face and graciously accept the inevitable."

Mrs. Channing hesitated, then nodded and smiled weakly.

Jack turned to Teddy. "What do you say, Teddy? Come with me? See the world?"

She stared at him for a moment, then laughed. "I knew you weren't really a banker."

"We'll have grand adventures, see things not everyone does, go places most people only dream of going. We'll spend five weeks in a balloon or make it around the world in eighty days. Or less." He grinned. "Carpe diem, Teddy." He grabbed her hand and pulled her into his arms. "Venture into the unknown. Marry me."

"Jack." She stared up at him and for a moment she could see a future with him as well as a future without him. Neither was perfect. Both came with regrets. She braced herself. "No."

He paused. "No?"

"No."

His eyes narrowed. "What do you mean—no?"

"I mean . . . no." She shook her head. "I can't."

"But I love you and you love me."

"I never said I loved you." She lowered her voice. "You should probably release me now. Everyone is staring." The room had indeed quieted as if those present were holding their breath.

"I don't care," he said but released her nonetheless. "And you didn't need to say it."

"It wasn't real, Jack, remember," she said firmly. "The engagement, none of it was real."

"Not the engagement perhaps but this is real." He gripped her shoulders and stared into her eyes. "You love me."

"Goodness, Jack I . . ."

"You are a stubborn creature, Theodosia Winslow, and you may deny it all you wish but I know. I see it in the look in your eyes and the touch of your hand. I feel it in the strength of your trust and the depth of your concern. I know it as I have never known anything before." He took her hand and pressed it to his chest and his heart beat beneath her fingers. "I know it in my heart, in my very soul, and you know it too."

She stared up at him. Not so much as a glimmer of doubt shone in his eyes. And it destroyed her. "Yes, God help me, I do. Of course, I do." She shook her head. "But I never intended for you to know that. I thought it would be better, easier for you, if you didn't know how I felt."

"You thought thinking you didn't love me, that you didn't share my feelings, would make things easier?" Disbelief rang in his voice. He dropped her hand and an aching sense of loss swept through her.

"Obviously, nothing will make this easier. But loving you . . ." Her voice cracked. "Apparently I'm not very good at hiding my feelings but then I've never truly been in love before."

"And you are now."

"It doesn't matter, Jack. It only makes this harder." Her gaze searched his. "Don't you see that?"

"No, I don't." His gaze bored into hers. "If you love me—"

"And I do." She nodded. "Truly I do. But—"

"But you have plans for your life."

"You know full well I do." She glanced at the others watching them closely. "Perhaps this would be best discussed in private."

"Oh, don't mind us," Dee said. "Pretend we're not here."

Jack ignored her and glared down at Teddy. "And those plans do not include me."

"No, they don't." She'd seen him annoyed but she'd never seen him angry before. And angry was exactly what he was. Angry and hurt. It showed in the hard line of his jaw, the tense set of his shoulders, and the look in his eyes. "You are the heir to Millworth Manor and a title and exactly the kind of man I always expected I would wed. The kind I was supposed to marry. In that, it seems I have come full circle." She forced herself to continue. "It also seems it's no longer what I want. Odd how quickly life changes."

"So," he said, his tone measured, his gaze never veering from hers. "You are choosing your . . . your pursuit of business over a life with me?"

"Good Lord." Mother groaned.

"No, I'm choosing to pursue my own . . . well, my own challenge if you will. My own adventure."

"I'm offering you adventure. The kind of adventure you've always wanted."

"I've always thought love a grand adventure," her mother said in a soft, hopeful voice.

Teddy shook her head. "But it's your adventure, not mine."

"It can be ours." The firm note in his voice did nothing to dim the growing realization in his eyes.

"I have plans—"

"Good God, Theodosia, plans, expectations change with circumstances or desire. My plans certainly have, for my life, for my future."

She struggled against the lump that lodged in her throat. "Mine haven't." Her gaze searched his. "You of all people should understand."

"I don't understand. I don't understand any of it." He glared down at her. "You've admitted you love me and I've declared my love for you. That should be the end of any debate. We should be planning a life together. It seems to me when two people find each other, against all odds that they would even meet, mind you, they would be fools to throw it away."

"Then I must be a fool." She drew a deep breath. "All my

life I have lived up to the expectations set out for me. None of which, by the way, I had any say in. You're exactly the same, Jack. You followed all the rules, met all the expectations. Now you intend to pursue a completely different path. You intend to do what you've always wanted to do, be who you've always wanted to be but never had the courage. Is it so hard to understand why I would wish to do the same?"

His voice softened. "You have nothing to prove, you know."

"One could say the same about you."

"She's got him there," Beryl murmured.

Jack scoffed. "That's an entirely different matter."

"Why?" she said sharply. "Because you're a man?"

His jaw clenched. "Exactly!"

"Even I know better than to say that," Sam said under his breath.

"Come now, Jack, you said yourself that you knew any number of women who successfully manage businesses."

"I said they rise to the occasion of their circumstances. I never said they were successful."

"It was implied," she said sharply.

"Nonetheless." His tone hardened. "I do think women in business is unseemly, I don't think they should be allowed in the Explorers Club, nor do I think they should vote!"

One of the ladies gasped.

"I don't believe you for a moment." Teddy glared. "I know you, Jackson Channing, you're just saying that to . . . to annoy me!"

"Furthermore." His jaw clenched. "Those women of business had no choice. They had to take care of themselves. You have a choice."

She stared in surprise. "To allow you to take care of me?"

"It's what men do."

"Well, I don't want to be taken care of, thank you very much. I've been taken care of my entire life. Indeed, I expected I would be taken care of for the rest of my life. But as you said—plans change."

"Brava," Lucy said quietly.

"I would never ask you to give up what you want," Teddy continued. "Is it right for you to ask me to give up what I want? Is it fair?"

"Yes!" he snapped.

"Ouch." Grayson winced.

"You don't mean that. You're nothing if not fair." She grabbed his arm, a desperation she couldn't hide in her voice. "Think about it, Jack. Please. Can you be happy if I'm not? If your happiness comes at the expense of mine?"

He stared at her for a long moment. "How long?"

"How long what?"

"How long will it take you to prove what you need to prove?"

"How on earth would I know? I have no particular deadline." She released his arm and stepped back. "What do you want me to say? If I'm not successful in a year, two years, five years, that I'll give up and meekly become your wife?"

He scoffed. "I don't expect you to do anything meekly."

"Good! I would hate to shatter your expectations!" She glared. "Let me ask you the same question. How long will it take you to decide how you want to spend the rest of your life? One year, ten, *thirty*?"

The colonel grimaced. "Poor form, Theodosia."

"I've already decided! I want to spend the rest of my life with you! Which does seem a rather significant decision." Jack shook his head slowly. "But I won't wait for you."

Indignation washed through her. "Nor did I ask you to."

"I will love you forever, Theodosia Winslow." His gaze locked on hers. "But make no mistake, I am not my father. I will not waste thirty years of my life waiting for you to come to your senses."

She gasped. "Come to my senses?"

Jack's brow arched.

Mrs. Channing huffed. "Oh, I don't think *come to my senses* is at all accurate."

"That is a bit harsh," Lady Briston murmured.

Teddy clasped her hands together. "Just because a man has decided he's in love with me, am I expected to throw away everything I want to acquiesce to his wishes?"

His gaze locked with hers and for an endless moment neither said a word. She wanted nothing more than to throw herself into his arms and tell him she was wrong. Nothing was as important as being with him. Admit that she was being stubborn and foolish. That this was the worst mistake of her life. But she knew as she knew nothing else in life, that if either of them abandoned what they wanted, what they needed, it would eventually destroy them both.

At last he shrugged, as if he didn't care. "Apparently not."

"I don't want to part like this, Jack." She struggled to keep her voice steady.

He smiled, defeat sounded in his voice. "I don't want to part at all."

She pulled off his ring and held it out to him, more than a little surprised at the steadiness of her hand. Her hand was apparently far more loyal than her traitorous heart. "You should take this."

He shook his head. "I never intended for you to return it."

"I can't—"

"Keep it, Theodosia. As a memento if nothing else." Jack reached out and closed her hand over the ring. The feel of his hand washed through her and wrapped around her soul. And shattered her heart. "It has indeed been an honor and a privilege to be your fiancé." Resignation shadowed his blue eyes. "Even if it wasn't real."

She nodded, afraid if she said anything her voice would break and the tears welling in her eyes would flow.

"That's that then." Jack nodded and turned his attention to the colonel. "Father, if you wouldn't mind, I have a few ideas I'd like to speak to you about. In the library perhaps?"

"Of course." Colonel Channing nodded and followed his son from the room.

Teddy stared after him.

Dee stood up and moved to her side. "You're not going to follow him, are you?"

Teddy choked back a sob. "No." She shook her head. "I can't."

"I think perhaps we should return to London today," her mother said quietly.

Teddy nodded.

Lady Briston rose to her feet. "Right or wrong, we must all follow our own path in life, my dear." She cast Teddy a sympathetic smile. "And hope we don't live to regret our choices."

"Goodness, Lady Briston." Teddy sniffed and opened her hand, staring at the ring twinkling in her palm. The vision blurred with the tears in her eyes. She had made her decision and now she had to live with it, however hard that would be. She had no illusions, regardless of her plans, of what she wanted for her life; it would be empty without him. The blasted American had swept into her world unexpectedly and right into her heart. And there he would stay until she breathed her last.

It was the right decision for both of them. She had no doubts about that. Although it didn't seem fair that doing what one knew was right hurt so very much. That doing what was best for both of them came with a price so high she might never recover. It would take a long time for the pain she felt now to fade and she wondered if it ever would.

She closed her hand over the ring, reminded herself there was truly no other choice, and forced her most optimistic smile.

"I already do."

Epilogue

Thirteen months later,
Somewhere in the deserts of Egypt . . .

"Eight," Teddy said and slapped at the dust on her practical traveling skirt. She refused to consider how hot and dusty she looked, which was probably no worse than she felt. Of course, how was one expected to feel after nearly a full day on a camel? Blasted, nasty beasts. Mrs. Channing had warned her, when she met the colonel and his wife in Cairo, that adventure was unfortunately not the least bit tidy. Still, this was not how she wished to look when she saw Jack again for the first time in more than a year.

Jack pulled off his glasses, rose from the chair behind the camp desk in his tent, not so much as a hint of surprise at her unexpected appearance in his eyes. Eyes that looked even bluer against his skin, now tanned by the sun. His jaw was shadowed as if he hadn't bothered to shave, his shoulders seemed somehow broader and, goodness, had the man grown taller? Surely not but there was an air about him of confidence and adventure and even danger that made him seem bigger than life. Good Lord, he looked like a bloody hero! Her heart skipped a beat.

"Eight?" he said in a casual manner as if he had last seen her yesterday and not thirteen months ago. "Eight what?"

"Eight months." She pulled off a glove and glanced around his tent. It was spacious and sparsely furnished with a folding desk, cot, several stacked trunks, and a Persian rug that obviously served as flooring. She did wonder how he kept the sand off it although judging by the grit beneath her boot—she suspected he didn't. The room was littered with stacks of books and maps and notebooks. Chunks of broken pottery and statuary and assorted artifacts were piled high. Spades and various tools leaned against the tent's posts. "It took me eight months to understand that being independent didn't necessarily mean being alone."

He sauntered around the desk, rested his hip against it, and crossed his arms over his chest. There was no mistaking it now, Jack was definitely his father's son. "Oh?"

"I didn't like that at all. It was most distressing. I became rather cranky." She wrinkled her nose. "Not at all like me. I'm usually so pleasant." She pulled off her other glove. "It's all your fault, you know."

"I would have thought it was your fault." His expression was nondescript. It was enough to drive even the sanest of women quite, quite mad. Why on earth did she have to go and fall in love with a banker?

"In the spirit of compromise, I am willing to shoulder some of the blame and apologize."

"Accepted."

"And?"

"You expect me to apologize as well?"

She slapped her gloves against her palm. "That would be nice."

"All right then." He shrugged. "Sorry."

"You should be." She sniffed. "I have been following you from one place to the next. Some of them most uncivilized and very nearly impossible to get to. One would think you were hiding."

His eyes narrowed. "I wasn't."

Teddy wouldn't have found him at all if it hadn't been for his parents. But she suspected if anyone knew where Jack was, his parents would. From what Dee had told her, they had accompanied Jack on his new life of adventure at least initially but then had gone their separate ways, only meeting with their son now and again in places like Algiers and Constantinople. While the colonel had always been notoriously bad about correspondence, Mrs. Channing was apparently a good influence and at least a handful of letters had made their way back to the rest of the family. Teddy had retraced their steps although, at times, it had been like following bread crumbs. Still, she refused to give up. Jack was at the end of those bread crumbs. She was both astounded and grateful when she had at last found the Channings in Cairo.

According to his parents, Jack had joined a group of scholars and treasure hunters searching for a lost city and evidence of a lost pharaoh or something of that nature. They directed her to this makeshift tent village filled with the most disreputable-looking men but had assured her she would be perfectly safe. Especially as the colonel had arranged for his most trusted guide and escorts to accompany her. Under other circumstances she would have been curious and intrigued but now there was only one thing on her mind.

"I must say, you haven't made it easy for me." She dropped her gloves on a chair that had seen better days. "I've been traveling for five months. You've been bloody hard to find."

"Have I?"

"You know full well you have."

"Again, my apologies."

"Even in this day and age it's damnably hard for a woman alone to travel to the places you have been. Why, I had to engage an elderly couple from Kent to accompany me as chaperone." She aimed a pointed look at him. "Fortunately, they are of an adventurous nature."

"That is fortunate."

She wasn't sure what she had expected but aloof and restrained wasn't it. Certainly she hadn't thought he would be overjoyed at the sight of her, take her in his arms, straight to his bed and back into his life. That would be entirely too much like a novel of romance or adventure. Still, she had hoped.

"You don't seem surprised to see me." She took off her hat and tossed it on top of her gloves.

He shrugged.

Very well, obviously he was going to make her pay for her sins.

"Perhaps you would like to know how I have spent those eight months? Before you shrug again, allow me to explain." She meandered around the edge of his dwelling, her gaze drifting over the jumble of artifacts and assorted piles of paraphernalia that might well have been supporting the tent itself. "I have always heard that hard work is the best way to keep one's mind off of something they'd rather not think about but think about nonetheless."

"And that was?"

"You know perfectly well what it was." She cast him an annoyed look. "Apparently when one has had a hero, one finds it difficult to go on without him."

"And?"

"And so I worked. I solicited new engagements, tripled our revenue, hired three widows whose late husbands were idiots, to run things and work with Mother who is, by the way, proving to be most efficient. Although she is leading your uncle Dan on a merry chase and I suspect she intends to allow him to catch her soon." She picked up a small stone carving of a cat and examined it. "In short I proved to myself, if no one else, that I could do what I set out to do. I can do whatever it is I set my mind to."

"I never doubted it."

"I did."

"And you are your greatest critic."

"Next to my mother."

He nodded. "I see."

She shot him a sharp glance. "Do you?"

"It's obvious." He studied her for a moment. "Having now accomplished what you set out to accomplish, you've decided to turn to the next thing on your list of what you want. Me."

She started to deny it, then realized it was pointless. "I wouldn't have put it quite that way." She replaced the cat and turned toward him. "I have never actually had a list but yes." She drew a deep breath. "You win, Jack."

"Do I?"

There was every chance he no longer wanted her. He had a new life of adventure and perhaps even a new woman in that life. It was a possibility she hadn't wanted to consider but it was always in the back of her mind. She had realized long ago what a risk she had taken but she would do so again. And for the same reasons. Regardless, she hadn't come all this way to give up without a fight. She gathered her courage and drew a deep breath.

"Yes, you do." She took a step toward him, ignored the butterflies trying to beat their way out of her stomach, and met his gaze directly. "I have missed you from the moment you walked out of Millworth's dining room. Every minute, every hour, every day. You have never been far from my thoughts and you have been most persistent in my dreams."

"Have I?" The slightest twinkle of what might have been amusement glittered in his eyes. It was a good sign.

"I'm not saying I made a mistake, I didn't. I was afraid, you see, that if I gave up my plans for my life, if I didn't *try*, I would regret it and eventually resent you for asking it of me. And there would come a time when we hated each other. I would rather let you go than take that risk. I would never want you to hate me." If she had the slightest chance of winning him back, she had to tell him everything. "In the back of my mind I thought, I hoped, that you'd come back to me." Her voice broke and she cleared her throat. "You didn't, of course. I never heard from you, not that I blame you but . . ." She shook her head. "I know you said you wouldn't wait for me but you also said you would love me forever. I took that as, well, a promise."

He didn't say a word and she hurried to fill the silence.

"The moment I realized that I had indeed achieved what I wanted I knew I had to find out if . . ." She squared her shoulders. "If it was too late."

He considered her silently.

"I didn't know I needed a hero until he—until *you*—were gone. I don't want to live my life without you. And I would very much like to share your adventures." There, it was all out. Now, it was up to him.

He stared at her for a long moment but said nothing. Her heart plummeted.

"Is it? Too late, that is?" She held her breath.

"There's something you should know," he said slowly. He straightened, turned, and rummaged through the piles of papers on his desk. "I did write."

"I never received anything," she said cautiously.

"I never posted them." He selected a stack of pages and held them out to her. "I too was afraid."

She reached out, her hand trembling.

He caught it, a troubled frown creasing his brow. "I don't know why but I always thought you'd be wearing your ring."

"I am." Her free hand went to the chain around her neck. The ring and the peacock dangled from it, hidden by her clothing. "I never take it off."

He released her hand, gave her the letters, then turned back to the desk. "There's something else you should see." He shifted a few papers, then grabbed a folded packet. "This includes passage to England."

She stared at him. "You were coming back?"

"I promised myself I would not make the same mistakes my father had. I would not wait thirty years. One was more than enough."

"For me to come to my senses?"

"Yes. And for me to come to mine." He shook his head. "Adventure isn't nearly as much fun without someone to share it with." He blew a long breath. "It didn't take me eight months to realize that. I knew it almost from the first. But apparently, I am every bit as stubborn as you."

She swallowed hard. "Everyone said you were perfect for me."

"And were they right?"

She choked back a sob. "Yes."

"Good Lord, Theodosia, we've wasted a lot of time." In one quick move he pulled her into his arms, crushing her against his chest. His letters fell from her hand. "Once again, Teddy, marry me. Share my adventure, share my life. Seize the day."

"No."

"No?" He stared in disbelief.

"I couldn't possibly accept that proposal." She scoffed.

"Why in the name of all that's holy not?" His brows drew together. "You followed me across the world. You tracked me down in the desert. What do you want?"

"Well, you called me Teddy, as you did the last time you asked me to marry you, but you've always preferred Theodosia and I must say I like—"

Without warning his lips claimed her, her words smothered in a kiss determined and filled with magic and entirely too long in coming.

Jack raised his head. "I warn you, Theodosia Winslow, as that is the only way I have ever found to shut you up, I intend to do it frequently." He grinned down at her with that infectious smile that lingered forever in her soul. "And with a great deal of enthusiasm."

"Goodness, Jack." She smiled up at him and wondered that her heart didn't burst with the joy of at last being back in his arms. Now and for the rest of their days. "I would expect nothing less."

In his later years, when Jackson Quincy Graham Channing reflected back upon his life he marveled at the twist of fate that had turned a banker, whose entire life had been planned and laid out for him, into a man who relished the adventure to be found in the unknown and the unexpected. And marveled as well at the stubborn, independent woman of business he had found to share that life.

The woman who was his first adventure.

And his greatest.

Books by Bestselling Author
Fern Michaels

___The Jury	0-8217-7878-1	$6.99US/$9.99CAN
___Sweet Revenge	0-8217-7879-X	$6.99US/$9.99CAN
___Lethal Justice	0-8217-7880-3	$6.99US/$9.99CAN
___Free Fall	0-8217-7881-1	$6.99US/$9.99CAN
___Fool Me Once	0-8217-8071-9	$7.99US/$10.99CAN
___Vegas Rich	0-8217-8112-X	$7.99US/$10.99CAN
___Hide and Seek	1-4201-0184-6	$6.99US/$9.99CAN
___Hokus Pokus	1-4201-0185-4	$6.99US/$9.99CAN
___Fast Track	1-4201-0186-2	$6.99US/$9.99CAN
___Collateral Damage	1-4201-0187-0	$6.99US/$9.99CAN
___Final Justice	1-4201-0188-9	$6.99US/$9.99CAN
___Up Close and Personal	0-8217-7956-7	$7.99US/$9.99CAN
___Under the Radar	1-4201-0683-X	$6.99US/$9.99CAN
___Razor Sharp	1-4201-0684-8	$7.99US/$10.99CAN
___Yesterday	1-4201-1494-8	$5.99US/$6.99CAN
___Vanishing Act	1-4201-0685-6	$7.99US/$10.99CAN
___Sara's Song	1-4201-1493-X	$5.99US/$6.99CAN
___Deadly Deals	1-4201-0686-4	$7.99US/$10.99CAN
___Game Over	1-4201-0687-2	$7.99US/$10.99CAN
___Sins of Omission	1-4201-1153-1	$7.99US/$10.99CAN
___Sins of the Flesh	1-4201-1154-X	$7.99US/$10.99CAN
___Cross Roads	1-4201-1192-2	$7.99US/$10.99CAN

Available Wherever Books Are Sold!
Check out our website at **www.kensingtonbooks.com**